Under The Blood Red Sky

A Novel

William Ellis

Table of Contents

Under the blood red sky

By William Ellis

Notes by the author

While this work is one of fiction several sources were consulted as part of the overall research for the book. Namely the Los Angeles times, the Borderland Beat and blog del Narco, just name but few. Research through the internet and several newspapers in Mexico brought to my attention several truly horrific incidents that occurred in the region of San Fernando and its state of Tamaulipas. While the nature of these horrific acts has been documented, my story has merely provided a fictional account of what occurred, namely during the very well documented San Fernando Massacre of both 2010 and 2011. My story merely provides a fictional account of what surviving eye witnesses have described.

Acknowledgements of the author

To Mai Wong of @happy_paintgirl for her hard work and excellent and breath-taking front cover design. A true genius and one for the mainstream. To my many friends who supported me through my writing and never doubted me for a minute. But the true acknowledgment goes to the very people that are the essence of this story, my inspiration and the one group of people that, without them in my life I could never apply such feeling. To my wife and sons, I love you and I thank you for all your support.

Chapter1

San Fernando, Tamaulipas, Mexico

24th August 2010

The gunfire has stopped — they are all dead, Papa is dead.

I lie under the bodies with my eyes closed; I am trying hard not to cry, I can't let them hear me — If they discover me then they will certainly shoot me. I run my hand through a pool of blood, that flows from the open wounds of the dead that lay around me. I see the face of a young girl — I remember her from the bus ride. She was around my age Her face twisted with pain and fear. I wipe the blood over my face. Got to convince them I am dead. Papa is slumped over me — he doesn't move. I pray he didn't suffer, please dear lord, help me now. Tell me that my Papa didn't suffer.

Why us? why stop our bus? why did they want to kill us? They shouted things we didn't understand; cursed us, beat us, tied the hands of the men. They demanded answers to questions that no one could answer. They accused us of traveling from El Salvador to work for the cartels. We cried and begged and prayed to God for these evil men to spare our lives — they didn't stop, they laughed and laughed. We just wanted to get to America, we meant no harm to anyone. They took us to the deserted barn and then began to beat us. They lined us up — put us on our knees. They held us for days then shot us like sick dogs. Papa grabbed me and pulled me into his arms. I felt his body twist, and heard him cry out. The roar of gunfire stifled my screams. They fired into the heap of bloody bodies — just to make sure. Make sure no one ever told of the evil that happened here.

I pull my hand over my mouth. They will hear me — he will hear me. The one with the tear drop tattoos, the one with the evil eyes. The

one who removed his mask — just so he could smile at us.

The one who sang, whilst we begged for our lives. He had the voice of an angel, yet he was as wicked as the devil himself. I can hear movement — they heard me. They are coming to pull me out, from under the bodies. I tremble — unable to control myself. My heart racing, crying loudly, getting ready to die.

In a last-ditched attempt, I try and pull myself out from underneath Papa's lifeless body, and the other unfortunate ones who died alongside him in this stinking shack. I wriggle free — where do I go? As I break free a hand grabs mine — I am pulled off the ground and I see the face of a man who has blood pouring from his arm. He is young; obviously, a passenger. I then realise, like me he survived.

'Run little girl, run like the wind I will run with you.'

The man runs — pulls me by my hand. There is a gap in the barn door. We

squeeze through and run into a wide open

field. I see trees and a cattle fence ahead, I run and run. The man lets go of my hand — shouts for me to head towards the trees, he runs in another direction. From behind me I hear shouting, lots of shouting. I hear machine-gun fire again. I see the ground explode in front of me, as the bullets strike. *My breathing heavy on my chest, I don't look back. I see the trees and the fence getting closer. As I run I realise I am still crying. Crying for my Papa, crying for the girl, crying for the dozens, and dozens who were murdered in that barn. Murdered because we were searching for a better life. I jump the fence and run through the trees — can't stop running.*

***

Waking from my dreams and returning to my reality is by far the worst part of my day. Night after night I dream of being with Laena and our boys, laughing and being happy, like we once were. In our special place, down by the Rio San Fernando, our picnic blanket laid out, kicking the football with Tomas, building the den with Joaquin and watching them play with Laena. Laena my wife, mother to Tomas and Joaquin, the love of our lives the tie that binds all of us together. I see her only in my dreams; I remember her young and beautiful and always smiling. The boys are laughing and joyous, playing as children should. But like everything good in life, it comes to an all too brief conclusion. I wake up — back in the reality that I have come to despise, and the despair that my own doing has orchestrated. A world where the boys laugh and smile no more, where our special place down by the river only reminds us of happiness long ago. Laena is missing. Before I go to sleep each night, I pray that I will see Laena again. So, what happened? How did it get to this? How did the woman I love so much and swore to care for become one of the tens of thousands of people who have gone missing in the land I was born? I could lay blame at the Los Zetas or Gulf Cartel or the Municipal Policia, but the truth be told, it was all my doing. The children know it, I know it.

I lay in bed looking up at the ceiling, watching the fan push the hot August air around my room, thinking how it all came to this. Questions going around in my head — over and over, the same rhetorical questions. Why her? why me? why us? She vanished without trace — one fateful day in March of this year. It's as if this god-forsaken place swallowed her up — along with the thousands of others, who suffered a similar fate. Laena is gone, the void that she leaves is immeasurable, the love that our family once shared, now replaced with resentment and guilt. Resentment from our children toward me, but the guilt is all mine — my burden, my cross to bear.

My friend, Alejandro always joked that soon she was going to regain her eyesight and finally see that for all these years she was married to the Felipe Hernandez that everyone else sees. Tall and lean, her long dark hair hung to her shoulders and when she smiles, her face lights up any room. I met Laena thirteen years ago; she was twenty-one. I was twenty-nine.

Our eldest boy, Tomas is twelve-years-old and the brightest boy I know, probably smarter than most of the adults I know. He senses my guilt and shame, and can't bring himself to look me in the eye — let alone even speak to me. Our youngest child is Joaquin; whereas Tomas has metaphorically broken communication, Joaquin has ceased to speak at all. Not a word in months: not to me, his brother or anyone else for that matter. Joaquin is six-years-old, and has witnessed more horror and despair in his short lifetime than many adults will, in a full lifetime. Witness to the reign of the cartels and a fucked up government that chose to start a war. A war that cannot be won, that has no ending, and the only losers are us — the people who are stuck here.

The man I was when I first met Laena is different from that I have now become. I met Laena at a dance near to the Rio San Fernando. Back then I was confident — ready to take on the world. A boy from the barrio, who ostensibly should have flunked out of school and went to work in the fields or a road gang. I got an education and got out. Back then I was a budding journalist who had a degree from the National Pedagogic University in Mexico City. I learned construction from my father, which helped me pay my way through college. With a degree and working for a San Fernando newspaper as a metro reporter, I was certainly a different man than I am today.

I am now is a general repairman in San Fernando, travelling around in a beat-up Datsun truck working for whoever can pay for my services. That pretty much translates to peasant, but once upon a time I was not that man. I was not the short squat manual worker with a belly hanging over his baggy pants, with wisps of receding hair combed back in an attempt to cover the bald patch and a face creased through age and the burning Mexican Sun. The usual four-day stubble now greying over my lined and tired face.

I climb out of the bed and dress in the ragged clothes of a peasant handy man. I look in my mirror and feel ashamed by my own pathetic reflection. I go into the living area of the house we call our home. I clear the cerveza bottles from the front porch where my friend Alejandro and I spent the previous evening drinking; putting the world to rights, putting forward our views on Fucking Felipe Calderon, El presidente of a country that prides itself nowadays on having one of its citizens being listed amongst the richest in the world, and incidentally being the most hunted and celebrated Narcos in the free world. This is what we have become, always renowned as being a nation of hard working and proud people and now we are becoming like those Yankees, making celebrities of Narcos and gangsters. Alejandro and I continued our drunken and political satirising repartee until one am. Making sure we didn't procrastinate too loudly, as despite the booze we were all too aware of the listening ears that would tell the Narcos and sure enough our ugly heads would be on a pole in the town square.

The evening drinking marathons have become more frequent than ever and, as always, move away from Politics to Alejandro's favourite topic of what Maria, a local woman and good friend of mine, breast size is likely to be. Maria is the mother of Tomas' friend Luis, who go to the same school, and probably talk about breasts and the like as much as Alejandro does. Difference being they are both twelve and Alejandro is my age. Maria and Laena were good friends and Maria has since become a friend to me; which is why I tell Alejandro constantly about his lustful thoughts. Despite his talk, it's obvious that Alejandro would like something meaningful with Maria but like a typical man, he can't bring himself to ask.

It's seven am and the morning sun burns down onto the front porch as I clear the empty bottles and cigarettes. Our house is basically a shack in amongst other shacks on this particular street in the barrio. The street is filled with old style Japanese and American cars that the neighbours use to go to and from their back-breaking jobs. This neighbourhood is thankfully occupied by families and hard working men and women who represent what Mexico has always been renowned for. We look out for each other, raise our children and suffer the loss.

This fucking place, this fucking war, we don't hold guns or drugs, yet we are the ones who lose the most. The streets are dust laden and uneven, yet the pride of the people is evident. The houses and gardens are maintained, each house a palace for those who live here. In only a few hours the Narco youth gangs will crawl through here in their stupid fucking trucks with their stupid fucking Narco music blaring out looking to mess with someone — just for kicks — just because they can, who is going to stop them? me, I am a coward, a nobody, a peasant who pissed away his college education dreams of being a journalist because he is a coward, a nobody who couldn't even protect his wife. A proud peasant who wore his own wife down with his pride, she stayed with him in San Fernando and worked the fields for money. A beautiful young woman of class and substance who came from a good family, who loved her husband and children, who stayed here in this region because I couldn't swallow my pride and take us away to El Paso. How did I ever repay her? I continued to let her go out on those highways, alone to work the fields, for her never to return. I still see Laena's face — that morning before she left for work just like it was yesterday.

In the distance, I can hear sirens and trucks like they are in convoy. I can tell the sound of SUV engines as I have heard them so many times previously. SUVs belonging to the military, driving at speed and it sounds like there are many of them. I wait for the next sound which I can predict with definite certainty. Within minutes it comes, despite its distance it still startles me. The unforgettable sound of machine-gunfire. I immediately go inside the house; from inside the sound of gunfire becomes muffled.

Time to wake Tomas and Joaquin, I go into Tomas and Joaquin's room and pull back the drapes. Grumbles come from the mattress on the floor that they both sleep on. Tomas is tall for his age and athletic just like his mother. He is a handsome boy and although he is easily embarrassed by it, he is popular with the girls. Since his mother disappeared I notice the way he looks at me. He doesn't say it but the look says 'It's your fault that she's gone.'

The bedroom they sleep in is bare, some soccer posters on the wall, Joaquin's toys in one corner and Tomas' comic books in another. Their clothes hung in the closet, threadbare and worn which clearly says they are the clothes of the sons of a peasant. Joaquin begins to stir; he opens his eyes and looks in my direction. While Tomas is very much like his mother, Joaquin is certainly my son. Short, stocky build with a belly that sticks-out over the top of his pants. Both Laena and Tomas have the Latin good looks that the world speaks of.

Joaquin looks at me with a smile. Despite the boy's daily struggles with life in general, he pretty much takes things in his stride. The school that Joaquin used to go to is closed now. A shoot-out between the Gulf cartel, or the CDG as they are otherwise known, and Los Zetas two months ago, saw to that. Six teachers and nine pupils die by gun-fire while leaving the playground. Joaquin saw the whole thing; some of the pupils were friends of his. Before the shootings, Joaquin was a boy, just like any other; played rough and tumble, got himself into trouble, was generally a kid, just like any other six-year-old. I remember collecting him from the school yard, he was pale, I gazed into his eyes and, only to be met with eyes that seemed devoid of any life left behind them. He didn't speak, he hasn't spoken since. For weeks, he barely did anything. That once playful, mischievous but loving boy was gone, just a shell of his previous self. There is no school for Joaquin now, he comes to work with me. He has become adept at maintenance and building, always carrying his own tools. While I am aware of my failings as a father, I can't send him back to any other school. When the story of the school shootings was covered by the local newspaper, the journalist who wrote the story was beheaded in front of his wife and children. That's why I like to be the man no one looks twice at.

I hug Joaquin when he gets out of bed and kiss his cheek. Tomas looks at us, he smiles but I can see the melancholy in his face. I hug Tomas, but it's all a little strained.

'I am going to see the cop again, Tomas, to see what he has found out,' speaking of the Detective in charge of Laena's case. I try to treat Tomas like an adult as much as I can, to let him know I am trying to do everything to find his mother, that I am doing all I can. It's all words; he knows that, I know that. I wouldn't know where to start. Now, I am just trying to keep my head above water, to raise these boys the way Laena would want me to.

'Let me know what he says,' says Tomas, trying as hard as he can to have belief in my efforts.

The boys sit down for a breakfast of Chilaquiles with chicken and cheese, leftovers from last night's supper. From the living room, I can hear gunfire going off in the distance. Tomas looks at me, he knows the sound, he knows what's going on. I look at Joaquin, he tucks into his breakfast at speed. He is hungry he has Chilaquiles around his mouth, but soon that ever-familiar sound, that he had previously heard up-close in that playground, causes him to jolt upright. He stops chomping away at his breakfast and freezes. The sounds are intermittent and off into the distance. I sit next to him and hold him tight. Tomas appears conditioned to the whole thing, paying it no more attention than someone hearing a car-horn sounding. It's just another day in Tamaulipas; gunfire to someone in this place is like hearing the sound of gulls in a seaside town. It's just background noise.

I suddenly think back to my father's old records in his collection. I don't know why, but a certain song jumps to the forefront of my mind. "We gotta get out of this place," absolutely god damn right. I suddenly drift back to those times of hearing my father's records playing in the background, while he sat sipping cervezas on the porch of his old house. Telling me of his time living in America, before returning to Tamaulipas. I can remember sitting and listening thinking that he was sharing some of life with me, as parents do. Well as good parents normally do. But then it would strike. At times, I thought there was a connection between my father and I, that he actually wanted to share his thoughts and feelings with me, waiting in hope that he put an arm out to me; pull me in close, kiss me on the top of my head, tell me he loved me, that he was proud of me. The booze made him whimsical to start, then that melancholic and spiteful side of him would come out. The side that had come to the forefront of his every day nature, then the comments, the bile, the resent. My father called me 'Flip' when I was a boy. He called me this because my name, Felipe Hernandez was a name given to those men of stature, of substance and of strength. My father said I didn't deserve to carry the Hernandez name or get to use his own first name, so he named me 'Flip.' Despite being an absolute bastard he could predict my strength of character and tell me my future. When I gave him my departing repartee before setting off to Mexico City for college he said: 'You will be back, runts always return to the litter.'

'American kids are spoiled, just like you, Flip. Never worked for anything in their lives, had it all handed to them. You listening to me, Flip you spoiled little shit.'

I remember noticing the empty bottles under his chair on the porch, that squint in his eye, that growl in his voice, that ever so slight slur in his speech.

His hands were large and rough like that of all Mexican men who worked in manual labour. His face was hardened by the cruel sun that burned down on him day after day, working on the roofs of San Fernando, Nuevo Leon and Monterrey. His skin brown and tough like leather, his body hardened and solid. His eyes — that squint, pointed in my direction whenever he was angry or needed to take his frustrations out on someone. The same eyes — that had witnessed the horrors in Vietnam when he was a young man, drafted because he was a poor Mexican who had to enlist and fight to earn his place. Those eyes that burrowed deep into me and saw what I was really made of.

I wished he would just hit me. At least then the pain would be tangible, would be something that would heal eventually. The beatings would come in time. But as a boy of eight, not much older than Joaquin is now, I had to come to terms with the fact that a fathers' love was something omitted from my childhood. You fucking son of a bitch, I thought to myself, even now it fills me with a juxtaposition of resent and that longing of wanting him to be father that I needed.

Tomas gets dressed for school and I pack up Joaquin's tools ready for him to come to work with me, we get into my old truck and drive along the dusty and uneven road of the barrio. We pass the murals painted by the street gangs, declaring war on each other as well as the Army and Federal Policia, drive past the lost souls who are stumbling to and from their menial jobs working in factories or the fields, into the evanescent sound of that gun-fire that has been ongoing, I keep thinking of that old song: “We gotta get out of this place.”

Yes Flip, you’re right —you’re absolutely god damn right.

Chapter2

San Fernando, Tamaulipas, Mexico

August 24th 2010

Papa's truck bounces along the uneven dusty road, out of our neighbourhood. Papa drives me to my school through Villa Del Mar, he never drives on highway 101. When I asked Papa why we never drive along highway 101 he told me that evil moves along the highway and snatches those who dare take the route, it's always the people from our neighbourhood who get snatched away. Papa hung a Crucifijo Catôlico, a crucifix on the dashboard of his dusty old truck to keep Santa Muerte away from us.

The barrio where we live is next to highway 101, as we drive through Villa Del Mar the roads are asphalt and smooth the houses around us are Stucco and look well maintained, unlike where we live. All the boys and girls from our barrio go to school in the city, so we must take the daily journey into town. The school bus no longer comes into the barrio; the bus company had lost too many buses because the Zetas shoot the drivers and steal their buses.

We join highway 101 within the city where it's safe. I can see the big police SUVs with machine-guns mounted on the roof. The policemen wear masks over their faces. All of them carry guns on their hips and machine-guns slung over their shoulders. They are lined up on the highway — their eyes peering at us. They look like Roman gladiators ready for battle.

As we get into the town square, the city looks like something from the books about Mexico in the 1800's, old stone and cobbled roads. Papa Antonio showed me those pictures when I went to America to see him. I miss him so much. I miss Mama all the time.

As we get closer to school I can see policemen stood around three bodies lying on the ground. The bodies are covered in blood and have a banner pinned on a wall above them like a message or celebration. I read the banner:

"This is what happens to pigs who side with the CDG, stinking motherless fucks. We will kill every last one of you. Signed Los Zetas"

I look again at the bodies and see the dead, lifeless bodies wearing police uniforms, one body has no head, and they all have pictures of their wives and children, that would usually be kept in wallets, pinned to their chests. One of the dead men has his underpants around his ankles; I look away when I notice his private parts have been cut away. There is blood all over the sidewalk. I look back into the cab of the truck, I see Papa looking at me, and he gives me that reassuring look, the one that tries to show me everything is OK. The one thing that is apparent is that some of the sights we witness don't shock us as much as they used to. Joaquin is staring at a hammer and screwdriver he has in his hand intently. He never looks out of the window anymore.

'Hey boys, how about we go down by the river this weekend, kick a ball around, and take a picnic with us. We could spend the weekend down there maybe camp out overnight. I hear that the fishing this time of year is good. Maybe you could bring Luis with you if you ask his Mama,' says Papa, desperately trying to distract me from looking at the horrors of the roadside.

Typical Papa, burying his head in the sand, doing all he can to hide me away from what is going on in this place.

'Sure, why not,' I try and appear enthusiastic about it, but without Mama it's just not the same anymore.

I can't bring myself to get excited about it. No matter how many trips to the river we take, it doesn't change a thing. It just makes me sad thinking of the fun we used to have with Mama, before she disappeared. Every time we have gone down by the river, Papa tries to remind us of those days and evenings down there and I hear the cracks in his voice and how sad he becomes. I have heard him crying when we sleep in the tent, I have looked out of the peep hole and saw him sat on his collapsible chair with a beer bottle in one hand, a cigarette in the other, looking out across the steady flow of the river. Completely silent, just gazing, he would sit like that for hours. Papa didn't make her disappear; he didn't bring the horror or the violence to this place or wish upon any of this. What he did, what his greatest failing and deepest regret is, that he couldn't see what this place was fast becoming. He didn't want to come to El Paso to live with Papa Antonio and Grandma. He believed that we could make it down here; he believed that one day this would all end. He was wrong, and I can't forgive him for this. I don't want to think about Mama, it hurts me too much. I don't want to believe that she could be dead, or that she suffered. We can't leave this place now because we must find her; we must try and find her.

'Papa, are you going to the police station today, to see that Investigator,' I say, knowing full well that he said similar earlier on today.

'Of course, I said that this morning and I will, as I do every day, Roberto is a good guy, he may have something for us, you never know,' Papa says, talking like Roberto is a friend to us, like he has a chance.

Papa tries hard to treat me like I am older than twelve. I heard him on the Porch the other night with Alejandro, talking while they were drunk. I heard him say that twenty-eight thousand people are dead since the drug wars began.

'Tens of thousands have gone missing since this cluster fuck started,' I heard Alejandro shout. I heard them both saying that the President and the military "Couldn't catch the clap in a Tijuana brothel." Papa and Alejandro, drunk and shouting off about how it's all gone wrong. What utter bullshit, I thought. These two men like to talk; like to get drunk, but what are they doing, what is Papa doing to find Mama, apart from kissing that cop's ass. I am a kid, so why is it obvious to me that twenty-eight thousand dead people, my Mama is never going to be top of their list to find. She worked in the fields, she lived in a shack in the barrio and all because that's the way Papa wanted it. Cops don't care enough about people like us to bother searching for.

We pull up outside of my school. I can see Luis waiting by the gate for me. I lean over to Joaquin who still has his hammer and screw driver in his hand. I take his face in my hands and I say: 'Have a good day and I will see you later.'

He look sad, he smiles, but it takes great effort, I keep thinking that he will respond to me, but it's been months since he last spoke a single word. I kiss him and give him a hug; he puts his arms around my neck and gives me a gentle squeeze. Papa reaches over and puts his arm around my shoulder as I return to a seated position.

'Have a good day at school son, and good luck at Soccer practice, I will collect you after.'

'Soccer practice is tomorrow night,' anything else you want to forget and get wrong, I think as I climb out of the cab. 'Let me know how it goes with the cops,' I say and run over to Luis, who is growing as impatient as I am over the time it takes for me to get out of my Papa's rusty old work truck. As I get out of the truck, I see a girl jump out of a car and run up the steps to the school, tears in her eyes, I recognise her from school, but didn't know her name. No doubt she saw the same as us, maybe she isn't as well adjusted to these sort of things as we are.

'Did you see the tits on that girl from high school, they were jumping everywhere, she ran into school and across the lawn,' said Luis. 'You probably didn't because you were talking in the truck with your Papa about fixing fences and repairing roofs and boring ass shit like that.'

Luis and I go to Junior High school, we are the youngest grade in school, but to hear Luis talk anyone would think that he was some big-time player, constant talk about women, gangsters and more to the point how many girls he had and how many gangsters he associated with. All in Luis' own imagination I might add. Luis is my friend but also he is the biggest bull-shitter I had ever met. We knew each other since we were four years old. He used to tell people that his Papa was El Chapo Guzman, the head of the Sinaloa cartel and that when El Chapo was on the run, he visited our barrio and had sex with his Mama and that's how he was born. The only thing he and El Chapo have in common is that they are short. Little does he know that my Papa told me, when he was drunk one night and I asked him about Luis father being El Chapo, Papa's reply was just as I expected, when he had been drinking?

'Luis father was a road digger from Soledad de Los Reyes, who drank Tequila from sun up to sun down. The reason he isn't around anymore is that Luis' Mama caught him balls deep in her sister's ass in her bed. She pulled out a carving knife and chased that deceitful cheating little pecker-head down the street. Although he was small in size that schlong of his was like a baby's arm holding an apple. Legend has it he got on a bus bare ass naked and left for Durango.'

I remember Papa laughing-out-loud as he told me and although he shouldn't have said it that way, I laughed lots, so much so I couldn't catch my breath.

Luis lived in the same barrio as us. He lived three blocks away from my family. Luis' Mama, Maria was good friends with my Mama. Like me he loved Soccer, we played for the barrio soccer team. Luis was fascinated with the gangs that hung out where we lived and he would often hang out with them. Although they would laugh at him and tease him, he would do anything to be part of them. The street gangs in the barrio were the lower ranking gangs that belonged to either Los Zetas or CDG. Luis told me about how the Los Zetas went to war early this year with the Gulf Cartel after they split, both used to be allied against the Sinola cartel and they have been fighting each other since. Luis told me how they would ask Luis to run errands for them that usually meant getting Cervezas and cigarettes for them, stealing from the local store or passing messages to other gangs in the barrio. Luis loved the attention and always updated me on the gang wars. He always said that if I wanted to, I could hang out with them also.

As well as gangs and football Luis loved to talk about girls. He would tell tall- tales of how he “Fucked that girl,” usually pointing at the girls in the upper grades of junior high, when we passed any attractive girl, it was usually followed by Luis saying: “That girl blew me behind the gym,” I would just laugh when he said these things as I knew damn well that these girls didn’t even know his name or ever look twice at him. We were kids, and poor kids from the barrio at best.

Girls and boys from all over the city came to our school, some rich, but most were poor; a few were “Narco kids,” that meant they are the children of some of the Gulf cartel heads in Tamaulipas. No one messed with them, or even spoke with them, unless spoken to.

‘Did you see that shit on the road side — that was bad ass, they killed those cops and cut the nuts off them,’ said Luis, the tone in his voice sounded sincere and slightly afraid.

‘Yeah, I did, why do you think they did that, the cops are only doing their job, doing what they are told to do,’ I said although I am intelligent for my age, or so the teachers have told me, I still didn’t understand why this sort of thing happens.

‘Those cops worked for the Gulf Cartel, didn’t you see the sign. It just happens that way sometimes. Revo and Angel told me that the cops are too afraid to go up against the cartels, in fact they work for them, or most do anyway, if they don’t take a side they die, but if they take a side, then they get killed. Did you hear that shooting this morning, way off in the desert? That was the cops and the Army blasting it out,’ Luis said with blustering excitement.

We walked and talked while climbing the steps to the front of the school and going into the halls.

‘That could have been anything,’ I said ‘there’s that cow shed a few miles out, the cattleman could have been shooting cows for beef, not everything is a shootout,’ I said this trying to reassure myself.

‘That cow shed ain't been used in years, I know because I screwed Isabella from my Math class in that cow shed just a few days ago, she said I was the best she would probably ever have,’ said Luis saying it so convincingly that I think he believed it.

‘No,’ I said ‘There is definitely cattle in those sheds because I screwed your Mama in that shed and she moaned so loud that the bulls cleared out.’

When you’re a kid, it’s all about the Mama jokes or talking shit about the unobtainable: girls, money, exploits on the soccer field. You name it, we bullshit about it.

'You asshole,' said Luis, he punched my arm and we both laughed. Mama jokes were the best, but Luis never made jokes about my Mama, although he could be a jerk sometimes, he was my friend and looked out for me and I did the same for him. As we walked through the halls we saw Miguel and Sebastian standing and talking quietly to one another. Both boys came from our barrio and played soccer with us for the school and our barrio team.

They looked nervous and quiet and didn't seem pleased when Luis shouted out: 'What's up with you pussies.'

Normally they would have played the usual game of verbal abuse-tennis, but today Sebastian only replied: 'Up your ass.'

'That's how your Mama likes it,' says Luis, one love to the short irritating loud-mouth. I can tell something is very wrong as both look very serious indeed. We may only be twelve years old but we have all seen a lot in our short lifetimes and grew up quicker than we should, but something was really wrong here.

'What is it, you guys are scaring me now,' I say.

But I am not scared yet, not scared until I hear Miguel give his reply, and when I hear those three words come from Miguel that's when I know the true meaning of fear?

'Rojo is back!'

***

I lay in the bush covered by the undergrowth looking back towards the cow shed. My breathing is heavy and my chest hurts. I look for the angel who pulled me out of that place. It must have been a sign from God, but already I know that God left this place a long time ago. Just a few hours ago, I was a fourteen-year-old girl on a bus with my Papa, heading towards the US border to meet a man who would help us cross. Those men in masks took us all, that devil with the tattoos on his face and neck, those eyes and that smile. I can see a truck with Soldiers pull into the ranch. I can see men in masks run into the fields in the opposite direction to where I lay. I can hear the gun-fire again and I see some of the masked men fall to the ground. I see Soldiers run to the men on the ground and kick and punch them. I see them hit them with sticks — knives are pulled. Throats are cut — blood pours, screams are loud. Soldiers killed the masked men.

Soldiers run into the cowshed at speed.
Soldiers come out of the cowshed at speed.
Soldiers fall to their knees.
Soldiers say prayers.
God doesn't answer them in this place.

Chapter3

San Fernando, Tamaulipas, Mexico

August 24th 2010

'Sweet Jesus,' I say as I drive through the uptown traffic heading toward Roberto Suarez office at the State Police building. I say building; it's more like a duplex building aside the Municipal Police station. Police and Army trucks are all over the road heading towards highway 101, their blue lights and sirens sounding. Everyone in Kevlar helmets and face masks, masked cops in turrets, pointing machine guns in the direction of their line of sight. I wonder if it's anything to do with those sounds I heard earlier this morning. I see no Narcos on the street, but then again, it's eight-thirty in the morning and those lazy bastards won't be pulling in a shift at the factory or plant or working the fields or putting up fencing like me and my six-year-old will be doing today. Those bastards won't see daylight until this afternoon. Someone should visit them all in their sleep and slit their throats.

I pass the mural of all the missing — the families stood there in hope or as I call it, desperation. As I get closer to the station I see nothing but cops spilling out and jumping into vehicles. From the front entrance, I see Suarez coming out — clipping his gun to his hip; my God he seems to age every time I see him. He reminds me of one of those old movie matinee idols from years gone by. I always think of Dean Martin when I see him; I remember those old records of my fathers. Suarez looks good for a middle-aged man, but the ever-present strain and burden of being one of the only honest cops in the region is taking its toll.

As he slips his suit jacket on and gets into his car, he looks in my direction as I approach.

'Not now, Flip I will call you later.'

I follow him to his vehicle, not wanting to be pushed aside again, no more brush offs.

'No way, how can I keep explaining to my boys that in five months you're no closer to finding their Mama. These boys are starting to hate me because they think I can't follow up on my promise to find their Mama, that's your job remember!'

I am normally very placid, even submissive some might say, but I can't take the look Tomas gives me, the look of disappointment in his father.

'Trust me, not now,' Suarez shouts.

Joaquin is by my side in the hope that this may sway him. He looked and sounded spooked. Suarez and another cop then jump into their car, lights flashing and sirens blaring in convoy they head away from the station. Well that told him didn't it, you silly son of a bitch. You really covered that — Tomas will be so proud of his father.

I get back in the truck with Joaquin who doesn't notice or pay attention to the foul language I curse as I drive along the well-worn route I take the route back towards the barrio. Off highway 101 to the north east of San Fernando the truck rumbles off the highway onto Manolito Chavez's ranch. Chavez is in his seventies now and struggles with the upkeep of his land. He is one of my regular customers and pays fairly well. He pays in cash which I save in a box in the house. I work on the fences surrounding his land, repairing and replacing the posts. As we arrive, the sun is burning down on us; I put a cap on Joaquin to keep the sun of his head. The sweat is pouring off me already and I peel my vest and the short sleeve khaki shirt away from the sweat patches now forming on my body.

As I hammer nails into the posts and panels I can see Joaquin studying the off cuts of wood with the tool-set I purchased for him. To occupy him while I work I set him tasks where I will get him to construct an object using wood and his tools or repair or remove locks using his tools. His attention to such detail is remarkable for a boy of his age. With his tools, there is nothing that fazes him. The concentration on his face, while he works away is second to none. I watch him in deep concentration, his tongue ever so slightly poking from his mouth. His eyes staring at the task in hand, the studying of each tool and the movement of Joaquin's eyes and hands as he tackles his task.

When Tomas or I speak with him about fixing things or building great houses that reach into the clouds, his eyes light up, as I describe the great tower we will one day build. Although he doesn't respond verbally, the joyous look in his eyes is ever prominent. Joaquin still has a habit of wandering off at times; I must keep him occupied, because like any six-year-old, exploration is something that he will still endeavour to do. Slowly he is re-building himself, slowly but surely, he will be the boy he once was — before the Narcos took away his innocence, before the Narcos drew blood in front of his very eyes.

While thinking of this, I walk over to him and kiss him upon the top of his head. I lean over and ask what he is making. Always trying to encourage a response. He continues with making his house from off-cuts of wood. His attention to detail seldom breaking.

Our environment is hard, yet it doesn't seem to affect Joaquin anymore, Tomas is more of a sensitive and somewhat astute boy who sucks it all up, absorbs the horrors around him, which fuels his frustration with me. His resentment grows each day. Joaquin on the other hand carries on without any acknowledgement; in regards to his mother, this was just another traumatic event coupled with the many he has learned to endure.

San Fernando wasn't always this way; it was a place of honourable intent with honourable people. Four years ago, Calderon's war on drugs started in Mexico, Laena's father and mother left for El Paso, and purchased some land a little while later. Antonio offered me work, and for Laena, the boys to cross over and live with them. Laena's father and mother were good people, generous and loving towards their children and grandchildren. They built a ranch on the plot of land, out in the western regions of El Paso. The work was hard and Antonio, even now in his sixties still undertook many of the cattle drives. He was a proud man who lived life believing that hard work never hurt anyone.

I had never seen the ranch, but I imagined beautiful landscapes offset by the mountain ranges of Juarez to the south. Laena went to visit the ranch two years ago, and went with the boys. When they returned, it was all they could talk about. They spoke of El Paso, like it was the Shangri-La of the western-world. They were happy, but in their joint happiness, I felt isolated. I had never travelled outside of Mexico. By this stage of my life, I was not the young and enthusiastic go-getter that I set out to be. I was the man I am now, the one who lays alone in the bed, he once shared with his wife, wishing she were still here. Praying each night, that once his head touched the pillow, he would pass out in the usual drunken deep sleep, and vicariously relive his old life again. Only in my dreams, do I feel the happiness and love that once was. Where our family was complete — where we were together again.

Why didn't I take the position? Why didn't I just go along with Laena and the boys? Indulge them, cross over and go live in America. Just one of the moral quandaries that I reflect upon, I think of Tomas and Joaquin sharing a bed in the neighbouring room in our excuse for a house in the middle of the barrio in San Fernando. Why I ask? Pure and simple — fucking pride — pure Male Spanish pride. Laena told me about this, she told me that I wouldn't be forfeiting my sense of pride by going to live and work with her family, it was an opportunity of a lifetime, a chance for us all to go live in the US and have a better standard of life, not to have to work ourselves into the ground for minimum wage, to get the children out of the barrio away from the gangs, away from the temptations that await them when they are older. Away from the violence, to live without fear of becoming a victim of the ever-consuming horrors that this war on drugs now holds when you're just a normal working family in Tamaulipas or anywhere in Mexico.

My pride was all I had left of my own identity and I held onto it like a pennant. In fact, it was a poisoned chalice, because by staying here, our situation is as Laena predicted. My fucking pride is why Laena is missing. I can feel my eyes fill with tears again.

My town was full of men and women who worked hard, raised families went to church and lived in peace. Then the Narcos arrived, then Calderon and his merry men marched through the various border towns and cities with SUVs and tanks — armed soldiers and cops. The war on drugs became the war of attrition, Narcos and soldiers fighting it out in the streets. The honourable men and women became targets. Once this unholy clusterfuck started it couldn't stop. Like a runaway freight train veering towards the station, never losing momentum. Now we the people pay the price: raped, tortured, shot, robbed and splayed out into the streets for CNN news to eventually capture on camera, but never broadcast because wars in the Middle East were the ones that mattered.

In March of this year the Red Cross refused to treat the wounded in Mexico because Sicarios were shooting at them. The US Secretary of State, Hillary Clinton came to Mexico with the defence secretary, Robert Gates where they pledged to assist Mexican forces in fighting the Cartels with offers of gunships and aid. March was the same month that Laena disappeared. Thanks Hillary, give my regards to Bill, tell him I wouldn't mind getting blown by big chicks as well, hope you enjoyed the Mariachi show, the piñata, the bull fights. I bet you didn't catch the headless naked corpse swinging from the underpass show.

I curse my back-breaking job and curse the lack of money and having to bring my child to work with me, because he has no school to go to any more. I curse having the lack of fortitude to fulfill my dreams. All my hopes and dreams had faded long before the recent violence had erupted with such perpetual motion. I had given up long before that. I gave up journalism and took to handy work for minimum wage. The college education I worked so hard for in my younger years, wasted. A once promising career in journalism gone, because I couldn't stand up and be counted, because the sounds of my father voice yelling

'You will never amount to shit, you're weak,' rang through my ears, I still hear it now, although the words were said when I was a child, they were still as clear and as hard-hitting as if it were yesterday. Coupled with being witness to a cartel Sicario, walk into the San Fernando office and shoot my editor in the face — because he published an exposé about a cartel member being responsible for throwing four heads into a local discotheque. This ground me firmly into the reality of the way things were in Mexico. The New-world-order had taken form. It was the era of the Narco.

True to form I quit my job at the newspaper, like my father always predicted, I was a loser and a quitter and good for nothing. Just a runt from the barrio, a 'Nobody, who would fade into the world and out of the world, never making your mark.'

Being a 'nobody' holds no occupational hazard. I look like a peasant, I am a peasant, my children are peasants and no one looks our way. My philosophy is if no one notices me, then no one is looking at me, and if no one is looking at me then I will keep what's left of our family alive. I could see the environment around me change; I could see the streets of where we lived, occupied by the cartels and gangs, the violence in the air, the gun-shots at night in the distant corners of the barrio. At night, when the shots were being fired in the street, we would all gather in our room and lay on the floor under the bed with our arms around the boys. I still remember Laena telling the boys: 'It's all right, it's just firecrackers.' She would hum nursery rhymes to them and sooth them off to sleep.

I wipe sweat from my eyes and ask Joaquin to go to the truck, which is parked near to the front of Chavez place, to grab some more nails and a nail bar. I watch him walk off to the truck, head hung low. I feel great sadness in the knowledge that my once care-free boy has been reduced to this. I curse this fucking place and those who brought this shit-storm down upon us.

***

It feels like I have been running for hours — maybe I have, through wide open spaces, dusty farmland and hills. After what I saw on at that ranch and In that shed, I don't think I can go on. Papa oh Papa I just left you there. I am dying I can feel It. It's deserted out here; I can no longer hear the cars racing towards the ranch, the place had soldiers and men in uniform everywhere. In El Salvador, it is difficult to trust police or soldiers, so I don't want to start now. I am thirsty, my throat is burning and dry, I feel weak and I can't shake that face —

that grin — those tattoos and that singing, why would someone with such a beautiful voice do such terrible things to people. My tennis shoes are old and worn anyway, but now I don't recognise them through the dust and the blood. I can see another ranch up ahead, it looks old, maybe I could hide there maybe someone there may help me, there is a road that leads to the ranch, maybe it joins a town in the far away distance, but in those towns may be more men with mask and guns or maybe that boy with the tattoos and that evil face lives there. I run again towards the ranch, it's not far, I can see a truck stopped just outside the big gate. There is a boy and a man stood by the fence, it looks like they are fixing the fence. The boy is walking away from the man and heading towards the truck. The boy looks young, he is short and stocky, a little belly poking over his pants and he is wearing a cap. Maybe he will help me, maybe he has water, just have to make it there, so tired, so scared, keep running.

***

I know Papa is sad and I know that he wants me to be well again. I am frightened all the time. I just can't stop thinking about my friends. I can't stop thinking about the noise of the guns and seeing my friends from class fall to the ground. My teachers jumping in front of us, watching them as they fall to the ground — screaming and crying out. My teacher, Mrs Rivera pushed me aside, she saved me, she saved a lot of the children. I remember her falling to the ground — the blood was everywhere. They ran around the school-yard shooting at each other, the noise frightened me. I want to leave this place, I have no friends, I have no school, all I want is to live without being afraid.

When I build my Sky Scraper I want to live on the top floor with Papa and Tomas and Mama. I don't know where Mama has gone. Papa says she is lost but will be back, that's stupid as Mama knows where we live; he treats me like I am stupid. They whisper around me, they don't know that I listen in. As I search through Papa's truck I struggle to find anything, it's such a mess in the back, tools, nails and fixings thrown everywhere. Maybe I will tidy this truck after I give Papa the nails. Found the nails and find the nail bar at last, better get — A girl, there is a girl stood at the back of the van, she tries to speak to me, she has blood all over her face and her clothes, her hair is stuck together with blood and dust. Maybe she is one of them — maybe she wants to hurt me — got to run away, got to get Papa; she might try and hurt me, maybe she wants to hurt Papa as well, I can feel my grip around the nail bar get tighter, the girl puts her arms out to me, she is trying to speak, she tries to climb into the back of the truck —

***

'What the fuck — Joaquin, what is it? what's happened? why are you crying.'

He runs at me, not stopping. He jumps into my arms and is crying aloud. I can't seem to stop him crying, he only ever cries like this when distressed or when he is scared.

'What is it,' I say in a lower than normal tone, 'Tell Papa what's wrong.'
He is still looking at the truck and sobbing. I don't know why I am asking, when I know a response isn't coming anytime soon. He won't take his eyes away from the truck and no matter what I say, he won't stop crying. 'Shhh, don't cry,' I say.

I am scared now, he isn't usually like this unless he has been startled or something out of the ordinary, or Joaquin's definition of ordinary happens. I walk slowly towards the truck; I can feel Joaquin's grip get tighter. It's only about thirty metres away, but I can already see someone on the ground adjacent to the back of my truck.

'Did someone hurt you,' I can feel anger building up inside of me. It's deserted out here; there is no one around, who could have startled the boy like this?

'Who is that on the ground,' I say, still unsure why I am even asking such a series of questions. Suddenly I am hit by a lightning bolt, did Joaquin do this, I can see the bag of screws on the ground and the nail bar lying beside the person. Just my luck, in the land with the highest murder rate outside of any war zone and my six-year-old son has killed someone and now I am about to be convicted of third degree murder of some shit heel bandit trying to rob my truck. It's funny how spontaneous the mind is and how rapidly it thinks. Before I have moved five metres I am trying to remember if I have a shovel on the truck and can I bury the body, or should I buy some lime to put in the grave. I can't let my son take the wrap I would have to say it was me — then the boys would end up in a state home for delinquent children, only to grow up to sling drugs for the Narcos and I would have failed them.

Put the brakes on that over active mind of yours Al Capone, you're planning hijacking a Boeing seven-four-seven and demanding a flight to Egypt when you don't even know who or why someone is lying on the ground. I go over to the body on the ground.

It's a girl — not much older than Tomas; she looks Spanish, maybe Mexican. Long dark hair, dusty and what looks like blood on her face. The blood looks dry, so at least that confirms Joaquin didn't hit her with anything when he was spooked. He is known to lash out when angry or scared. Both Tomas and I have the bruises to show for it.

'It's OK Joaquin,' my voice sounding less panicked: 'It's a girl, just a young girl who has fallen over. You're my helper and the best helper I could ever wish for. Go into the front of the truck and get some of those spare bottles of water will you.' He runs to the front of the truck and returns with the water.

I clean some of the blood away and quickly see that she is alive and well, the blood didn't come from her, the blood on her face has not pooled anywhere and looks smeared, although there is a lot of it.

'Stick that in your ass Suarez,' I say to myself: 'you're not the only swinging dick cop around here after all,' strangely I start to congratulate myself after solving the mystery of noticing that the blood didn't come from the girl.

A wave of anxiety comes over me. I am nervous and slightly ill at ease with being faced with such an oddity. How on earth did this girl get here? Where did she come from? She is so young; surely she wouldn't be mixed up in all this Narco shit. Although the teenage gangs are fearsome and deadly, she doesn't look the type. Most gangbangers look exactly that, just take Rojo for example. No time to be thinking of that sadistic little Bastard.

I pour some water gently onto her lips, let her taste the water. Joaquin gets a rag from the truck and passes it to me. It's strange how I notice that in times of need Joaquin is quick to think on his feet and always seems to know how to deal with problems. I pour a little more onto her lips and onto the rag and squeeze it gently onto her forehead. The girl wakes suddenly and jumps up; I fall backwards onto my ass. She looks afraid, she is startled.

'No, no, no,' I say in haste 'I am not going to hurt you, I am trying to help, you need water — here take the bottle, my little boy and I fix houses and fences, we mean you no harm, I swear.'

I stand up slowly and put my hands out to the side, the international sign that says I mean you no harm, just look at me I couldn't fight my way out of a bar full of rowdy Nuns.

'If you run, you are miles from any town, you wouldn't make it on foot, let me help you. I am Felipe, but everyone calls me Flip and this is Joaquin, I have another boy also about your age, his name is Tomas,' that declaration usually calms a distressed child, but this girl looks terrified. 'What happened to you, are you hurt.'

The girl shakes her head, but stares at me blankly. She understands Spanish, that's a start. The blood and dust has run away from her face owing to the amount of water I managed to pour over her, I can see that her skin tone looks slightly darker than that of girls from around these parts of Mexico, maybe southern Mexico? Guatemala? Further into Central America maybe. She is of slight build and what is apparent is how pretty she is.

The girl breaks down and begins to cry, she cries aloud before falling into bouts of heavy sobs. This can mean only one thing, I recognise those very same cries, I have heard them from my own children when I told them Laena disappeared. The cries rip through to my soul. She falls to her knees. Do something, don't just stand there. I can hear Laena say it now as though she was looking over me now from wherever she may be. I stand over the girl; wary that she is distraught and probably very scared. I place one of my hands on her shoulder and hold it there for what seems like an eternity. I look back towards the direction she must have come from to get here, over the low ground up onto the hill where Chavez's ranch is situated. It's a little far but it's the same direction I heard those shots ring out from earlier this morning. Christ, she has made her way nearly ten miles over desert ground. What on earth would make someone do that? What did happen there? What danger is she in now?

Chapter4

San Fernando, Tamaulipas, Mexico

August 24th 2010

The teacher is lecturing us on history of the Catholic Church, I can see Ms Lupo mouth the words 'Cyril of Jerusalem' and his lectures when he was a Bishop in the year 350AD. I see the movements of her mouth but I can't hear the words. The only words I hear and have heard ringing through my ears and my head are 'Rojo is back.'

The halls of the school have echoed the very same things throughout the day. Some kids buzzing with excitement, because to them the whole Narco gang member thing is something they aspire to. I like the word Aspire, Papa told me what it meant, again when he was drunk he said 'Son, I aspired to write in newspapers, but what I really wanted to do in life was, more than that was to paint houses, repair roofs and garden walls and lay concrete in gardens. I truly aspired to become a fuck up.'

I laughed when I heard Papa curse, because Mama didn't like that talk, Papa spoke this way when he drank beer, he lightens up when he is drunk. I often like him more when he has drunk beer because he admits that he messed everything up. He does not hit us, like some fathers do when they have been drinking beer, in fact he hugs both Joaquin and I and starts to laugh and fool around. Usually Alejandro is with him and they drink beer together. I find their conversations funny when I hear them shouting off about what they would do if they were in power.

My mind is going everywhere; I forget where I was now. Some kids Aspire to be Narcos, others are just plain terrified, and with Rojo they have good reason to be. As school finishes Luis is still talking about Rojo. Secretly Luis is as frightened of Rojo as I and other kids of the barrio are. Many months ago, Rojo left town, the reason behind him leaving has become that of legend. I remember Luis telling me the story of why he was hunted. Before this, Rojo was feared anyway because he was a killer, because he was crazy and because he didn't care. He wasn't like all the other gang bangers who just wanted to be Los Zetas and played tough and talked shit and carried a gun but couldn't hit a cow's ass with a banjo (another saying I got from Papa) he was a killer.

For every person he killed, he had a tear drop tattooed on his face. He started from the corner of each eye, now he has three rows of tears down his face. They say that he has started on his chest and arms now, I don't know how Luis and the other boys know this, but I am sure they got it via the bullshit express — another line I got from Papa.

Rojo went to a Gulf cartel member's house in the south of the city with a group of boys from the barrio, to initiate them into the gang. To make it into the East Side Demons, members must kill to prove their loyalty. Rojo was trying to impress the Zetas and help recruit barrio kids. Rojo had to test the kids, so he planned on doing so by sending them to the Narco's house and kill him. Luis tells me that they busted into the house carrying guns and found the man sat having dinner with his family. There were two young boys about nine and twelve and two girls who were six and fourteen. Also, there was a baby in the house.

I remember Luis' voice changed at this part of the story — he sounded sickened but didn't want to say so, but continued to tell it. First the boy who was to be initiated killed the wife in front of the family by stabbing her: forty times to the face, neck and chest. The gang, under Rojo's command took the family into the living room, the Narco, was put on his knees and had his hands tied behind his back. Rojo raped his two sons in front of his very eyes while the other boys raped his fourteen-year-old daughter. Once they had finished, the children were killed in front of the Narco. Just when I thought the story couldn't get any worse; the boy, who was to be initiated was told to get the baby. He was then ordered to swing the baby by its legs and hit its head against the table to kill the child. The boy was so sickened that he said he couldn't. The heads of the entire family were taken and placed on wooden spikes on the front lawn. The baby was never seen again or even spoken of. It was at that point Rojo announced to the initiated boy that the man of the house was not a Narco, but a local bank manager and he wanted to test him — to see if he could do the job, because he failed them, he would have to go to the police and tell them that it was he — and he alone who murdered the bank manager and his family — or the boy's family would suffer the same. Rojo had qualified to join the Zetas because he was willing to do what others couldn't and wouldn't do. Rojo went to Nuevo Laredo and joined the Zetas. They had heard of his evil wicked ways as he wanted them to and they welcomed him with open arms. The devil of San Fernando as he is now known, a sick evil rapist, killer, torturer someone who butchered his parents and other families just to add to his reputation.

All of this and Rojo is still only fifteen-years-old

After our soccer and meagre lunch, we have gym class. You can always tell the barrio kids and the kids from the nice parts of the city. They all wear gym clothes with names or fancy logo's or men on horses and all that other shit. The boys and girls from the barrio wear rags. We studied Dickens in class and that is how I imagine what they would look like. I have good grades at school and in sports, but I always feel like I am not worth as much as some of the other middle class kids who are in my classes. Luis, Miguel and Seb are in the lower classes so I am left to face the comments from the kids in my class about how poor I am or if I beg for food, or if my Mama disappeared because she was some kind of drug mule or a whore. I mainly ignore the comments, but I occasionally let Luis know about them. This then ends up with Luis and some of his crazy friends from his class beating the shit out of those assholes. It's funny how I let stuff slip out accidentally.

I like school because I feel safe here; the looks and name calling are just par for the course. Home just reminds me of how much I miss Mama. I hate Papa because he is weak and a coward. It's his fault we are still here in this place, no matter how much Mama asked, even begged him to go to El Paso, he resisted. I heard him say to Mama 'We have a life here, this is just fucking typical of you Laena, always wanting to change things, you're ashamed of me, of this house, of how we turned out. I am a man; I'm not heading off to live with your family in America and get a job with your father. I am no fucking charity case. Why did you even marry me, I thought more of you than that I thought you wanted me regardless?'

Papa left the house that night very angry and Mama cried. Mama, Joaquin and me had just returned from El Paso and we nagged at Papa about leaving here and moving. Mama told me that it was wrong of her to make Papa feel that way. When Papa came back he said sorry. She never mentioned it again. Within a few months, she vanished. Vanished because Papa was too proud to leave, because he didn't want people to think he couldn't care for his family. He didn't care for us because if he did we wouldn't be here now. Mama would be with me when I got home and would tuck Joaquin and I into bed and sing to us and tell us stories. I feel so alone. Joaquin doesn't speak at all. Papa doesn't speak because he knows it's all his fault and I hate him for it. I hate being scared all the time, I hate all the killing and shooting and the gangs. I hate that all the good people are slowly leaving the barrio and moving away because of the drugs and gangs. We stay here because one day Mama might walk back through our door.

The girl is limp and lifeless as I carry her out of the back of the truck and into Chavez house.

'Over here Flip, on the cot in the other room,' old man Chavez says as he leads me to the cot at the rate only a seventy-six-year-old man can. More of a shuffle than a walk. Hunched over after years of gruelling hard work, thin as a whip, his shuffle taking speed. I lay her down on the cot, a young stable hand follows carrying water and rags. Joaquin stands by my side while I kneel and mop the young girl's brow. It seems that whenever in doubt about medical attention, try wet rags on the patient's forehead.

'Where did you find her,' Chavez says as he looks over the lifeless body: 'how did she make her way here, there is no other place around here that is in walking distance for miles.'

'Seven,' I know how far the next place is. 'Seven miles is the nearest place, that old ranch with the cow shed out back. The guy who owned the ranch took off some time ago. But why would she come from there, there's nothing, out there.'

My bewilderment is a front for what I truly suspect; the old man's beady eyes scan over my face until we lock eyes.

'I may have been born at night Flip, just not last night,' the old buzzard's X-ray vision can see through the front. 'Just because you're a smart guy, don't treat the rest of us like jack asses; talk to me, I can see the cogs turning in that head of yours.'

'Hear the cogs, not see the cogs you senile old crow.' I can get away with this kind of talk; ten years ago, a backhand would be coming my way. 'Must remember that the older you get; I must start upping my fee to not fix your shitty old fence.'
He laughs and I put my hand on his shoulder. I am starting to feel a sense of doom, for years the cartels and the drug wars took the lives of people like us, but we were just collateral damage. Caught in crossfires all along the border, but now I had a feeling that now it was beginning to reach out and touch us. Rather than observers, the people of Mexico were becoming a major part, and as always, the real losers, those who didn't have a choice and didn't want an invite to this dance of death. Looking down upon the blood stained and unconscious girl, I knew that she wasn't part of this but has now inadvertently entered my life and possibly brought trouble with her.

'Chavez, did you hear that gunfire earlier today,' I can tell by the look on that worn face of his, that those old ears work occasionally.

'I walk like John Wayne with shit in his pants and get up for a piss three times a night, what makes you think my hearing is tip top,' always jocular in his delivery. I always wished he was my old man.

'There were shots coming from north of the barrio this morning and suddenly cops and soldiers flying out of the city heading out toward the direction of that derelict old ranch. I hear gunfire every day and cops don't rush to it, but today something was different. Remember that Federal Cop I told you about, Suarez.' I pause to check we are on the same page. He nods; good Chavez still has his marbles.

'I told you before he was honest and a good cop and cool as they come, well he looked spooked, like really spooked as he rushed out of the station. That tells me that it's not Narco shit, it's something else. Cops either throw parties over dead Narcos or start fretting over where their next pay off is coming from. Also, there were three dead cops laid out for all to see with a Los Zeta banner spread out announcing that they were responsible,' My mind is working overtime as I relay my suspicion. 'Something has changed, the Gulf cartel only fucked with others in that line of business, but this is something else.'

I see Chavez look down and take a moment to process this. No witty or acerbic comeback. I must go to Suarez, tell him about the girl, it's not my problem, it's not my war. I hope Laena doesn't think too badly of me. Apathy equals survival in my book.

I don't want to take Joaquin with me to find Suarez, but he couldn't stay with Chavez and his employees, it would unsettle him. Even if they found something to occupy him he would potentially wander off. That puts a lot of strain on others. Whatever went on at that deserted Ranch and caused the girl to end up at Chavez place is something I don't want a child to witness.

My truck bumps over the spine roads that connect to the dreaded Highway 101. Bandit territory, the routes that the Narcos take to deliver shipments and money and buy guns from Yankees to shoot down innocent Mexican children and mothers.

I am not far from the ranch, I travel along one of the spine roads, up a hill until I get to the top where I look down through the dust covered windshield, I see the ranch about half a mile down the road. The ranch is swarming with Policia and Soldiers. Armoured SUVs — men in uniform stood around the perimeter — guns pointing off into the brush covered deserted fields and roads. Lights still flashing on top of the marked police vehicles. Ambulances are there. I continue down the road, expecting someone in a black uniform with his face covered by a balaclava point a machine gun in my face and pull me from the cab of my truck. I can see a huge white marquee tent erected at the rear directly adjacent to the cowshed. What the fuck, I think to myself as I get closer. I slow my speed down so not to end up with a bullet either through the windshield or my engine block.

I stop about fifty yards from the front gate of the ranch. Its chaos here, I can hear voices shouting aloud and orders being given from within the compound of the ranch. I can see many men in suits, many of them now in shirt sleeves; sweat pouring from them, shirts stuck to their backs. Cops in uniform stood around, probably around fifty cops at the ranch and several soldiers scattered within the compound. I have never seen such a gathering; men writing on clipboards, doctors stood around talking with federal cops. The doctors don't seem rushed or panicked. That can mean only one thing, there is no one left to treat, whatever has happened here happened some time ago and medical attention is no longer required, all torches have been extinguished, adios Muchachos. Maybe the place was being used as some kind of Meth Lab or Cocaine processing lab. I notice the Tamaulipas coroner's truck, or as I always knew it when I worked at the newspaper — the meat wagon parked at the rear. As I got closer I notice lots of meat wagons parked inside the compound. Sure enough, a cop is walking towards me, what the hell to do I tell him, how do I know that he isn't on a payroll, how do I know that he won't sell me off later down the road?

'Go back,' he yells 'You fucking deaf, I said get out of here.'

'Senor,' I get back to obedient peasant mode 'I have to see Senor Roberto Suarez of the Federal Policia right away, it's something very important.'

'You tell me what it's about and I will get the message to him.'

'Senor,' peasant oozing from every pour 'he asked me to bring him something very important, he called me and asked I deliver it to him right away, I had to give it to him personally. I am so sorry and don't want to cause offence, but it was an order. I am a courier and I cannot disobey my orders.'

I now favour subservient passive aggressive, something I have mastered over my entire life. Try living with my father and talk shit, you would be in the ground.

The Cop pauses and then uses his Radio which is connected to his Kevlar vest, his covered head tilts down to the radio as he asks for Suarez to come to the main gate. I stand solemnly, my head looking down to the ground, I am waiting for thirty minutes before I even see Suarez making his way towards the sentry through the main gate of the ranch. I notice everyone inside the compound is hurrying here and there, I can see people in white suits with gloves, face masks and shoe coverings coming out from the cowshed, not in full view, but I can see enough that tells me there are dead bodies in there, probably Narcos. The one thing that stands out to me is the tone of the place. The faces that I see look horrified or disturbed. The expression I saw on Suarez face this morning is replicated over and over on each face I see. Suarez is heading towards me, he looks Pissed, really Pissed. Probably thinks I am here about Laena. He walks toward me like he is about to hit me. I put my hands out and feel I must say something first before I take one on my glass jaw.

'Senor, I have brought you something you needed, it's what you really wanted,' this year's academy award goes to Felipe Hernandez, Suarez immediately detects something as he is just used to my Submissive tone. 'Come to my truck it's in there, just like you asked.'

Suarez seemed surprised that I was not the sad sack pushover he always had me down for. Maybe I should throw in a little: 'Hey fuck nuts what about finding my wife rather than pulling bullets out of those who deserve it.' Maybe too soon.

We stand by the truck; he is dust covered and sweat soaked. He has aged even since this morning.

'What is this Flip,' he is becoming impatient, 'can't you see that I am into something here, don't tell me you dragged me out here to take another look at your boy in the hope that this will make me feel guilty. You know I am trying to find her, as well as hundreds of other missing people.'

'I didn't come here for Laena, it's about a girl I came across a few hours ago at Chavez place. She came from this direction and was alone and on foot. I heard the commotion earlier today and thought it was all connected.'

I can see Suarez look at me attentively, my tone is much more assertive than he is used to. His eyes squint as he is joining the dots as quick as I can get the words out.

'She was covered in blood, but appears to have no injuries and is unconscious, probably heat exhaustion. She is just a kid; I mean a normal everyday kid not some gang banger hanger on — '

'Where's Chavez ranch — who is Chavez, can he be trusted,' his voice getting quieter and he looks around as though someone might be watching.

'It's about seven miles north of here, she is lucky she found the place, she could have died out there. Chavez is a good man; he is one of the good people around here.' I try to convince Suarez, but he still has the air of suspicion about him. 'What is all this anyway?'

'You don't want to know,' Suarez says, 'get the girl way out of this region, maybe take her back to the city; you have my cell phone number let me know where.'

'No, no way I gave you information, I am not a cop I am not bringing this shit on my door step, maybe that girl is some Narco mule or something and you want me to take her somewhere, I have children of my own, she is your witness I only wanted to help because you need all the help you can get and I would want someone to do the same if they knew something about Laena, that's why I came here.'

'Officer Rodriguez,' Suarez shouts, 'I have to take this man into the compound to gather something for me, is that OK. Just keep an eye on his truck and his son.'

Officer Rodriguez walks towards the truck. I give Joaquin another drink of water from our bottle, because if I don't he wouldn't necessarily think to have one himself and I wouldn't trust the Stasi Commando. I place Joaquin in the back of the truck as he has taken a liking to sorting out the ungodly mess that is the back of my truck. That will keep him occupied until I get back.

I follow Suarez inside the compound through the armed sentries, the uniformed cops and soldiers are standing around and keeping observations on the surrounding landscape, no doubt to see who is watching them. No one looks at me or even pays any attention. I get to the forensic tent, where Suarez pulls back the folding door, inside I can see up to ten people in white suits with masks and gloves and covers over their shoes. There are large metal suitcases containing all sorts of forensic equipment such as swab kits, with powders and tweezers and collection pots and test tubes. Suarez enters through a ready-made citadel, I follow; where I reach the mouth of the cow shed, people in white suits stood with cameras, flashes going off inside the shed. I fix my gaze into the shed — oh Lord, oh God.

Bodies stacked up against the left side of the wall of the shed, bullet shells everywhere. The bodies drenched in blood, dried blood pouring from the mounds of tangled bodies. I can't tell at this point who is male and who is female. I can see faces looking up at me with grimace, contorted with pain and horror. Their last facial expressions before being machine-gunned to death, bodies on top of each other, each face possessing that same look. At a rough guess, I can see up to twenty bodies. As I compose myself my breathing switches from shallow to controlled. I can feel my blood pump and my heart race as I slowly realise that the faces looking back at me are people just like us, just like me. Not a Narco looking bastard amongst them. The inside of the shed is riddled with bullet holes, as I look to my right in the far corner I can see another pile of bodies, more people in amongst that pile. I don't enter the shed; I can smell something I had never really smelled before in such great concentration. The smell of death, the heat inside the shed is unbearable, the bodies starting to rot, the blood drying on the ground. Hair matted with dried blood — faces missing flesh, where the bullets have torn through the skin. Heads with scorch marks where the ungodly bastards shot them at close range.

I look again around the shed and see a third pile of bodies — I turn to walk out of the shed, when I look to my left I notice body bags: lined up after another, after another, after another. I move outside of the tent, I bump into a white suited clad man, who says 'Get this man out of here,' I feel Suarez take my arm and lead me outside. I feel sick, as I get outside I see dead men on the ground, gold chains, Narco wear clothing, earrings, pearl handled pistols in their dead hands.

'These bastards and others like them did this,' Suarez says making his point loud and clear. 'Those people in there were not Narcos or gang bangers or mules; they were from Guatemala and El Salvador making their way to the US.'

He leads me to the very back of the ranch. I immediately see buses; several buses — deserted, the doors open, bags and suitcases still inside. Bags and cases that were packed while these poor people thought they had hope, thought that they were escaping a land they no longer recognised and flee to a land of freedom and opportunity. I can see a teddy bear on the floor of the bus, it's pink, it belonged to someone young, too young to ever be here, someone who probably carried it throughout the journey, someone who sat with excitement and giddy enthusiasm knowing they were about fifty miles from the Border to the US. Belonged to someone who's last memory would have been dragged from the bus and led into this place, holding their Mother and Father's hand, not knowing what fate awaited them.

'Now you see Flip why I can't have that girl come here, so far we have nearly fifty bodies and we are finding more all around the ranch in other places, I can't let anyone know about her. Another man got away, he's with the army as we speak — he led us here, and already I have heard other cops, my colleagues on cell phones no doubt telling those responsible they have left a living witness. I can't protect that man, but I will protect her. That's why I need you, take this.' He hands me a manila folder; I look inside it contains nothing. 'If anyone asks you, stick to the story you had to drop something off and I asked you to deliver this to my partner Benito, you got that.'

I nod, Suarez suddenly stands up, I look behind me and I see a man in a state police uniform. He is about fifty years of age with very dark slicked hair combed to the side. He is tall and slim and is wearing mirrored aviator sunglasses. He has a match in the corner of his mouth. He certainly caught Suarez attention. He wears no mask or face covering or Kevlar and seems to be of rank, I glance and notice his name tag has Captain. I don't catch his last name. His skin is tight to his face and he has a pencil thin dark moustache. He is exposed to everyone around him and not in disguise, probably because he doesn't fear the Narcos, his swagger and sinister grin tell me that he runs with the hares and the hounds and doesn't care who knows it.

'Get this sorry sack of shit out of here,' as I guessed he was as much of a bastard as he looked, his voice never raising above monotone but enough for me to get the picture.

'He's with me, I asked him to run an errand for me and now he's leaving,' Suarez stands defiant.

'I am a Captain you jumped up little shit, that top Investigator mantle you hold so dearly doesn't mean shit to me.' He stands nose to nose with Suarez, Suarez doesn't budge an inch. Suarez knows what this guy is and that's why the respect angle doesn't cut it.

I leave immediately, I don't hear any more of the conversation, I look back and see the Captain staring directly at me, those mirrored shades radiating the hot afternoon sun in my direction, I get a bad vibe from him. I head past the tent and curiosity gets the better of me, I look in again and see body bags and people in white suits and camera flashes and people moving around. I head towards the main gate, masked cops and soldiers carrying their guns at shoulder height, just in case another attack comes.

I can't make sense of what happened there, not in my own head, why those people, what did they do so wrong. They travelled from other countries to get to the US. They were poor working people, just like me, so why do this to them? What did they do or what did they pose? I get Joaquin out of the back of the truck and into the cab. So much for my fucking apathy!

Chapter5

San Fernando, Tamaulipas, Mexico

August 24th 2010

Where in the hell is that asshole I told him I didn't have Soccer practice after school. No doubt he has been working and probably had some Cervezas at the end of work with that old man on his ranch. I am angry — I have seen this all too often now. Papa has turned up to collect me from school and I have seen Cerveza bottles in the cab of his truck, he usually has some bullshit reason, like he finished a job and it's his little celebration or he was paid extra for finishing before time or the Sun rose today in the east. I have been waiting half an hour, I can see the Narcos riding around the streets near to my school. The young Narcos looking to start some trouble somewhere or generally patrolling; searching for the enemy, or the older Narcos collecting children from school. Bastards; dripping in gold, nice fancy cars, beautiful and younger women by their side, cowboy hats, leather cowboy boots, the huge belt buckles, all here to collect their brat children who look down their noses at the likes of Luis and I and call us names. We don't say anything because we don't need that kind of trouble.

Papa's truck screeches to a halt outside of the school. 'Quick Tomas — get in.' Fuck you I think, why the rush. I walk slowly, just to prove my point, 'Come on, hurry.' He genuinely looks and sounds concerned about something, maybe it's news about Mama.

'Why the rush — where have you been, I told you I didn't have practice tonight,' I don't hide my annoyance.

'Something happened today, while I was working at Chavez Ranch that's why I was late.' He sounded sorry about being late, but the way he said it sounded like he had purpose, like it wasn't just some excuse. 'I will tell you everything before we get home.'

Throughout the thirty-minute journey he tells me everything; finding the girl, Papa going to the deserted ranch outside of the City, to the murders at the ranch and the bodies found and how Suarez has pleaded with Papa for help in hiding the girl until he got to our house. Papa described the bodies piled up on top of each other, the bullets on the ground and in the walls, the blood and the flies and the smell. As he told me the story he looked dead ahead and the story just seemed to pour from his mouth, almost like he was telling an adult the story. His voice quaked and cracked as he told the story, I could see the one eye fill with water and he couldn't look at me at all. Papa even stated that he took Joaquin with to the ranch and how stupid he was for that. I looked down at Joaquin who had a ratchet screw driver in his hand and was looking at it and was twisting the ratchet so it made the clicking sound.

It took the entire journey for Papa to tell me everything. We arrive at our house and go in. Luis mother, Maria was at the house and on Papa's bed was the girl he spoke of.

She was filthy dirty — dried blood streaked around her face. She wore denim jeans and a pale T shirt and tennis shoes, all her clothing was filthy. She looked like she was Mexican, long dark hair down to her shoulders, although now it was scattered over the pillow. Despite being covered in dirt and dried blood I could tell she was pretty, the longer I looked at her I realised how pretty she was. I didn't recognise her from around the barrio and I remember Papa saying that the people found at the ranch were from other countries.

'Listen Tomas,' Papa says, breaking me away from looking at the girl, 'It's very important that we speak to no one about this, we don't tell a soul, and Suarez said the same thing. Maria won't even tell Luis because he couldn't keep a secret if his life depended on it.' Papa looked at Maria, she nodded her head in agreement.

Maria sat on the edge of the bed next to the girl and spoke softly to her, trying to wake her. I liked Maria she was gentle and kind and treated Joaquin and me very well since Mama disappeared. She often came over to the house and spoke with me about it, her voice and the things she said soothed me, it was almost like having a replacement, well almost. Maria is a larger lady, the boys joked about the size of her breasts, much to Luis annoyance. She had long curled hair and a kind face. She also had a terrible temper; it was something that could erupt, with very little provocation. Luis had a talent for making her angry, by the way he would talk back at her and use bad language in front of her and the rude magazines he would smuggle into his house. Maria worked in a factory on the outskirts of the city, she worked hard and long hours, which generally meant that Luis would come over to our house and eat. Maria would also return the favour when when needed. However, more and more Luis would go and hang out with the gangs in the barrio. Many occasions Maria would go up to the gangs and grab hold of Luis and drag him back home. She was not afraid to call them names, some names I had never heard before and even hit them with her broom.

Papa had called Maria at work and asked if she could finish early and come to our house. Luis had gone home with a couple of kids from High school who have a car and are part of the gangs, as they drove off I saw one of the boy's hand cigarettes out and Luis light one up. I didn't let Maria know this.

'Hey boys,' Maria looked at both Joaquin and I, 'Why don't you both have a look in the refrigerator and get something prepared for dinner. I have to run a bath for this young lady and try and clean her up, she is very tired and needs our help, just until the policeman gets here.'

As I go into the Kitchen, I hear the girl wake; she doesn't speak but makes a grumbling sound and then shrieks. I hear Maria and Papa speak with her and try to calm her, I look into the bedroom and see the girl sat up, she is huddled into the corner and looking at both Maria and Papa. Both introduce themselves and ask her name, she doesn't reply, the girl looks terrified, she doesn't speak at all. Joaquin and I make Burritos as Mama taught us, for almost an hour I can hear both Papa and Maria speak with the girl, telling her she is safe, they ask her nothing, just try and reassure her. Maria convinces her to come with her to the bathroom, where she tells the girl to have a bath. Maria leaves the girl to bathe. Both Joaquin and I are told to stay away from the bathroom for the time being. Maria moves from the Kitchen to the bathroom, which doesn't take long as our house is so small. Every couple of minutes I hear Maria go back into the bathroom to check on the girl, we don't even know her name yet, she hasn't said a word to any of us.

***

The bath is warm but I can't stop shaking, these people are trying to help but no matter what they say and do I can't tell them what happened. How do I know I can trust them, they look like normal people, they look like friendly people but I just don't know if I can take the risk. I can see that the man and woman are not a couple, the woman talks with him like a friend, they speak in Spanish but I am too shaken to truly understand what they are saying. The man and woman are caring, I can tell that they are both parents just by the way they speak to me, they know what to say and do. They don't question me about how I came to come by that farm. They clean me up because they understand that it's distressing having blood on my face, on my clothes and on my hands. they both spoke of a policeman coming to speak with me, to take me away. I won't go, I will run away again. It's best I don't speak, let them think I can't speak or am too distraught to open my mouth and let the words come out. I can't stop thinking about Papa, dying in that place with the others, hearing the screams and the guns sounding and then just the laugh of those animals and that singing, I hear the voice again over and over. He wasn't a man, he was a boy, probably similar age to me — tattoos — taking drugs — laughing, that horrible grin and singing the way he did. My mind keeps wandering, I can't stop the thoughts inside my head, it's like a television that I can't switch off. I am so scared. The police in El Salvador are not to be trusted, I wouldn't trust them here either. I don't know where to run I could end up back in the hands of those evil men again, but If I stay what will the policemen do with me? I heard the man say that the Policeman is a good man, an honest man, but the woman didn't think that any of them could be trusted, she sounded like she was suspicious of any policeman that was honest. She called him Flip, she would often place a hand on his shoulder, Flip has a look of sadness on his face, like a man who is guilty of something and has the world on his Shoulders. He looks tired, not just because he works hard, but that look of a person who just doesn't seem to want to carry on. My Mama looked the same when she was dying, she had that look that said she had enough of life. Maybe he has lost someone, maybe even killed someone. No, I don't think so; I see the way he looks at his children I can tell that they are everything to him, even if he didn't say it. The woman looks strong, like she is someone who tries to help everyone, even if that means she goes without. She is a large lady, but still pretty. She hugged me when Flip took me to his house. I pretended to be asleep. Her humongous tetas almost suffocated me, but she did it because Flip had told her everything and she wanted to comfort me. I like her, I like Flip, I am just not sure if he is strong enough to be able to help me. The smallest boy was sweet, very young, small and chubby, with his vest and cap on. When I saw him face to face I could tell that he was scared. He smiled ever so slightly but then became afraid. When I stumbled towards him I saw him swing something at me, maybe a wrench or something hard. He didn't mean it really, now I have seen what he is like, he was just scared — like me. They all think I fell over because I was exhausted, I was, but I don't want to get the little boy in trouble. I heard his brother call him Joaquin. The older boy looks sweet also, but looks different to his father and brother. He looks lean and tall, a little younger than me and very handsome, but again looks sad. His hair was neatly combed to the side and was dark, his voice sounds like it is breaking or starting to break. He is quiet and has not said much since he came home from school. Maria stayed with me while Flip went off with the young boy Joaquin. This feels like a family home, but no Mother around. from peeking through semi closed eyes, I could see photos on the wall of a beautiful

woman, she looked like a model, photos in a wedding dress, photos in the sea, photos with the children and with Flip. Maria comes back into the bathroom and scrubs by back and washes my hair and puts soap on my face and arms she holds a dress in her hand. The dress is blue and she says to me that it belonged to her when she was young and slim, she warned me that it might be too big around the bust for me, which I know it will be. She makes a joke about her tetas saying that she notices men looking down her cleavage all the time and that when she catches them doing it, she slaps their faces. I feel a smile grow on my face and Maria smiles back at me. She doesn't push it any further. She says that the men in this house are gentlemen and wouldn't do that she says I am safe here. My smile slips away and my mind races away again — back to that cow shed — back to being lined up again and the men in masks. Back to that boy lifting his mask, where I saw his evil grin and those tattoos on his face. Teardrops, yes they were teardrops three lines of them coming from his eyes. I remember his arms from underneath his jacket, I could see lots of tattoos on his arms also and the line of his neck, more teardrops. All over his neck and the top of his chest, killing my Papa and all the other passenger — I can't switch it off it keeps coming back.

***

I stand out on the porch, mentally preparing myself for the dinner that Tomas and Joaquin prepared. I wish to god that Maria hadn't decided to occupy their time by getting them to prepare a meal; my stomach is in knots at the moment, the last time they cooked for me I spent the following day sat on the toilet with Beelzebub himself poking my ass with the flames of hell.

I look out towards the fields, beyond the highway. The sky is blood red; it looks like it's trying to burn a hole through this region. The dusk sky in Tamaulipas is mesmerising, my favourite part of the day, aesthetically mesmerising. The sky, beaming red with the sun going down over the skyline of the City. I think today however it's best to keep ourselves hidden from the rest of the world. I feel anxious, almost like I expect those responsible to bust into the house and mow us all down for being complicit in aiding this girl. Maria announces that she cannot stay for dinner, which is a shame because without her I don't know what to do for the best for the girl. No conversational skills with women of any age. I just hope Suarez gets here soon enough.

We sit at the table and Maria brings the girl through, she looks like she can walk unaided. We all stand for her; although we are poor and from the barrio, we know how to greet a lady. I look over at Tomas and I can see him staring at her attentively. Tomas is a polite and caring boy and it is abundantly clear that Tomas is growing up, I remember the first time I started noticing the girls, I probably had that slightly embarrassed and awkward look on my face that he holds now. He is doing all he can to look at some other fixed point in our shack of a house.

It must be said the girl is pretty; her skin is olive, long dark brown hair, no longer matted with blood and dirt. She looks a trifle thin; I guess she is about fifteen-years-old. Her facial features are very prominent; she has that slight look of the orient about her, which is common in some females from Central America. She is wearing a blue dress that Maria found for her, it's obviously Maria's as the bust is hanging a bit too low and the straps over the shoulder have obviously been adjusted. On many occasions, I have been unable to avoid the Canyon that Maria has for a cleavage, I don't think she ever noticed me looking though, as I would have been beaten to within an inch of my life. Laena caught me peering once, rather than try and lie my way out of it, I pointed out it was unavoidable. The girl looks ill at ease in a dress; however, I have her clothes soaking in a bowl in the kitchen.

We engage in small talk at the table, generally our dinner table is quiet anyway. We have all run out of things to say to one another. Joaquin's silence only amplifies and brings to the forefront that Tomas and I are growing further and further apart. Maria stands and announces she is leaving and gives everyone a kiss on the cheek while they are seated. Joaquin always gets the biggest kiss; he smiles when she does that. I walk Maria to the door, out of ear shot of the table.

‘Thank you so much for today, I will let you know what happens, are you sure you don’t want to eat with us before you go.’

‘Flip, you’re so predictable, it’s time to brush up on girl skills, and it’s going to have to be you who speak with her tonight. As for Tomas, I think you need to try harder with him. I know how you feel maybe he needs to hear this from you, tell him how you feel about Laena. Maybe then he will open up.’

‘Maybe,’ I say with a hint of pessimism, ‘but maybe I won’t want to hear what he has to say.’

‘Try; also, tell that asshole Alejandro to stop slowly driving his bus past the factory when I am going into work and when I leave, I know his game.’

‘Why don’t you give him a shot, you never know,’ I do know Maria’s feelings about Alejandro and all men to be honest.

‘What are you going to tell Alejandro about the girl, as and when he shows up on the porch carrying beers for you both to drink into the early hours,’ Maria, directing her eyes at me as if to state what I hadn’t thought of.

‘She will be gone by then; it’s strange, usually he would have called me by now, maybe he is working late.’

‘Now you mention it,’ Maria barks with suspicion, ‘he didn’t follow me this morning, my day was almost incomplete without some horny degenerate staring at my large ass with his tongue hanging out.’

‘Sometimes he drives the long-distance buses so maybe I won’t see him tonight, Good night Maria, will speak to you tomorrow.’

‘Yep, now time to go and find that little shit of a son, probably out with another bunch of wannabe gangster assholes, talking shit and telling them how he scored with some seventeen-year-old high school chess club members.’

Maria walks away, she does make me chuckle. I sit back at the table and we eat. The boys are chomping away, but both look in the direction of the girl. She wolfs the food back and doesn’t care how much of it is over her face and mouth, but the eating is one of starvation rather than enjoyment. I know that feeling myself, when my father used to throw me out of the house, because his mood took him that way and wouldn’t allow me back in until morning. I would plough food down my neck hurriedly and he would sit there watching me — staring right through me, calling me a disgusting greedy pig and that I was no son of his.

After our meal, I sat at the table, the girl sat with us. She still had not said a word or even looked up at us. Joaquin started building his model sky scraper again. I talked with the boys again about writing some messages to Mama and we could attach them to helium balloons and launch them. Before I could finish, Tomas jumped off his chair and went straight to his room. Well I fucked that up again. It all starts to come back to me again — when Laena disappeared. I remember telling Antonio about Laena going missing, and his offer to come back to San Fernando to help with the children, to take them to El Paso and to help me look for Laena. I declined his offer yet again; we spoke over the phone which was a good thing because the shame on my face was like a mask I couldn't remove. He never said it, but I knew what he was thinking, the same that Tomas shouted at me when his mother didn't return home that day in March: 'It's your fault, why didn't we leave when we had the chance.'

Tomas cried for two days straight after that. We took a picture of Laena to the town square and put it on the plaque amongst the hundreds of other pictures of missing people. Hundreds of smiling faces looking back at us, timeless photos capturing happier times. Photos of young and old faces: male and female, mothers and fathers, sons and daughters, husbands and wives. The faces of the missing, all smiling back at those who chose to cast their eyes over the plaque. Handwritten messages from families, pleading for information. Begging for the safe return of their loved ones. Many of the families of the missing people of San Fernando, return to the plaque every day in some form of hope that their appeals will encumber the black hearts of those responsible and return our loved ones back to them.

Before Laena disappeared, we would go to the Rio San Fernando every Sunday. Nearby, a vendor would sell helium balloons and we would write messages on paper and tie them to the string of the balloons and launch them into the sky. 'Let it go Mama' Joaquin would shout, once it was launched he would run after it until it went out of sight. During the journey home, Laena and I would tell Tomas and Joaquin to look into the sky and see if the balloon was still up there. We would tell stories of where the balloon may settle, and who may read our messages. I always felt guilty about being cynical about the message writing, it was our family's way of believing in hope again.

I snap myself out of it, I look at my watch; where the fuck is that asshole Suarez, Mr Top Dog Investigator, he should have called by now or at least let me know what was going on. I look off into the horizon in the direction of the abandoned ranch; I can see convoys of vehicles, blue flashing lights providing an eerie juxtaposition against the dusky skyline. No sirens just lights and a fleet of meat wagons. Thoughts of that cowshed; the images replaying — taunting me. I look back at the girl and think you poor baby.

Chapter6

San Fernando, Tamaulipas, Mexico

August 25th 2010.

Laena is wearing that beautiful summer polka dot dress with her hair flowing down to her shoulders, she runs after Tomas and Joaquin. Running in circles around and around, the boys laughing uncontrollably, their faces alight with joy. She reaches down and gathers Joaquin in her arms; he is smiling and leaning in to kiss his Mama on the lips. Tomas is smiling looking up, his face a true picture of happiness, childlike happiness, his smile beaming from ear to ear. We are on the beach, the beaches between San Fernando and Matamoros. A warm breeze blowing in off the Gulf of Mexico, I can see Laena's dress and hair blowing about from the breeze. The boys are dressed in their smart tailored shorts and shirts. There is no-one else around. The beach is our place, the Hernandez place where we go to be a family. Laena still has Joaquin in her arms and is twirling around, Tomas running around her in time, keeping up with her. They're getting further and further away from me. I can see them in the distance, but I can't make out their faces anymore — I run towards them. They don't look in my direction, I call out to them but they don't look in my direction. Laena, Tomas and Joaquin are locked in a timeless moment where they refuse to disconnect because if they do it may be infinite. I desperately want to be part of the tryst, in our special place we share with no other, our family together with a bond of love that no one can break. I run and run toward them but they seem to be further away. The faster I run the further they seem to be away, the whole time I cannot see Laena's face. I am frantic, running and calling their names but they don't hear. The horizon is the only thing in my line of sight, my family have gone and I suddenly jolt back into consciousness.

I open my eyes immediately, waking from the dream — a dark fever dream, that once I had awoken from I never wanted to have again. I wake on the couch so I take thirty seconds to compose myself, find my bearings in the place that was once my family home but is evermore starting to feel like a shell that once replicated a loving home is now more like a haunted house, where the memories linger of what was once present but have evaporated.

I look at my watch and it's five am. Fucking Suarez is full of shit. Take care of the girl, she is important, don't tell anyone else and don't let her out of your sight. I check my cell phone, no missed calls. It's a piece of shit old cell phone but it does what it's supposed to do and makes and receives calls and has not let me down in the three years I have owned it. It's clear that he hasn't called or even sent one of those annoying text messages that is so popular and has single handed ruined the art of conversation. I punch Suarez number into my phone and call him; it rings and goes through to Suarez voicemail. No, don't leave a message, what if he has lost his cell.

Without consuming any beer the previous evening, I feel less melancholy than normal; however the dream has vexed me somewhat. I seek some Freudian explanation to its meaning. I drift off to sleep each night, wishing I will see her in my dreams. I have tried Solace in my church, but now I take the boys to Sunday Mass out of trying to instil the values that Laena wanted, rather than my belief in the Catholic Church. My faith dwindled some years before Laena went missing. I ponder the hypothesis that the dream is a message, forewarning me of impending doom. However, if this were the case then why wasn't I warned before she vanished? Too deep, my paranoia taking off again. Full flight.

I go out onto the front porch and light a cigarette, blowing the smoke into the warm early morning air. The dawn sky is beautiful, yet terrifying in equal measures. The red and black sky now appears sinister considering what I witnessed yesterday or should I say the aftermath I witnessed. My mind starts to go over some of the facts. A high number of people taken from buses and murdered just off highway 101, three cops murdered and mutilated on the city streets with the Los Zetas announcing that they were responsible, two survivors from the ranch, only one is known to authorities with the exception of Suarez, who has not made contact like he said. That Captain with the mirrored sunglasses seemed off to me? Watch out Flip you're using that brain of again, for a moment I think back to those days on the Metro desk at the newspaper and then my editor's brains all over the window of his office and the Sicario casually walking out, staring towards the office full of journalists who couldn't meet his gaze.

I sit at the dining room table, clock watching so not to disturb the three children I now have in this house. The door comes flying open, where Maria comes crashing holding a copy of the San Fernando paper. 'Have you seen this,' out of breath like she ran to my house, her voice loud and certainly sounding alarmed, 'The front page read it now.'

'Read it,' I say, 'I was there Maria, why would I want to read this.' I look at the front page and I am truly shocked, I didn't think it possible: "72 people dead bodies found on outskirts of San Fernando."

The article goes on to describe the scene as a Massacre, there are quotes from Suarez, but they are all to brief. It describes the scene and how the bodies were found and how Mexican soldiers were alerted by a young man who was wounded and managed to escape and alert the security forces. It then describes a fire-fight between Narcos who were using the abandoned ranch as a base of operations, and Soldiers, where several Narcos were killed. The article goes on to say that the people were abducted while riding on buses and taken to the ranch. The article is devoid of any one naming or wishing to be named, we all know why that is.

'I can't believe it, seventy-two confirmed dead, that has got to be the largest scale murder in the country, it has to be,' as I pick up the paper and scour through the rest of the paper, looking for any sign of any mention of any other survivors or witnesses.

'What about Suarez, any word from him,' Maria poised — awaiting a positive answer, it looks like the realisation has hit home that this is some serious shit.

'Nothing — he could still be over at the Kill sight,' the old Journo speak drifting back to me. As I scan the newspaper article, I started collecting information and analysing it, breaking it down, checking for misdirection or any Government stamp over the article. The Government and law enforcement are synonymous with stepping on Journalists, and forcing Freedom of Speech to become anything but free. Journalists have a habit of getting killed or disappearing down in Mexico when they write about affairs relating to Narcos or any kind of investigation that leads to uncovering conspiracies between police and Narcos. We used to call them conspiracies, but today it's such common practice for Narcos to pay off cops that it's better described as reciprocity.

'Hey fuck-head,' Maria is annoyed at my lack of response, 'Never mind reading the thing — what now, this is huge and that little girl is in danger.'

'Wait,' I put my hand up to her, she doesn't like that, 'can't you see that there is no mention of who is involved, no actual comments or observations as to who is involved, or why this occurred it's just plain reporting. As news, it sells, but I bet this house on the fact that this story will be buried within a week and won't ever be mentioned again. Someone will apply pressure on the papers and not a mention will come of it.'

'What about the survivor they speak of who alerted the Soldiers, what if he told them about the girl and those who are responsible come looking, what about Suarez, what if he mentions it in a report or when his corrupt pals threaten him and his family, do you think he would stand up to that, I doubt it — would you!' I know I wouldn't and I know Maria, also knows that.

'Look at the facts here: the survivor is supposed to have made it to a check point, which was about ten miles east of the Ranch and alerted the Army, how would he have made it in that time. I believe that the Army were tipped off by other means. Those people were from Guatemala and El Salvador, Suarez said so, they wouldn't know where to go to whom to speak to, they are unlikely to trust Soldiers! Look what their military infrastructure and how they treat their own people.'

Playing Devil's advocate to Maria is vexing her, she doesn't share my enthusiasm. Although I am concerned and slightly scared, I find it exhilarating, the thought of nefarious happenings, taking place in our back-yard. For so long I have been Flip the peasant, who bummed his college education and Journo' job and went to play poor little peasant boy, fixing roofs and porches for pittance, trying as hard as possible just to acquiesce and be what my father always said I was. 'Listen, I will talk to Suarez about the girl, I had better get the boys up, Tomas has school and I can't be seen to break routine as it arouses suspicion. Joaquin and I will wait around for Suarez. I will call him at seven am when he starts duty. Our excitement will be over by mid-morning. Hey maybe we could play at being Woodward and Bernstein,' I say being jovial for once rather than the usual sad-sack.

'We can't be Woodward and Bernstein,' says Maria, 'I can't sing to save my life.'

I stare at her in amazement wondering if I had just heard what I thought I did, and then she breaks a wry smile, she had me.

***

The girl looks peaceful while asleep in my bed. The covers pulled up to her chin, she lies on her side facing the doorway. I look at her while stood there, a coffee cup in my hand and feeling fresh after not consuming vast amounts of beer the previous evening and actually having something to occupy my mind. I didn't have the usual wave of melancholy rushing over me, thinking about Laena. The dream still haunts and perturbs me, but I don't have the option of burying my head in the sand and pondering over this too long. The girl wakes up and almost immediately slips into an upright position, she looks at me, her face is emotionless and expression blank. The girl's facial features are soft and I try and imagine what she would look like smiling. I smile at her, because I don't know what else to do. I tell her that I have prepared breakfast and to come through when she was ready.

I went through the usual ritual of getting the boys out of bed, Tomas ready for school and Joaquin to come to work with me. The girl joins us at the table; she is wearing the clothes we found her in, except they were now clean. Maria even managed to get the blood out. We eat together, the girl eats, but this time without the same energy as the previous evening. She soon appeared to lose her appetite and just sits motionless, her eyes only peering down, to avoid any eye contact. It's abundantly clear that whatever shock or trauma she has suffered has had a profound effect, Joaquin is living testament to that. The Hernandez family need no tutelage in that field.

I cleared the table and prepared a meagre lunch for Tomas, looking at the wrap filled with black beans and feeling the shame of not being able to even feed my children satisfactorily. I call Suarez cell again and then his office, I get the answer machine and voicemail. What the fuck is he playing at; this is a shit thing to do to me.

I manage to get a neighbour, Mrs Ortiz to stay over at my house while I take Tomas to school. I tell her that she is my niece from Monterey. Mrs Ortiz doesn't ask anything further and I forget to explain that she doesn't speak. Mrs Ortiz is hard of hearing and just shouts at the girl asking mundane questions about school and Monterrey and complaining about the government and El Presidente.

I get the boys into the truck and take the same well-worn route to Tomas' school. Joaquin sits in the middle of Tomas and I, in the cab. Despite our close proximity, we are oceans apart when it comes to being a family. Joaquin sits in complete silence and devoid of any facial expression; he holds his beloved hammer in his hand, with his tool bag between his legs. The tools he carries are never far from him. Each day, the silence becomes deafening. I try to break the ice any way I can. Must try a new tact, I saw the way Tomas looked at the girl, maybe this will be my in.

'So Tomas, what did you think of the girl?'

'Nothing — like you said, that cop is taking her away today, it doesn't matter what I think because she won't be around when I get home.' Tomas' delivery remains cold; I guess I could try appealing to his near teenage sensibilities.

'She's pretty and I can tell that you think so to. I was your age once you know, a boy in love and all that,' I say in a teasing fashion, trying hard to be best friend and father at the same time.

'Papa,' Tomas shouts, which silences me and fast removes that idiotic grin I know I am sporting. 'Have you forgotten already how you came to find that girl, it was only yesterday. What is wrong with you, we don't know where she came from or who she is. How can you say something so stupid?'

I do know what happened and where she came from and he is right. Possibly in my top ten of insensitive comments, since I became the boys' sole carer. I feel so fucking stupid, always trying, but failing with every breath I muster. I should tell him about the newspaper reports about the ranch. Fifty-eight men and fourteen women murdered in our town, only a few miles from our barrio but I can't seem to treat him as the intelligent and mature boy he has become.

'Tomas, I'm sorry and I am an asshole, that wasn't funny. I'm trying Tomas and I know I'm failing,' my voice cracks and the tears appear in my eyes, desperation sets in. 'Please Tomas, I need you to stop hating me, I am sorry, sorry for everything; your Mama, our predicament, living in this hell hole, everything.' We stop at the lights three blocks from the school, I put my hand on Tomas' hand and say, 'If I could change things, if I could change places with your Mama, then I would, just to end your pain, I would do that.' Tomas looks at me, his eyes are red, 'You can't change things.' he gets out of the truck and walks the rest of the way.

I sit in the cab and watch Tomas walk away, his head hung low and as he gets further away I notice him wipe his eyes. What a piece of shit I am, I have ruined his life and I expect him to be happy about it. I forget he is only twelve years of age sometimes. He works like a dog, he cleans and tidies the house and on weekends it's usually spent helping with Joaquin or accommodating me, listening to my drunken ranting and blaming the entire world for any and every thing that has gone wrong.

I pull away and head through the now busy streets of San Fernando. I don't recognise the town any more. Always an industrial and industrious town full of hard working people just trying to make their way through lives, but now it's gangland. Slowly but surely its residents are moving away, now all that seems to be left are those that are planning to move away and those that can't. I fall into the latter. The wide-open streets, with broken pavements and asphalt, the shacks that were once stores. The market places bustling with people and the old exhaust spitting cars crawling along the streets, honking horns this looks like the San Fernando I know. I pass by the Church of San Fernando most days and look at its beauty, but it's what is lurking in the shadows which have everyone scared. After what I saw yesterday at the ranch, in that shell like, stinking, fly strewn cow shed I am beginning to think that the shadows are now coming out to prey on us all.

I arrive at the police station, Joaquin holding my hand and ask at the desk for Suarez. The cop on the desk looks me over and tells me that no one has seen him. I ask to speak with his superior officer, the cop on the front desk, who is sporting three-day stubble and is about twenty pounds' overweight looks at me and say 'Go fuck yourself, what do you think this place is, a Police station.' He lets out a mighty laugh to which other cops in the background do the same. I tell them it's about my wife, this makes no difference.

I leave the station hoping that cops next shit resembles a porcupine and he howls for mercy, fat prick. I sit in the cab and think. Joaquin has his hammer and screw driver in his hand, also he has taken small nail punch from my bag and claimed it as his own. Fuck it, go back out to the ranch, maybe he hasn't gone home and he is working through. I take the spine roads that crawl through this territory. I arrive at the same check point I arrived at yesterday, where I bump into the same charismatic and enthusiastic cop wearing his balaclava again.

'Excuse me, senor I am here for Detective Suarez again, he wants me to courier more things again.'

Super peasant to the rescue again. He calls on his radio, without even acknowledging me, where I hear him call to the Detectives down at the crime scene. No answer over his radio. He looks at me and calls again. I wait as I am instructed to do nothing else.

After around twenty minutes an older man in a grey suit appears the check point. He is lean and at around five feet ten he sticks out, like Suarez did as Mexicans we are generally shorter than most of the men in the Americas. His hair is thick and fluffy and greying all over, the dark can be seen just through it. He has a thick moustache, which unlike mine complements his face quite well. I would guess he was in his mid-fifties. He walks up to me directly and extends his hand to shake mine.

'I am Benito and you are please?' his voice low and polite, rather the usual myopic tone attributed to cops. I almost fall over, he is well mannered and it doesn't seem to bother him that I am just a normal person.

'I am Felipe, but people call me Flip, how are you senor.'

'Please, it's Benito,' he smiles and has a look of sincerity about him. Is he trying to ingratiate himself to me because he wants what I have, or is this genuine? 'Let's go over here a minute.'

Now I begin to think the coup de grace is coming, is he the enemy, the smiling assassin that I hear so much about when it comes to cops these days. We walk to a parked vehicle and he sits on the hood. 'I am Roberto's partner, he told me about the girl, he told me because we have been friends and partners for a while now, so your secret is safe.'

'Where is Suarez, I have been trying to call him for hours now,' I am beginning to think the worst as I say it.

'Roberto has not been seen, his wife has also been making the same calls to me and to the station and I don't know where he can be. May I be candid with you Felipe?' He leans in to speak closer, just to my right ear. 'Get away from here; don't mention to another soul the girl or anything that Roberto has told you. It's because of this place and those bodies that I think we will not see Roberto again. Roberto is diligent and honest and they know he will uncover what happened here and that's why I am starting to suspect that they have done something terrible to him.' His voice shakes.

'Who Benito? who are they.'

'Us and them?' he looks about the ranch, at the Cops around the sealed and cordoned Cow shed. 'I am telling you because I don't know who to trust anymore, I am hoping that I can trust you. Keep the girl away, no one other than Roberto and I know about her. I swear on the lives of my children and grandchildren I will not utter a word about her.' He looks into my eyes, his eyes are full of tears, I can see his lip quiver.

'Why would they want to protect those responsible, just tell me your thoughts I need to know, if I am to protect this girl.' I'm intrigued but at the same time terrified.

'Because there is a new world order in Tamaulipas now, much worse than anything we ever saw before. We all know who is responsible, who they are, just not why. The truth be told; we will never find them because we don't want to find them. Roberto is the first casualty. I know him like I know my own brother, for him to go missing like this when duty calls is unusual. Also, I found this in my mail box this morning.' He holds out a piece of paper, the words written in what looks like blood.

"Keep your mouth shut old man or you will suffer at our hands, we will kill your family and make you watch we promise
Signed
Z."

The Zetas generally sign everything with "Los Zetas" when they hang the naked and mutilated corpses of their enemy, but Benito needs no formal introduction. He knows who the “Z” are, pretty soon so will everyone. He puts his hand on my shoulder and walks away, back into the ranch, to go through the motions, make it look like he is investigating this macabre scene of mass murder. Make it look like they are investigating this, but never coming up with the answers; or, having the answers but never wanting to commit to them. I realise that I will never learn of what happened to Laena at this point. I look over at Joaquin, sat in the truck I think of Tomas almost in tears getting out of the cab today and I think of that girl at home. All in the knowledge, that we will never have the answers. I failed one person before, the only woman I loved, the mother of my children. I won’t make that mistake again, I won’t fail the boys any more, I won’t fail this girl. I must keep her safe.

***

We all sit at the dinner table later that evening, the girl sits with us, she stays looking down at the table, in the twenty-four hours that she has been part of our household, and she has not said a word. She is clearly in shock and may not ever come around. Two children locked away in their own rooms, both through the suffering and pain they had endured. Both in their own private worlds they have found each other. If they can resolve the issues and struggles they both have, then I will be damned if I can’t resolve things with Tomas. I am determined I am not going to lose my family through blame and guilt. For all too long I have lived under my own cloud, blaming myself each second of every day and it’s getting us nowhere. I won’t lose my family to this god forsaken war, to these bastard Narcos with their Sicarios and gangs. I won’t lose them through starvation and poverty. I build it up; the table is silent as always, I work up the courage to say what I must say

‘I have made my decision,’ I have started, no going back now, I clear my throat, ‘It’s time we started working together rather than against each other. I have made my mistakes, I have truly fucked up,’ Tomas lifts his head and looks at me, noting my cursing at the dinner table where his Mama would definitely not allow such language. The girl looks up as well; cursing at the dinner table is obviously frowned upon in El Salvador or Guatemala or wherever she is from as well. ‘I wish I had done thing differently, I miss your Mama so much and I have never loved another woman as much as I did her, and I never will. I won’t lose you the same way, I can’t lose you’. My voice is breaking, I look at Tomas he is focused on me, his usual cold look is showing signs of warming, I can see his lips quiver; his eyes start to fill with tears. ‘It’s time we got out of here, leave this place behind us. I don't want to leave your Mama, but the longer we stay the more likely it is something bad will happen. All our neighbours are trying to get out, most of the people in the barrio are slowly slipping out of here or being killed and it's only getting worse, yesterday was just the beginning. As for you,' I look at the girl and see her acknowledge me. 'I want you to come with us. We must raise the money to leave, so I will keep working and save and save and save. I am going to call Papa Antonio, in Texas and tell him we are going to leave here. I have worked it out and by later this year, I hope to get out of here.'

'Mama, what about Mama,' says Tomas.

'I promise we are going to find her first, then all of us will go to America, it's what we all want, to be safe, not to have to live this way. Live with Papa Antonio and Grandma.'

I am probably building this up a little high myself, but I have got to try and appeal to everyone, it has to be me who stirs everyone up. I omit the fact that we must leave because if the Zetas find out about this girl, then we would all be killed. We could leave now, I think, but no way am I turning up cap in hand to Antonio, no way. I do still have a little pride left and I won't be supported by anyone. I know Antonio is a good man and would never ask anything of me, but I am who I am. I will do this for my family, for those boys, I lost the one true love of my life and that I am to blame. I won't be consciously responsible for the loss of the children. I lost Laena because although the signs were always there that I chose to ignore them. Laena, going out every day on Highway 101, to get a bus to work, then coming home of an evening. That dreaded stretch of highway, synonymous with death and loss. I could have worked harder so she didn't have to; I could have left when she said we should, I could have refrained from making her feel guilty about mentioning leaving, I could have grown some balls and stayed at the Metro Desk of the newspaper and maybe not have ended up living in a barrio and made my name as a Journo' and worked in the capital.

I notice Tomas looking at the girl 'What do we tell people when they ask about her.' Again, he makes a good point.

'Febe,' we all look up and toward the girl, her voice soft, slightly broken with emotion. Holy cow, she spoke and it's like a great wave has come over the room, even Joaquin acknowledges it. 'My name is Febe, you can tell everyone that I am staying here to take care of Joaquin, or I am your long-lost cousin or that you won me on the lottery.' Febe smiles and the whole room notice it, especially Tomas. It is at that point I can see that Febe has a sense of humour and a mischievous nature about her. I can see that Tomas is won over.

'Would you like to come to America with us,' says Tomas.

'Sure,' she says her accent stronger than ours, but Spanish none the less. 'That's where I was going anyway; I just ended up getting slightly lost along the way.' She will get on fine in this family and I can already tell that she is enjoying playing around with Tomas' serious nature already, hopefully she will be the anecdote he needs to be that cheery little boy who doesn't have a care in the world.

We sat and ate our meal and we asked Febe about how she came to be here. She told us everything, about her Papa, where they were from in El Salvador, how her mother died and how Papa was trying to cross the border to Brownsville, Texas and how he had a coyote, which is someone who arranges for immigrants to get across the border, already lined up. When Febe tried to tell us about what happened at the ranch, she couldn't, but we already knew the outcome. She spoke of the Man who pulled her out of the pile of bodies and got her out. I asked her about the lump on her head, I noticed her eyes meet Joaquin's and knowing how prone he can be to having an explosive temper, I knew what had happened. Febe stuck to her story, that she must have banged it when she fell to the ground; despite the fact I found her led on her back. Tomas and I both have the bruises from Joaquin's occasional outbursts; however, I have conquered this by letting him get his own way most of the time. Laena would be furious if she knew.

After Supper, I nipped away to the street vendor who sold odd bits and pieces in the barrio and bought four helium balloons. I took them home and told Febe of our little tradition. We each wrote our notes, our wishes and tied them to the balloons. Joaquin as always with help from Tomas, wrote how he wanted to build the biggest sky scraper in the land so he could live high above and look down. Tomas, this time wrote how he wanted to find his Mama. For the first time, I joined in. I wrote my note wishing that the boys would find happiness, that they would smile again and we would all make it out of here, that I would find the money as quickly as possible and we could flee. I had never been to America; despite my father living there before, I was born here and had never left Mexico. We launched the balloons and Joaquin ran, as he always did after the balloons, to see if they made their way into the dusk sky, the burning red sky that lit the street. It was a sight to behold. I wished that this night would never end, as it seemed like we were family again. We just had to make it through the following weeks and months and I had to get the money soonest, because true to form, the longer it went on, the less likely it would be for us to ever get out. But I promise myself one thing, before I leave this place I will find out what happened to Laena.

***

Toot toot, fuck me that is goooooood shiiiiiiiiiit, it burns my nose — hurry up motherfucker — not long now until it reaches my brain. I love this shit, this coke is the best shit around. Straight from the Colombian Farms: straight to the Mexican springboard, over the border to those Yankee motherfuckers. White puto bitch motherfuckers, handing stepped on shit around frat parties in San Diego; Austin, Miami, New York, Chicago, Houston, Los Angeles, Atlanta and all those other white fucking puto neighbourhoods. We get the real shit, before it gets stepped on, pure Colombian white. Oh shit its making its way there now — woooooow I am reaching for the fucking sky. The boss said I can take some for my own stash, I love this shit, can't do without it.

The boss put me in charge of my old barrio: recruit, recruit, recruit. We need soldiers, young soldiers; we need this town to hold the good shit until we bounce it over the border to those greedy white and black motherfucking sons of bitches in the states. Fuck those pussy motherfuckers, they want a war, those American gangs ain't shit compared us, Los Zetas forever; you fuck with one of us you fuck with us all. From now on I will call myself King Rojo, I am going to turn this piece of shit barrio into a ghost town. There is a new king on the throne down in the barrio. Wait 'til they get some of me. Motherfuckers are gonna be running when they see me coming, by the time I finished with these disloyal fools, I am gonna have teardrops down to my swinging dick. They been hiding CDG Sicarios in the barrio; well I will burn them all out of their homes, make them give them all up and when they do, those disloyal sons-a-bitches are gonna wish they was dead. I'm gonna skin them alive in front of their children and then rape their raggedy ass kids and wives while they hang from a lamppost screaming in pain watching — with no skin covered in fucking rock salt. I'm gonna burn the place to the motherfucking ground and burn those CDG fucks alive — let those ungrateful traitors in the barrio watch, before I blast those fools.

I got all sorts of shit running through my head, I can't sleep, I can't eat, I can't concentrate on anything. I keep seeing things in my head, all the time, everywhere. I can't trust anyone, they're all talking about me, I need to shut them up, all of them. Those motherfuckers in that shit stinking cow shed, they ain't talking about me no more, I saw them, laughing about me, talking about me, they dead now. The boss was not pleased about that, fuck him, one day I will be boss man one day. I will prove that I am the one who will lead the Zetas, straight into Culiacan and Juarez — wipe them all out —kill every last one. Rojo, the badass king of Mexico.

'Where's my Ice,' I shout at that pathetic bitch on her knees with tears rolling down her stupid fucking face.

'Please, let me go Rojo, let me take my children and go, I won't tell anyone.'

Fuck this bitch. I should make her suck my dick. She don't even know it yet, but she is dead. Her fucking no good Gulf Cartel Husband — dead on the floor, he's looking up with dead eyes, mouth wide open, his brains all over the carpet, in his living room, with his dirty whore of a wife on her knees begging for her life and the lives of her kids. I want him to see her like this, watch motherfucker, look at her now.

Slaaap — that bitch takes a backhand across the face quite well, look at her crying, it is pissing me off.

'Where is the Ice in here, get me some Ice, some Meth, I know that worthless, dickless piece of shit got Meth in here.'

One of my boys grabs her and drags her away, he looks scared, his eyes wide. I must sort that puto when we leave. She comes back with the bag, her husband cooked great Ice. Not any more, fucking pussy ass bitch. Not now though, not ever again. I laugh, I load that shit into my pipe, light it, hit it hard. Ooooooh Fuck yeeeees. It smashes my head; I am back up on cloud nine again. I yell out at the top of my voice. I look in the mirror at myself, I see a beast, a monster, King Kong about to smash shit up in San Fernando, — yesterday, in that cow shed, was just the beginning. I can hear that bitch's kids crying from the other room, those boys who work for me now, trying to keep them quiet, they know crying and screaming makes me mad. They don't have the balls to blast those kids.

I look over at two useless shit heels, supposed to be east side Demons, my ass: 'Take that bitch, get her to show you where the money and the rest of his Ice is at, and don't come back 'til you got all of it.' They nod at my orders — too fucking scared to talk back at me.

I walk into the childrens room, two kids in the pen, they can't catch their breath, they crying so much; red eyes, big ass tears and snot all over their faces, two boys. The kids of puto CDG. I sing to them — a lullaby for the children, I used to sing when I was small. I was an altar boy, sang in the church. I can still see the face of my Mama, she used

to cry when I sang, said I had the voice of an angel. I liked to sing. The kids are looking at my teardrops down my face and my neck, so I sing a little louder to them, 'rock a bye baby on the tree top, when the wind blows the cradle will rock.'
I think of my Mama, so proud in that church, the priest's face as I sang "Ave Maria." He looked like he was gonna cry as well. Before my teardrops — before I killed so many — before I killed that bitch whore mother of mine for being a traitor, trying to give me medicine that she said would help me. I think of those boys in the barrio, who used to call my name when I walked home in my altar boy dress. 'Gael, Gael, Gael the Girl. Hey you faggot fucking queer.'

They beat me to the ground; I was different then, they beat me — I pissed myself — they saw — they laughed and laughed and laughed. I puked on the ground when they kicked me, they rubbed my face in it, and they ripped my altar dress. I walked home, my Papa kicked my ass some more, he said I was a sissy. I can't bear to hear my first name anymore; I just go by my last name: Rojo. I killed three people for calling me Gael, when I hear that name I fill with rage, my vision goes shaky and my head hurts, its screams out 'KILL, KILL, KILL,' I don't disobey the voice in my head. It tells me to do things, even when the boss tells me to do things, I don't. I listen to my true leader, that voice way up inside my head. The boss said he will kill me if I ever cross him again, like I did yesterday, he didn't like it, that those stinking fucking border-jumping Guats and Salvadorans were killed and left like that, he said they should have been buried, fuck him — the voices said, leave them out, send the message Rojo is king.

'Leave the kids,' I say to my little band of wannabes, 'let them grow up — if they want to come after me, they can.'

The rest of the boys look at me, they better not talk about me when I can't hear them. Once I take over San Fernando, these motherfuckers are dead.

We got the shit, we got the money. I put my gun, my 45 in that bitch's mouth. I wouldn't get hard with that bitch's mouth around my dick, it wouldn't do anything for me. But now I got her mouth around my pistol I am hard. I fire — her brain sly out the back of her fucking head and all over her dead, Puto sissy bitch husband. Now I cum in my pants, that's what makes me shoot. I take out my lighter and put some more Ice in my pipe and light up.

'Shiiiiiit, I am a fucking Olympic psycho killing murdering bad ass Zeta.'

I can't help it I got to yell it out. I take some more of that magic powder and rub that shit into my mouth and my nose. I am orbiting now, ready to fly to the moon. I take my lighter and set fire to the couch and pour Tequila over the living room, the flames go up.

'What about the kids, shall we get them out,' says one of the group, I don't know who, because I am at warp speed — into the midnight sky, straight to the stars.

'I changed my mind, I wanna live forever. Let those fucking kids burn, with their puto-ass parents.'

I promise myself, that before I am done, every one of those barrio shit heels is gonna die, those kids who beat me and called me Gael, they are dead already, my Papa and Mama, I gutted them both like fish, but I can still hear 'Gael, Gael, Gael,' crying out through the streets of the barrio, soon to be drowned out by the one true sound, my own lullaby 'KILL, KILL, KILL, KILL, KILL, KILL, KILL, KILL, KILL, KILL.'

Chapter7

San Fernando, Tamaulipas, Mexico.

August – September 2010

Papa has been trying hard lately; I have noticed the change in him. He tries harder with Joaquin and encourages him to speak again. He sits and reads with him and talks and tries hard, to overcome this hurdle he now faces. Despite his efforts, Papa does still mess upon occasions. After all Papa is Papa and he will mess up, but at least he is trying. Papa has tried harder with me; he seems to write things down that I tell him, so he won't forget. Although it is becoming annoying at least he doesn't forget things like my Soccer practice, my lunch for school although school is soon out for the summer. He remembers groceries and tried buying less beer and more fresh fruit and vegetables. He tries hard but has on occasions forgotten his note pad and then can't remember a damn thing; he seems to rely on this book more and more. Rather than smother me, he lays off and lets me come to him when I want to talk. I remember him at the dinner table, the day after we found Febe telling us he wanted us to get out and I was relieved. He seems very sure that we are going to get out and he is working extra hours and saving all he can to get us all out of here.

Every day since Febe came to live with us, she has become stronger and more talkative. I often hear her pray at night for her father and cry for him. Febe has told the story about what happened to her, she said that she was taken off the bus two days before we found her and taken to the warehouses and cowsheds of the ranch, where they were forced to stand there, blindfolded and eventually they were beaten first, and shot later. She tells how her father gathered her in his arms at the point of the shooting and she fell underneath him. It fills me with horror when I hear her talk about it. All I can think about is my own Mama. For many months now all I could think about was her coming home to us, now I am not so sure. If she died, then I hope it was quick, I hope she didn't suffer. We launch balloons every week now carrying messages and chase after them. Always wishing for the same thing. Always that we will find Mama and she is OK. Febe stopped telling us about what happened when she was taken from the bus as she can see what it does to us, not knowing where our Mama is.

It's the last day of school before summer vacation; our school break is different in San Fernando than most other places; we were buzzing with excitement. Luis was buzzing more than anyone else; he hates school and just wants to get out.

'Hey, I heard that the Zetas killed those people up at that ranch,' Luis says, 'I was told by Angel, that the Zetas heard those people on the buses were heading to work for the Gulf cartel, that they were the enemy, sent here from down South to kill for the Gulf. So, the Zetas took them off and shot those motherfuckers.'

'What did you just say,' Mr Lingala, the school principle stood there, he overheard everything, Luis is in the shit now. 'Say that again Luis, you heard what.' Luis repeated his comment again; Mr Lingala replied in a voice that would have awoken the dead: 'Those Zetas are scum, murdering scum. How many Pupils do you think we have lost because of these Murderers — and you stand around talking about them as if they are heroes, like Robin Hood or something? We have had thirteen children, no older than you, killed by these cowards, these monsters.' Mr Lingala's voice is cracking; 'If I hear another word mentioned about these Zetas or any other gang then I will expel those responsible immediately.'

The entire hall is listening; many, like me feel shamed, embarrassed and agree with Mr Lingala. But there are many that don't; boys like Luis are influenced by these guys. That's because they have not lost loved ones like I have or some of the other pupils. Only a few days ago Luis told me about Rojo, killing some Narco and his wife and burning their house to the ground with their children inside. The children were small; I don't know if the children lived or died. I walked away while Luis told the story. Luis is a good boy really, his mother loves him very much and he is my best friend, but now he is hanging out too much the boys in the barrio who tell such stories.

'Fucking Puto,' Luis mutters under his breath as Mr Lingala walks away back to his office and we head to class. 'Hey Tomas, what you up to over the Holiday, you want to hang out, some friends of mine drive and offered to take me to Nuevo Laredo, you want to come.'

'To do what.' I think I know the answer already.

'You know, chase some girls, start some shit, you know, maybe have something called fun, you ever heard of that. Maybe get to get your hands on some big titties in table dancing clubs.'

'Why go there to see big titties, when we can go to your house and hang out with your Mama.' I always have a Mama joke to come back on; Luis is lost for words because he doesn't break the friends' code of talking about my Mama.

'Oh, fuck you, your Mama was so fine, I just wish she was here so I could come back at ya.' He punches my arm, because that's where his height allows. 'No seriously I mean it, the boys are OK, they won't get us into trouble or any shit like that, just ask your Papa.'

'He wouldn't allow it, plus I got a visitor staying with us now from Monterrey she is the daughter of a friend of my Papa's.' I must remember that story, now I have laid it out, I got to stick to it. 'I got to look after her and Joaquin, my Papa is working a lot these days, why don't you come over we could kick a ball around or go to the river or the beach if I can get Papa to take us there.'

I can see by Luis face that he is not impressed with that idea.

'Come on, we're thirteen soon, we can't keep doing that child shit, no one going to mess with us up there, plus some of the boys got friends in the Zetas, no one would mess with us if they think we with some Zetas would they?'
Luis is trying to assure me, but I can't think of anything worse. They probably think I am scared, well I am. I just don't like to admit it to anyone. I don't want to be part of any gang; I just want to get out of here as soon as possible. I will miss my friends, but they could always come to Texas to visit.

'Look,' I say, just so it doesn't sound like I am a total spoil sport, 'I want us to hang out and we will, you go and have a good time and come over and tell me all about it.'

'Your loss,' Luis puts his hands out to the side as if to indicate that it was a kind offer, 'see you over the holidays — my Mama been coming over a lot lately, is it to do with that Alejandro guy?'

'Yeah,' I lie again; I hope she doesn't drop us all in it about Febe. 'see you later then.'

From my Math class, late that afternoon I heard two loud bangs. I recognise those sounds, so do the rest of the class. The teacher tells us to get down on the ground and stay away from the windows. We scuttle on our backsides out of the door — panic sets in amongst the class, someone is shooting in the school yard. The teacher makes us all walk to the assembly hall; we are joined by the other classes in junior high. From the hall, we can see into the car lot. I can see a man walking towards a black SUV, with blacked out windows. He is wearing a black vest, like those worn by cops and soldiers. He turns and looks towards the Hall, but he doesn't seem to notice us. One of his hands is covered in what looks like blood. He is older, maybe twenty-one or so. Tattoos on his neck, black hair combed back, wraparound sunglasses on his face. He gets in, the SUV drives away.

We don't go back to class, the teachers try and hold us in the assembly hall, we are panicked, the crowd spill out of the main entrance, down the steps and into the main car lot. I can see a car with the door wide open. I don't know why but I run over as I can see the door open — blood all over the inside of the car. I don't recognise the car, but I recognise the man led inside the car; with two huge bleeding wounds to the side of his head. Mr Lingala — eyes wide open, a look of fear on his face. He saw it coming; probably begged for his life. I look at the wind shield; drawn in blood, covering the entire wind shield the letter Z. Killed for speaking out, for condemning the Zetas. I try and remember if I had ever said anything. I look across the car lot and see Luis stood watching. He looks shocked, he looks upset — he looks guilty. I remember what he said to me earlier, "No one going to mess with us up there, plus some of the boys got friends in the Zetas, no one would mess with us if they think we with some Zetas would they.'

***

I am literally working as hard and as fast as I can, since telling the boys we are getting out of here, I can't take my time like I always did in the past. People around here don't pay much for work, they can't, and they're poor. So rather than make a job last as long as I can, I work faster, take shorter breaks and move on to the next job. Cutting lawns; fixing and repairing fences and walls, odd plumbing jobs. It's only been five days since my decision, but I have put my ass in gear. Tomas breaks up from school today for the summer. That means I don't have to collect him from school and I can work on. The weekends and evening are time I want to spend with the boys and Febe.

Febe's presence holds us as a family tighter than before. Since Laena vanished we became further and further apart. Speaking less and less, but sometimes tragedy can do that. I remained in touch with Benito, the massacre has caused a shit storm down here. The mayor is being asked questions by the state governors, as is the police chief. Amnesty international have even sent people down here to ask questions. Felipe Calderon, himself has become involved, he even mentioned Roberto Suarez himself in the papers, sighting that he was the top investigator and it was announced that Suarez and another policeman disappeared a day after the massacre was discovered. I may have been one of the last people to see him alive. Saw him talking to that Captain wearing the mirrored sunglasses. I can't tell anyone. He probably had forgotten about me anyway. No one remembers me anyhow.

The ranch is still crawling with cops and forensic investigators. The local San Fernando papers have gone quiet about the story, probably threatened. I remember reading the story, "nineteen eighty-four" when I was in college, instead of room 101, we have highway 101 and Big brother is always watching. The cops are out in full force on the streets, they have been flooding the barrio since a Narco was killed a few days ago and his house set on fire. Again, the local papers didn't follow the story. Most of my old Journo friends have been killed, all of them for doing their job — for reporting. The local papers have silenced some of their more aggressive reports for fear of what might become of them. The barrio is being hit hard by local cops, looking for Zetas who are taking over the region. Many local boys have been dragged away by the cops and not seen again since. There have been beatings of local boys by the cops in the streets. Word around the bazaars is that its cops working for the Gulf cartel, trying to protect their side income, 'time to earn your wage,' I can hear some fat cat Narco boss saying to them. It's time to pay the piper — you run with the hares and now you run with the hounds and all other assorted analogies.

I keep busy, keep my nose to the grindstone and work so we can have money to get out of here; our visas and travel don't come cheap. But I don't want to cross the border like so many others do. I want to cross with my head held high, just like Antonio did. He went across because the Americans wanted him over there, he was a master of industry and they wanted him, wanted his ranch, wanted his business and now he well esteemed and well thought of in El Paso. I am no charity case, my family and I cross with pride. That's the way I am.

Febe has made good progress; she sleeps in my room, while I take my rest on a mattress in the living room. I hear her cry out in the night sometimes. Her dreams torture her, dreams of her time at that deserted ranch. Neither government nor police have released any of the names of the dead. Rumour is that it was the Los Zetas killed them because they believed that they were hired hands for the Gulf cartel.

Alejandro finally showed up after working away, he seems morose since his travels. He puts it down to hearing about the massacre and how his hometown has changed for the worse. His drinking has become more frequent, Tequila of a night on my porch instead of beer every other night, its hard liquor every night since he got back from his travels. When he talks, it's with a venomous rasp, like he has become haunted by something. Rather than the usual drunken pious rantings of how he would make things right, it was now spat with hatred, something had tipped him. It was also becoming boring. Maybe it was always like that, but I was drunk as well. Lately I would join him for one beer then leave it at that. Last night he stormed off the porch, bottle in hand accusing me of cowardice, stating I was just a peasant and insincere about fighting the system. Of course, I was fucking insincere, I am not about to bear arms and take on the Cartels. Certainly, got the wrong man in mind.

Alejandro told me that he heard that Rojo was back in town and that Rojo was involved in the murder of that Narco the other night. He also said he heard that Rojo was one of the Zetas now and that he was present at the massacre. When I challenged him about this, he clammed up and put the bottle back to his lips. Fucking Gael Rojo is fifteen years old. I remember him from the barrio, he sang at Church. Some say he could have gone to the capital and sang for the Monsignor; his voice was like that of an angel. I worked for his parents on occasions. His mother and Father were snooty, far too good for the barrio, but not good enough for the other parts of San Fernando. They moved to the barrio from Calle Mariano Abasolo, they used to live in a large Stucco house, but the father lost his business and they ended up here.

Mother Rojo was an older woman who stifled the boy. The father was a shit heel who hated the fact that the boy Gael could do no wrong in his mother's eyes. When I worked at their house I noticed things that I thought were off kilter. Gael, used to sit on his mother's lap and suck his thumb all day, he wouldn't move. I saw him once firing a catapult at stray cats and called them "Vermin." I also heard him mutter the words, "KILL, KILL, KILL," as he did so. Gael was young then, ten maybe eleven. The father was a lazy brute of a man, if given the chance, would have beaten the boy all day long. Gael was spoiled by the mother, to the point that she would hear nothing of the father's procrastinations about how he thought Gael was sick; that he was evil, that he did things only crazy people do. I also worked for the neighbours of the Rojo family. They stated that they saw Gael jerking off in the garden when their small children were playing in the hot sun. He seemed fascinated with cross bows, guns, and catapults anything that inflicted pain. He would hurt animals and once he even placed a cat in a cage and used a magnifying glass to burn it. One day I saw Gael being beaten by the local boys on his way home from church. He was dressed in his altar dress. It was torn; he was covered in vomit and had pissed himself. I chased the boys away and walked with him to his house. His fuck head of a father slammed the door in my face, where I heard him and mother Rojo join forces and tear strips off the boy. I felt for him, there only seemed to be bad love in that house, it seemed unhealthy. I remember hearing Gael crying out, begging for his mother and father to leave him alone and stop hurting him.

Their house is like something from a ghost story. Urban legends floating around about what happened to the parents. About how Gael murdered them, butchered them. Gael haunts the barrio like a ghost, his new founded membership into gangs and now the Los Zetas was long overdue. Evil can prevail where good men do nothing. Gael is no more; the name is not mentioned anymore — only Rojo is the name to be used. I have not seen the boy in years, but he haunts the barrio like a spectre. In later years, when anyone saw him heads go down, eye contact is a never. He is crazy, he is evil — he is just a boy. While I struggle to believe all of what I hear, I hear more and more about this young man. He is not a product of the war; he was always this way. His genetics, his upbringing and now he can operate with impunity in the madness that has engulfed this once fine place I call home.

It's time to collect Tomas from school. I turn the radio on in the cab, where I hear the news: 'Teacher shot to death at local high school, panic everywhere.' No, not again — not Tomas. I gather Joaquin in my arms and throw him into the cab. My piece of shit truck has never moved so fast in its life.

***

The cops show at my school, asking around, putting tape around Mr Lingala's car, taking photos, marking the ground where the shell casings have landed. I have seen this hundreds of times in the barrio and in the town. Mr Lingala was a good principle, a good man, he didn't care for the gangs or the Narcos and wouldn't allow them in our school. I had never heard him get quite as angry as I did today. It's always the decent people who get killed. Our school always felt safe, Mr Lingala always held our Summer vacation at the end of August, just so we wouldn't mingle with kids from other schools in Tamaulipas, he always thought it best that we remained apart from other state schools. They usually break up in the end of July. It did work, but now that will be all over, who would want to be a principle in our school now.

The girls in school all stand outside or sit on the steps crying, all hugging each other, all of them scared, all of them wishing they were somewhere else. The boys stand around talking about it, dozens of voices talking about what happened, all saying how they heard the shots and looked out of the window. None of them talking about the man they saw get into the SUV with the wrap around glasses. Cops speak to pupils; all pupils tell the story — every one of them misses out the part about seeing anyone there. Not one sighting given to the cops. A cop speaks to me and I tell him the same as everyone else, as our classroom was overlooking the lot, it was expected that someone would have seen something. We all saw something, but wc would never tell.

After they finish with me I see a woman screaming outside of the police tape. Cops are holding her back, she is screaming and crying and yelling, I hear her say, 'Not my Marco, not Marco, please, please, please tell me it's not true.'

There is an older cop with grey hair and a moustache who is smartly dressed holding her, trying to comfort her, she is wailing loud. Stood next to her is a boy, a bit younger than me. He is still — he doesn't move, he is just staring at the blood splattered car, the woman has her hand on his shoulder, she hugs him while crying and wailing. His face doesn't change; he doesn't cry, he doesn't shout, he just stands there looking. For a while it doesn't click, but after a few seconds it comes to me that they are Mr Lingala's wife and son. Her screaming and calling out his name will stay with me forever.

I look around for Luis, and there he is, stood away from the crowds, hanging back. Normally he would have been buzzing around and offering his own opinion on this, telling everyone the gun used and how he had probably fired one similar, or escaped from some ambush by gangsters who fired such bullets at him or some other bullshit. He was quiet and just staring into space, away from the car lot. He looked upset, he looked frightened, he looked confused, and he looked like he knew more than he would ever let on.

'You know anything about this,' I say at him, I am angry.

'You think I had something to do with this,' I could see the red eyes, where he had been wiping them, I knew that look on his face, I knew Luis better than anyone. 'Fuck you Tomas, you think it was me because Mr Lingala shouted at me in the hall, you think I went straight on the phone and called them. There were lots of kids there, anyone of them could have called them, told the Zetas he was talking shit about them.'

'You said the Zetas,' Papa taught me to be aware of lies, to pay attention to what people say, 'who said it was the Zetas, it could have been anyone, it could have been another gang or Narco or some ex-pupil who hated him, I didn't mention them.'

'No, but I did,' he replied 'I was talking about them asshole, don't try and catch me out, I am nothing to do with this, he shouted how they were cowards in the hallway and they found out and killed him, don't try and be smart with me.'

I know it was him, his face told the story; I just didn't think he thought it would turn out this way. I walked away from him; I couldn't be part of what Luis wanted. He looked up to the gangs and the Narcos. He saw the way they lived; the fancy clothes, cars, girls, money and liked it. But deep down, he was a scared kid, just like me, just like all the kids in the barrio, even the ones in the gangs feared one thing or another. Luis stormed off, not saying anything. I should go after him; I should try and speak with him. But I just let him wander off.

At the front of the school there are queues of parents collecting their children, all of them in tears of joy when they saw their children come out, alive and well. Papa is running towards me, holding Joaquin's hand as his little legs struggle to keep up with him. Papa is covered in sweat and dirt, his clothes ragged and dirt covered. His cap pulled back so he can see. Joaquin holding his hammer still. Papa grabs me in a hug; he kisses the side of my face. He doesn't let go, almost crushing me. He keeps me like this for what seems to be forever. I put my arms around him and hug him back.

'You're OK, my boy is OK,' he is talking to himself. He is crying, he doesn't care who notices him. He takes hold of my face, he kisses the top of my head again and hugs me, like his is checking he has got the right kid. I feel Joaquin put his chubby little arms around me also.

He drives us home, when we get there, he tells me to get the soccer ball and he takes me to the local play area. He is trying to provide a distraction; I know Papa better than he knows himself. Joaquin and Febe come as well. We play soccer, Papa is the goal keeper, we all take it in turns to shoot at him, he tackles us when we have the ball, and he cheats and pushes us all to the ground. He is smiling, he is laughing, he is shouting aloud in celebration when he scores. Febe seems to be enjoying playing with us, she wants to be on Joaquin's team and they play against Papa and me. I get the feeling that she just wants Papa and me to be together, to play and be a team. She looks over at us when we celebrate and gives a little smile. It's almost like her entire plan is to get us to be a family again. I am glad she stays with us. We play soccer until it gets dark, we head off back home and eat and wash up to get ready for bed. Papa cleans up and shaves, although I wish he would get rid of that moustache. It makes him look old. Maria comes over to see Febe and they talk for a while. Maria brings over new clothes for Febe and Papa gives her the money. I hear Papa and Maria talking in the living room from my room.

'It's horrible what happened in school today, Luis came home and went to his room, I have not seen him since, he went out, but I can't find him now,' Maria says, she sounds concerned and she should be.

'Tomas hasn't spoken about it, I won't push it, maybe Luis would like to come over during the summer vacation, maybe we can get the introduction to Febe out of the way. Speaking of which did you tell him.' says Papa.

'No, he's not that bright to put it all together, I am worried about him Flip, he seems too interested in those idiot kids in the gangs than to bother playing with Tomas like he used to. I just don't want him involved in it. When I say to him that he should come over to your house, he dismissed it. When I mentioned Tomas to him tonight he went quiet, like they had fallen out or something.'

'Tomas didn't say anything to me, give him a few days and I am sure it will all blow over, you know what kids are like.'

'Yes, I know what kids are like. Speaking of which,' I hear Maria pause; like a lecture is coming, 'Alejandro said that you and he had a falling out, say it isn't so?'

'He had the falling out with me, he just went for me. He doesn't like it because I am not drinking as much, that's probably it.'

I listen in over Joaquin's gentle snores; he is sound asleep. His book of sky scrapers is in the bed with us. It's a hardback, so I usually wake in the night with the thing poking into my ass. One day Joaquin, one day we will go see some sky scrapers, when we get to America. I continue to listen in to Papa and Maria talking.

'Alejandro has been coming over a lot lately,' I hear Maria say, now my ears home in. 'I see a different side to him, I have told him the drinking has to stop, he actually asked me out and I said I would think about it.'

'Good for you, despite being annoying sometimes and speaks before engaging his brain, he is a good man. Unlike that dipshit pecker head who was bending that large thing of his into your sister.' Papa laughs as he said it and I chuckled too, it was funny to hear some of the things that came out of his mouth.

'Me and my sister are talking again; she said she was sorry, did you know that?'

'No, I didn't, how long?'

'Well,' I hear Maria say 'For a while now, but not after I beat seven shades of shit out of her first. You should have seen it; we rolled about on the ground in the street, tits and big asses everywhere. But eventually the bigger sister won.'

Papa laughs, Maria leaves and takes one last look in Papa's room at Febe and then in on us, I pretend to be asleep. I think about Luis; I hope he is alright.

The summer starts, and over the following weeks I love the fact there is no homework, no class and no need to get up early. Papa works and works hard; sometimes coming home late, but he has money and he saves some and buys decent food and on occasions gives some to Febe and me so we can buy sodas or candy. Most of the stores sell old and out of date goods, but still it's nice.

Joaquin goes to work with Papa as usual. I call for Luis on several occasions at the start, but he never seems to be there, his Mama leaves early for work so I never know if he is avoiding me or just plain not there.

Febe and I end up spending the days together, there are times when she goes quiet and I can tell she is thinking about her Papa. We build dens, we play soccer, and we leave the barrio every day and play in the fields. She teases me, by taking my hat and running off. I chase her, but she is fast. When I eventually catch up with her, she holds it above her head. I am the same height as her, when I reach for it I can tell she is physically strong. I like Febe, she is not like some of the other girls in my school, all they care about is make-up and looking good and wanting to be models or going on about how good the last episode of Keeping up with the Kidachians, or whatever it's called that they watch on their satellite TV's. Febe liked to play and didn't mind working hard around the house, as all of us did when Papa set us chores. She could play soccer, but did like to cheat. My shins and legs are marked from all of the high and late tackles she would throw at me. She didn't seem interested in other boys or how she looked. She was beautiful, but a tomboy to go with it.

Papa set strict rules in the house around washing and showering, that we must always knock on the bathroom door before going in, now a lady was present. Joaquin had an annoying habit of wandering in when I would shower and sit down and take a dump, the rules came about after Febe encountered that very same thing, when she had to wrap the curtain around her while he sat down reading one of his books about buildings and looked at the pictures while taking a dump. Febe found it funny, Papa not so much.

We sat down each night and ate together, Febe liked to cook, after she became ill after eating one of our burritos carefully made my Joaquin and I. Joaquin had been building a mud pile on the patch of dirt that we call our front lawn and didn't think to wash up before preparing. Again, she just laughed it off. Once a week, we got balloons and attached our wishes and let them go into the sky, Joaquin always chased his. As a family, we spoke about America. Papa told me that he had contacted Papa Antonio and told him of our plan and how Papa Antonio said to come as soon as possible, but Papa, being Papa didn't want to come without first making the money to pay his way. I liked that about Papa, although I couldn't wait to leave.

Every day during the summer I spend the days with Febe, we got on a bus to Ciudad Victoria which took about two hours. Papa said it was OK and we got on a bus that Alejandro drove that day. That was the condition that Papa set for us. We left early that day. Papa dropped us off at the bus station in town; this was the first time Febe had been to our town. We pass lots of empty houses and vacant lots, people seem to be leaving San Fernando these days. I remember when people did live in those houses, but more and more it seems people are moving away.

The bus ride is two hours, Alejandro is our driver. He always played up, when people he knew were passengers on his bus. As we got on, he stood up and leads us to the back of the bus, I am dying of embarrassment.

'Well hello pretty lady,' he says, he takes us what he calls the best seats in the house. I turn red as Alexandro is loud and the other passengers look over and laugh along. 'Prepare to be dazzled by the most beautiful countryside Mexico can offer, you love birds sit here, it's the best view from the bus.'

Febe seems to take it all in her stride, she doesn't get embarrassed like I do, I wish I was a bit more like her.

'Well thank you kind sir,' she says, she even manages to play along with it.

Throughout the journey, I tell her about Ciudad Victoria and what we can do there, the markets, the play areas; I also warn her that it can be quite dangerous there as well. I am trying to impress, trying to be like her bodyguard, but I don't think she needs it.

'With you here to protect me, I am sure we will have no problem.'

Febe jokes around on the bus, she pulls faces out of the window at other people driving by, they do the same back, she laughs out loud when a bus full of younger children do the same and when one gives her the bird. Febe is always on the move, since she first started talking, after those first two days, she is full of energy and life. After what she went through, she has shown us all, that despite whatever happens you can always pick yourself up and get on with it.

When we arrive, we go to the markets and some of the stores; the stores here are much fancier. The store owners look at us, they know we are barrio kids and keep an eye on us at all times, just in case we steal anything. We go to a clothes shop in the Plaza San Rafael. Febe is looking at a dress in the store.

'May I help you young lady,' says an older assistant, probably the first we have seen that appears friendly and not snooty.

'May I try that dress on,' Febe says, the dress is white and looks expensive. The assistant goes into the changing room to help Febe get into it. I wonder what Febe is up to. When she comes out I can't believe my eyes. She looks beautiful, not like the tomboy Febe I have been used to seeing for the last few weeks. Her long dark hair is worn up; the dress looks like something a movie star would wear. I could always see that Febe was pretty, but at this point I looked at her differently. Before she was just my friend, someone I would play with, who would annoy me and tease me, who was loud and always clowning around or playing about or who wold go quiet and get upset all to herself. I looked at her and realised I was staring, I had to break or otherwise the game was up. I had a funny feeling in my stomach, like a giddy feeling you get on a rollercoaster, I could feel a smile had grown across my face. She looked beautiful. She wore shoes that had a heel on them, nothing too high. The dress made her look like a lady; she didn't look like that scruffy girl always in jeans, sneakers and boys T-shirts any longer. I didn't know where to look; I didn't know what to say. I know what I want to say to her, but I can't. I am confused; I have never seen a girl like this before or even thought of another girl like this before. Oh shit, so I like the look of her or is it just unusual for me to see her dressed so nice. She looks in the mirror at herself and says to me:

So, what do you think, is it good enough for the prom?'

'Um, what, what did you say, oh yes the prom, definitely it's very nice.'

I sound like an asshole, I can tell now that Febe is just fooling again, trying on dresses just to have a bit of fun.

'Can you hold it back for me please, I have to go get some money from my father and then I will buy it,' says Febe, always the joker, as for me, I am still wondering what's going on.

I then start to remember what Mama said to me, how she met Papa and how they were in love and how they danced together and how Papa asked to meet her again and how he asked Papa Antonio for permission to marry his youngest daughter. Why am I thinking this way, what is going on?

'My date to the prom, will come back later today and buy it,' says Febe, shit she is looking at me and so is the assistant. My face is burning, 'Isn't that right Tomas.'

'Yes, of course, anything for you,' I stammer and try and play along.

We leave the store and Febe laughs about it, she says that she has never been to a big city like this before and wanted to enjoy it, how she lived in the countryside in El Salvador and how she liked it here. I am still stunned and can't quite shake the feeling I now have, am I in love with Febe — don't be stupid, I saw her in a dress that was not like the one Maria put her in which made her look like an old woman and now you're suddenly ready to ask for her hand in marriage, time to snap out of it.

We go to the Plaza de Armas and visit the local cathedral, we look around, I follow Febe wherever she wants to go. I have been before, but to her it's all new and she takes everything in. I am just happy to follow. Along the street, we see families stood around with boards with photos of relatives; the sign says they are missing. There are hundreds of photos of young women on the boards. The mothers all stood there, people who walk by look at the photos.

When it's time to leave, we head back to the bus station, where we were dropped off. Its late afternoon and Papa wanted us home before it gets dark. Febe starts to drift off to sleep no sooner has the bus left.

'Sit still will you, let me rest my head on your shoulder,' says Febe. That feeling in my belly is still there, it has been all day. I wonder if it's been there since she arrived, maybe I just never noticed it before. She lays her head on my shoulder and snuggles in. I can smell the shampoo from her hair; she rests her hand on the arm rest. I put my hand on her hand. She doesn't move it.

'Thank you for today Tomas; I had a really nice time. I never thought I would ever laugh again, but I have since I found you.'

I look down and almost kiss the top of her head, I stop. Am I getting the wrong idea, I don't want to do anything that would upset her, what if I did kiss her and she ran a mile. She is fourteen and I am twelve, well thirteen soon. Febe stays this way the entire journey. I stay awake; I enjoy the fact that she is resting her head on my shoulder. I have that giddy feeling all the way home.

Chapter8

San Fernando and Nuevo Laredo Tamaulipas, Mexico

August – September 2010

Fuck Tomas, the little bitch-ass queer. Fuck his fat pussy of a dad and his little retard brother. Fuck his stuck-up bitch Mama, I hope she never comes back. Tomas could never have known I made that call about Lingala. I didn't know that they would kill him. I say a prayer every night to God asking for forgiveness, asking for the cries from his wife to leave my head. It won't stop, please lord help me; please take her face from my mind.

I thought the summer was going to be the greatest. At our stupid school, we take our summer break separate from other schools, Lingala's stupid idea. I thought Tomas was going to grow some balls and hang out with me. I thought we would hang out with some of the boys in the barrio rather than just play stupid kids games, playing soccer and chasing each other around the fields like dogs. He is my best friend and I feel bad that he doesn't want to hang out with me. Well fuck him, the boys are going on a road trip to Nuevo Laredo and I am going with them.

I realise I don't know their names, one of them is called Tuco, one is called Javier. They look bad-ass. Tattoos on their arms and necks. They are east side demons. They are packing guns in their trunk of their car; they have lots of money in their pockets, girls always hanging out with them. Their sixteen or seventeen, I don't know. They know Rojo, they don't like to talk about him, they say, 'Rojo, he baaad, he Craaazy motha fucka. He got himself into the Zeta clubhouse, membership for life ese, no one ever leaves, you want in little chicken hawk.'

'Sure,' I say, 'I am sick of this kiddy-shit, running around stealing cigarettes from stores for you, I want in.'

Tuco and Javier laugh and laugh and laugh. I am furious, I feel myself going red in the face.

'What is your name again ese.'

'It's Luis.'

'Well then Luiiis,' says Tuco, making fun of me, 'Come to Nuevo Laredo with us, we got a little job for you.'

Javier drives, Tuco sits up front. Two other boys are in the car. They don't speak to me. The journey is long; it's hotter than hell in the car. It smells bad in here. They pass around yerba, the smoke from the joint makes me feel sick. They pass it to me; I take a hit. I choke and cough so much I almost puke.

'Come on Luiiis, don't be a pussy, get on that motha fucka.' Tuco gives me the whole thing, I take smaller hits, I do the whole thing. Feeling woozy — the inside of the car seems like its spinning. They pass me a cerveza, I drink it, a whole tin — then another and another and another.

When we get to Nuevo Laredo I am all over the place, legs heavy and my head feels light. We go into a bar, full of men in white and black cowboy hats; leather pointed toe boots, jeans with big gold belt buckles and shiny black and white cowboy shirts. Outside hummers and SUVs parked with boys my age guarding them.

'Fuck you lookin' at punk, puto bitch,' one of them says to me. I look away and scurry into the bar. Even Tuco and Javier keep their mouths shut. I am given a bag, like a sports bag and told to ask for Leno. They wait by the bar, El Tigrillo, Narco gangster music blaring out of the sound system. I am scared; I don't want to do it.

'If you don't do this, I will personally fuck you up, you little pussy ass bitch,' Tuco growls this into my ear.

'Who is he, where is he,' I ask.

'Ask about,' Tuco says, playing tough but looking scared.

I walk about the bar, there must be fifty guys in here, it's hot and stinks of sweat and yerba. A big fat guy grabs me. Lifts me up by my arms. Goatee beard, gold teeth top and bottom, breath reeks.

'Hey little man,' his friends all laugh, I start to cry. I think he is going to hurt me. He is fooling around. His friends all laugh at me crying. I run off, one of them squeeze my ass. I wipe the tears and go asking about.

One man says to me, 'you stupid little punk, you want to tell everyone your looking for Leno. Come with me.'

The man is around twenty-five, he looks mean, it's dark in the bar, and he is wearing shades. He leads me to a room behind the bar. More men; all dressed the same, in the middle of the room is a penned off area. Two dogs are fighting in the pen. Both covered in blood, snarling, biting, and clawing at each other. They are big, but I can't see what kind of dogs they are — they have ripped each other to pieces. One of the dogs bites the other around the throat, blood spilling onto the sand covered ground. The howls are like nothing I have ever heard before. It's horrible — I just want out.

I notice uniform cops in there as well; drinking with Narcos, laughing and passing money around, betting on the dog fight. I feel sick, I feel very scared. I am taken to Leno. He is old, like Flip's age or something. He is fat, big fat. The fat under his chin hangs down to his blue cowboy shirt which is soaked in sweat. The man takes the bag from me, I turn to leave, but my arm is grabbed. Leno looks inside the bag —

A flash of orange light comes from the bag and then I hear the bang. Leno screams — his face is ripped to shreds. Nails sticking out of his face, flesh burned and peeling away — blood covered skull peeking out behind the hanging, oozing flesh. The men around him are running in all different directions, covered in blood, nails sticking out of faces and limbs, screaming and bleeding.

'Arghhhhhh, help me, help me, help, help me, fuck, help me.'

I run, I don't think anyone noticed me walk in. In all the confusion and the inured, screaming people I run out of the room into the main bar. All I think is that Tuco and Javier set me up — used me to hand a bomb to someone because they knew no one would suspect a small boy of this. I wonder what he thought a twelve-year-old boy was doing there, was he stupid. But then again no one suspects a boy. Everyone is running into the room as I try and run out.

'It was that fucking kid, stop that little shit.' no one has grabbed me yet, I get stuck in the crowd. I fall to the ground. Cowboy boots crush me, people fall on me, I can't breathe, I am scared and I panic. I piss my pants. They're going to kill me.

Suddenly I feel Tuco grabs me from the floor. A Narco shouts, 'He's here.' No one hears him above all the noise and panic; no one notices him or what he is saying. Tuco pulls a knife and shoves it into his neck — blood sprays everywhere. The Narco falls to the ground, gargling blood.

We get outside. Javier is shouting, 'He's here, I got him, I got that motha fucka.'

I am dead, but then I look on the ground, he has a small boy pinned to the ground, I recognise him as one of the kids guarding the cars when we came in. The one who talked shit to me. He is screaming and crying. Javier is telling everyone that it was him who went inside with the bag. He saw him talking to some Zetas before he went in. Tuco shoves me down the road. What kind of fucked up plan was this. The men grab the boy off the ground. The boy is screaming and crying and telling everyone that he didn't do anything. I hear the shot fired. I don't hear the screams anymore.

Tuco keeps pulling me towards his car, the other two guys are stood by the side of it, they don't say anything. Javier comes running to the car at full speed. 'Get us the fuck outta here, start that bitch up.'

We jump in the car, its engine roars, I look back at the direction that Javier came from, back towards that bar. Narcos are running down the street, they have guns in their hands.

'Move it,' Javier shouts — he sounds frightened, but also has that nervous laughing sound to his voice. The windows of the car explode as bullets tear through them. I am on the back seat; I lie down into the foot well. The two guys in the back, pull guns and start shooting out of the back of the car, where the window used to be. Javier drives the car extremely fast, it turns and screeches and turns again. Shots can be heard coming from behind. They are chasing us; I have never been so scared in my life. I look up to see the two boys on their knees holding guns and firing out of the back window. The noise of the shots ring through my ears, the sound is horrendous. One of the boys falls backwards, his back hitting the front seats, blood spraying all over the inside of the car, he collapses on top me. The back of his head is just one huge hole, like a crater. Blood pours out of the back — all over my face, the weight of him; I can't turn myself over to stop it pouring into my face. I then feel pain in my arm; my left arm hurts real bad. I touch where it hurts, there is a nail stuck in my arm. I was about ten feet away when that bomb went off, I was lucky I just got that. I pull it out and scream in pain. I lie under the boy, suddenly I can't hear any more shots coming from inside the car, and I twist my body to see the second boy is lying on the back seat. Blood pouring from his chest, I can see bone and flesh from the hole in his shirt. His mouth is pouring with blood. He starts to shake and then his body starts to jolt about. He pukes blood, lots of blood out of his mouth all over his face, it sprays inside the car. I can feel pools of it running into the foot well. I lie in it because I can't do anything else.

The car is still moving fast, I can't hear much else, I don't hear Javier or Tuco talking. The car starts to slow down; I have no idea how long this went on for. What happened in the bar seemed like years ago? It lasted only a matter of minutes, but seemed like an age. Eventually the car pulls to a stop. I hear Tuco shout: 'Hey, you OK little man, you hurt.'

'No,' I try not to cry again, 'get me out of here.'

Tuco and Javier pull the boy off me and get me out of the car. Javier pours what smells like gasoline onto the back seat, all over the boys as they lay there, covered in blood, gaping holes with bone sticking out, and throws a lit match onto the back seat. We all run away. I hear the boom of the car and I can feel the heat on my back as the fire catches.

I have no idea where we are. We are in a barrio; it's much bigger than the one we live in. The houses are run down, the pavements are cracked and broken, and there are lots of alleyways, narrow alleyways. We run down the alleyways, lots of young gang members looking at us, I can see Zeta tattoos on them. They are in black, what looks like army style clothing, all of them carrying pistols, some machine guns. Some of them show us where to run. We get to a hut, nine or ten men this time — all dressed in black army style clothing with bullet proof vests on. They are not teenage gangs; they look like men. They look like the army, muscles bulging out from underneath their tight black T-shirts. They look tough, they look mean, they wear sunglasses, they don't speak to us. Everyone looks at me; I am covered in blood, blood from Leno, blood from the boys in the car. We are put into the back of a truck — blindfolds are put on us. The truck drives away. Javier and Tuco were happy to have the blind folds put on them; I still don't know what the hell is going on. The longer this goes on, the more I think that I won't be killed after all.

Fucking Tuco and Javier could have told me what their plan was. Would I have gone through with it if I had known? I seriously doubt it. That was quick thinking of Javier to blame that young boy, to say it was him who took the bomb to Leno, they were not fooled for long though. I sit blindfolded in the truck, where I can only hear the engine. No one speaks; no one smokes yerba or fools around. This is serious. The weapons the Zetas were carrying were the shit, not old rusty guns I see the barrio kids holding and that bomb didn't blow everything apart, it was meant just for Leno. What a fat fucker, he must be Gulf Cartel; he must have upset someone real bad.

***

The truck stops — we have been driving for hours, I am taken out and the blind fold is taken off. It's night-time. We are in a place with high metal fences with barbed wire on top. Boys in black are guarding the gate with machine guns, I can hear whistles being blown, I look to see groups of people in black; practicing knife throwing, taking machine guns apart and cleaning them, rows of young boys stood to attention while a man, also in black shouts at them, tells them they are stupid, useless fucking barrio shit birds and they will never make the Zetas. They are all forced to run at full speed. Then push ups, then run, then push ups. The place is basically an army base, for Zetas.

I go into a tent, with Javier and Tuco. Inside the tent are bottles of beer and women. Some of the men have the girls sat on their laps, kissing and saying dirty things to each other. They are drinking beer and I can smell yerba inside the tent. There are twenty or so men in here. They are around eighteen to twenty-one years old.

We take a seat on folding chairs away from the other men. It is then I see Rojo come into the tent. Holy shit, look at those tattoos; on his face and on his neck, rows of tears from his eyes, down his face and over his neck. His eyes are wide open; he doesn't seem to blink. His head is completely shaved, bald as a baby's ass. I can just make out the outline of his hair; it goes into a point at the front. He looks like the devil himself. He is in black, black combat boots, black cargo pants and a black vest. His arms and hands completely covered in tattoos. Not one patch of skin can be seen accept those parts of his face that have not been covered yet.

'We got him Rojo, motha fucka bleeding like a stuck pig,' says Tuco.

'How,' Rojo's voice is soft, he sounds like a girl — no sooner as I said it he looked at me. Shit, did he read my mind, I am dead now — don't be stupid you're just imagining things.

'We used the bomb you told us to take. The kid here took the bomb in, he is one crazy mother, I can tell you, real balls of steel.'

Rojo takes a chair, he sits opposite me — real close. He stares at me; he doesn't say anything for what seems like hours.

'You're from the east side barrio, on the outskirts of town.' I nod; I am too scared to speak. 'Leno controls the barrio where you live, where your family live. Now he is gone, we will run things down there, we will make sure that no one else in the barrio dies because of that fat lump of shit. You did a good thing today, without him; the barrio will be a better place. The Zetas will take care of everyone. No one else need die needlessly. But we must rid the place of Gulf spies, there are lots of them, would you like to help us. Kill those filthy fucking shit eating scum.'

I nod, and say 'Yes.'

'Good — good. Now don't be fooled, the spies are everywhere and they are likely to be your friends, your family, your own mother and father. I know who they are, you have to trust me, do you trust me?'

I nod, but I don't know if I do trust him. I want my Mama, I feel scared.

'If you don't want in, you can leave now. You did a great thing today. It was Leno who killed those people on that bus and his Gulf scum will kill more. Z40 is building an army and he asked me to lead an army — to hunt rats and there are lots of rats to hunt. Are you a rat hunter or are you a rat?'

He can tell that I was going to ask to leave; I shake my head and say 'No Senor.' I call him Senor because I hope that this will help me.

'I asked Javier and Tuco to deliver that bomb and because they are disloyal pussies they got a kid to do it. But a kid with the heart of a lion, and the balls to match. Now do you want in; become a Zeta, we will train you, teach you to kill, teach you to become a soldier, do you want that or do you want to go back to the barrio in San Fernando and pray that I won't come to your door and kill you in your sleep.'

No choice, I feel tears roll down my face, what about Mama?

'I want to join, but Senor,' I pause — his eyes glare at me, his face is getting closer to mine, his eyes don't blink. I look down into his hand, I don't know why but I do. He is holding a toy car, 'My Mama, please don't hurt my Mama she is good, she isn't a rat, I will do anything for you, but please don't hurt my Mama,' I sob, I can't help it.

'Come outside with me,' says Rojo.

I walk outside with Rojo, Javier and Tuco follow. Rojo shouts over to a group of boys all around fourteen or fifteen years old.

'Gather round, we have a new member of the Zetas, but first he has to go through the initiation.'

Now I look about, the other boys have evil in their eyes, they grin, they want blood. Javier is pushed into the middle of a circle of the group. Tuco is then pushed in as well.

'Now then, if you want to be a Zeta, you must take the challenge, all of us had to do this and if you want in, then you must do this. If you refuse, then you will die.' Rojo throws two baseball bats into the middle of the circle, nails driven through the bat, sharp, shiny metal nails. 'Don't go for those until I tell you, the rules are simple, you fight to the death, the survivor gets to be a member, the loser goes straight to hell.' Rojo looks at the baying crowd and smiles, the crowd of Zeta kids are screaming, all baying for blood.

'Fiiiiigghhhhht,' cry the crowd. Rojo joins in.

Tuco is first into the circle, he grabs the bat. Javier side steps and picks up a bat. The boys hold me and make me face the circle. One of them whispers into my ear, 'Don't you dare look away, look at this.'

Javier and Tuco both look pleased to be accepted, they both look like they want to be initiated. Javier swings at Tuco's head, Tuco moves and the bat drives itself in the ground. Javier turns and faces Tuco, who swings the bat. It hits Javier in the leg, the nails stick in. He screams — blood pours from his leg — Tuco punches Javier in the face — nose explodes, blood down his mouth and chin. Tuco tries to pull the bat, but it's stuck in Javier's thigh, every time he pulls I can hear flesh tear — blood pours down his leg and pools on the dust covered ground. Javier moves away, the bat hanging from his leg, he swings his bat at Tuco, Tuco moves back. Javier hold his own bat in his left hand and takes the bat stuck in his leg, he pulls the bat out of his wound — blood squirts out of five or six holes now in his leg. Javier now has two bats. Tuco panics and tries to run out of the circle, the boys push him back in.

He weeps, he screams, 'No Javier, no please, please don't, not like this, I don't want to fight anymore, I am sorry I did that, I just want to go home.'

Javier holds both bats above his head, he brings them both down on top of Tuco, the nails tear though Tuco's face — the top of his head — his mouth is ripped open when one of the nails drags its way across the corner of his mouth to his ear — he screams and sobs and now when he shouts his voice now unrecognisable, fear and pain can be heard in his screams.

The next hit is in Tuco's eyes. He is screaming and stumbling about. He is blind, he falls to his knees. Please end this; I don't want to see anymore. Javier drops one bat and takes the other in both hands. Javier's face is white, he is weak, he is losing blood, and he can barely walk. His brings it down on top of Tuco's head. The crowds of boys' yell and cheer and chant. I can't believe this. The circle goes quiet again; the bats are taken and put back into the middle of the circle.

Javier is pushed back in again; Rojo takes my arm and brings me into the middle. I scream and try to get out — I am pushed back in. The crowds go wild; they scream and shout and want more. I don't want this; I want my Mama I scream. They push me back in. I look at Rojo, his grin is huge, and he is laughing. I don't want to die this way — not here — not like this. I beg with him, I tell him I am only twelve years old, Javier is stumbling, he is covered in Tuco's blood, he has fury in his eyes, he looks at me, he sizes me up — he was ready to kill me. I realise that it's useless — they will kill me if I try and run, Javier will kill me because he doesn't want to die. I try and calm myself, I stop screaming, I stop crying, I stop asking for Mama. I can see that Javier is slow and limping. My only way out, I look at Rojo, he screams out at the top of his voice:

‘Figghht.’ As fast as I can I run towards the bat?

Chapter9

San Fernando, Tamaulipas, Mexico

August – September 2010

I break my back working long days. The sun beats down on me like a cruel tormenter — burning my flesh; while I put myself through this. The end goal is to get out of here. Poor Joaquin works with me, but he understands to stay in the shade. Keep building son, keep learning and studying, but don't be like your Papa. Despite the problems you face day to day, keep observing and keep building. Maybe, one day an architect or an engineer, don't lose faith like your Papa, go straight to the top, don't look down.

I rip down walls; I build new ones back up. I take down roofs I put new ones back. I am not much of a bricklayer or a carpenter for that matter, but I keep trying, it all pays. I go home soaked in sweat, covered in dust and mortar. The sun crucifies me during the days, weeks and months that pass. When I get home, I am ready to fall into deep sleep. I undergo the same rituals every night and day. My priority is the family, Tomas, Joaquin and our new edition, Febe.

Tomas and Febe have become good friends, spending the entire summer together. Over the passing weeks it has become apparent that no one is looking for Febe. She is believed dead. The monsters that did this are not trawling the barrio seeking her out. She has been seen with Tomas, the questions have been asked and the pretence maintained. She is a family friend from out of town, she will be staying with us for some time, she is not a girl who has attracted attention from any other parties, except Tomas. Rather than hide her away she is visible — furtive behaviour arouses suspicion. Living in my house, no one attracts the attention of others. I am just the handy man, raising two boys and now another has appeared. No one cares; everyone has more important things to discuss. I have heard the rumours of who the local people suspect was responsible, but I pay enough interest when it's discussed, just to keep anyone off the scent.

I keep in touch with Benito, he usually he meets me out by Chavez place. We discuss how Febe is bearing up. I tell him how strong she is, how positive a personality she is. I tell him we are going to leave this place.

'Why wait Flip, why not go now,' Benito sound intrigued and a little puzzled at my reasoning for making the money.

'I am no one's charity case, especially indebted to Laena's father. I owe it to him and the boys to earn my way, not to just turn up like hoboes and paupers with our hands out. I want to pay for our travel, get our visas and have some money to pay him for housekeep. When I get there, I will earn my way.'

'Do you know what it will take to get to the States Flip,' Benito says, now sounding slightly patronising. 'They won't just allow you to hop across the border and hand out visas and the like. They will scrutinise you, they will want sureties that you're not going to be just another border hopper looking to drain their system.'

'For god's sake, I work harder than any of those overweight, reality TV show watching narcissistic, pampered Yankees any day of the week. Plus, Antonio is sponsoring me, we are his family. Plus, his other daughter, her husband and son all live over there, no questions asked.'

'You have a point Flip, but let's run through this and I am sorry to be so bold, but isn't he likely to blame you for what happened to his daughter, I mean you told me that he offered to take you all in years ago, and has done so since, but you refused. I am sorry for pointing this out, but might this just be a trick, where you go over and then he takes the boys from you, their social care system dictates that if children are likely to be at risk of deportation, then they can seek asylum in the US. But where does that leave you, deported back here minus your kids, think about it.'

My heart sinks, it's not something I have given much thought to in the past, but he has a point. My head goes down.

'You don't know him or the rest of the family, they wouldn't do that to me, despite what happened, he has never said anything to suggest that he hold any malice against me.'

'Of course, he wouldn't say that Flip, if he upsets the apple cart and you take off and move away or break contact then he has lost them for good. You're a college educated man, surely alarm bells must be ringing by now, surely you're not so naïve.'

'If that is the case, then at least the boys would be safe and would have a fresh start and a chance in life, not living in this place, surrounded by crime and murder and dirty backhand cops.'

I thought I would throw that in, I hope he feels as shitty as I do. He grins because he knows that I am telling the truth.

'Maybe you're naïve Benito, maybe it's you who has to have a fresh perspective on life in general. When Suarez disappeared, do you think that he just one day thought, fuck my family and my responsibilities and the oath I took, I am going to head to Tijuana, sip margaritas, watch a donkey show. No, YOUR people saw to that, they killed him, or made him vanish or wherever the hell he is. What place on earth, during one of the biggest massacres this country has ever known, and then stands by while the person investigating disappears and then looks back and says that it must have been one big coincidence? What horse shit!'

'Flip, you are a wise man and quite a Pit bull when you want to be. You're right, but this is Mexico, the judicial system has always been fucked up.'

'No, thousands of miles away the Yankees were ripping through Baghdad and Kabul in tanks. Just over their border they stand back while tens of thousands have been killed in four years. Why don't they intervene? Because of exactly what you just said? It's Mexico and it's always been fucked up. If we can't sort out our bad apple barrel, then why would they. You criticise me for wanting to get my children out of here, you think I want those boys to grow up where apathy is all around. This place used to be home to some of the most prosperous and hardworking people the world have ever seen; now it's full of Narcos and murders.'

I don't know what the purpose of this discussion was all about, usually he meets me to talk about the investigation into Laena's disappearance and how Febe is getting on, but today seems like there is an element of finality about it. I watch him as he ponders his next move.

'Flip, I too have been warned off. Not by Zetas — fuck those assholes. I too was visited by that man you saw, the one with the sunglasses, the captain. He is overseeing the situation and he has told me that I am to close the book on all investigations of this kind. What I tell you now stays with us and does not go any further, you understand.'

I nod, I know the drill, I am the holder of secrets these days.

'The attorney general and the government are paying particular attention to this region after what had happened last month. Questions are being asked as to why seventy-two people were killed and it's also starting to raise awareness of the many hundreds of people who disappeared in this part of Tamaulipas. The Captain had it passed down to him from above; under no circumstances are the other disappearances to be listed as suspicious. List them as runaways or beaten wives who fled from violent homes or if they are children, then list the parents as either physically or sexually abusive towards the children, so to explain why they ran away. Within those files, evidence has been altered to give that impression already. If any of the relatives ever question our decision, then they could face arrest and prosecution under the belief that they could have been one of the abusers. The file on Laena has already been altered by the municipal Police and that file has been back dated so it shows that Laena had made a domestic abuse complaint against you.'

I am silent; it's hard to comprehend what I have just learned. Benito is staring at me and his delivery of that revelation is done with sorrow and shame. He can barely bring himself to say anymore. I look away from him, I look over the vast fields surrounding Chavez place, back towards the town in the distance. The town I so loved as a child, the church where I went as a boy, the soccer pitches I played on, the Rio San Fernando that I love to sit and stare out across its still waters. The place where I first met her. The memories I hold now seem like they have been shattered, my belief in our system is just an illusion.

'Nothing I can say or do will bring any justice for you, but I did look through the file that the municipal Police originally held for Laena, before the state cops took it over. Suarez, as you know was Federal. But he found someone who used to work in those fields with Laena a man by the name of Bertrand. Bertrand is believed to originally come from Belize or somewhere like that but worked the same fields that Laena worked. Suarez had contacted a witness who said that Bertrand and your wife were close. His next action was to locate Bertrand, who is somewhere in the state. If it helps, Bertrand is black, so that may help. That is all I know.'

My day is just getting better, now my mind is doing back flips thinking that Laena may have had relations with a man she worked with. Benito leaves and I try and put this all together. I had to think rationally, All Laena did was work and come home, she got the bus early that day, her pay was always the same, never short so she couldn't have been skipping out with another man and she would be home for the boys. So, who is Bertrand and why may he be so vital or why did Suarez think he was so vital.

I think back to that day again, In March. Laena left for work, she took the bus everyday near to the house. I would take Tomas to school in my truck and she would take Joaquin, walk him to his bus and ensure he got on it. Before his school closed forever. She kissed me goodbye and left. It was the same as any-other day. When I got home that afternoon, the house was empty. We waited for an hour and thought maybe that Joaquin had been held up coming home and she was at the bus stop waiting for him. When we arrived at the bus stop, Joaquin was stood there alone. He was crying uncontrollably, his face streamed with tears and mucus and continually asking for his Mama. I picked him off the ground and hugged him, thinking Laena would never do this, she was never late for Joaquin and she would have been going out of her mind if she thought she was late for him and he would have been stranded.

With the boys in tow, we went to the super market, the bus stops, we drove to the field where she worked, it was deserted. I had never been there before so I recall it was strange to visit the place where Laena worked. It was desolate, no one around to ask if they knew her or seen her. That night I went to the police and informed them. A report was taken by a cop in uniform, who might as well have been taking a grocery order, he cared not, and the questions he asked implied that maybe she was just lost or out with friends and would likely come home later, he didn't know my wife, yet he assumed everything. I didn't argue with him because that's how I am, submissive, passive and trusting that the police would do their jobs.

For days, I would go to the cops and ask and for days they said that a report had been taken but no one assigned to the case. Tomas cried throughout those days. At night he would cry himself to sleep; he wouldn't eat, he couldn't think of anything else. I would say I was going out to look for her, but I would drive around aimlessly, no plan in mind, just in the hope that I may just magically find her. The Municipal police continued to ignore my calls and my visits to the station. Maria and Alejandro were good friends to me, they supported me. I started to drink heavily, when I woke up, before bed, during the day. Anything just to drown out the thoughts that I had going through my head. The children were not fed or bathed; I left them to fend for themselves while I spent four weeks in a downward spiral of self-pity and alcohol. When I phoned Antonio, and told him, he said he was coming down. I played it down, I fobbed him off. I told him not to come and that it was in hand. Eventually I begged him and promised that the cops were taking care of things and that potentially the town was in some sort of lock down by the federal authorities because at that time the Gulf Cartel and the Zetas had parted company and started their war for territory. I knew that if he came down, he would be packing a gun, he would shoot every mother fucker in the barrio until someone told him where she was.

I am ashamed of my lack of effort — I am ashamed that rather than pour my heart and soul into trying to find answers, I poured alcohol down my throat. Eventually Maria took charge; she took the boys and looked after them. She gave me a piece of her mind, told me to snap out of it and that I had a job to do, a job as a father and sole carer of the boys. When I sobered up and collected them, they were mere shadows of themselves, withdrawn and totally wrecked. Their hearts were broken.

I cursed her at first, blamed her for leaving the boys. Thought that maybe she left us and sought a better life outside of the town she longed to leave. I was cursing myself, blaming myself. I still do and will forever more. I think about burying what I had just learned, why go looking for Bertrand? but Laena had never mentioned him before and I wanted to find him, maybe he had some answers.

I decided to drive once again to the fields where Laena worked. The one and only time I had ever been there before was the day she vanished. The fields were deserted, over grown and uncared for. No work force in the field at all. The day I went there before, the fields looked kept, like they had been harvested, but now the fields were unploughed and deserted. Where had that workforce gone? Why had they left? The land didn't even look like it was up for sale. I drove up the narrow dusty road towards a farm house, the house looked empty. Windows smashed, like kids were using it to play in or just fool around breaking windows.

I got out of the truck and knocked on the door. No answer, shit, fuck, what now. You fool, you're being nosey — you're overthinking this. But it's too late. Joaquin and I pick padlocks at work, when companies buy property and need to gain access when locks have been fitted, but the keys are no longer to be found. I taught Joaquin how to do this, I only showed him the once, now he is a professional. Maybe a cat burglar will be his new-found occupation. Stop it Flip, your mind is wandering. I pick the padlock and enter. The house is dirty, in the kitchen there are cerveza bottles lined up on the table, ash trays full of cigarettes, old food gone bad, the smell hits me like a heavy weight punch to the nasal passage.

'Hello is anyone home?' I call out, already knowing that no one has probably been home in months.

The house is all on one level, no upstairs. The furniture is ripped, but looks like it belongs to someone elderly. I look on the sideboard. In a frame is a photo of a man and wife on their wedding day. The photo looks old, like it was taken in the fifties or early sixties. They look neat and tidy and proud. The man looks young and handsome, the lady regal and elegant. They look happy, they look in love. All the belongings look old and judging by the photo a couple in their sixties or seventies would have lived here, they would have owned the farm.

Although the house is dust laden, in the kitchen area there is a patch of the wooden floor that looks cleaner than the rest. It is a square of about ten feet in diameter. It looks at odds with the rest of the dust and grime, like something had been left on the floor and had covered it, hence why it was cleaner than the rest. Maybe bags of grain or corn as it was a farm. If that were the case then someone removed it very recently, like within a matter of days. The fields have not been seen to in months, so it couldn't have been produce from the farm, what else usually comes in large very bags? — Oh, you are an asshole.

I run out of the door and get into the truck. I look around, but if anyone was here by now I am sure I would have known about it. You stupid fucking nosey, journo wanabe, you have put not just your foot, but your head and fat ass into the hornets' nest now. I drive down the dusty road, when I see a black SUV parked across the roadway, blocking me in. Guns are pointed at me. Men shout for me to stop the engine and throw the keys out of the window. Never before have they witnessed such compliance. In true ass-kissing form I throw the keys out of the window before you could say, 'Is that a melted snickers bar inside your under wear, or have you just shit yourself.'

Stood to the side are two men. One white, short, about late 40's, stocky with a beard around his mouth. Next to him is a black man, tall, like six three, short hair, handsome looking dude and unusual to see a black man. He looks athletic and in his mid-thirties. At first I think I have found Bertrand, but then I notice he is wearing a Kevlar vest with three dreaded letters on the front — DEA. The black guy walks towards me; he is cool and collected, calm and somewhat confident. He leans down and looks at me, I smile at him. Not to be cocky, but afraid and to make sure I give the impression that I am what it says on the tin, just a peasant handy man out looking for work. He smiles at me; he has that passive/aggressive demeanour about him.

'Get out of the van asshole.' No sooner as the word 'asshole,' was mentioned the door was open and I was on my knees with fingers interlocked behind my head.

And so, it begins, American agents arguing it out with the Mexican federal police. They shout at each other, they're blaming each other. The White American Agent, who I imagine is called Hank or some other stupid Yankee name, then accuses the Mexican authorities of corruption and taking bribes and there was a leek, that's why the house is empty. All this while I am on my knees, hands behind my head wondering why the war on drugs is such a Cluster-fuck of the highest proportion. Hank is then shoved in the chest by one of the Mexican cops; he then accuses the Americans of being observers, not wanting to get their hands dirty and of cowardice. Hank then starts to push back and before I knew it, there are cops restraining cops, spitting on the ground and cursing and making observations about each other mother's and how they perform fellatio on various animals This goes on for minutes, I hope the old couple who did live here are not witnessing this from wherever they may be — this life or the next. The sheer incompetence and playground fighting between the great American DEA and federal police has truly renewed my faith in anything authoritarian.

As I watch this fiasco, I notice the other agent just looking on, a wry smirk on his face, looking extremely tired of the whole thing. He probably thinks Hank is as big an asshole as I do and the Mexican cops are pumped up, macho boys out of their depth. He looks at me, I am looking at him. I give nothing away, keep the story the same, and don't let anything on. You're knocking doors, looking for work. I had that plan as soon as I was out of my truck, which I might add has not yet been searched. The fighting, or should I put it squabbling has ceased, Hank is back beside the other agent, who dwarves him by at least a foot in height. The black agent looks down on this little pit bull runt and stares at him with disdain for even getting into such a pedantic and futile squabble. He walks over to me and goes down on one knee.

'What's your name my friend.' Fluent Spanish, I like him already; Hank looks pissed because he can't join in.

'Felipe Hernandez, I am a handy man, I came here looking for work, someone told me that the house was in a bad condition and an old couple live here, I do lots of work for the elderly for a reasonable rate in these regions.'

'Who told you about the house, what's their name.' The agent is probing.

'I don't know senor, he was young looking, about late teens, he said that he used to work here about six months ago, picking in the fields and tending crops.' I am hoping that the agent may give something away, in his gaze, in his voice or even say something.

'Where do you live,' Short and to the point

'In a barrio, just outside of San Fernando, literally only a few hundred meters and you're in the town limits. This was the first time I have ever been to this place senor.'

I look behind me towards my truck, the federal cops are searching the rear of the truck, one is inside the cab. I can still hear them cursing Hank. Hank obviously doesn't speak any Spanish at all, because otherwise he would be throwing pathetic little girl like punches again as I can hear the cops passing judgement that his cock is probably like a shrivelled walnut. The other agent however continues to try and stifle laughing, only ever so slightly. This one is too cool for school.

'My name is agent Curtis, I am based in Nuevo Laredo, overseeing operations in this region. I need people like you, eyes and ears on the ground as it were, here is my card.' He speaks low and sincere; his card only has a telephone number on it, no logo, no official title, nothing that says he is DEA, except it is on his Kevlar vest. On his right arm, I notice a tattoo, it's a Marine Corp tattoo, my father had one just like it. 'You know what I am here for and I am sure you see things; I am here to rid this place of people that kill the people in your barrio and get away with it daily. You probably have a family and wouldn't want any of them to get hurt; I can help your people.'

Superman to the rescue; what's he going to do, fly into our barrio and rid the place of incessant evil and oppression and get a cat out of a tree while he is at it. I don't mind being patronised — I am Mexican after all. But he tries to sound sincere, he sounds like he believes it as well. Maybe I could barter with the guy, without sounding like I was here for any other reason other than the lie I passed out. I look like a peasant, sound like one too. This is my armour, this is my shield, go on play him like a cello at the philharmonic.

'If you need money, I will pay for good information,' he sounds desperate, like all the intel' so far has been for shit. I remember hearing of counter-intelligence. I remember hearing that the Zetas were particularly good at this sort of thing.

'I did here there was someone who may know something about this sort of thing senor. He wouldn't talk with you, but he may talk to someone like me, the only problem is I can't find him. If you were to find him then I could speak with him, for you senor. I don't want money for that, just to help.' If Machiavelli could see me now, he would be proud.

'Who,' agent Curtis says, sounding like he is buying it.

'He is a black man, came up from down south somewhere, they call him Bertrand.' I slip him my cell phone number and it was as easy as that.

Chapter10

San Fernando, Tamaulipas, Mexico

September – October 2010

I can't stop thinking about Febe, we are due to start school again very soon and I have spent every day with her. I feel stupid for thinking about her, I stutter my words out when I speak to her. She has, at times noticed and teased me for this "What's the matter TTTTomas" she would say and laugh. We have played together all over the summer break. She doesn't like to lose when playing soccer and my legs have more welts and bruises over them than I could count. Only yesterday, she pulled me to the ground and lay on me, she was laughing while she did this. I felt funny; my stomach felt like it had butterflies going haywire inside. I didn't like to admit it, but I liked it when she was close to me, I liked it when it was just Febe and me. I couldn't think of anything else: just being us together. I even became jealous when she would play with Joaquin, I feel so stupid, why do I feel this way. I look at her and I notice how pretty she is, I want her to just want to be with me, no one else. I don't want her to speak with anyone else just me, to play with me only.
Things have been strange around the barrio; Luis is missing and his Mama is looking everywhere for him. She came over to our house to see Papa and she told him all about it. That was the day he went out and came back shaking like a leaf, when I asked him, he said that police had pulled him over in his truck and pointed guns at him, but he wouldn't say anything else. He has been working very hard recently and has not been drinking beer. Maria came over and was crying, crying very loud, I could hear her from the kitchen; Papa called me in and asked me if I had seen him. His Mama had looked everywhere for him; she had hassled the gangs and even went up to the Narcos and asked them outright if they had seen him. Papa said she was crazy for doing that, but deep down I think Papa wished he had the same courage as Maria. She went to the police station twice daily, shouted at the cops; even hit one of them when they laughed at her. She wrote letters to the government, the mayor, anyone she thought would listen.

I feel bad about Luis, because I had shouted at him and accused him of being responsible for what happened to Mr Lingala. I shouldn't have done that, I couldn't tell Maria that; although I know I should. Some friend I am, I just left him all summer, I should have tried harder. I feel bad because all I wanted to do was to be close to Febe. I just wanted to be with her.

Febe is now enrolled into our high school; she was older, so she wouldn't be in any of my classes. She showed she could read and write OK, and during the summer I sat with her and we practiced math and writing. She seemed embarrassed that she would struggle at school. I told her that she would be fine and I would help her. She asked about the girls in school and I told her how some were stuck up and thought they were better than the rest, than those of us who lived here. 'Fuck them,' she said and I laughed.

I enjoyed our time together, but the more time I spent with her the funny feeling in my belly was beginning to hurt. I couldn't imagine a time without her. I looked forward to her coming to America with us. We would both be strangers in a strange place; we could hang out together and always be that way. I hoped that she felt the same way as I did about her. I had to tell someone, because I don't know what to do. I have feelings that I had never felt before. I couldn't stop looking at her, she was beautiful and I always thought about the time I saw her in the dress, she looked like something from a painting or a movie. I couldn't tell her how I felt before speaking with someone, Papa was probably best, but he seemed busy all the time.

The day before school began, Febe and I went for a walk to the nearby fields and we sat down under a tree. I could feel myself wanting to talk, I felt at complete ease with her.

'Febe, have you ever been in love, like with a boy I mean,'

'What do you mean, like a boyfriend?'

'Yes, like a boyfriend.'

'I do like boys that way, but I haven't seen any boys other than you. The boys around here all want to be tough and in gangs and I don't like that. Look what happened to me and my Papa, I couldn't like someone who was like that. I like nice boys who treat girls nice. Anyway, I have my eye on a boy.'

My heart starts to hammer at my chest, will I like the answer or not. If I am the boy, then it's the greatest day of my like, if it's not, then I don't know what I will do, probably cry.

'Who is it,' I say, trying to play it cool, like I am not bothered, but I know my face is burning, and it's not from the heat of the afternoon sun.

'It's Joaquin, he is my little boyfriend and a great kisser,' she laughs and then shouts, 'Race you.' Up she jumps and runs back to the road we came from. I get up and am slightly disappointed that Febe is always joking around, always on the move and can't be serious ever. I run after her and we go home.

When I get back Papa is at home with Joaquin. Febe and Joaquin play in the yard. I must speak with someone. Papa is probably the best person to talk to. He did meet my Mama and without being cruel, he is not the best-looking man in the barrio, so he must have done something right, because Mama was beautiful.

'Can I speak with you Papa.'

'Sit down son, what is it? is it Luis? is that what is bothering you? Alejandro and Maria are out day after day asking about, down at the police station. He has been gone for weeks. Maria seems to think he went off with some older boys from the barrio, have you ever heard of Javier or Tuco.'

'No, I don't think so, but it's not about that.'

'Ok, what is it about then.'

'What did you do — when you met Mama, I mean how did you ask her out, at that dance you both talked about?'

'Well, I just went up to her and started to talk, not about anything really, I didn't make it obvious I liked her, I saw that she was different, she wasn't impressed by the boys who talked about themselves or who tried to make out they were better than they were. I took a leap; I did something that I wasn't usually fond of doing. I took a chance, a risk and asked her. I got to know her over a couple of hours and just went for it, why do you ask.'

'It's nothing Papa, I just wondered.' I didn't want to say, I just wanted Papa to ask me.

'It's Febe, isn't it? I see the way you look at her and the way you are around her. You know, it reminds me of how I was with your Mama when I first met her.'

'I like her Papa, but I don't want to be a fool or look stupid, I don't know what to say or how to ask, what if she doesn't think the same way? I mean she is older than me. I am just a boy, she is fourteen. I don't know any girl at my school who would go out with a twelve-year-old boy, they would just laugh and tell everyone.'

'Maybe, but that may be most fourteen-year-old girls, but I don't think Febe is one of those girls, she has had the worst in life happen to her and look at how she has bounced back from that. I know she still gets sad, but she is tough. She is also mature, she has had a hard life, she isn't spoiled like some of those Narco kids who wear makeup and watch American TV shows on cable and worry about their nails and hair. That's what I liked about your Mama. She was the most beautiful girl in this region, but she was also tough, she worked the ranch, she was smart and she didn't go for the types of boys that were full of shit. She saw through all that, she liked how people were on the inside. That is what

Febe is like. She can see you are a good boy and a caring, very much like your Mama was. I can't tell you what to say or how to say it, but if you feel this way, only you can do it, no stupid lines or try and be fancy, be yourself. I have spent my life wishing I did this or wishing I did that, I wasted so many years of my life not doing what I wanted to do or taking your Mama for granted, when I should have treated her like a princess. Don't waste any chances or live having regrets.'

Papa puts his hand on mine, I can see that he wants to cry, I have never heard him talk that way before, but it makes sense what he is saying. I squeeze his hand back. 'I love you Papa, and I wish I had been better towards you recently.'

'When we get to El Paso, you can buy me one of those milkshakes, the ones with the cream and strawberries on top — deal.'

'Deal,' I say, I leave him to rest.

***

When we arrive at school, Febe looks nervous; she is dressed in a chequered school skirt and the white blouse that all the girls wear. She hates it, she likes jeans and sneakers and T-shirts. Her shoes are polished; her hair is in a ponytail. I think she is the best-looking girl in the school. When we get to the halls before our new classes, she waits with me. I can see those horrible girls staring at her; I can see the boys look at her as well. Before we got here, Papa reminded us of the story that she is from Monterrey and is staying with us; she is the daughter of a family friend. I start feeling angry that boys are looking at her.

We have a new school principle, he holds assembly where he introduces himself. He isn't like Lingala; he never will be. He seems weak, he seems scared, when he speaks it's quietly, with a nervous stutter, it's very awkward. It's like he is reading from a script that he rehearsed before coming to school. He then mentions Luis, how he has been missing for three weeks now and if anyone has any idea where he may be then come to him or the police. In the halls, there are posters of Luis everywhere. It's not until now that it hits me. I feel terrible. I have been so wrapped up in Febe, that I put him to the back of my mind. I hope he is OK, I hope this isn't because of me and what I said to him before summer break. Maria has posted his picture everywhere; she arrived at school before start time and put them up.

I see Miguel and Seb after assembly. Seb looks at the poster, and then it comes out of his mouth: 'Luis is dead, I know it.'

'Don't say that.' I reply, not even sure if Seb's comment was aimed in my direction, 'you shouldn't say that; you don't know that.'

'Really shitbird, what the fuck do you know. I know that he went to Nuevo Laredo with four guys and none of them come back. I talked with Revo and Angel; they saw Luis get in a car with Javier and Tuco. They are tough motherfuckers as well. Revo said that Tuco was talking about Rojo, about doing something for him. Rojo's a Zeta now, and he's running things. He has his eye on taking our barrio. Revo said that the Zetas have some kind of training camp — near the border, they train kids how to shoot and build bombs and cut heads off and shit.' Seb doesn't sound the same excited way that Luis used to, he sounds afraid.

'So what are you saying, you think they went up there to become gangsters.' If Seb knows something, I need to get it from him.

'That Fucking Tuco has a big mouth, he told everyone before they went up there — they was going to do something for Rojo — when they never came back, stories started to fly around. You would have heard them too if you weren't playing doll houses with that new girl.' Sebastian laughs at me, I give him the bird, he carries on, 'We heard that to get into the gang, boys was being made to fight each other to the death — knives and chains and all that shit, whoever wins — they get a membership to Los Zetas. The loser, he gets buried in the desert somewhere. Well the five of them go up to Nuevo Laredo right! but the only one left standing was Javier. He sent a message to his Mama, saying he wasn't coming back and that he was safe and well and for her not to worry.'

'Did you tell Luis Mama that story,' I say, I am pissed that they would keep that from her.

'No fucking way, she has been to my house already, my Papa, he was pissed at me, gave me this big lecture on if I know anything then I should go speak with her right away. I ain't saying anything, she been around the barrio like a mad woman. She hit Angel with a club — around the ass and legs when he tried talkin' shit to her, calling her chica. She beat his ass — she was with some guy in a bus drivers uniform, and he looked as scared as Angel did. Revo, he's in hiding man, he knows she's crazy. She has started rounding up people from the barrio, I mean like normal people to go around and start asking questions. She has been outside of every building in town with the posters, but now it's not just about Luis, it's about all the other people gone missing around here. Fuck man, my Mama and Papa have even joined her. She been writing and putting stuff on the internet and everything. If Rojo finds out there could be big trouble.'

'She's not afraid of him,' I say, I know this firsthand, 'where is Rojo, you said he was back, yet no one has seen him.'

'Raising his army — those CDG in our barrio had better watch their backs, Rojo and his army are coming; Revo said the same, not only the barrio but the Zetas are taking over and it's happening now. Those people in the ranch, they was all killed by Zetas; those cops, Mr Lingala and now Luis, Javier, Tuco and the other boys, all killed by them, they just warming up. The wars that been going on in the other towns and cities, well its coming here as well, I been told.' Suddenly Seb stops and looks over my shoulder, I look around and Febe is stood behind me. Her face is blank, she looks upset, she heard what was being said and she walks away.

I follow her, she walks fast, she obviously doesn't know where she is going.

'Wait,' I shout 'Febe, wait up, those boys were just talking nonsense.'

'Really Tomas, well it looks like you were enjoying it all, the stories about these men, who killed my Papa and others like him. All boys are the same, I thought you were different Tomas, I didn't think you went for all that stuff.'

Febe's eyes were filled up with tears, she stormed off. I tried to touch her shoulder to get her to come back, but she kept on going.

At lunch, I tried to find Febe, but couldn't. Girls in her class all asked me about her, they made fun of her. They didn't know me and had never spoke with me at all, but did today, just to tell me they thought Febe was weird, she didn't talk, she didn't wear make-up, she was probably a lesbian or a serial killer, that they didn't want her in this school. I heard some horrible things today, things I didn't ever want to hear again. About Febe, about Luis.

When school finished, Febe waited outside of the school for Papa to show. She got into the cab, she didn't speak with me, and she gave Joaquin a big hug and kissed his face.

Papa asked how school went and Febe lied, she said it was OK, that she made friends; she thought the people were friendly, but not once did she look at me. When we got home, Febe went straight to what was now her room and closed the rickety old door. Something she never did before. Papa looked at me, he knew something was up; he looked towards the door of her room.

'Go on, show her you're better than, whatever this is.'

I knocked and Febe answered, she walked away from the door and sat on the bed, I went inside and closed the door again.

'Febe, I'm sorry, but I want you to know that I don't like what has happened or; whatever is going on. Miguel and Sebastian, they are stupid, they are not bad kids, they're just dumb, that's all. They were only telling me what they heard; they just speak that way sometimes. I have to tell you something that I have not told anyone before, about Luis and about what happened before summer.'

I felt relieved and a somewhat cowardly as I told her about Mr Lingala and what I had said to him and how I blamed myself. She listened, normally Febe would say something or talk over me, but she remained silent as I told her. I became upset as I told her how I felt.

'Also I want you to know,' choosing my words carefully, 'that I would never do anything to hurt you Febe, not ever. I am sorry if it seemed that way, but I am not like other boys. It's horrible what happened to you and your Papa and I don't want to think about it, but the same could have happened to my Mama as well. I hate not being able to talk to you, for us to be like we were before, please believe me Febe.'

I stopped talking; I waited to see if she would say anything. Febe stood up and came over to me, she hugged me, tight. I felt her put her hand on to the back of my neck. I shivered. She held onto me and looked at me.

'You know what you have to do, don't you,' said Febe.

I nodded, 'yes I will, tonight.'

Febe kissed me on my cheek, it was the best feeling ever, my stomach had butterflies again, and today I was filled with dread that she would hate me forever. This was the closest we had ever been, it felt natural to be honest with myself and to speak like this. I felt that I could tell her anything. What I truly wanted to tell Febe, I couldn't, not now anyway.

'Tomorrow, if any of those bitches speaks to me that way again; there is going to be more than a beat-down coming their way.' She laughed and I was glad that school didn't scar her forever.

I knew what I had to do. It was the longest walk I had ever taken. The garden path seemed like I was walking to one of those firing squads we read about in history classes — where deserters and traitors met their end. That's how I feel now. I deserted Luis, when he needed me most. I stand outside the door, waited to catch my breath and then knocked on the door. Alejandro answered the door; he was living there by the looks of things.

'Hello Tomas, what can I do for you little man, or should I say big man,' he says.

'Is Maria there please, I need to speak with her right away.'

'Sure, come in,' he looked puzzled and he led me in. Maria was at the table. I could feel myself getting upset. Maria welcomed me in and sat me down. I told her everything and I mean everything. About our argument, about how I suspected he made the call about Mr Lingala and about what I heard Sebastian tell me today and how he heard it from some boys called Revo and Angel. She listened and didn't become mad, I cried as I told her and said that I should have said something to Luis rather than go off for the summer and not bother with him. I told her how he invited me to go to Nuevo Laredo before summer break. I was so ashamed as I told her.

Maria came over to me and hugged me, 'don't get upset Tomas, this isn't your doing. We all know Luis is easily led, but I am going to find him and find out what happened to him, if it's the last thing I ever do. Now you go home and don't worry about it and I will go and pay Revo another visit.'

Chapter11

San Fernando, Reynosa, Nuevo Laredo, Tamaulipas, Mexico

September - November 2010

I wish I stayed at the seminary, at my age I could have made it all the way to the capital by now. Instead I am a fifty-nine-year-old police Detective. I have seen things in my life time that I cannot ever erase from memory. I left the seminary because I felt I could do more with my faith, I thought I could go out into the world and solve life's ill's, make the world a better place. Help the people of my homeland. I love this place; I have always loved this place. The people of this state are good people, honest people, my father always lived here, he was a hardworking, a man with values, who loved his church, a gentle man who loved his family and would have done anything for us. I tried to be like him, my sons have moved away at the behest of my wife Magda. They are men now, grown up with children of their own. They visit when they can; they live far away from here; living in the capital, in decent well paid jobs, raising families like my father before me. I live for my family; I used to live for my job. Everything has changed, I am old, I am broken, I have seen the very worst in life.

I go to confession and tell the priest of my sins. The sin of apathy, the sin of acquiescing. I tell my priest of the letter I was sent by the Zetas, I tell him I am scared, that I don't have the moral courage to stand up to them. I tell him of being weak, of the fear of my family being used as a pawn. I tell him that I have now joined the ranks of the corrupt and the wicked. Cohesion has been formed between these drug traffickers and my people: the police, those that swore an oath to protect the people — all have now bowed out and work with them. Evil prevails when good men do nothing; I remember that proverb from the seminary. I used it as the backbone when I first put on a uniform nearly forty-years-go. Now it seems I have succumbed to the evil that pollutes this once great region. I beg God for forgiveness, to overcome fear. My priest tells me that I should say ten Hail Marys and five our fathers. He tells me that it is not a sin to fear and not to give into fear.

That day I go to work, I see a car in the middle of San Fernando. Windows shot out, three dead men inside, the letter Z scratched on the driver's door. This is nine thirty am. Before I even manage to sketch the scene, I am called to highway 101 just on the outskirts of the city. An SUV containing members of the Zetas are found at a gas station. The attendant tells me that they pulled in to buy sodas and when they get back into their vehicle, three vehicles pull up and shoot them all dead. Blood in the foot well, blood over the windows. I check out the SUV, it has been sighted in the barrio just outside of the city near to 101. The same barrio where Flip lives with his children. Where Febe lives. Previously the cartels and its members lived outside of the city limits. The battles in these regions were sporadic, the casualties and deaths would be high, but generally infrequent. In the major towns and cities, the Marines and the Army have flooded the streets, the cartels don't care, and they match them for firepower. They install their psychological war on the Army by placing banners taunting the government, the Army, the police. Telling El Presidente to get his forces out of the cities or else. Calderon will not relent, he continues the war on drugs — a puppet dancing around for his American masters, when he shows no signs of relenting, the cartels murder more people and now they have chosen to kill civilians, as a way of demonstration. The Army has moved out of this area now and flood the larger cities.

San Fernando has generally, over the years been a place where the cartels and the war on drugs has not greatly affected. The government had adopted something called Operation Nuevo Leon – Tamaulipas, a state-wide operation to combat the cartels, and it has been bloody. Since the Gulf cartel and the Zetas parted company earlier this year, things have gotten worse. The Zetas are a different kind of enemy, like the bogey man, the ones you fear more than most. They have no fear; the founding members are all ex Special Forces and combat trained. They kill indiscriminately, they don't care who gets in their way. The barrio outside of San Fernando has been said to be the nest, I am hearing more and more that they are moving in, taking over properties and storing weapons and drugs, ready to take over the border. The massacre in August has now been officially pinned on them. I am off the case; after Roberto vanished the Attorney general has taken over the investigation. He is no further forward.

I think of Roberto every day: he was a threat, a threat to the cartels, to the Zetas and now it seems that the Zetas are the most powerful cartel in Tamaulipas. Even before the massacre they operated near to San Fernando, but now they are pushing the CDG out, bit by bit. The CDG still fight back. It's a futile game where there will be no winners.

I start to take photos of the scene, remembering that I still have to go back into town, for what was the precursor to this murder. My phone rings and its Maria, that poor woman, her son Luis is missing. She tells me of a camp, where Zetas train young children to fight for them, that Luis is died at the camp, that he was killed by some other barrio boy and that the boy has been sending text messages to his family, telling of how he survived and is alive and well and not to worry. She is hysterical and crying uncontrollably, she says that if I don't do something soon, she will take action. I try and slow her down and talk to her, she tells me to fuck myself and tells me that I am corrupt, just like all the others. The phone goes dead.

At midnight, I get back to my office; I have the files for Laena Hernandez and Luis on my desk. The photos looking up at me, with that wholesome innocence of youth, their faces haunt me. They are the innocent ones, the ones that we didn't protect — we took money and drank tequila with these murdering bastards. They are the forgotten ones, the real casualties of war. I vow to find them, I tell myself that I will dedicate my time to find them both; I must, for my salvation, think about the seminary and why you left, to bring propitiation to your life and the lives of others. I fall asleep in the office, the fourth time this week, when I wake its daylight.

I walk out of the office with the files; the Captain is stood there, those fucking mirrored sunglasses still on his face. He is indoors for heaven's sake.

'Pack your shit, you're off to Prison,' he says, facial expression remaining the same.

I call my wife, she is concerned about me, but I tell her I love her. I pick up clothes from the locker and head off. I go alone to meet other state Detectives who are already there.

September 10th, eighty-five inmates have escaped from the prison in Reynosa. When I arrive, there are other state Detectives already present, all scratching their heads. The fence is still sealed and intact. No tunnels that can be seen. The prison is just over the border from McAllen, Texas. Maybe they jumped the border, but I doubt it. All the eighty-five were cartel members, we don't know which cartel, but it was confirmed they were all serving time for drugs trafficking and murder. What in the fuck kind of place loses that number of prisoners? By the end of the day we launch an investigation into the warden and the guards, by the end of the week they are all arrested.

The investigations pile up; the bodies pile up also. The violence in the state of Tamaulipas is the highest in Mexico, even outweighing Juarez at this point. Throughout October it's daily, one murder scene to the next. Sometimes three separate murder scenes per day. At each scene, anything up to ten people dead. Often civilians caught in the cross fire. Women and children are playing in parks, soldiers shooting at cartel members, cartel members shooting back. In the middle the very people we should be protecting. All mowed down by gunfire.

DEA come to me, asking to speak with me. Agent Curtis and some short fat fuck asking about some farm on the outskirts of town, they say that half a ton of cocaine had been stored there and now had been moved. They explained they were working with Federal cops trying to find likely spots this side of the border where major haulages were stored and prepped for going over the border. I ask about the murders and if they are here to assist in anyway and they tell me their mandate is drugs only. You couldn't make this shit up. They didn't know any of the key Zeta or CDG players and probably never wanted to. I tell them about Roberto and how we worked together as part of a state and Federal operation in this region and how he had disappeared. I may as well of told them I was Santa Clause; they probably would have nodded in agreement. They weren't listening. I told them the place was a farm, where workers picked the field; I knew the place, I explained how Laena Hernandez was last seen heading there back in March. I told them the date. It seemed to register something with them, but when asked what was significant, he said it was classified. I spoke with them in English, just so fat fuck could understand. Curtis on the other hand seemed a sharp character, intelligent and ruthless. He looked like a football player, big shoulders and arms, narrow at the waist and hips, tall, with an element of intellect, but by his accent, which sounded like it was southern I am sure he was from working stock, but attempted to disguise his roots with a thin veil of opulence. Probably had to, these American agents can be an uppity bunch. He gave me a card with just a number on it and said he was up at Nuevo Laredo, should I need him.

One night I receive a call at home, told to get down to San Fernando. Four dead cops. I was expecting at the hand of the cartels. The captain was present, mirrored sunglasses worn, even at night. He's in full uniform. He doesn't speak, he just observes. The street is cordoned off. Lots of cops present, all hustle and bustle. Shell casings from handguns, departmental issue. The breakdown of our society was here for all to see. Cops had shot cops. A witness, who wouldn't go on record saying that they were drinking on duty, one group approached the other. They argued and cursed each other. Each of the two groups shouted allegiance to the CDG and the Zetas. Then the gun battle broke out and spilled into the street. Not only on the payroll to look the other way, but now murdering each other and taking the names of the cartels they are affiliated. I look around the cordon and all I see are faces in uniform, the faces of men who look like the gangsters. The uniform, the same State uniform I once wore with pride. If there was such a thing as the apocalypse, then it was taking place here and now in the twenty first century.

The captain approaches me while inside the cordon, he steps on shells, he contaminates any possible forensic evidence. I should shoot this motherfucker, right now and have done with it.

'Keep it clean,' the captain says, 'write it up right, these men have families, the Gulf cartel did this, they have been preying on us for some time now.'

Ah, you get paid by the Zetas, they're your paymaster.

'Captain, I can't do this, I know what happened here, this isn't right. We need a full investigation; how do we know that more of our men won't end up this way. I can't manipulate this even if I wanted to, to like the way you say it is.'

'You petulant old fuck, I should write you up for insubordination right now. Word to the wise — you work with these men; they protect your old ass when you climb out from behind your desk and prance around with your camera and notebook. They watch your ass and make sure you don't end up with a chalk mark around your decrepit old body. If they were to learn that you went up against them and went to the AG, do you think they would watch out for you, maybe the next door you must go through and need their assistance, you may accidentally end up getting shot in the back, or the head or the —'

'Why you motherfucking bastard, it was you who left that note for me, signed by the Zetas,' I can barely hold my rage, "where's Roberto? it was you wasn't it, you and your pals?'

Before I can say anymore, he leans in and takes hold of the lapel of my jacket, 'Just remember who you are and who I am before making accusations. You have been told — if that happens, if you follow the rules as I set them, you and your family will be fine, do we understand each other.'

The thinly veiled threat takes effect when my family are mentioned. The Captain walks away. I go back to the office. I write it up as a revenge shooting by Cartel members. I can't do anything else. My position is obstinate; but if I can get that bastard any other way, I will.

October goes much like September — as it dawns to a very bloody conclusion and November looms fast I receive a call from Flip. I arrange to meet him at Chavez place, I remember Chavez when he and my father were friends, they used to play cards, smoke cigars and drink together. I get to Chavez place; he is looking old, probably is old, and must be in his seventies at a guess.

I meet Flip and we exchange handshakes, he seems different from when I first met him, he makes eye contact now, not always looking at the ground and mumbling, he doesn't come across like the man I first met at the scene of the massacre.

'How is Febe,' I ask.

'She is doing well, she is at the same school as Tomas, they are quite the pair together. She has her off days, shall we say, but generally she is doing well.'

'What is the purpose of this meeting, if you don't mind me asking Flip.'

'Well,' he says like this was something that he had thought out, 'I understand that Suarez has not been found, same for the police officer, who disappeared with him, is that still the case senor.' He still calls me senor.

'That is correct, why do you ask.'

'I have heard that someone may have seen them, the day before they vanished. Now I know that it would be very dangerous for you to go snooping around, but if you could find that someone then I would speak with them and let you know.' He sounds sincere, it is then I notice another side to him I had not before. That he held a modest intellect about him, one that he never shows to anyone else.

'Who is the person?'

'I have been in contact with another party — they found out some information for me, they informed me that this person may be in Matamoros.'

'What people — who in hells name would give you such information and what would you have had to do in return.' I wonder what in the hell he is playing at.

'Let's just say that, these people want to know about things going on in the barrio, and came to me. These people have traced, through immigration the man you need to speak to; he is from Belize. He has been in trouble in Mexico and they traced his movements because he was arrested in Matamoros recently for some kind of misdemeanour to do with drinking; now he apparently works there, in a bar. What I would need you to do — using your connections up in Matamoros, to locate his address. It is apparently on the file, so it shouldn't be a problem. I can't go approaching the police asking for that sort of information, it would raise suspicion. I must speak with him because he won't talk to police, too scared, but may speak with me.'

That's it, that's the way to find some leverage on that bastard, and then I don't put myself in the firing line. Maybe this witness could finger that bastard Captain, and that would be fine. I take out my pad and pen and pen, 'Go on Flip, the name.'

'Bertrand Le Vell.'

Chapter12

San Fernando, Nuevo Laredo Tamaulipas, Mexico

September - November 2010

I have searched frantically for Luis; every park, every soccer pitch, anyone who knows him. I can't sit still, I can't eat, I don't sleep. My little Luis; my lovely Luis, he plays tough, but he's not. He is sensitive, he is scared, he is all alone out there. The more I think that way, the more my heart breaks. All alone and scared. I can't think of the possible, I won't think of the worst. I just won't, I will do everything in my power to find my little boy. I have spent all the Pesos I have on posters; I have put them everywhere. I look at those poor parents stood down by the mural in town, stood next to the hundreds of faces in photos lined up next to each other. I hope they are together, keeping each other warm and safe, looking after my Luis.
Alejandro goes with me. I have put Luis face on every bus that Alejandro drives. He hands out posters to all his passengers. When he goes to Ciudad Victoria or Matamoros or Nuevo Leon, he does the same. I have been with him on these journeys, walking around, handing the posters out, wandering aimlessly, desperate. I don't know where to start. Every city I go to people wish me luck, because many of them have suffered the same thing as I am going through right now.

Flip has asked Tomas and Tomas doesn't know. I have been to the barrio and asked all the kids. One of those little bastards called me 'Chica,' I beat him with a broom that I found outside on a porch. I don't know what I am doing, my mind is doing backflips. I can't stop; I go on for days like this. I think I am losing my mind. Some days I don't even drink water and by the end of the day I am sick. One day I collapsed from exhaustion and thirst. Some women from a store came out and sat me up, brought me into their store. I looked in the mirror, an old lady seemed to look back at me, I have aged since this happened. Please, Please, Please Luis, come back to me. I will do anything.

I even managed to get word to Luis father, the useless little shit, he said he hadn't seen him. That was that, not even an offer of help or assistance. Thank god, I have Alejandro. I snap at him often; he is trying to help and be reasonable but sometimes I just snap at him. I know I shouldn't, I know I am wrong to do it, but I can't help myself.

Weeks drift by all meshed into one. Each day is just as painful as the first. Then Tomas comes to the house to see me. He is such a sweet boy, but I can't help thinking that if Tomas had not of pushed him aside at the start of summer break then he would still be around. That was until Tomas told me everything. He told me about Tuco and some shit head called Javier and what he had heard in school and this Revo guy mouthing off about what he knew. Tomas tells me the whole story and I am angry: not with him, never with him. He is a boy who has suffered enough.

My boy is dead. That night I cry and cry, Alejandro doesn't know what to do, he knows how I have been and I don't blame him in not trying to comfort me. I keep seeing his face and try not to imagine how scared he must have been, being made to fight like that, in the way these bastards make them. Just kids all of them, boys who think that these Narcos are heroes and something to aspire to. My boy is dead; Luis is dead and we know this because Javier is alive and texting his mother from wherever he may be. I have work to do, I can't sit back like Flip and wait for the police to do something — because they won't, and they never do. We have suffered enough; the good hardworking people have suffered enough. I scream at the top of my voice; I am screaming and screaming — these bastards have killed my boy. I can't stop screaming. I feel hands on me, its Alejandro and Flip, they are both trying to restrain me, I have lost control. I punch Alejandro — he hits the ground. I struggle so much Flip can't hold me. I run into the street. I scream his name. It then goes dark.

I wake to find myself on the sofa and I can hear Flip's voice. I must have passed out. I hear Alejandro thank him for coming over so fast. I keep my eyes closed. I feel a kiss on my forehead, I know that was Flip.

'Goodnight my sweet,' he says.

I don't sleep — over and over I can see his frightened face, surrounded by a pack of dogs, shouting and cheering as he is butchered by some shit-heel from the barrio — some shit-heel bled my boy, just so he could carry the name of Los Zetas. I try to switch it off, but it stays with me. All the letters I wrote — all for nothing. I even managed to get letters sent to some of the families in Guatemala who perished on that ranch. Urging them to travel to Mexico — to demand justice, to demand answers. Well that's what I am going to do — I am going to get my justice!

I have received letters from towns-people in Culiacan and Nogales, saying that they are sick of the murders, sick of the army and police and saying that most of them are corrupt. They tell stories of the army taking people off the street and never being seen again. They say that they are going to rise and take action, they will fight the Cartels themselves — they will raid towns, kick the bastards out. They speak of justice and getting it themselves. They are speaking of an uprising. Groups who rise and fight the cartels. They are preparing and arming themselves all over Mexico — normal people who are sick of this scum.

I head to the house where I know Revo hangs out. It's late in the afternoon, all his friends will be there, smoking yerba and drinking. There he is, sat on that old car again. Probably belongs to some innocent person who lives here, but is too frightened to tell him to get the fuck off. I have my shopping bag by my side. I may be older, I may be out of shape but I am ready to start confronting people — I want answers. That shit head Angel is there as well as some younger, nasty looking barrio bitches. As I get closer they notice me, they all turn around.

'Hey Chica,' shouts Revo, the gang laugh, 'hey sexy Mama, are you here because you want to chase me around again. Can't get enough of old Revo.'

I drop the bag, I reach inside. My father's old billy club inside, I take it out, there's Revo's knee. Whaap, whaap, whaap! Oh, look, now it's gone — no knee Revo from now on, that's your name shitbird.

He screams, probably louder than I did when I found out my son is dead. Let's put him through his paces — but first the others. Angel is slow off the mark, as he runs I hit him over the back of the head, he falls. Now the legs — I turn him over, he is unconscious. Poor little Angel, this will wake him up. Whaack — left knee first. Whaack — second knee cap. Now he's awake.

Barrio bitch number one gets her hair pulled out by the handful as I take her to the ground. That made up little face is about to get made a whole lot uglier. I hit her and hit her and hit her. Face swollen, blood from her nose and mouth. I feel some skinny little bitch jump on my back and dig her nails into my neck. Obviously, she knows nothing about me. She doesn't know that I lift sacks of grain by the kilo at work. I throw myself back and land on top of her. I turn over and take her hair. I punch her about the face and kick her in the gut. I pick her off the ground and kick her in the ass. The other bitches think better of it. Thank god they didn't go to my bag. The bitches run off.

'Go tell your gang friends what happened here today, go tell them.' I shout.

I reach into my bag — my father's thirty-eight snub nose revolver. Revo is still screaming, he can't move. He sees the revolver which I point at him. He covers his face, he is crying like a baby, a seventeen-year-old baby I might add.

'No, no, no please, please, I didn't do anything, what are you doing this for. I didn't do anything to your boy, I just hang out here.'

'Open your mouth, come on, this Chica wants to play, come on faggot, you can take two inches of steel in your mouth can't you. Open up or I shoot the knees.'

He opens his mouth with great reluctance, I put the gun inside. I cock the hammer.

'Now tell me everything you been telling everybody else, I want details and I want to know where Javier lives.'

He spills his guts, not literally but I am in the mood for it, should he show me any reason to. He tells me the story; I try not to get upset. I am conditioned for that now. He tells me where I can find Javier's mother and father.

'I see you or those other bitches again — or you,' I the gun point at Angel, who has just finished puking into the dust covered road while screaming in pain, 'and I will certainly fuck you up. Not gently like this time, but permanently, I mean with blow torches and nail guns.'

I take out my father's old camera. I take photos of them both, lying on the ground. Angel — a slobbering, crying puke covered wreck and Revo, with his piss stained pants and tears of pain etched into his face.

'I will show these photos around, I will show these people, what shits you all are. These East Side Demons are first, then I am coming for the rest of you.'

The street is filled with people; shop keepers, mechanics, laundry and textile workers, manual labourers, old people, young people. Everyone looking at me, they all look amazed; some slightly scared as I am the true definition of crazy bitch right now. Men and women of all ages come out to see what the fuss is about. I tell them not to worry, not to be scared anymore. I tell them to be at my house on Sunday and bring friends.

I make my way to Javier's house, it's not far, I can walk it. As I walk down the street, people come out of their houses. They have just witnessed those barrio bitches running down the street, blood splattered and beaten. They have heard the noise and already people have been going door to door telling everyone of the sight of some overweight crazy-bitch beating up on the East Side Demons. I arrive at Javier's house, its modest; the garden could do with some work. The porch has a shrine to god, a catholic family. I knock the door and a woman in her mid-forties answers. She looks like she has just come home from work.

'Hello, how can I help you?' The woman's voice sounds much like any other woman. She sounds gentle, like someone you would expect from a good catholic home.

'My name is Maria; I am the mother of Luis, who is a friend of your son Javier. They went to Nuevo Laredo together some weeks back, but my son did not come home. He didn't come home because your son has killed him, just so he can prove his worth to those Narcos, just so he can join their gang. I understand he sent a message to your phone — show me.'

The woman became upset and started to cry. A man came to the door, he was covered in dirt, he wore a vest and pants with work boots on.

'What is it Jenny,' he looked at his wife; he put his arm around her, 'what is this all about, why have you come here.'

I told them the story, I couldn't help myself, I broke down and told them exactly what I had heard over and over and how Luis had died. The man invited me in; Jenny, as I now knew her got me some water. Javier's father sat me down at a table in the modest kitchen; the house was tidy but bare. A rosary above the picture of the family, there were other children in the photo.

The father told me of his disappointment with Javier, how he had become a kid with no brain, with no direction. How he tried to tell him, pleaded with him that the road he was going down was the wrong path. The man was the same or similar age to Jenny. His hair was greying, bushy hair in need of a cut, his skin dark, like leather, hands with dirt ingrained into them. As a family, they appeared much the same as any other family. They seemed like they had little money and were struggling just like the rest of us.

Jenny got her cell phone out and showed me the message, it read:

'Mama I am safe and well and don't worry about me. I am live and well and will speak to you when I can.
Lots of love Javier'.

'They told me that only three of them made it to this so-called Zeta camp and were made to fight. That means who ever sent that message is the only one that survived. That means my boy is dead, that means this Tuco kid is dead. My boy, no matter what would have contacted me. He has a cell phone, he was given it by some of your son's friends, for doing god knows what in return, he would have told me he was OK. He is only twelve years old.'

I start to cry again. Jenny puts an arm on me. I hit it away, she looks startled. It's not her fault, but I can't, I just can't do this. I stand up, they both look lamented, they have had to face the fact that their boy is a murderer, and they have had to mentally assimilate this, in a short period of time.

'If I ever see your son, I swear to god above, I WILL kill him and then I will kill those god forsaken bastards who stood and cheered and buried his poor little body in some shit infested dust ground.'

I get up and walk out of the house. The neighbours, who probably heard all about the scene down the street stand looking at me. Some with sorrow, some with expressions of furtherance. I was waiting for that car to come screeching down the street followed the sound of machine gunfire, and then I would be no more. The car or the gunfire never came. I went home, Alejandro was waiting for me. He threw his arms around me and I cried again.

Sunday came and I was astonished to see people standing outside of my house. At first I wondered who they were, why they were here. I then remembered what I said, the day I attacked Revo and Angel.

A man walked onto my porch, 'We are with you Maria, whatever you need, whatever we can do, we are with you. We are sick of these gangs, sick of these Narcos. If you meant what you said, we are with you. My four-year-old boy was killed at that school. He died coming out of that school-yard. When I got there his teacher was draped over his body, it looked like they had shot them while they were dead on the ground. The police never found anyone and never will. We are with you.'

And so, it started, day after day, week after week. We would meet, not at my house, but at an old abandoned store, eventually word got about and we went from a dozen, to over thirty people. Our group became public knowledge, so much so, that the cops started trying to find out who we were. Yet we had not done anything. We had taken no action. Eventually Old man Chavez started letting us use his ranch outside of the barrio. Each of us bought guns, some hand-guns or hunting rifles and stored them up at the ranch.

Flip tried to talk me out of it, he said this was crazy, that we stood no chance against the Zetas or the CDG, they were too powerful. At first I started with a march through the town, holding banners — demanding justice. The police came out to break us up. Some shit-bird with mirrored sunglasses pushed me, so I spit in his face. I was arrested and taken to jail. I was looking at a sentence, but a lawyer came to represent me, free of charge and got me off with a fine — that he paid. He too had lost a daughter during this war.

We held further marches and demonstrations, anything to get noticed. If the cartels wanted to display banners, then so would we. We demanded justice; we demanded that no more people should be killed because of this war. That the cartels be brought down. I was the voice, the woman who lost her twelve-year-old son. We stood outside of court houses, we stood outside the mayor's house with loud speakers, and we marched through the barrios in the west, south and north.

Hundreds joined in. TV cameras and newspapers came to see us and all wanted to hear our story. The police stopped trying to confront us any longer because for every arrest that was made a lawyer would come to defend us, some travelled from all over Mexico. One even came from America.

Justice was not coming, so it was planned, by me of course, that we would have to find our own justice. My first course of action was to surround a known stash house in our barrio. We were armed and ready to fight. When they gave themselves up — we put them on their knees outside of the house and filmed it. The three men were members of some other gang form outside of Tamaulipas. That day we probably did the CDG and the Zetas a favour. We filmed their confession (they did have guns trained on them and a pre-filming warning that if they didn't confess — they would lose their knees and then their balls). The confession was put onto the internet for the world to see, it went viral, I thought that was bad, but I am informed that means good in the parlance of internet terminology. We tied them up and poured the Cocaine all over them, bags and bags of the stuff, kilos of it all over these shit-birds and then left them for the cops. Later we heard they were from Sinaloa. El Chapo's men.

Every action incurs a reaction; one of our members was shot getting into his car leaving for work. He worked in a warehouse just outside of town. He had three teenage boys and a wife. The wife said that her husband was killed because of us; we had gone too far; the cartels would win because they had the will to kill. We held a meeting, over fifty people attended. We had halved in number because of this. People started running scared. I announced the group.

'I am sorry for what happened to Lupe, he was a good man, I understand if you people want out I really do, but this was always the way it was going to go. We must be willing to do what they are willing to do. To fight fire with fire. I am willing to show you all what I am prepared to do.'

Sure enough the numbers depleted down to twenty, they were scared, they had good reason to be. For the next few weeks we attacked gangs in the street, demanding to find out who killed Lupe. They played tough and when they did — I shot out their knee caps. I was a different person now; I didn't play by the same set of rules. I was willing to go that next step further.

Alejandro left, because I told him to go. I could see that he didn't have the stomach for this, he and Flip tried to reason with me, but they couldn't. I had gone down the rabbit hole and was not likely to come back. After days of attacking shit-bird low level Narcos we found out the name and address of the person involved. He was in a bar on the south side of San Fernando. His name was Pepe, but everyone called him El Toro. Such a cliché, he was a Sicario for the Zetas, twenty-seven; he'd been with them after he skipped allegiance with the CDG when the Zetas captured them and demanded they switch sides. El Toro did just that. Rather than the Bull, he should be called the rodent.

I am now our leader, whether by surreptitious means or not, that is how they all see me, so lead by example. I went to the bar while the others waited outside. I told them if I didn't come out then they should shoot the place to shit. The plan was to take his knee caps and I swore that I would be the one. I walked in; I looked like nothing more than some woman looking for a drink.

There he was sat at a table having a cerveza, typical sleaze bag had a teenage girl sat on his lap. His head was shaved, some straggly hair on his chin, tattoos on his arms surrounded by other shit-birds, they looked smashed; they looked like they been hitting the powder. I looked around the bar, no one of note in there other than some boys playing pool on the other side.

I walked over to the table, my heart is pounding, I feel out of my depth, I look about and the only way out is the way I came in. I don't think I am going to be lucky this time — well the going was good while it lasted. At least my story got out there. El Toro, looks at me.

'El Toro,' I say, while I knew it to be him, I felt it the most appropriate thing to say.

'Yes Mama,' he says in a high pitched annoying squeak of a voice; he grabs his crotch and squeezes it, 'You heard why they called me El Toro.' Predictable, just another fucking man-boy misogynist who believes this is how women should be treated; I am sick of these pigs, I am sick of being treated as a second-class citizen because I am a woman. I feel the fury burn deep inside; I am going to enjoy this. "Because my Cock is the same size as —"

My right arm comes up and I squeeze of three rounds from my thirty-eight into his murderous horrible little face. In my left, I have a forty-five. I raise it, I look at the bartender and the boys at the pool table — no one moves. The other men at the table don't move. If they are carrying they're far too slow.

'You take one of ours; we take one of yours, next strike I start taking out three, to every one of ours. You kill any more of our children, I will kill all of yours, get the fuck out of the barrio — go back to where you came from — go hide under a rock, go back to Nuevo Laredo or whichever rock you crawled from — you hear me!'

They hear me alright, they don't move. They nod their stupid fucking heads. One of them says, 'viuda negra.'

'Black Widow.'

Chapter13

San Fernando and Matamoros, Tamaulipas, Mexico

October - November 2010

The seed has been set, the lie is too big to come back from now. I have set about finding Bertrand Le Vell at any cost. The DEA has labelled him a person of interest in relation to drug trafficking in the region, the federal Police the same in the disappearance of Suarez and another officer, Benito has gone along with me on this, he has falsified reports in order to specify that Bertrand Le Vell is a man sought in the connection of Suarez's disappearance. What Benito doesn't know, is that my intention with Bertrand are less than honourable or merciful. On every occasion, I have stipulated that I am the only one that he is likely to speak with, that he would confide in me only and that any form of agency would likely fail should they try. He is a witness and source of important information. I have channelled this carefully and corroborated this with phoney intelligence of my own. I have exaggerated, impeached, embellished and damn near twisted as many truths to fit the lie that I have manufactured. There is no going back now. I must find him. He is the only thing that lies between me and finding out where Laena is. I only wish I would have acted sooner. I have encumbered State, Federal and international agencies with my lie. I have carefully manufactured my duplicitous act. Just the right amount of bullshit will keep them on board. Through interagency cohesion Bertrand is believed to be in Matamoros. This has taken weeks of planning and execution. I have acted as agent provocateur in leading the authorities into believing that he is likely to be the source in major activity into drug trafficking in the region and be a font of intelligence.

The truth is I have no idea who Bertrand is. He is an unseen face, a spectre that haunts me, he is my quest, the Holy Grail or maybe poisoned chalice. My mind does not focus on anything other than him. Who is he to Laena, her secret lover that was more attentive than I ever could be? A close confidant, who she found herself being drawn too. Were they to run away together, to find an Island in the sun that they could share? Or was he her killer? her kidnapper? is she in fact waiting for me to find her, tormented by this mad-man who has her locked away in some room without windows, some fortress somewhere? On the face of it, what I have learned about him is nothing. He entered

Mexico legitimately, he has coasted around undertaking work and would then drift off unnoticed. The only thing that sets him apart is the colour of his skin, the only real reason why people have remembered him. I envisage that my quest is indicative to those of the conquistadors, like Francisco Pizarro González meeting Atahualpa and then murdering him for his empire. I have not yet thought ahead for what I am about to do, I lack the certitude or the conviction to become an assassin.

At night, I dream of Laena, as before, but with the thought of her with another man. I see her down at the Rio San Fernando, instead of me being at her side on our picnic blanket, another man is there. Bertrand, but my dreams have given him another face. A face that I imagine for my tormentor. He is young, handsome and bound in charm and sophistication, Laena is happy and content, she looks in love, while I, an observer, someone on the outside looking in. I see her lean in to kiss him. I wake, it is dark, I can't catch my breath, I must gain my bearings and compose my thoughts. Remind myself it was a dream and that the tormentor is my own subconscious.

Days and weeks go by; I find myself attuned to the fact that unless I find Bertrand I will never find peace. I will never learn of Laena's fate and I will continue to poison my own memories of her. I switch from believing that she is in fact not the woman I married and that she is in fact betrothed in some clandestine affair with another, to believing that some harm has come to her. On a threadbare fact, I have formed two conclusions, none of which I can sustain or consider or rationalise. I am losing that spark that I thought I had regained.

I am becoming less attentive towards the children, paying less attention to them and just wallowing in my own self-pity, while continuing to create subterfuge with the authorities, while they believe the lie I manufacture and continue to manufacture daily. I have taken the role of stooge for the police, feeding them things I have learned — when in fact I have learned nothing. I take a fact and manipulate it to fit in with my objective, to fit the need to locate Bertrand.

The violence in the barrio is worsening, in my Machiavellian role I pretend to hear things; I pretend that I am the eyes and ears of the barrio and that I make sure that it all travels along one road, the road to Bertrand Le Vell, my tormentor, the man who is now haunting my sleep and my sanity.

I am ashamed to say that when I learned of the murder of Lupe, the man from the barrio, who was a friend of Maria, I even implicated Bertrand in that as well. I stated that he was on the periphery, that he was somehow connected. No sooner had I ensured that this lie would reach the authorities I felt shame. I was using the misfortune of others to better my chances of finding him.

I was neglecting my family; my friends, those who needed me most. It was Maria whom I needed to pay attention to; it was Maria who had lost the most. I couldn't imagine the pain that she was going through and it was hard to face her in the knowledge that she was mourning the loss of a child. The look of pain and sorrow in her face was almost too much to bear.

Rather than withdraw and take it, she decided to fight. She fought the establishment; she criticised the regime, in public, on air, in front of cameras and on live television. She led the masses through the streets of San Fernando and other cities; she had become a folk hero in as many weeks and months. She was the bastion of hope, a beacon of light, she was the voice of the common person and she certainly had her voice. Both Alejandro and I tried to talk to her and tried to warn her of what may happen if she continues this line of passive/aggressive protest. She accused us both of being weak, of being cowards, she was right.

Maria had not only become something of a legend, but she had also inadvertently become the voice of empowered women from all over. She refused to bow down to any totalitarian suppression of the truth that was becoming evident in our country, she spoke out about the lack of action in relation to the massacre in San Fernando in August of this year and how the authorities had shelved facts about the case to conceal their inaction against the cartels responsible. She spoke out about how it was the worst kept secret of who was involved and how the authorities and the police were in cahoots with cartels. How she had personally learned of the fact that cops in San Fernando had opened fire on each other, where officers were killed, all because of their allegiance to cartels. This statement sent shit flying I can tell you! State police had attended my house looking for her after that one; it was damaging for the reputation of the Tamaulipas state police. They issued a warrant of arrest for that one, but by then it was too late.

Maria has now slipped into the shadows. Her group has been branded a militia by the police and the authorities. She is now an outlaw, hiding away. Maria and her followers have taken the name of autodefensas, which is a name of similar minded people in other states in Mexico. She has taken to fighting the cartels and arresting them and filming their confessions and placing them on the internet. Until the murder of Lupe, she was branded a folk hero. But recently rumour has spread that she has taken to murder, that she was now wanted for the Murder of a Zeta Sicario by the name of El Toro. The police have branded her and her group as murderers, no better than the cartels. The people however have vastly different opinions, she is their hope, their patron saint, she is now known as viuda negra, the Black Widow. Her actions are now documented in the newspapers and television. Her voice only heard now on recordings that she has left at scenes of her vigilante crusades.

People from the barrios harbour her, give her shelter, feed and clothe her before she moves on. Her actions are becoming nationwide news. The cartels have chosen to act with swift and fast retaliation. She shows no mercy; she shows no sign of giving in. Her numbers are growing. She taunts them, she strikes fear into the hearts of the low-level gang members and runners. She has chosen to take lives to make her point known. But in return the cartels have chosen to start their campaign of terror on the very same people she chooses to fight for.

The barrio is becoming a no man's land. The town of San Fernando has not yet recovered from the atrocity of the massacre some months ago. The streets are becoming a war zone. SUVs containing Sicarios from both sides patrol the streets with impunity, bodies are strewn out onto the highways after being brutalised and mutilated. The cartels fight each other; the autodefensas are starting their assaults, both the police and the army are fighting everyone. The lines are blurred; there are casualties on all sides. It is only a matter of time until the innocent again, become the true victims in this war of attrition.

My true quest is to keep the children safe, I cannot fail, I must not fail. I will get them out of here, but first I must learn about Bertrand Le Vell, I must find him. Either way I must punish him.

I had contacted Benito and subsequently appraised him of the Bertrand situation. When I say appraised him, what I truly mean is that I have lied to him. I have used his Achilles heel against him; I have now placed Bertrand as the last person to have seen Suarez alive and the potential key to this entire riddle that vexes Benito. He has taken the bait, like me he has become obsessed in finding his bogey man. He now lives in a constant state of paranoia and fear. He is privy to the corruption awash within his establishment and yearns to wipe it out. My moral compass points very far away from north, I have learned that good guys finish last. I just hope that I can come back from the brink. The lie I have orchestrated is that Bertrand is currently in Matamoros near to the border. The DEA learned this because they think he has major links to supply to the US. Through their contacts in Mexico he has been identified as living there. Benito has done the rest. Through his informants he has obtained the current address of Bertrand, in Matamoros.

The tangled web of lies I have created is vast and I am careful to keep a mental note of this. I will travel to Matamoros with Tomas, Joaquin and Febe using the cover that we are skipping school to go up there to celebrate the day of the dead. I buy costumes using a small portion of the savings. Benito, who was impressed with the cover story, has appropriated funds to put us into a small and modest hotel for the celebrations. To find the path to the truth I have taken a detour along the trail of bullshit. I could end up in jail if I don't get a streak of luck, but to compose myself I think of all the times the cops have put me at the bottom of their pile, made me wait and generally sat back while Laena remained missing. Fuck them and fuck those who may judge me for what I have done and will do.

As a family, we always celebrated the Day of the Dead. Laena would usually make costumes and masks. This is our first without Laena and probably Febe's first ever. We left San Fernando on the first day of the celebrations. The Cartels have been fighting constantly over the last few days, so now was a good time to get away. I gathered the children into the living space that night and we slept on the floor while machine guns roared in the streets and alley-ways near to the house. The night before we left for Matamoros, I dreamed of Laena again. I met her by the river, we stood at the bank, it was warm and hibiscus was in bloom. She came to me and told me everything was going to be alright.

I awoke in the early hours; to the deafening sound of silence, the gunfire has stopped. I looked across, to the children sleeping on the floor. So peaceful and still. I start to wonder what kind of world I live in, where the sound of gunfire acts as a cathartic lullaby, and the sound of silence discomposes peaceful sleep. I watch over the children until it's time to leave for Matamoros.

The children are excited; little do they know of my ulterior motive for going. It's seven am, I call Benito. He answers straight away.

'I am leaving this morning; I will call you when I have made contact,' I say wincing as I spin my duplicitous yarn.

'Bullshit are you, I'm coming with you. Do you honestly think I am going to be responsible for your death if it goes wrong up there? I will hold back until you knock his door. I have it on good authority that he is still in the city, my sources will find out the exact location of where he is living.'

That fucks things up for me; I can't very well take the life of my wife's lover or killer or whatever the fuck he is, with Benito, the straight arrow standing the other side of the door. I don't have an address now, fucking Benito doesn't have it either, I am just biding my time for him to come through on this one. We get ready, eat, dress and get on the federal highway 101: the road to hell.

Zeta checkpoints all along highway 101, Narcos and Sicarios everywhere. This stretch of road is now known as the most dangerous in Mexico, if not the world. I pass the old farm where Laena and Bertrand used to work. I look to see if there are any sign of police or DEA, especially after my last encounter there. Nothing! — the law has given up here. The army, police and cartels all pass one another on this road. Running from San Fernando to Matamoros. The highway of death, as it is now known. It runs alongside the desert, telegraph poles running parallel to the highway, the mountain ranges in the distance looking like looming monoliths. This road is a no go area at night. No one drives along here at night —no one.

It's a two-hour drive to Matamoros, I drive at eighty, I don't break, I don't stop, the truck rattles and shakes. We remain quiet throughout the journey. The scene is like some biblical epitaph, almost too true for words. The ditches that run alongside the highway are littered with bodies, littered almost every five hundred yards. Some singular, some in groups. The old picnic stops now hold cars splattered with blood and bullet holes, the blood dried and streaked over the chassis, flies and feral animals dining out on the cadavers. Most of the bodies are unrecognisable, decomposing in the extreme desert sun and pulled apart by coyote packs and left hanging out of the open car doors. If I could imagine an apocalyptic end of days' scenario of plague and pestilence, then this highway is the closest semblance of such horror.

Armed soldiers and uniformed police drive up and down the highway —faces covered, machine guns mounted on roofs of black SUVs, eyes alert, trigger fingers itchy. The cartel Sicarios drive along bearing similar army fatigues and firepower.

From the open windows of the truck the rancid smell of decomposing corpses drift in. Even at this speed, we can't escape it. Army checkpoints feature the closer we get to Matamoros. At the first checkpoint, we see Cartel members on their knees, guns trained on them — soldiers asking questions. The responses don't come — highly polished leather army boots, crash into faces. Teeth spill onto the dusty road in a cluster of red mucus and saliva. Necks are grabbed, faces pushed into the dirt. Clothes are torn off and battered and bruised bodies are cavity searched in public. Vehicles are torn apart, seats slashed and ripped open. Handcuffs are placed around broken wrists. Faces of disdain and venomous threats are directed at soldiers.

'You fucked up, ese we gonna find you out on them roads and cut you to pieces, you can't hide behind those masks, we will fucking find you and cut you piece by piece and post them back to your families.'

The response by the soldiers is swift, the naked and blood splattered bodies are lifted from their knees. An army knife comes out of a belt. No more threats. The children shouldn't have to witness such things. Today is the day of the dead; now three more join the twenty-eight thousand dead so far since this war started. Febe looks mortified — her eyes wide, her face without expression. Tomas looking at her, he reaches over and touching her hand, 'It will be OK, we will be there soon.'

Soldiers move us through, the lines are blurred, no good-guys, just gangsters everywhere. Gangster-cops, gangster-soldiers, all working for the establishment. I notice uniformed police stood to the side; they must have witnessed what we saw. They stand by now; they allow this sort of criminal behaviour; cartels and cops, sicarios and soldiers, they all seem the same. As we pass by in the truck, there are some high school kids lined up outside of their car. No doubt off to the celebrations. They are on their knees and naked. No sass from them. Three boys and three girls, the girls no older than sixteen. Uniformed cops running their hands over these naked and extremely upset girls. Tear streaked faces. Blubbering and crying begging for the so-called protectors of the state of Tamaulipas, to leave them alone. The sounds of cop voices asking where they keep their travel money. The boys being shown the now lifeless bodies of the now dead Narcos.

'We know you got more, hand it over or you can get some of this.'

The boys cry, the cops taunt them about how their girls are going to find out what real men are like. The girls are led away behind a portable cabin. They scream and beg — the boys take fists and kicks and fall to the ground. The screams are drowned out by the laughter of cops. As I pass through the checkpoint I realise I am yet again a silent and passive witness, I tell myself that I say and do nothing because survival is more important. I carry on to Matamoros. The day of the dead is upon us.

Chapter14

Matamoros, Tamaulipas, Mexico.

The day of the dead

November 1st 2010

Papa has been very distant and quiet. He seems to be in thought, deep thought most of the time. The journey up to Matamoros was something I never believed possible. Papa was usually such a worrier that I never thought he would ever take us out of San Fernando. Since Ciudad Victoria, Febe and I have been on strict instructions not to go too far from the house, especially since Luis was murdered and since the fighting had gotten worse. The journey here has shown me that the world can be a cruel and terrible place.

Febe tells me I worry too much; she tells me that she locks her bad memories in a box and never lets them out. She says that sometimes they escape, but she always manages to get them back in again. Febe is the only one who truly understands me. In front of my friends at school I must play tough, like what goes on around me has no effect. In front of Febe, I don't have to act that way. I can tell her I am afraid; I can tell her that I miss my Mama and Luis. That every night I pray for them.

We go into the main town of Matamoros for the celebrations. Matamoros is such a big city. The main roads in take us through the barrios that are much bigger than ours. Houses built on top of one another, painted houses of aqua blue against salmon pink. Metal shutters and bars against the windows, people in the streets getting on with their routines. Police and the army are everywhere here. Guns in hand; watching the people, never knowing who the enemy may be. The streets are full of gangs and Narcos, but not the wannabes like in my neighbourhood, they look like they mean business. The cowboy hats, the steel toe-caped cowboy boots, silver and gold pistols tucked into their jeans. The younger ones dress in plaid shirts with oiled hair and basketball sneakers. The streets are full of this kind of Narco. You can feel the danger in the air. At any moment, it feels like trouble may happen. The main streets are wide open streets with large grocery stores and outlets. Burned, or shot out cars infrequently scattered about the busy streets, the police seem to be there and the wrecks are moved out quite quickly. Not like where we live.

People from San Fernando are thought of as hicks or hillbillies, stupid and unsophisticated. This is what Papa tells me.

We go to the cathedral of Matamoros where the main celebration is taking place, I can't remember the last time I saw so many people all in one place. There are hundreds, all dressed as ghouls or ghosts or skeletons. Joaquin had a tight grip on Papa's hand. Unusual and crowded places made him uneasy and on a few occasions Papa had to tell him it was all OK and everyone was there to have a good time. I dressed as a skeleton, with an all in one black costume. Febe painted my face white with black rings around my eyes. Febe wore a white dress, like one from the old days in rural Mexico, again with her face painted the same as mine. Joaquin was a vampire and wore his old suit that he used to wear to church, which was now far too small for him. He didn't seem to be getting into the swing of it, but we all knew that this was hard for him. Papa wore no costume, he stated he was ugly enough without makeup or a mask, none of us bothered to remark that he wasn't.

The streets were filled with music, people dancing to the continual loud drumming. Parades that lasted for miles went through the streets and passed the cathedral steps, where we congregated.

Men dressed as ghouls danced with women dressed as Santa Muerte. They spat tequila against naked flames and watched them erupt into fireballs. People laid cigars and drinks at the Santa Muerte shrine, laid out in front of the cathedral. The skull under a shawl certainly sent a chill down my spine. We stayed out until dark, where Papa took us to a taverna on one of the narrow side streets, where lots of bars and tavernas celebrated the day of the dead. Mariachis played and people danced and sang. Papa spent most of the day trying to reassure Joaquin, both Febe and I took in the sights and enjoyed the magnificent parades and celebrations. We ate dinner in the taverna, mainly consisting of jalapeño poppers and chilli with black beans and peppers. We washed it down with soda, while Papa drank some cervezas. Papa told us some stories of when he went to school in Mexico City. The stories were always about drinking beer and getting up to mischief, but we found them funny. He laughed with us and Febe told us about how she poured Tabasco sauce into the girls gym slips, to teach them a lesson for laughing at her when she first started this term.

'You should have seen them running from the gym,' she said, laughing to the point where she struggled to get the words out. 'They reached for anything and everything that might take away the burning sensation from their assholes. One teacher was relieved of a pot of chilled yogurt that his kids made for him. Can you imagine having to explain when he got home, that he didn't eat the yogurt, lovingly prepared by the children he so adores — because some snooty spoiled Narco kid swiped it from his hand and poured it over her asshole and Cooch.'

We all roared with laughter, especially Papa who had to dry tears from his eyes because he laughed so much. He wasn't aware of the story, which was now legendary at our school. Febe had never admitted to anyone that she was responsible, although everyone suspected. The sight of the schools richest and bitchiest girls trying to force their bare asses into drinking fountains was a sight to behold.

It was good to see Papa laughing again. Lately he has seemed like he has the world on his shoulders. What with Luis being killed and Maria getting herself into major trouble with the Narcos and the police, he has been preoccupied. The good thing is, he is still serious about us getting out of Mexico. Things have become so bad now, that we sleep in the living room, away from the windows. The gangs and the Narcos are everywhere. People are leaving their homes and moving to other towns. This all started after the murders at the ranch; seventy-two people killed, and nobody knew why.

The only good to come from any of this is I now have Febe in my life. She came to us like an angel, fallen from heaven. I love her with all my heart. I want her to be with me forever and never lose her. I finally worked out what I was feeling: it was love. For so long I was unsure, it was like a spell was cast over me, an alien feeling that I had never experienced before. The love for Febe is certainly different than the love for Papa, Mama and Joaquin, but it's just as strong. I look at her and the way she looks, her beauty fills my heart with happiness. Even now, I find I can't take my eyes off her. One day I will tell her, one day I want what Papa and Mama had together, with Febe. I just don't have the words.

It's good to spend the time celebrating together. The final day of the three-day celebrations we spend together. Papa takes us to the Brownsville-Matamoros Bridge; we stand looking over to the United States. Papa bought four balloons, we all wrote our messages and launched them over the Rio Grande towards America. Each of them taking flight and making their way towards Brownsville, Texas. Each balloon carrying our message to a place where we believe provides hope and safety. Papa has never crossed over to America, he has never left Mexico. He told us that his father once lived there, many years ago. Papa doesn't talk about his father, we never met him. I don't even know if he is still alive.

We stand and watch the balloons in total silence. Each of us wanting the same thing, we don't wish for wealth or expensive possessions. We wish to survive this war, to live in peace, to not lose any more of our loved ones. We wish for what others take for granted. We didn't ask for our country to turn out this way, we didn't deserve this. Yet its people like us who suffer. People like Luis and Maria, Mr Lingala, Febe, the seventy-two-people dragged from buses and taken to a farm, then slaughtered like animals. I watch my balloon take flight until it's out of sight, towards the tall buildings of Brownsville. Joaquin stares in amazement. Papa, who usually looks either tired or sad, was happy, he was having fun. We were making memories together. I felt a hand slip into mine as we stood facing across the Rio Grande. It was Febe's hand in mine. I never wanted this moment to end. The last time we were complete, was when Mama was here. I wish she were here now.

We stay in Matamoros after the celebrations end, Papa doesn't tell us why and we don't ask. We go to museums, we go to the coast, and we watch street entertainers. Our hotel room holds all of us for our time here. The city is so big, that we don't see the shootings and killings that we would normally witness. We can see America from this city. We can almost see the people of Brownsville walking around, happy, smiling and not having to think about if they might be snatched off the street and held for money or gunned down for looking a certain way.

I wake up to hear Papa whispering, he is talking on his cell phone.

'Calle Sexta,' he says, 'where is that.' He is nodding while writing on a pad, I can hear a male voice on the other end of the phone. 'Downtown, you say,' Papa pauses while the voice talks, 'Just remember what I said,' Papa says, he sounds more direct than normal, like he is calling the shots, it sounds unusual, 'he will only speak with me. Stay out of sight, I will go to his apartment and as I promised I will get the names from him.'

I duck under the covers when Papa flips his cell off. I wait for Papa to fall asleep; I can hear him snore like a bear. I check Joaquin and Febe are asleep. I creep over the sleeping bodies led on floors and beds of our room, over to the small bedside table. I don't recognise the address that is written on the pad. There is a name at the top, Bertrand Le Vell!

Chapter15

Matamoros, Tamaulipas, Mexico

November 5th 2010

Downtown Matamoros has a certain energy, like electric searing through my body. Maybe it's the surge of adrenaline coursing through my veins, the fear, the anxiety, that feeling of impending doom. For what feels like so long now I have been searching for Bertrand Le Vell. I am expecting trouble; I am expecting violence, I can feel it, that impending sense of doom. For so long now he has been my nemesis, he has been in my thoughts, sharing the dual role of the clandestine concubine to Laena and her killer/kidnapper. He is an ogre, a monster, Goliath to my David, I have visualised him in my thoughts and dreams as an imposing spectre, who wanders the towns and villages of Mexico, orphaning children and widowing husbands. In turn I have changed, I am a different man. I have used deception and duplicity to find my foe. I have no regrets; I have lost all conscience I once had. I am a man travelling through the busy streets of downtown Matamoros, hunting my prey, seeking justice for my children, for Laena — for me.

The children ride in the truck with me. They will not be witness to my crimes; they will be unwilling patsies, my cover. If ever asked about the crime I am about to commit, I can say, 'who me? why I am a mere peasant handyman with children, what kind of monster do you take me for.'

The children talk on the journey; they look out of the windows and talk the way children do. Tomas seems to be studying the streets; we arrive at the address I received from Benito. He is due to arrive today in Matamoros — in the expectance that I will unveil the star witness, who will reveal the persons at the root cause of Roberto Suarez's disappearance. I should feel guilty about the lies I have concocted in order to snare Bertrand Le Vell, but I don't. Benito is my pawn.

I park the truck at the address, a tenement block, two-storeys high. The building looks dates, probably was once plush and modern, but now outdated in the era of modern architecture. All white stone, metal fences and sliding doors; the building is structured into squares, square courtyard surrounded by each block. A washing line, little dilapidated play area, probably used mainly by Narcos now. I park the truck away from the block; I take my lock picks out of the glove compartment. I should take Joaquin with me as he has become a competent lock picker, but my morals have not become that questionable just yet. As I get out of the truck I tell the children to stay put that I was just looking at some work that a man in a bar asked me to look at.

'No you're not Papa — where are you going? I know you're up to something.' says Tomas, looking at me unflinching. Shit he knows; he must have heard the conversation with Benito on the phone.

'I am — for god's sake not everything has to be an argument!' I regret shouting at the boy, Tomas, Febe and Joaquin all look in my direction; they have never heard me raise my voice before, that I can remember anyway.

'I heard you,' says Tomas, his eyes look like he is about to cry, his lip trembles, 'You are here because you're looking for someone, you were talking and you sounded like it was serious. What is it, drugs, guns, have you decided to smuggle for the cartels for money.'

I almost took the opportunity to say yes, as it would be a damn site better than reveal that I may kill someone in those apartments. That feeling, that momentum was beginning to lessen now realising that my own children have discovered that I was up to something.

'You wouldn't understand Tomas.' I say realising I was patronising a very intelligent boy, despite his age; I was using the oldest cliché in the book. I am half out of the truck, beginning to question my intentions. 'Sometimes a person can feel compelled to do something, something that he feels is right, when actually it may not be. I can't tell you because I don't think you would like what I am about to do. It's something I must do, I don't want to lie to you, but I cannot tell you now. I will be back in a short while, just don't get out of this truck, and don't talk to anyone, just stay put.'

I slam my door and move toward the block of apartments — the apartments where I will find Bertrand. I can't face explaining this to the children, if I delay any more then I will fail, I wouldn't go through with it. An eye for an eye. Heart is beating fast. If Bertrand is Laena's lover, then why should he pay for that? I had become inattentive, I had become stubborn, and I had pushed her beyond the breaking point. I rebutted all her suggestions — just so I could live my life in my town, in my way. To live in the town that I was raised, the memories I had of this place were not good memories, like memories at that age should be. I was poor then and I am poor now. I was a peasant child, and now I am a peasant as a man. I had no confidence or self-belief and that has not changed. I aspired to be something great, but I reverted to what I had always been at the first sight of confrontation. I have always been a coward. She could have been anything; she was beautiful, she was intelligent, she was glamorous and had the strongest of will in any person I ever met. Rather than taking an opportunity then, I chose to remain in the place we now call home. Ridden with Narcos and murderers — of poverty and desperation. I couldn't see it before; I didn't have the foresight to realise that things were getting worse. She could have been anything; instead she worked in the fields, doing back-breaking work, because of this she met her fate — she met Bertrand Le Vell.

I take the stairs to the first floor of the two floor apartments. People are coming and going, they pay me no attention, I am the grey man, no one ever notices me. I could be the maintenance man; delivery-man, living out their days in ramshackle apartment blocks, living in fear of the violence and mayhem that exists in the streets and neighbourhoods. I get to the door; my pick is in my hand. The craft knife I use for work is in the front pocket of my baggy pants. At that moment, my childhood flashes back before my very eyes. My father in the front yard, boxing gloves on, hitting a heavy bag. Sweat covering his hard-chiselled body.

'Come here Flip, spar with your old man. Come on, what's the matter chicken – shit, you scared?'

I remember putting the gloves on, being thirteen again, already scared stiff of my father, putting up with daily bouts of verbal and psychological abuse and torment. Being called a, 'No good Bastard, you're no son of mine, your no Hernandez, you can change your name, you're not having mine.'

Watching him circle around me, my hands by my side. The United States Marine Corp tattoo on his left bicep. The look in his eyes, I was not someone he loved, but someone who he wanted to punish. The human punch-bag. Once it started, it wasn't ever going to stop. I had finally reached the age, where I could take some of this. His hands moving fast, the blows to my face, my cheeks, my nose. That feeling of blood running down my chin. Crying in pain and fear.
Hearing his voice:

'Come on Flip, come on fat-boy, you some kind of fucking pussy, hit me.'

I followed through, trying to hit him, not because I was angry, but because I was afraid of what he might do if I didn't — he moved fast — I missed, he hits me again, and again and again. I cry and eventually beg him to stop, he laughs at me. I can see the scars on his shoulder from injuries in Vietnam. I can see the look in his eye — he is crazy, he hates me, he wants to punish me. I am soft; I don't have that mean streak that he possesses. What have I done to him that is so bad that I deserve this? My mother just walks about the house, knowing what is going on, just allowing it because it's easier that way. I cry again begging for him to leave me alone.

'Not until you get mad and hit me, come on, hit me, I'm hitting you.'

I feel rage — I run at him, throwing punches, I make contact with his body, he takes the blows — his body is like oak, I hit his arms and try to hit his face, eventually he hits me on the side of the head and I fall to the ground. I tell my mother; I tell her that I hate him. She slaps my face, the face that is bruised and cut from my father's blows. She tells me I should be ashamed. My father never hit me, unless it was in the yard with our gloves on. That was his excuse; he said it was to make me into a man, to make me into a fighter.

I feel that rage building inside as I think about it. It spurs me; I am ready for whatever happens now. I enter the apartment. I get hit alright, with a dense and overwhelming smell. It takes any fighting spirit or adrenaline I had before. Unwashed plates with food in the sink, thick grime over the floors and kitchen surfaces. The apartment is open planned and in the living area is a filthy mattress, surrounded by empty cerveza and whiskey bottles, cigarette butts, rotting food. A pile of filthy clothes stacked in the corner. I search the apartment — that doesn't take long. No Bertrand — someone lives here. It's got to be Bertrand; the condition of his apartment simplifies things. He is a deviant, a man who lives like this must be dirty to the core. It's something sinister; Laena would never be with such a man, a man who lived like this. I think of a torture pit or putrid place of evil and decay. I start to think that he disposes of his victims here, mutilating them and killing them. I think that he must resemble some kind of deformed beast who trawls the underbelly of cities seeking his next victim. I sense evil and wrongdoing. My thoughts turn towards Laena again, what ungodly act could have been committed against her by this man.

From the neighbouring apartment, a tall, thin man opens the door and looks at me, he is around thirty with tattoos over his body. There are others inside the apartment. I can see them stood behind him, peering over his shoulder.

Got to think fast, he looks like a Narco. 'Good day Senor,' I say, making sure I keep up the pretence, just an innocent man looking for my friend. 'I am visiting from out of town, I am looking for Bertrand Le Vell, he lives here, do you know him,'

'The fuck you knockin' my door puto, who fucking asked you to knock my door. Who the fuck you talkin' about.'

'Sorry, I just thought you may know him senor, I will leave you be.'

It dawns on me that I have been set up, this guy has no idea what I am talking about, he looks nervous, he looks shaky. A pistol comes out through the door; another man is stood behind him. I then notice several people inside. In the background, I see the rumpled and rugged face of a man I recognise, a face I have seen before, in the papers on TV. The mugshots all over the news. He can be seen over the other men; he is taller than I thought he may be; heavy set, large build. It hits me how much shit I am now in. The face I know is that of Antonio Ezequiel Cárdenas Guillén, aka Tony Tormenta. The leader of the Gulf cartel. I look away from him, trying not to show any recognition at all. Holy fucking shit — how does this even happen? Bertrand lives next door to the most wanted man in Mexico right now?

I am frozen stiff, the pistol in my face. Guillén, is no longer in view, just his henchman.

'I am sorry senor, I am just here to see Bertrand, he is my old friend and I was told I could find him here.' I feel my legs shake — got to get out of here.

Before I could get a response, I could already hear boots charging through the courtyard. Suddenly the men inside the apartment run out, they push me aside like I am nothing, I don't register to them, I am just some dumb-ass peasant. They start banging on other doors within the apartment, men spill out of the neighbouring apartments — wearing Kevlar vests and carrying machine guns, magazines being loaded into machine guns. From the ground, I see through the railings at what comes running towards them, Federal police, heavily armed and in their full warrior attire. Men are spilling out of the apartments on all levels. Police take cover in the courtyard. From the first-floor landing, looking down into the courtyard, the Narcos start firing down.

The sound is unbelievable; the roar of machine gun fire is terrifying and continuous. I crawl on my belly across the floor towards the flight of stairs. Narcos have positioned themselves on the stairs firing down towards police as they try and climb them. On the stairwell, I can see two cops on the ground — they are on their backs, they are wearing masks, blood is coming from their torso, it pours down the stairs, like a fast-flowing rapid river. I roll down the stairs on my front, staying as close to the ground as humanly possible. There are battalions of cops making their way onto the courtyard.

From surrounding directions, black SUVs containing Narcos drive at speed towards the cops pouring into the apartment block. Machine guns pointing from the open blacked out windows, they fire at the police. Cops fall to the ground —five of them hit the ground — some scream in pain, some dead as they hit the ground. Cops turn in the direction of the SUVs and open fire. One SUV crashes into a telegraph pole, cops run at it — still firing. They point guns into the vehicles and still fire. An explosion of crimson coats the inside of the windows.

I look towards my truck which is now right in the middle of the firefight. I don't see any of the kids: I try and run towards the truck — I am grabbed by a cop, who pushes me into the concrete pavement.

'My children are in the car, my children are in the car, let me go, bastards, let me go.'

I am face down looking towards the truck. Narcos are coming from all ends of the street, in every direction. The cops are in a cross fire; the bullets are striking anything and everything. The cops are outnumbered. The bullets whizz overhead and some hit the pavement by my head. I try and get up again, a cop pushes my face against the pavement. I feel something go around my wrists. I am restricted, I can't move my hands. I have been tied and left face down. I can't hear anything but gunfire, its continual; there has been no break from the shooting. All along the cops were waiting to confirm if Guillén was in that block. It looks like my stupid actions led them there. The realisation hits me hard. All around me, I can see Narcos and cops with machine guns firing at each other. I can see Narcos and cops fall to the ground in equal measure. To my right, I look to see an elderly woman, face down, blood coming from her face, she doesn't move. Her elderly Husband lying next to her, he is crying uncontrollably. Windows are shot out on apartments; Narcos shooting from elevated positions on cops. More SUVs arrive, those belonging to police and those to Narcos. More men pouring out of the vehicles, the fight is becoming more ferocious, now in great numbers. They equal each other in numbers. Within a matter of minutes, this once quiet neighbourhood is now a warzone, I can now hear explosions. Bullets ricochet close to my face. I see bullets hit the front end of my truck. I see the windshield get blown out by Narcos firing at cops. I try and lift myself off the ground, I can't move my arms, I can't pull these ties away, I can't break away. I must save them; please lord above — not them as well. Cops take cover behind my truck and return fire. I scream and scream and scream.

***

Covered in glass, lots and lots of glass. Tomas and Febe are trying to push my head down and keep away from the windows. It's so loud out there, I can't stand it, I must get out. Febe and Tomas pull the passenger seat, trying to get into the back. They are stupid, trying to do it that way. I reach underneath the seat and pull a catch that operates the back of the seats to fold down. As I do this the seat folds. Tomas pushes me through the gap into the back of the truck. I slide to the back of the truck, I look out. Men in masks everywhere, running around, shooting at each other. My ears hurt, I am frightened, it reminds me of before; back in the playground, watching my friends and teachers die.
I look out of the window of the back of the truck, I can see Papa, I can see him on the ground, he could be hurt. I can open the back of the truck from the inside, I must get to Papa, I will help you Papa, I will save you. I reach down towards a latch that with a flat head screwdriver I can flip open if I lever it. The pops open.

As I jump out I hear Tomas and Febe both shout and call my name, 'Joaquin, get back in here, get back here, don't go outside.'

I slam the back of the truck, Febe and Tomas don't know how to open the door like I can, they will try and stop me, I want to save Papa.

The gunshots go off, bullets buzzing around my face and head. I can hear loud bangs and crashes. Cars are on fire. I look over at Papa, he is screaming, he must be hurt. I start to walk very slow, I look over at the men in black, with masks, one of them pulls his mask down and is shouting, 'Get down, hey little boy get out of the way.'

He runs towards me and suddenly falls to the ground, blood sprays over the ground. He is on his front, blood coming from his mouth, he is still shouting the same, he stops shouting, his eyes roll into the back of his head. I run across the road, pieces of concrete from the pavement explode, it's like someone is using a drill or jackhammer. It's so loud, I can't stand it, but I must save Papa. I make my way to where is laying, Papa is shouting and screaming at me, 'Please Joaquin, get to safety, I am OK, run away, run away.'

He is crying, so he must be hurt. I am stood in the middle of the street. On both sides, men are shooting at each other, there are men all over the ground, they are hurt and bleeding. I run as fast as I can to Papa.

I can see that he has his hands tied; I recognise the binds to his hands, cable ties. I remember seeing him slip a knife into his pocket before he got out of the truck; I reach into his pants pocket. Papa raises his hip so I can reach it. I feel it and take out the knife. The knife is sharp, it cuts the binds with one cut each.

I feel something hit me in the back, really hard. I can't breathe very well. It hurts and I cry out. It really hurts, but I am drifting off, I fall down onto Papa's back, I feel weak, I am getting sleepy, I can't keep my eyes open, the pain is drifting away, so am I, it's like a dream. I can hear Papa calling my name; his voice is getting quieter and quieter. Don't cry Papa, I saved you, I saved you….

***

'No, no, no, no you bastards, he is just a boy, my little boy, no, no, no you fucking bastards.'

I can't catch my breath; Joaquin is like a rag doll, blood coming from his his shoulder blade. He is weak, I can't get him to wake up, please, oh please lord god, no, please not him, not my little boy, don't take my little boy.

I gently tap his face — the expression doesn't change. Compose yourself, check for breathing. It sounds like he is struggling, he is struggling to breath, he is dying. I open his mouth, blood on his tongue and around his teeth. Internal bleeding — he is dying. I can't wake him. Got to get him out of here — got to get him out now. If Joaquin got out of the truck, why didn't Tomas and Febe. Oh no, oh Jesus Christ. Before I even know what I am doing, before I even think of anything, I run towards the truck. The fastest I have ever run — head down, straight to the front of the truck — they're not in there. The seats are flipped down. They got in the back, how on earth Joaquin got out of the back is a mystery to me, it's near impossible. I duck down and head to the rear of the truck.

I open the rear and Febe and Tomas are huddled down, they're both crying, they are distraught — they're petrified. The roar of machine gun fire is still as loud as before but becoming evanescent in the knowledge that Joaquin is dying and I must save the children, I must get them out of here. Out of the situation I created. I am a curse on this family; I am the one, it's me who should be dying over there. They are both crouched down, they are frozen stiff.

'I have to get you out of here, come with me, don't be scared, I will get you out, just follow me.'

I try to remain as calm as possible, despite the fact Joaquin is splayed out on the nearby sidewalk, fighting for his life.

'Where is Joaquin,' Tomas shouts.

'He is by the roadside, don't be scared, come with me. Hold hands, all of us, we will go together.'

Febe doesn't cry, she is shell-shocked; this isn't her first time in such a scenario; Whereas Tomas is talking, Febe is still and frozen, she is unresponsive. Almost back to when I came across her after the massacre. All those memories flooding back. I grab them both and pull them towards me, Tomas starts to scream, 'No Papa, I can't, I can't, I'm scared Papa, I can't.' He trembles and shakes with each gunshot that echoes throughout the immediate vicinity.

I lean forward and say to them, 'It's OK, I am with you, I will never let anything happen to you.'

Bullets rip through the front of the truck again; one pierces the side of the truck, missing me by a few feet. As I slip out the truck, I notice cops at my feet, dead. Cut to pieces by gunfire. I hold both their hands, I look into Febe's eyes as she is the most likely to resist.

'I promise, I won't let anything happen to you, it's not far, trust me.' Nothing, she starts to panic, her current catatonic state starts to shift to absolute fear.

I pull them both out, their feet hit the ground. I drag them in the direction of where Joaquin lays. We run — bullets still ploughing through the concrete — bullets whizzing overhead, we stoop down, we run. Fast, fast, fast. It's about twenty-five metres to where Joaquin lays, but feels like miles. Febe falls to the ground. I can't lift her up; Tomas is pulling at me. I grab Tomas, leaving her sat in the middle of the street. I gather him in my arms and run the rest of the way, back to Joaquin. I dump Tomas on the ground.

'Joaquin is hurt, real bad,' I shout, 'Keep trying to wake him, try and get him to breathe, try breathing into his mouth, try something. I will get Febe.'

I dart back across the street. How I have not been killed by now is a miracle. Febe is sat down, she is hysterical. I grab her, lift her off the ground. As I run five metres, I trip and we both hit the ground. I look up and see Narcos in Kevlar moving forwards, they have ski masks on. At the back of the group I can see Guillén. He is holding a machine gun in his hand; he is trying to escape. He looks down at me — a glimpse of recognition. Yes, I was the face at your door; I was the one who was snooping around before the cops crashed the apartments. He looks angry; he points the gun towards me. Here it comes, my death, shot down like a dog in the middle of the street, with what I have been through, I am accepting of my fate, but let me save my boy, don't let my little boy die this way. I will do anything, let me save him and I will personally come see you — you can behead me in the street, shoot me to death or whatever you want. I grab Febe, I stare back at him, I stand up. No way, not now. I don't care who you are, saving the children is more important than you, now and forever, amen motherfucker.

I stand up with her in my arms. The group is stationary; shooting at cops, only Guillén is paying any attention to me. He knows me. I don't care, I should be trembling, but I am not. I will save the children. I will kill you if you stand in my way, I don't care who you are. He is still pointing the gun at me; he raises the gun to the air and turns away from me. I turn and run back towards Joaquin and Tomas. I hear the roar of gun fire from the group, they have engaged the cops again; me, I am forgotten about — for now anyway.

I get to Joaquin; Tomas is doing mouth to mouth on him. He is pushing down on his chest, he is working hard, he is frantic. He is focused, he is not panicked, he is trying to save Joaquin's life. I rip my shirt from my back and tie around Joaquin's shoulder. Already the shit T shirt I wear underneath is blood soaked — Joaquin's blood. I tie it off to try and contain blood loss. Joaquin has a pulse. He is breathing, but shallow, it's better now than before, time to move, time to get Joaquin out here.

I gather him in my arms, he is like a doll, his body flops, his face is lifeless and pale. We run — run into lanes and alleyways, staying away from the main streets. The gun-fight is bigger than before and getting bigger. I can hear gun shots way off in the distance. Cars screeching, through the dusty and overgrown alleyways, Narcos rush through on foot, like commandos heading towards the fight. I hear them shouting to one another, how the cops are here to get Guillén —they must fight to the death.

We run as fast as we can, try to find a hospital or an ambulance. We are lost; all we know is to get out of here. Get out of the middle of this thing. We run for ten minutes until we find a police road block. We run towards it, I signal that my child has been hit. A medic runs to us, stuck at the side trying to get to anyone who needs his help. I lay Joaquin on the ground and the medic checks his pulse and breathing. He pushes down on his chest over and over. Tomas is crying, pleading with the medic to save his brother. An ambulance arrives and we jump in, blue lights all the way to the hospital.

Joaquin is rushed into theatre. I try to speak with doctors and nurses, who tell me they have no time to speak with me now; they are trying to save his life. We wait outside of the theatre. It is then Tomas looks at me, disdain and hatred in his eyes. Now I must face up to things, that all of this is my doing.

'Tell me now Papa, was it worth it, was it worth Joaquin getting shot, he could die in there, he could die and if he does — I will never speak with you again. I will go to El Paso and leave you here; you had better tell me what this was all about!'

He stands up and hits me in the chest, in the stomach, tries to hit my face. I grab his arms and pull him in tight.

'You're a fucking loser Papa, you can't even keep your family safe, that's your job, that's what you're supposed to do.'

I try and pull Tomas in close to me, attempts to comfort him are futile, he breaks away, Febe takes him aside, she holds his hand while he sobs for his brother.

'He is tough — that little boy in there, they will save him, they will keep him alive.'

I turn to Tomas and I tell him everything, from the start, about lying to the police to the DEA, trying to find this man Bertrand, what I think has happened, how I think he may have been the one who took his mother. As I tell him he looks at the ground, his head between his legs, taking it all in. I want him to understand, I want them all to understand why I did these things, I hoped it would be cathartic, I hoped that I would unburden myself, explain what I had been so reckless. Tomas just glares at me.

'Mama can read people better than you — do you honestly think that harm would come to her? from this man? is that what you think? I would have trusted her over you any day. You're a fool Papa, you suddenly decide to do this now, why didn't you do this back then? when you had the chance, when it was in the beginning. You're not a man Papa, you're weak and stupid and could have got us all killed. Joaquin saved your life; in return, he ends up in theatre. It should have been you!'

Tomas is right, too little too late as always. All that effort in trying to repair this family and now I have made things worse. I get my cell phone from my pocket and call Benito. He answers.

'You motherfucker,' I say to him before he gets the chance to say anymore.
'I hope you're happy with yourself? were you baying for a promotion or are you now on the payroll? You knew that Bertrand wasn't staying in the apartment; you used me as a pawn, someone who wouldn't attract trouble. You sent me to an apartment next to Guillén to see what reaction you got and knowing me, you knew that I would step into the hornets' nest. Well my son is in theatre, he was shot today, and he might die.'

'No Flip— 'he replies, I stop him there.

'You call me Felipe, Felipe — you got it. Only my friends call me Flip, you old bastard. You set me up and almost got my whole family killed. Now this Guillén will probably have me killed as pay back.'

'Flip, I mean Felipe, it wasn't me I swear. My captain, he rumbled me; he told me that I was to tell you to go there; I didn't know what the plan was. I am in Ciudad Victoria today on another case. It was his plan all along; I wouldn't do that. I wanted to find Bertrand myself, you have to believe me, you told me he knew about Suarez, I wanted him as much as you did.'

'Well fuck you old man, you played me like a mariachi guitar, you put me onto that name as a way to lure me into coming here, you knew I would take the bait and you could use me any which fucking way you liked. Is he even real? Did he even work with or even know Laena — tell me you old fuck!'

My shouting attracts the attention of a nurse who signals toward me to be quiet.

'I swear Felipe, he is real, Suarez said so in his report, you know he can be trusted.'

'That's the point — I don't know who to trust anymore.'

'Please, trust me on this, I — '

'You can tell your captain to go fuck himself, and you can do the same. I should never have trusted any of you. You're all the same, if I was some Politician or oilman from PEMEX or a city official I would have had a first-rate service, but because I don't have money or power it's me who gets fucked.'

'I helped you Felipe, I lied for you, to my superiors, to everyone. We can still find him, with my help, we can find him, just tell me how I can help.'

'You can't, no one can. I have lost everything now.'

I walk the corridors. I catch the local news. The biggest shootout the city has seen. Up to fifty dead in shootout in the streets. Antonio Ezequiel Cárdenas Guillén, aka Tony Tormenta killed in today's gun battle between the Gulf cartel and police. The total casualty rate is not known. Residents are interviewed, people seen crying in the streets. White blankets over dead bodies, children crying for their parents.

A doctor comes approaches me. I freeze, my heart pounds, he's not smiling, no warm or comforting smile to ease my anxiety. Oh no, oh what is he going to tell me.

'Senor, your son survived the operation, he must stay with us for some time as we don't yet know the full extent of the damage. The next few days and weeks will be crucial; don't plan on going anywhere just yet.'

I drop to my knees and hold my hands together. Febe and Tomas come over to me. Tomas cries, I put my arms around him. I pull Febe in as well. Thank god, thank you god. I promise I will be a better man; I will be a better man.

Chapter16

Tamaulipas, Mexico

November - December 2010

I am both hunter and hunted. I am true to my word, if they kill any of us; then I take three of theirs, just to tip the balance. I am lost; I don't think there is any way back from this. I had a Damascene moment and decided that the path I was to take was one of retribution. However, I am now lost, there is no way back. I am the Black Widow.

The name stuck, the Narcos don't like to admit it, but they are wary of me. My tactics are subtle; the element of surprise is the only way to victory. For as many as I take out, more join the cartels. No sooner was it announced that Guillén was dead, we went to Matamoros, we picked off as many high-ranking Gulf Narcos as humanly possible. Last count; we took out four senior ranking members, nine mid-level and thirteen of the lower rung. We weren't taking knee caps anymore; we were taking lives. The Federal and state police are looking for us. No doubt it affects their payroll, the money that goes into their pockets from these scum is under review after we started hitting them, and hitting them hard.

We travel to Matamoros, Reynosa, Nuevo Laredo, El Mezquital, Soto la Marina, General Zaragoza. We gather our intel, we study and survey our targets. We watch their routines and strike with ferocity. We are the first of our kind in Mexico. We have taken the name of Autodefensas, but in other regions, there are rumblings of such groups. We have taken action; we have spilled blood in the sand. Many good people have lost their lives. When we strike; we hit hard: burn cocaine, meth, black tar heroin by the hundreds of kilos. We learn of their stash houses and hit them as well. We shoot the guards, we cut the throats of the chemists and mixers, we steal money to pay for more weapons — like the Narcos we use psychological warfare. We hang people by the neck in small towns and villages who work for, or conspire to work for the Narcos. We liberate houses taken over by these scum, we free the people who live in towns occupied under rule by the cartels and they love us for it. We always have food, always have shelter; these towns won't give us up.

This action however, doesn't come without consequence. To flush us out, the Zetas have lined up, what they call collaborators and shot them in town squares. They post the shootings over the internet; warning others, if they collaborate with Autodefensas, they die. If they assist the Zetas, they will live. Any information of our whereabouts will be rewarded. The Zetas resources and finances are unlimited. Our numbers are small, we hold around twenty-five active members now, we are untrained, but learning fast. We move about, town to town, never knowing when the betrayal will come, upon arrival in each town, we are met with cheers, as we ride in on jeeps and trucks. Usually I am up front, stood in the back of the truck for all to see, not showing fear, bullets on belts over each shoulder, criss crossing, like Emiliano Zapata. The Black Widow — that's how they know me. The people of the towns come out to us, giving us food, often we get new members, men and women from these towns, who have lost someone close to them during the war on drugs. They want to fight; they want to maim and murder and scalp Narcos. They shout my name; they want photos taken with me. I oblige — I am one of the people. We are equal, we need each other, we are one and together we will fight.

For every town that the Narcos make suffer; for every person, they strike down, I repay them. The Zetas are notoriously hard to find, but I have managed, where the police and army have failed. To seek revenge against them, I found one of their hide outs and captured the small house, located near Reynosa. The Zetas I captured were just boys. No more than sixteen. I tied them up and burned them alive, I filmed the scene. The sounds of those screams will stay with me forever, but I am becoming adept at fighting evil acts, with evil acts. I am lost; I am truly lost with no road back. Every time I think I will falter or be unable to follow up on my promise to the people, I think of Luis, the vision of him suffering, dying in pain, calling out my name — but I never came. I never took away the pain, I never rescued him. It fuels my rage and makes me do unspeakable things to those I hold responsible. The lines are blurred; I don't discriminate anymore. All Narcos; all collaborators, facilitators, associates and friends are deemed the same. Anyone who ever loaned money or harboured drugs and guns are thought of the same and will die the same.

Our numbers are growing stronger now. Within weeks, we are up to fifty strong. I have a new second in command. Manny is his name. Manolito, but everyone calls him Manny. He is a mercenary, originally from Ciudad Juarez, but lived in the US for many since he was a teenager. A graduate of Special Forces school: trained interrogator, explosives expert and marksman. A killer and a consummate professional. He is educated and has educated me, since he joined the group. He takes payment from the drug and cash houses we raid, His body is like chiselled granite, he is handsome, but not boyish handsome. He has that rugged look, black hair going grey at the temples, eyes in a permanent squint; he is lean, yet muscular. He has the experiences of Iraq and Afghanistan under his belt, hunting Al Qaeda and Saddam's military forces. To him, the cartels are chicken feed, they arrive in vast numbers, but numbers is all they have, they have no skill, no finesse. Manny trains us in the mountains and the deserts. I have lost over ten pounds in weight already and losing more. He makes us suffer; he punishes us with workout regimes and weapon handling and training. He has turned us around from a rag tag band of armed peasants into professional insurgents. He taught us to use the cartels weaknesses to our advantage.

'Let them get stone drunk and high, we will use that against them.' Say's Manny, always wise and pragmatic.

I offered him the leadership, on more than one occasion, and his reply was simple.

'You *are* the black Widow, it's you the people follow, they don't understand your tactics or how you get the job done, all they know is that you stood up to the cartels and the cops, it's you they care about, it's you they want to see. You are the one willing to make sacrifices and are willing to go that one step ahead, willing to go further than the average man. I don't want the glory or a name for myself, I would be a fraud. The people empathise with you, because you lost the one thing that everyone fears, you lost a child and they know that. Besides, I just want the money.'

He smiled upon telling me this, a sly grin that I found quite endearing and most of all quite attractive. Although I was the leader and Manny was the tactical one with experience, Manny always asked my thoughts rather than take over. For once in my life I was the empowered one. It was me, a proud woman who stood up when most men didn't. As a woman, I have needs and the need at present is to take Manny into my bed.

'So, second in command,' as I liked to address Manny in my hour of need "tonight its time you took charge.'

I felt stupid saying the words to him and a little embarrassed. It felt corny and slightly false, but fuck it, I didn't want to tap dance around anymore. It's either Manny, or I saddle up and mount old man Chavez, I have caught him on many occasions peering into my cleavage. Manny didn't laugh or tease me. He was a pragmatist and he knew that like all animals, we have basic needs, and one of those is sex. Although I found Manny attractive, I was no little girl, who was going to become all coy around him and give him longing looks every time he did something manly or heroic. I just wanted to take care of my needs and so did he. It was a business arrangement, a necessity. So, without making too much of a big deal, we had sex, and we maintained this arrangement most nights. He was good at it, better than Alejandro. We didn't fall in love or whisper sweet nothings or have pillow talk. We just did what had to be done, enjoyed it and went to sleep, in separate beds or tents or caravans or wherever we may be that night.

Although Manny was keen to strike, I devised a new way to hit back at the cartels and its associates here in Tamaulipas. By using surveillance and the recording of telecommunications. I wanted to expose the corruption that was evident and widespread in our state. Once exposed, I would take the evidence directly to the attorney general or any other government official. My word alone was not enough; I was an outlaw; my words and demonstrations were not enough. We took a vote amongst our group on what they thought. We should take our fight underground, become savvier. Gun fights in the street and attacking Narco safe houses was vilifying us to the public. Our actions were attracting attention, but for the most, officials thought I was just a terrorist; an eye for an eye was not what they wanted on their streets. I was becoming an inspiration to the people, but as time passed, the Zetas became more and more powerful. We stood no chance against them. They were occupying cities and slowly but surely driving the Gulf cartel out of Tamaulipas, out into the wilderness. The Gulf cartel was without leadership as such. They stood no chance. While we would never side with either, when the Zetas came to power, it was the beginning of the end for us. They were more powerful, highly skilled and trained and most of all cold-blooded killers.

Word got out that they were recruiting young boys and girls to fight for them. These young kids were walking around the barrios with machine guns and murdering whoever got in their way. They were trained by the elders and put to work. They would systematically turn against their parents if they spoke out against the Zetas. These kids were loyal and not afraid to die. The Zetas began to use them as human shields. Send them in to fight the police and the army. When the children were killed in the fighting by the army or police, the Zetas would then use this, as their propaganda. They would post this onto the internet, on banners in the cities of Tamaulipas. Requesting that the PAN government pull its troops out of Tamaulipas all together. The joint operation Nuevo Leon-Tamaulipas was losing momentum. So many state and municipal cops were now on the payroll that the Zetas were being tipped off about operations. The Zetas didn't care about murdering soldiers or cops in the street. The Zetas were originally a bunch of highly trained soldiers who deserted and started shop as the Zetas. More and more soldiers in our state switched sides. Fed up with the low pay, they jumped ship and joined the Zetas.

We couldn't fight that, we had to expose it. The town officials and mayors of Reynosa and Matamoros refused to admit they had a problem with cartels in the region, so it was now up to us to expose this. We used telescopic photo lenses to capture pay offs of city officials and cops by Zetas. We placed covert recording devices in bars where cops and Zetas would meet to discuss business. We began attending the Nuevo Laredo Border crossing and photograph and record shipments crossing the border — with impunity no less. We learned of Zeta hideouts near the border where the shipments would be prepared ready to go to the US, right under the noses of city and state cops. With all this information, we could highlight this to the United States and Mexican governments, forcing their hand to act against corruption. Over the weeks, we managed to obtain this sort of thing relatively quickly, how did we do this so fast? well the answer was already there? It was blatant, it was everywhere, it was a pandemic. Our plan was to release our footage, when we had gathered all relevant evidence. To do anything at such an early stage would be futile. To try and expose this now, half-cocked would tip them off and they would change the way they operate. I will make these bastards pay, I promise that, I owe it to the people, I owed it to the immigrants who were killed in San Fernando in August and I owe it to Luis. I received letters from some of the families of the dead; they were from Guatemala and El Salvador. They travelled to San Fernando and held banners and shouted and demanded justice, they marched on government building. News cameras filmed them and televised it. Calderon *must* have seen this, but still no action seems to come from it.

After weeks moving about, I go back to San Fernando — covertly of course. The barrio in which I lived all these years is slowly being taken over by Zetas. The good people are being forced out; some of their houses are occupied by the Zetas. Armed patrols of Zetas are walking about the streets. Houses are now stash houses. I hear the news that little Joaquin is in hospital in Matamoros, he was shot in the street, he must stay in the hospital, he is in a critical condition. I weep for them. I weep for that family; they have suffered so much. Alejandro is living at the house, while Flip stays at the hospital. Tomas and Febe are back at the house with Alejandro looking after them. They are going to school, they look like a picture of innocence, I notice as I watch them from a deserted rear yard that is now overgrown. I see Alejandro on the porch rushing out to his beat up old car, ready to drive the children to school. Flip doesn't allow them to get the bus, or go out onto Highway 101. I feel a tear build up in my eye, poor Alejandro. I never gave him a chance, I did love him, but he was not what I needed right now. I could only fulfil my thirst for vengeance; nothing else could stand in the way. I catch my reflection in the window. My hair is cut shorter now, I am gaunt looking, my eyes hollow. I am dressed for an invasion: khaki pants, vest top under a hooded jacket, a Glock pistol tucked into my waist band. Blood on my hands and vengeance in my heart. Part of my group is away on reconnaissance, obtaining what I need for the big exposure, but right now I can see what I need to do. From a deserted back yard; just beyond the fence that I am cooped; I hear singing — beautiful voice, like a child's. Ave Maria sang at falsetto. I look through the fence. I see a small figure sat down with their back to me. I see toy cars on the ground and it looks like it's a child pushing toy cars about while singing. I can't tell, but it's a child; singing and playing, without a care in the world. Suddenly I hear a voice, a man's voice come from the other side of the fence, obviously directing it at the child.

'Where the hell is that fucking kid, supposed to be — '

The man walks into the yard and the child jumps up, head shaven with a cut-throat razor, bald as a baby's ass, tattoos coming from each eye, like a flood of tears, tattoos over the hands. Can't see the rest of his body as its covered in what I now see, as the black uniform of the Zetas, the badge of the Zetas stitched onto an arm, its black in the upper sections and the Z is yellow with a map of Mexico on, from the neck I can see the Los Zetas Commando Medallion around the child's neck, obviously, he has taken lives to earn that. He looks only to be in his mid-teens, but is a freak show of a human being. Eyes wide, mouth wide with thin lips, nose pointed, like a beak. He was playing with toy cars and now has been found out.

'Hey,' the man shouts out, 'hey come have a look at this little queer, *ahhh* baby playing with his toys.'

'No, No I wasn't, hey stop that, please don't go tellin' everyone, hey please.'

The boy frantically tries to stop the man from calling anyone else in. The man, keeps calling, I look a little harder, struggling to see through the fence, the boy looks toward the fence, unable to see me through the knot hole. Its then it hits me, that must be Rojo — the boy Rojo. I heard so much about him, so many stories and still even now his name keeps coming up. Pieces of Intel, horror stories about his actions, the unspeakable things no one would expect a child to do. I pull my radio out of my pocket and hit the button, warning the others who are nearby that I need assistance. This kid is one that needs to be stopped.

The man is trying to shout out to other Zetas, Rojo is trying to stop him, obviously, he has a reputation to keep up, he doesn't want his group to know that he is still that child, who before butchering his parents, was just a weak kid who was beaten and humiliated by the other kids. I see Rojo pull a small blade form his waist band, the laughing Zeta, who is desperately trying to humiliate him doesn't see this. He wouldn't expect what was coming next. The flash of the blade, the small hand holding it comes up and plunges into the Zetas throat. Blood sprays over the tattooed grinning face. He is enjoying this. The Zeta goes to the ground, Rojo cuts across the throat — wide cut — veins and arteries spray blood. Gurgling sounds, blood coming from his mouth — he won't last long.

'So, how does that feel,' Rojo, grinning, that awful toothy grin, top and bottom teeth on show, like a clown. He is giggling, like a child does, but this is not the action of a child, 'does it hurt Leno, does that hurt? I bet you wish you never joked about with Rojo, I bet you wish you never teased and called me names now, don't you. I am going to make these fuckers down here, pay for this, I am gonna kill everyone down here, they laughed, just like you.'

I go to move and sure enough I scuff my boot. From the fence, I hear Rojo's voice, 'Who's there, who's there.' Suddenly he jumps up and his arms are on top of the fence, he is peering over. Blood over his face, I look back, he looks at me.

'You fat bitch.' He shouts.

I turn and make my way from the back yard to the neighbouring yard. I jump on the fence and sling myself over. I run through the side yard into the street. The jeep is here, Manny is driving. From the background, I can hear that voice again.

'It was the Black Widow, she slit Leno's fucking throat, she was drinking his blood, she went that way, oh no, oh god, I tried to do something, I really did.'

That fucking punk, little shit bastard, he truly is a disease that needs dealing with, crazy blood thirsty little shit. Loyalty to none and I first hand heard his true intentions. I crouch down and point my Glock towards the front of the yard, in the hope that Rojo is the first there, but sure enough the cowardly little bastard is nowhere to be seen, instead, three Zetas bound through — straight into a hail of my bullets. All of them down. I reload another magazine, walk up to the bleeding soon-to-be corpses, writhing on the ground, bleeding out on the pavement. I put one in each forehead — heads explode like melons.

Manny is out of the truck, AR15 slung to chest height, eye trained through the scope, SUVs drive at speed towards us. He sprays the vehicle with a steady rate of gunfire. In quick action, he raised his right hand to the magazine housing, releases the empty magazine and already is reaching for the second and has that one in the housing, before the Zetas jump out. Two in the chest then finish with a head shot, two Zetas go down. I am passed an automatic pistol, I spray the second SUV driver and passengers — faces explode all over the interior of the car. I reload and take cover, rapid fire coming from the rear open window. One of our group tosses a grenade into the rear of the second car. Before he can turn to run, he is shot through the back — chest explodes as the fateful bullet exits —chest bone and organs exposed, he falls to the ground. The SUV explodes. I see that little shit Rojo, he's running, so I give chase, down littered alleyways, through holes in fences, through yards, probably being lead into a trap, but I must stop him. As he runs I can hear him crying, next I hear in a panting, scared voice;

'Please, no don't kill me, please, I am just a boy — a child, please don't kill me.'

I am out of control and out of breath; it's like an out of body experience, breathing heavy, a burning hatred for someone so young, I was never this person before, I want to kill that boy so bad it hurts. It dawns on me, he is the type of sadistic little shit that would have been initiated and probably killed a boy to get into the Zetas, a boy like my Luis. I am out of my mind, I run and run and his youth is getting the better of me, He makes ground, so I take aim and shoot, I miss. Fuck, fuck, fuck! I see him running, he then turns back to look at me, he gives me that wide-open grin;

'Fuck you, Black Widow cunt; you're full of shit, ugly fat bitch. I hope you die, you stinking ugly cunt.'

He runs again. Out of sight — Lost him.

Chapter17

San Fernando, Tamaulipas, Mexico

November - December 2010

'Forgive me father, for I have sinned, it has been four weeks since my last confession I accuse myself of the following sins. Dereliction of my duties as a public servant and protector of the peace, for the obstruction of justice and allowing evil to prevail when I could have prevented this, and for the sins of the catholic church, pride and sloth being those sins.'

I pause in shame; I must tell my priest what I have done.

'I have been a lazy policeman, who has cowered away from challenging corruption and evil that is present in our everyday lives. I have failed in the oath that I once took to protect good people from evil. I have allowed such practices and never spoke out; I acquiesce daily; my behaviour is tantamount to complicity in the corruption I speak of. A small child is fighting for his life in a hospital bed, because of me because of my inaction.'

'What makes you complicit my son, do you take bribes.' The priest's voice sincere and non-judgemental.

'No father, worse than that, I covered up the murder of men, of policemen. I had the chance to expose this corruption, but I chose not to.'

'Why did you choose not to?'

'Because I was afraid father, because rather than stand up against evil and expose it to my superiors I did nothing. Had I of done something at the time, then I could have prevented what subsequently became.'

'You have to be more candid with me than that, my son? Why did one case of inaction, as you put it lead to something else?'

'My Superior needed a stooge, someone who was easily manipulated. Now, a child lies in hospital, because of me, all because of me. I am too ashamed to face the man, to face his child. I just want to make it right.'

'And how would you propose that you could have stopped that? we all answer to superiors, even I as a servant of god and the church, if we do not know of another's intentions then how can we predict them.'

‘The superior officer is one of the men involved in the cover-up I speak of. If I had spoken out, then maybe this wouldn’t have happened. He used me because I am weak, because I am afraid. He knew he could do this and I would never question his motives. I am just a weak old fool, help me father, I need to put this right. I need to make peace with the child, with myself and with god.’

‘While I cannot take away what you are feeling, I have to say, that to make this right is a tall order, one that requires you to find the courage. Just because you didn’t speak out before, it doesn’t mean that you cannot speak out now. Only you can decide my son, how best placed you are to resolve this. How do you propose to atone for this? A sin is not to be afraid.’

‘I need to atone father, tell me what I can do, what I need to do.’

‘I cannot tell you what you need to do, only you can do that, what I suggest is that you say — ‘

I am out of the confessional and making my way out of the church. The church that I love, and confessed my sins and sought restitution. The sins I have carried over the years. For being unfaithful to my wife, for lusting and yearning after women when I was at the seminary, for foregoing my learning as a priest, for envy, for pride, for greed. I do not know how to make this right. I must make this right, but not with god or myself. For a small boy, who was nearly killed, who is lying in a hospital bed, with his father next to him. In any way I can, I will put this right.

As I stand outside the cathedral of San Fernando, the Sun burns down on me. The air is getting cooler this time of year and being outside is bearable. I feel the breeze on my face, my old, lined face and it’s of comfort to me. I didn’t need the church to tell me what I must do; my own conscience is telling me that. The consequence of my actions will be swift and deadly, but that is the oath I swore to uphold. I must move fast.

As I arrive home, Agata is there. She sits on the porch of our small house, looking out onto the streets of our city. She is tired of it here, she stays because I stay, she endures this place rather accept it. Her eyes, as mine have watched this town change especially over the recent years. I am the only thing that keeps her here. I wished my love I would have treated you so much better, given you a better life, I think to myself as I kiss her on her on the top of her head. She smiles, but its only one of formality rather than a genuine one of content. I pour myself some iced tea and sit with her; I don’t look at her and look out onto the street.

‘I think it’s time you went to stay with Mateo in the capital.’

'What brings this on, why on earth are you saying this now.' Agata's face is one of bewilderment. 'We leave together, that was the deal. What's going on with you Benny? you have been so distant lately, so wrapped up in whatever has been going on at work, I always said that problems are shared, not bottled up, now you have sprung this on me — just like that.'

'Yes, just like that. This is how things are now; they happen, just like that, in the bat of an eye. It's not safe to be here, policemen are being killed daily, all over the state. The townsfolk are migrating out of here at such a rate, it's hard to keep track of. They have nowhere to go, but would rather live in fields or ditches than stay here. We have somewhere and we should go. I am going to leave the force, but before I do, there is something I must do. I can't tell you about it, so don't ask. Go to the capital and I will join you.'

'I am scared Benny, you're scaring me with all this talk, its furtive and very suggestive, like you're up to something. I know you, better than you know yourself; you try and keep things from me because you think that you're putting me in some sort of danger — let me be the judge of that, I am not scared of what is going on around us, I am scared that your guilt is going to make you do something that you may not live to regret.'

Agata stands over me, she doesn't shout, she never does, but her manner is enough for me to see that I can't keep her in the dark any longer. I decide to tell her everything, the cop shootings in town, how I had vicariously been responsible for little Joaquin being shot in Matamoros, because I used his father, how I lied to him about knowing the whereabouts of the man I thought connected to his wife's disappearance. How, had I done my job properly, once I had taken over his case, then maybe it wouldn't of come to that? My mind was a mess, guilt can do that.

'So what do you propose, to make things right,' said Agata, she could tell I was suffering, just by the change in her tone, more empathetic now.

'What I should have done in the first place, I should have told my superiors, gone above the captain's head and told them the truth.'

'But he threatened us, you said so with the letter from one of the cartels, how were you expected to do the right thing. I know you feel bad about what happened Benny, but what about *your* family. What's done is done, now it's time to take care of *your* family. Come with me and forget about this place. Forget about your self-righteous code of ethics, it's going to get you killed.'

'Not if I do this and flee, they will never know where to find us. But before I do any of that, you must get out of here first. If you refuse to leave before me, then I won't do anything and I will stay here and continue being a state Detective.'

It's hard, but sometimes a threat is the only way I can get Agata to budge. She walks off the porch and into the house. I remain seated, just looking out into the street.

By the end of the following day Agata has gone. I promise her that I will be there in a few weeks, just must tie up some loose ends — make things right. Agata takes the money from the house and goes to Mexico City to live with my son and his family. I go to the station, where I unlock my drawer, in there is the money that I was forced to take and keep. I was told that if I didn't then the men would be most upset. It's still in the sealed envelope, I refuse to take it, but I know how to dispose of it. I put it in a small jewellery box that my mother had and bury it out in a field, just beyond the barrio.

I want to make peace with Flip, but I understand why he wouldn't want to. If I were in his position, then I would feel the same. I go to his house, where I find another man there, looking after the place, while he remains at the hospital with Joaquin. The man tells me that Tomas and his friend from out of town are at school. The man is careful not to let the cat out of the bag, as he is quite clearly unaware that I am aware of the situation. I don't let on, I hand a letter to Flip, that took me somewhere in the region of a week to write to him. The man tells me that the hospital bills are very high and all the money that Flip had been saving is dwindling and he doesn't know how long he can keep this up for. I ask him to make sure he gives Flip the letter and I leave. I never tell him my name; I never tell him why. I will be long gone from here soon. I must make amends before I do. Make right with god, make right with myself.

I travel through Tamaulipas and Nuevo Leon, looking for the man I know only as Bertrand Le Vell. I had learned that on his immigration documents he lodged, that he worked the fields and road gangs. I don't know what to do if I find him, but I must try. I follow the trail, the dissipation of people through my homeland is immense, migrants come through Mexico on route to the US daily from South America. Le Vell is registered here; if he weren't then this hunt would be a difficult one. I follow the trail; he jumps from one road gang, to working in a field picking crops, back to the road gangs. I follow this trail, throughout the region. I must find him, it's important to Flip, it's what he lives for now. With every place, I visit; I leave a letter for him. He doesn't stay in one place long enough to form friendships. He is black, he is from South America, to many, he is not welcome here. Maybe he made it over the border? maybe he is now dead himself? Maybe he was one of the seventy-two we found? With that high a number and the level of decomposition on some of the bodies, it would be hard to tell what colour skin they had.

I travel in hope that I may find him, but the trail is going cold. I have nowhere else I can think of looking. I learn that he is a drinker, so I go to known manual worker hangouts and bars. Most are deserted these days. Like most commercial premises, the cartels and the violence have cleaned them out, no one wants to stay in the towns and cities anymore, they are fleeing out to the valleys, to live in exiled peace. Still I leave letters at each place, in the hope that they find him. I tip the bar staff and ask them, to contact me, should they learn anything.

I contact the hospital in Matamoros and ask how Joaquin is doing, they tell me that he is slowly recovering, but in no fit state to leave his hospital bed. They tell me that his father sleeps in the street every night after visiting hours and washes in the public bathrooms and eats in the canteen, just to be with him. He won't leave. They tell me that Flip's son and daughter come up on the weekend and stay at the hospital; they usually sleep in a bus that another man drives. They tell me that the medical bills are piling up and that his father doesn't have sufficient funds to keep this going. I tell them not to concern themselves and I pay the bills, plus an advance. I had saved some money of my own, that I kept just in case I had to flee town in a hurry.

My captain watches me like a hawk, he sends me out to every murder scene in the state he possibly can. He is now aligned to lead a state and federal police task force, but I have already sown the seeds to put a stop to that. I sent an anonymous letter to the head of the federal police, informing them that the captain was the last person that any of us know to see Roberto Suarez alive and that they had an argument, just before. While I cannot be totally sure of that, I feel it necessary.

I draft my letter to the Attorney General; I sign it faithfully. I tell him of the frustrations within the investigation of the seventy-two persons killed just outside of San Fernando, I write how Roberto Suarez was the only cop I could trust. I tell him that although he was Federal and I am state, we worked together and he was the finest cop I had ever had the pleasure to work with. I write informing of the ties to state and municipal police to the Los Zetas. I tell him of the shoot-out at the cop bar in San Fernando. I tell him how I have secured each fire arm of every officer involved and how ballistics will show that bullets found inside the dead and the scene itself will show that it was a cop on cop shootout. Gave the names of all the cops there at the bar that night and if weapons are seized, they could match ballistics, I laid out the reasons and their connections to the cartels, the payoffs, the protection cops provided over the shipments of drugs. I had it all laid out for him. I attached my letter of resignation to the memo and gave my reasons for it. I informed him of my sins, my knowledge of such wrong-doings and my years of obtuseness. How I wished I could have been a better man, a better cop. This felt like penance, I now realised that all the years I went to confession; this was a medium that felt just as rewarding. Wash away my sins. No Hail Mary's or Hail Our Fathers.

As I finished my handwritten confession I looked out onto the streets of San Fernando. I watch Municipal Police pulling vehicles over, not issuing citations, but taking money, hand over fist, car after car, hour after hour. I look around and see my so-called colleagues in the state police — meeting with known Zetas, in public of all places. Things have gotten out of hand. I must leave; I have to go now. It's been weeks since I packed Agata off to live with my son and his family. But I always think of what will be. What have I done? Will they hunt us down in retaliation for my penance? I can't keep putting Agata through this. I think of leaving the country, finding our own little paradise somewhere else. A place in the sun — a place of tranquillity.

The next letter I write, I might as well address it to Santa Claus. I seal my bets and write one to the Black Widow. I still find it hard to believe that she is the same woman I met back at Flip's house, all those months ago. How her son is one of the missing. I find it strange how one person can change. Maybe we have all changed. Since the massacre, a little of everyone died in this town. I find a young street vendor and empty my pockets to buy pistachio nuts and pass him the letter. A full and frank admission, nothing left out. I detail who is involved within the state police. I plead for her to refrain from attacking them, especially in front of their children. I tell her that the best way, the only way to cut the head from the snake is this way, subterfuge will be her best weapon.

I feel giddy, as I run through my master plan and wish I could be here to see it through. I have the letter addressed to the Attorney General in my hand. Ready to courier to his office. My cell phone rings, where I am told by a male stating he is part of a road crew in the eastern barrio, that a male I might be looking for is here. I ask who and he tells me Bertrand Le Vell. So, he has returned.

I ignore lights and junctions, driving as fast as my squad car can go. My heart races, I found him, I have him. The road is dusty and bumpy and takes me up into the hills, I look out and see the town, it's getting dark now and I see the lights from the streets and the houses. From up here, the town looks like any other. You can't see the despair that is going on now, or the human suffering. I drive, but can't see any sign of any road crew or in fact any works at all. What I do see is a police road block. Holy fuck — just for me. The road is too narrow to turn around. I turn the car in a widening of the road, but it's too late. I hear the gun shots; the tires blow out and the car dies in the road. I jump out; try to think on my feet. You stupid old bastard, you've been ambushed, to foolhardy and gullible.

'What the fuck is going on here, you morons.'

Cops in uniforms, beady eyes staring at me.

'Don't you recognise a squad car, when you see them, straight out of the motor pool.'

A flash of metal in the dusk light, a familiar sound of a bang. I hit the ground looking up into the sky. I twist my head to the left just to see the beauty of my town, one last time. Like it was before — like it was in the past. The captain stands over me; I see my reflection in those mirrored sunglasses. That hair oiled to perfection.

'Anything you want to say Benito?' his face like granite, his voice not even changing tone.

'Yes,' I say holding up my hand with the letters to the attorney general, knowing now that the game is up, 'Can you post these for me?'

He laughs out loud. I feel the pain in my shoulder; I taste blood in my mouth. The other pig bastard cops laugh along with him.

'You have been a busy boy Benito, we have been told that you have been all over the state, looking for some guy. Your car has been seen in all sorts of places. At first, we just thought you were being diligent old Benito, then it dawned on us, your wife has gone, your house is packed up, you're doing unofficial enquiries, so you must have been looking to betray us and run. Don't worry about your wife; you will be joining her very soon, along with your sons and their sons. We have friends all over the place, didn't you know.'

I let out a scream and I can't stop. The godless bastards look over me as I scream and cry and writhe on the ground. They laugh and spit on me. I have lost everything. Everyone dear to me is gone because of my doing.

The captain pulls his side arm; the others have their pump actions at the ready. I will see you in paradise, my love, we will get to that paradise and we will be together, for all time. As the sounds of gunfire ring out, I think of paradise.

Chapter18

San Fernando, Tamaulipas, Mexico

December 2010

If they put their hands on me again, I will fucking kill them. Nobody touches me, nobody calls me boy. They laugh at me, they call me a pussy, they made me dress up as a little girl and sing for them and dance. They drank and smoked the yerba and did lines. I cried and they laughed even more. They made me sit on Z30's knee. I had to blow Z30 in front of the gang; they laughed and called me names. All I ever wanted to be was a Zeta, I am a natural born killer and they made me look like a fag, like a pussy. I will show them — no more tears — no more crying, I will show them all what I am made of. I fought that kid fair and square at my initiation, I hit him square in the face with that bat, I tore the flesh from his face, I stamped on his skull until it split in two. I heard the loud crack, the blood everywhere. They didn't respect me for that. They all said that the only reason I won was because he was weak, because he was only thirteen years old, because he was handicapped, because he had limb deficiencies or some other crap. That fucking kid was made to fight, me I travelled there, I wanted to meet Z40, the leader, all I ever wanted was to become a Zeta, I wanted him to notice me, to see me. He didn't watch my fight; he didn't see what I could do. I killed that kid and the men just gave me shit about it. They said I was a fraud; I was just some sick little punk who hung onto people because no one liked me.

I got into the Zetas fair and square, I am a Zeta and I will kill the next person who says otherwise. I killed that fucking punk Leno, he laughed at me, he wanted to tell the boys that I was just a kid who played with toys; well the laugh is on Leno, because I fucking cut you up like a stinking rotten pig. Ha ha ha ha ha ha ha ha ha ha — die you fucking rotting pig, lump of shit bastard — die, die, die, die, die. That fucking fat ugly black widow cunt — she dies, I will cut her up too and hang her naked from a telegraph pole with her insides hanging out. How the fuck dare she point a gun at me, I pissed my shorts, she made me beg for my life. She doesn't know that no one fucks with Rojo, not anymore. Z30 put me in charge of training the Zeta youth, now I have an army, an army who will fight and kill for me. Z30 wants me to take control of San Fernando, of the east side barrio. My old home — the place I suffered, the place where I was a nobody, a place where they laughed at me. They won't be laughing anymore. Z30 runs San Fernando; I get to clean out the east side barrio. That's what he wants, that's what he will get. The streets will run red with blood. The East Side Demons want to join up with us. Those motherfuckers are the first to die. I don't want any of them talking shit to me, trying to relive the old days, when I was just a scared kid, when I cried and ran away when we fought the north side barrio gangs. Z30 said I fucked up when I killed that Narco, his wife and kids. They reported back, saying that I went too far, those treacherous assholes ain't Zetas anymore — they're dead. I told him that it sends a message, it says don't fuck with us, we are the Zetas. Z30 said that he didn't give that order, he beat me in front of the men, and they laughed. He sent me to the desert, to train kids, most of them teenagers. They are fucking kids; don't you see my tears down my face — a tear for everyone I killed. Those maggots in Matamoros, those truck drivers in Nuevo Laredo, those families out on highway 101, all those trucks and caravans and fucking nigger immigrant motherfuckers up and down that highway, that fucking disease spreading filthy pig fuckers from those buses. I killed many, I got the tattoos to prove it, my face and body bear the marks — I won't stop, I can't stop. My cock is hard all the time, thinking of killing more and more. I don't want any more truck drivers or immigrant cunts to kill, I want a mission, I want to take on the cartels, not just robbing and killing these barrio fools and travellers. I want to kill someone who is worthwhile, a worthy adversary. I want to take out that Black Widow and her Autodefensas.

'Get the fuck outta here, you piss ant kid,' Z30 is not happy with me as he hollers at me, 'you too crazy for any kinda work, like that. That Black Widow bitch will cut your dinky little balls off and stuff 'em down your throat. You only good for robbing people who can't fight back, you're just a sick little freak and if I had my way, I would get rid of you now. But Z40 wants that barrio in the east cleared out; he wants those houses ready for storing. That's your job; you're just some little two bit, girlie shit that cries when he can't cope. One day, you little crazy fuck I will whoop your ass like a man can. You get to recruit more boys and clear those houses out. Who knows maybe you could do that without killin' everyone in your way. What is it with you, killin' old women and kids? you can't take on some old man or some hillbilly or maybe they know all your little secrets? Maybe they knew you when you were called Gael, fucking Gael, that's a fucking pussy name if I ever heard one.'

He laughs at me; the others laugh as well. One of my band sniggers, Raffi sniggering as they call me Gael. Stood in some shitty little tavern south of San Fernando, being laughed at, being called Gael, by this fucking turd. Z30 sits with his stupid cowboy shirt half open. He used to be Special Forces, like many of the others, but now he is fat, he is old, he hates me and I hate him back. He thinks I am too soft. I will show that fat fuck, once I shown him, I cut his throat out and take this town over for myself. I hate that name; he keeps repeating it.

'My name is Rojo, fucking Rojo!'

Z30 stands up, he ain't laughing now, he looks pissed. He walks over slowly to me.

'What you say to me, I'm Z30, you want to start some shit — you seriously think you got any rank to talk back at me. Whatever I call you, whatever I say to you, you just take it or I put you back in that little dress again. The only thing you ever did well since you been with us — was take a mouthful of my dick.'

No one laughs — just in case. Hands move, quick as lighting, his right hand strikes my face and before I know it, I am on my face on the floor. Pain shooting across my jaw, tears rolling down my cheeks. Real tears, not the ones I got put on there.

'You think you can kill some kids and women and that makes you a man. Put some tattoos on your stupid little face and body and suddenly, you're like me. I stood up to Soldiers; I killed Sicarios from Sonora. What you ever done? You look like some freak show who got dipped in ink. Fucking singing and crying and playing with toys when you think no one can see you.'

Now the others laugh again, I lay on my front looking up toward him; I hold back the tears best I can. The shit he is saying, making me look pussy in front of the others.

'Get the fuck outta my sight.'

As I get outside the bar, I am followed by my so-called army, kids of fourteen and fifteen years of age, some younger. Dressed in black, wearing the medallion, trying to look tough. Raffi looks at me; he has a grin on his face, like he enjoyed this shit.

'You find this fucking funny, Raffi?'

I leap at him; I smash him in the nose with my fist. I pull the knife from my waist band and hold it to his face. We fall to the ground; I straddle him and hold it close to his eye.

'I will cut them both out, you hear me. I was put in charge of this band, you ever disrespect me again, I will mail you to your mother in Ciudad Victoria, piece by piece. Starting with your cock and balls and let you bleed out.'

He doesn't flinch; he is bigger than me, stronger, but not nearly prepared to do what needs to be done. I don't keep this up, because I need him. He is tough; he can fight and will kill. I need as many tough kids as I can get.

The East Side Demons, they hold the barrio now. I gotta clear it, I gotta prove myself. They're still tight with some of the CDG. They don't have any loyalty. My old gang, I was head of the younger fraction, but now it's time to take it back. They got bigger than before. The fucking CDG been arming them up, giving them guns, paying them many Pesos to try and keep us out. The day Leno was killed; we were out hunting them in broad daylight. These East Side Demons have become stronger, before they were just kids hanging out on the streets. When I was there, they didn't want me around no more. They thought I was crazy, they thought I was scary. They didn't like it when I started killing those kids who called me Gael, who beat me up when I was at church. No one talks about those days anymore. If they do, I will kill them. Kill, kill, kill.

We slip into the barrio one night. Its December, the nights are colder, Christmas decorations going up on some of the houses. Stores and houses with flashing lights and reindeer and baby Jesus. Just as I remember it, dusty streets with old ramshackle houses lined up, side by side. Stray dogs wandering the streets. Deserted houses with old cars parked outside. Old men drinking cervezas on porches; talking shit about the old days. Women carrying groceries through the streets, kids kicking soccer balls around. Pretending they are star players — pretending that everything is OK. They don't know the shit that is about to come to their doors.

The Demons hang out mainly by an old deserted house I recognise. Its ripped through, with no windows, no doors. Graffiti covering the walls. The name "ROJO" sprayed, like a mural across each of its four outside walls. They hang out at my old house. Where my Mother and father once lived. They use this place as their base of operations. Armed kids outside keeping watch for the Black Widow or Zetas. Some of them sit inside on old, piss covered sofas, Cerveza bottles and cans littered all the way through. The smell of yerba, floating across the cold night air. I am looking for Revo and Angel. They were supposed to be loyal to me; they were supposed to be Zetas. I have been back in the region on and off since August.

It was me who masterminded that fucking pig in Nuevo Laredo getting his stupid fat fucking face blown to bits. It was me who got word to the kids to come fight for the Zetas, but what have I got to show for it — nothing. I am spoken too like shit, like some stupid kid. Amongst the elder Zeta members, I am just being some little pussy, but amongst the kids, I am feared. I am the bogeyman. The one person that haunts their dreams. I will use this; I am going to do what I set out to do. I am back for good, and no one will topple King Rojo. Z30 will be proud of me; he will mention me to our leader, Z40. I will be king. One day I will run the Zetas, all across Mexico. I will take charge and wipe the other cartels off the face of the earth.

Raffi and I sneak up the patch, knives out, quiet. Tip toe, not making a sound. Like we were taught in our training. Two sentries, watching over the street. Unaware that we don't fight that way, we are soldiers, trained to kill. A little toot toot before we do our bad deeds. Hand over the mouth of the sentry, maybe sixteen years old. Knife through the back of the neck. Sixteen is as old as he will ever get. Dressed in black, like Ninjas, we slip through the main door. Straight into what used to be my living room. Where my mother and father fought; where my photos as an altar boy once stood, where I had tantrums, where my mother used to tell me that I was her little boy, the best little boy in the whole wide world. The Living room, where I fucking killed those no-good worthless bastards. The same room, where I am going to kill these no-good worthless bastards.

The look of horror and surprise on their faces is quite a sight. They all stand up, hands reaching for guns, mouths wide open, the air rushing out of their bodies as fear sets in. Boys in black, tattoos and machine guns on show. Zeta badges on our suits. Let's hear the excuses now shit birds.

'Look what we have here,' quick as a flash I have eyed up everyone in the room. Angel is here, nine others, know the faces, don't know the names. So long since I been here, so much has happened since then. Killed so many — lots of coke — lots of death. All about seventeen years old. Some Chicas here as well.

'It's like Goldilocks and the bears; you remember that story, don't you. Goldilocks breaks into houses that don't belong to them, breaks what doesn't belong to her, takes food that she didn't buy and sleeps in other beds that she shouldn't. This is the same, this is my crib — this is my barrio and soon this will be my town. As you can imagine, the bears were very angry. Goldilocks gets away in the old fable, but not in this one.'

The bitches start to cry and weep. They start begging for their lives. Angel looks at me.

'Hey Rojo, we didn't know you was back for good. If we did then we would have cleared out. Hey we Demons bro, we are kin, we the same.'

His voice irritates me, he is weak, he is scared, he may as well beg now. I look in the faces of the other boys, they look just as scared. I can tell they heard the stories about me. I take out my knife, one boy pukes on the ground, one starts hyperventilating. Angel starts trying to plead.

'Hey Rojo — it don't have to be like this man, we just kids hanging out, we ain't in the life, we don't want any part of this.' Shaking, eyes fill with water, he's about ready to scream and beg for mercy.

'You interrupted my new version of the story, Goldilocks ain't the hero of my story, oh no. She is a lying, thieving, treacherous piece of filth. She says she would never come back, but the bears know that once a lying, thieving, treacherous piece of filth, then always one. The only way to truly deal with this, is make sure she never comes back.'

I nod to Raffi, he hardly ever speaks, just smirks occasionally.

'Bitches' says Raffi, 'get in the back, get those skank clothes off and get on your backs. Any of you refuse, you die like these fools.'

The girls start hollering now, the rest of my band drag them back. I instruct five of my boys to fuck them, one after the other. The girls still refuse; one even tries to break away. They have guns trained on them, they don't see their future. The boys go to work — clothes ripped off — they havin' a good time now

'Get on your fucking knees,' I shout at the Demons. They kneel; their guns are taken from the sofa and their mine now. Girls screaming and praying to god in the other room. The grunts and groans of my boys can't drown out those screams. My cock is hard thinking about it. Not because of the girls, because of what I am about to do next. My band does as I say — when I say. They fuck on command; they kill on command. They only speak when ordered. They don't obey me — they die. I don't know all their names and don't want to know their names, they are my underlings and they do as I please.

Demons put on their knees. Their clothes ripped off. Sharp knives out, the order is given. Angel first — four of my band train guns on the others, make them watch. Five hold Angel down, another five doing their deeds with the bitches in the other room. I take my knife; I look him in the eye.

'Time to peel that lying, thieving, treacherous skin off that devious bone rack. Let's see if you're a coward underneath shall we.'

He screams so much, the air in his lungs runs out. He can't talk. I run the blade down his arms, skin being peeled away like an orange. Both arms and legs. He passes out about every two minutes. Pour Tequila on the exposed wounds, just to wake him up a little. Ha ha ha ha ha ha, I hope this hurts you fucking rat motherfucker. It takes me forty-five minutes to peel as much away as I can. I take his head off his shoulders with a machete. We do the rest of the Demons that are left. People come out of houses, but don't dare to come over to find out what's going on. We do the remaining Demons the same way, the boys get to have a go, some puke as they do it — some struggle. They don't do as I say — they die.

They don't refuse me, none of them do. We take all their heads — we line the garden with the treacherous little rat-faced heads. The faces still have that grimaced looks of pain, agony and fear. They have experienced about as much pain as anyone ever has. They can tell El Diablo, when they get to the fiery pit, that they met his match in Rojo. The heads are put on stakes in the front yard. The mutilated bodies hung from lamp posts in the street. I see faces from behind curtains; peek out at the horror show I have put on for them. Cops don't show, army don't show. The bitches are hopefully filled with little Zeta babies, are sent out to pass the message onto the rest of the Demons and any CDG still left. This is Zeta territory now.

Silent night, holy night, all is calm, all is bright. I sing this as I walk through the streets of this shit hole. December is going to be one to remember. The barrio is going to be alight. Night after Night, we attack the Demons. We shoot up their houses, we kill their families. We take territory; we take back stash-houses that they have claimed. We have gun battles in the streets. They fight back hard. They run around, blazing guns, all macho and cocksure. We move stealth; we creep up on the enemy. Before they know it, we are blasting them, we travel in smaller numbers than they, but we are fast, we are quick. They don't see us coming: we shoot up drinking holes, card games, stores that pay money to the Demons. They pay us now. We take over houses they used to live in. Before we killed them — before we put their heads on spikes in their yards.

I walk down the street with my boys. No one dare look at us. They look away, they are scared. They fear us; they don't know when their turn may be next. The young kids look at us, I can see their faces telling me they admire us, they want to be one of us. The Demons are in hiding, they have lost a lot of foot soldiers now. We attack them when they roam the streets in their fucking stupid Narco pimp wagons, guns pointing out of the windows into the darkness of the streets. Little do they know, the darkness is our ally — our friend. We lurk in the shadows and strike when the time is just right. We are the hunters; they are the prey. My army is loyal; the only thing they fear is me. Soon this place will be the same.

We recruit the young to come fight for us. Start small, get bigger, and take over. Our actions go unnoticed: we move fast, shoot to kill, usually take out anything up to ten at a time. What doesn't go unnoticed is what we leave behind. The heads of our prey — placed out like demented ornaments in yards, the fear and pain its victim suffered, frozen in time across their faces. It sends the message loud and clear. It scares these hillbilly fools. They won't rise up, like that Black Widow bitch, they can't. They know who rules this place. The cops don't come down here now. If they do, they die.

We learn of a big attack coming our way, the Demons and CDG are coming with full force to try and take us down. We are ready, we are armed and dangerous. We take out their shipments on highway 101, every night I send a team to intercept the trucks, kill the drivers and take the cocaine. I hand the shipments over to Z30.

'I am impressed little man. I never thought I would say it, but you are a true Zeta, merciless and deadly. They are getting the message down there. Once those Demons have gone, the place is yours — to do what you see fit. I may even trust you with our product; give you special operations to move the shipments across the border. But first things first. Get rid of them, get rid of them all.'

Fuck off fat boy — you will get yours, I am just waiting for you.

We hide in the town and move around at night, through the barrio. It's coming, the Gulf cartel and the Demons are coming back. The cops have found this out and run it back to us. Some old fucking guy with greased hair and mirrored sunglasses meets me to tell me. Z30 gave me money to pass onto him for his information. I can see my reflection in his glasses. Tears down my face, three lines from each eye. I am a mother fucking natural born killer.

With every shipment, I rip off, we keep some for ourselves. We are tired, we are out every day and night, hunting and killing. I can't keep track anymore, I stop inking tears onto my body now, I killed so many, I lost count. We snort it; inject it, smoke it. Without it we can't function. It keeps us alert. We shake when we don't do it, first thing, when we wake up — got to get some of that good shit. Its Gulf cartel shit usually, but it comes from Columbia, straight to us, bounce it over to Yankee college kids and stockbrokers and movie stars and singers.

We are alert; we don't sleep at all, our eyes bulging out of our heads, noses red raw. Kids on Meth and coke and killing is just a recipe for destruction. We don't have any mercy; it's just a big game to us. We love it; we can't get enough of it. We are Zetas and we always will be.

The day comes — we are ready. Thirty of us against the might of the Demons and a fleet of CDG SUVs, filled with their sicarios. AR15's slung over their shoulders taking aim out of the SUVs as they drive in convoys through the barrio streets. Everyone looking for us, we take the rooftops; one young Zeta is seventeen and already a sniper. He can hit a target from half a mile away. We have M60 machine guns, AR15's and Grenades; all ready to go. We have jamming equipment to knock out their cell phones. We have the training, cover and fire. Use elevated positions; constant gunfire, don't stop —show no mercy.

From the barrio, I can see the convoy coming from the north, heading towards the barrio. People still walking about the streets, going about their business, they will die — just like these fucking maggots. Once I have this place, these shit heal no good barrio rats they call people will die as well. My head spins with all the plans I have. I can't keep still — I am not frightened at all, I am buzzing. The coke runs through my brain; my body is light and pumped up. I am excited — I am ready. Z30 has men in the town, ready to come help us, if things get too hot. I will show them. One road into the barrio, all routes in from highway 101. The road to hell, the highway of hell, the papers call it. It's about to get hotter than hell in here. I have poured gallons of gasoline over the road in; it's just waiting for them. I have a long wick running between my hidden spot down in the gully that runs parallel to the road, the wick runs directly into the pools of gasoline all over the road. Ready to light as they arrive. I am twitching with excitement. Never had this much fun, since I was with the men, when we shot up those bus-loads of border jumping rat motherfuckers. I sang sweet songs to them, before we shot the shit out of them. Never been caught, never will. We are Zetas, we will live forever.

They are getting closer now. I pour a little more over, so it doesn't evaporate. We stole a fuel truck from the highway last night. Loaded the fuel into barrels and got it ready for our big offensive. Thank you, PEMEX, for your donation. The sun is in their eyes as they drive in. Fucking amateurs, don't they know that the environment is your greatest ally? My instructor taught me that at the camp, I loved it there. I think about that cripple kid, who fought me that first day. He was screaming for his Mama; he didn't want to be there. Some older Zetas, killed his parents and made this sick little crippled retard boy fight me. I killed his ass. People like him shouldn't be allowed to live. Maybe that's the first thing I should do when I take over. King Rojo. Rojo the conqueror. Almost there, come on, hurry up, drive a little faster.

'Here comes Santa Claus, here comes Santa Claus, riding down Santa Clause lan,' I sing, the boys look at me and smile.

We take our hiding positions. The boys have laid out the spike strip along the road and covered it with dirt, just at the head of the gasoline. As soon as that lead vehicle in the convoy tires are blown out, its roast Turkey for all of us. Cooking CDG scum in the barrio and serve it to all these fucking peasants. Close now — not far. One hundred metres away. Fucking amateurs, they don't break the long line of the convoy or split up at all. I count eight SUVs, plus what looks like some kind of armoured carrier at the rear, plus some cars at the back. Seventy-five metres, hold it. Sixty meters, hold it. Fifty Metres, hold it. Thirty metres, hold. Ten metres, nine, eight, seven, six, five, four, three, two. Blow out, both tires on the front SUV. Grinding holt.

'What the fuck was that,' can be heard from the lead SUV. I will show you what that was. All vehicles now stuck on the narrow road, unable to back up, unable to go around. One road into the east side barrio from Highway 101. The only road you fuckers are going to take out is the road to hell, you stinking, cock-sucking maggots.

One of the boys goes to light the wick. I stop him and have my zippo at the ready. Some of the CDG step out and their footsteps can be heard sloshing around in the gasoline. I want them to slowly realise the hell I am about to send them to.

'Light it, before they realise,' whispers Raffi looking at me as though I am about to mess this whole thing up. I light the gasoline soaked wick. It ignites, the fire travels along the heavily soaked wick, to the pool of gasoline — which now bathe eight SUVs. *Whoosh*, the fireball erupts. The flames go from three feet in height, to eight feet in seconds. Those out of the vehicles are engulfed straight away. One falls straight to the ground, killed outright. Another runs in a shroud of flames toward us. AR15's cut him down, he falls, still burning away. Scumbags trying to get out of the vehicles. Out of the frying pan, into the fire. They can't escape it, whatever they do, they're fucked. I get to a position where I can witness it. I feel a smile appear on my face. Before I know it, I am laughing — I can't stop. I am excited; cock hard, stomach doing flips. It's like birthday and Christmas all at once.

'Here comes Santa Clause, here comes Santa Claus, coming down Santa Clause lane.'

The screams coming from inside the vehicles, provides me satisfaction, I like to hear them — the louder the better. Many, many screams. I even hear one cry out for his Mama. Grown men crying for their mothers, while on fire. I shoot in my shorts. It's better than any sex. I can't get enough. The screams die down. The rear cars and armoured vehicle aren't harmed by the fire. The CDG jump out – guns at the ready. Confused, wondering what just happened. I signal the boys to get up here, engage them. We have guns out; we come out from our hiding places and start shooting.

AR15 gunfire roaring, they run to take cover. They hide behind parked vehicles and stone walls in alleyways. The roar of gunfire and exploding brick and stone, provide a cloud, almost like fog as the CDG fire all over the place. We are chameleons, we are hunters. We move quick and from out of the shadows. The shadows are our friends. They spray everything, they can't hit us. We move about, rather than stay still. The dust shifts, a mother and her two small children lay slain on the ground — Blood everywhere. Shouldn't have got in the fucking way, putos.

Windows of nearby houses are blown out; we throw grenades in their direction and blow out walls. We tell them to surrender, they shout:

'Go fuck yourself.'

Clever men — they know what we will do to them if they do give in. After two hours of shooting at each other, their ammunition runs out, they try and run. We have them surrounded — we blow them to hell. When they are dead on the ground, we keep shooting. Faces and bodies explode from all the bullets we fire into them. We pursue the ones that got away. One of them is limping, he is struggling. It's fucking Revo.

There are four of them now, they run into a house. Screaming kids and parents standing aside, letting them through. They escape out of the back and into neighbouring yards. We cover the buildings they are likely to use for escape. We have them surrounded. Fucking amateurs, they come to a barrio they don't know at all. When the Zetas go to a place, they have memorised the entire place by satellite photos, examining and memorising all routes in and out before going to war. That's why they will lose this fight — and this war. We shoot them down like dogs. All except Revo — I shoot his good leg. He falls and begs for his life.

'Please Rojo, I will do anything, don't fucking kill me please, please don't fucking kill me, I beg of you, no, no, no, no. Please, please, please I will do anything; I can help you get the rest of them.'

I like his screaming and begging; that pitiful sound of him wanting to save his own ass, by offering to turn over all his new formed friends in the CDG.

'We don't need you Revo, we can kill them all ourselves. We don't want the shipments, we don't want money, we don't need your fucking help, puto. What I really want is to hear you scream some more.'

'Rojo,'says Raffi, 'maybe we could use some of this, pass it back up the line to Z40.' He whispers this in my ear. He knows that if he speaks out again in front of the boys, I will take his eyes. 'What do you think? Z40 will be grateful for this. He would promote you, maybe even give some territory, some shipments to secure and give you your own show.'

Raffi is a thinker, a planner. He's right. Maybe I should listen to him more often.

'Revo,' I say, 'Maybe you *can* help us, but if you do, I don't want any bullshit. You tell us now, major shipment routes and the names of the main players in your organisation and where they are hiding out. You do it and you do it now motherfucker.'

Raffi and I sit with him for over an hour, we tie his leg, stop the bleeding. We give him a pad and a pencil. He writes and scribbles and hands it all over on a silver platter. We lift his heavy ass out of the yard and take him to the central most point of the east side barrio. The boys round up the locals. I want people to watch. Fucking Revo is stupid, probably the most stupid little shithouse scumbag I know.

'Listen up, the Zetas have taken over,' I shout, all listening, most remembering my face, wondering if they ever laughed at me or called me Gael or beat me or made jokes about me being an altar boy and singing in church, 'You all now work for the Zetas. To live here, you have to pay us. If you try and run away, we will find you and kill all of you and your families. No one, and I mean no one can out run us, or escape. I will fucking gut you all, if you ever try and rise up. If I find any Autodefensas or Gulf cartel collaborators in this town, I will burn the entire place, with you locked in your homes. I will kill your children; I will kill you. I will cut the eyes out of anyone who even tries to speak with the pigs or the army. This place is mine now. Remember me, I am Rojo.'

I see one man looking at me. He looks strong, probably about twenty-five years old. Obviously works the fields. Stood with his small child and a woman. Probably his wife — fucking peasants. One piece of ass and pussy for the rest of his life.

'You,' I say while pointing at him, 'you want to join; you want to be a Zeta.'

'No senor, I can't. I have a wife and child. I have to support them.'

Out comes my blade — quick, like lightning, he couldn't predict that. Two inches from his carotid artery. We learned the significance of the arteries in training camp, which ones can make a person bleed out.

'I won't ask again, you don't fucking refuse me. You don't ever refuse me; none of you ever refuse me. If I want to fuck that cunt whore of a wife of yours, you say, "yes Rojo sir, anytime you like." If I want that small boy of yours, to raise as my own, you say "yes senor Rojo, he is yours forever more" do you hear me.' The boys laugh, I look at them and I grin. 'So I say only once more, you want to be a Zeta.'

'Yyyyes, Senor Rojo.'

'What, I can't fuck hear you.'

'Yes, Senor Rojo.'

'How old are you.'

'I am twenty-three.'

'Can you fight, or are you a pussy, like most of this fucking shithole barrio.'

'Yes senor Rojo, I can fight.' Tears in his eyes, his lip is moving. Trying to stop himself. His wife is looking at him. Crying, knowing that it's lose, lose situation that he is in.

I toss a knife onto the ground. The boys know what's coming, we form a circle. I try and push him into the middle, but he is big and strong. He moves into it. Good man, don't fucking try and embarrass me, by showing I ain't strong enough. He stands there, tears rolling down his cheeks; he looks back at his wife. She is holding the child. The child reaching out to his father crying, 'Papa, Papa, Papa.'

I fucking love this shit — the locals look on in horror. Those who look away are told if they do that again, they die. They are told to watch or their eyes are cut out.

'Now I need a volunteer, to go into the circle and fight this man. Who's it going to be? Don't be shy, don't be scared. He is big and looks strong, but that doesn't mean shit. The fight is one of mind, not just body.'

I look over and Revo is passing cigarettes out to my boys and laughing, like he has the front row seat to the boxing.

'No one wants to fight,' I look around the crowd of forty to fifty people, 'OK, I will choose for you.' The crowd is made up mainly of old cow hands, factory workers, too old or too frail or women.

'Revo,' I say, 'as the newest member of the Los Zetas, who do you think should fight this man.'

'Well Rojo,' he says, all confident now, forgetting that he pissed his pants earlier and that his leg is bandaged, full of bullets, 'I think this cat, should fight that guy over there.'

He points at a man stood with his wife; the man is probably fifty, wrinkled face, dusty dirty clothes, probably a manual worker. The man slowly walks towards the circle through the crowd. He doesn't protest or argue. What balls on this guy? As he gets to the circle, I put my hand on his shoulder.

'Shit, wait I forgot — I forgot the rules of the Zetas for a minute,' damn well knowing I hadn't, I just wanted to fuck around for a minute, 'go back old man, but thank you for your participation.'

He breathes a sigh of relief; he looks like a hard-ass, for an old guy.

'Revo, as a new member, I can't remember you ever taking the initiation.' Oh shit —he suddenly starts to look scared again, realising he has been played for a fool. Raffi throws in a baseball bat into the circle, next to the combat knife. 'No, that's right, you didn't take the initiation. Every member of the Zetas must fight another person if they wish to join. They both fight to the death and the winner gets his badge. We all had to do it; every single boy you see here today had to do it. No exceptions —same goes for you.'

'No Rojo, my one leg is bad and I just took a bullet in the other, I can't stand up, I can't fight.' He starts to tremble and his voice shrieks.

'In life or death situation, you will be surprised what you can do Revo. That one good leg is healing up. I watched you run from the fight, like an Olympic sprinter earlier on. I am sure you can do it again. Boys, get him to his position.'

'No, no, please Rojo. Don't do this, not now. Give me a few days and I will beat this fucking puto, but not now.'

'We don't have a few days,' I say, enjoying fucking with him — and this man, who stands in the circle, shaking and crying and watching on as his wife and child cry and scream his name.

'Papa, Papa, Papa.'

Revo is in the circle, having trouble with his balance. Both stood a few feet away from the weapons. Revo, realising that the crying must stop — if he doesn't get into the zone now, he will die.

'The rules are simple,' I shout, 'It's like a Gladiators arena, you take a weapon and you fight to the death, the winner gets into the club, the loser, well he gets fed to the buzzards and the hungry coyotes. Fiiiiight.'

I stand back; I watch the reaction of the locals. They look on in horror. Realising the power, I hold. First hand witnesses, to what could happen if they fuck with us. I hold the key — I own them — I can do as I so please.

Revo, surprisingly runs to the bat, the man, breaks out of his crying and trembling and runs also. He kicks Revo's bleeding leg and grabs him by his stupid white cowboy Narco shirt. Revo screams out in pain. The man punches Revo to the face, once, twice, three times. Nose fucked and bleeding, Revo slumps to the ground. The man takes the bat and backs off. It looks like he doesn't have the stomach for cold blooded murder, but he does move quickly. Revo scrambles over to the knife, picks it up. Gets on his feet, blood and pulp over his face.

'You fucking piece of shit, come on motherfucker,' Revo screams at the guy, wiping bloody globs of mucus from his face, he lunges towards the man; off balance, leg giving out. The bat strikes his knife hand. Knife falls to the ground. A kick to his stomach — I am beginning to think that this man may not be all I first thought. He may be a peasant, he may be some good catholic boy hanging out here in the barrio, living in a shanty house wanting to raise as many kids as possible with his one and only love, but I notice that he knows what he is doing.

Revo is recovering from his ass-kicking. He picks up the knife, his hand is swollen. He dances about like a bantam punk, he thinks he can do this, he seriously thinks he can take this older man, this man who is tall and muscular. The more I see him and the way he moves, I begin to like him. Knife slashed at him, he moves and backs up, he dances about — avoiding the blade. I am frankly becoming bored. I want him to get on with it. I stand next to his wife and child, who are now in hysterics.

'Listen you pussy fuck. No more dancing about, no more holding off. You fight, or I kill them,' pointing toward his wife and child.

That was enough of a warning for him. He gets in close; the knife is flashed at him again. He swings — the bat hits Revo in the face. Revo: down on his knees, face crimson red, eyes swollen, nose flat, teeth falling out of his mouth. Another strike about the head with the bat. Revo face down. The bat strikes, once twice, three times. Revo's leg is twitching and begins to spasm. The man drops to his knees. He realises that this isn't over. The town look on in horror.

'Winner,' I shout, the crowds are not cheering. 'Take him away; get him ready, he goes to the training camp, today.' I walk over to him; I look him in the eyes. The fear is gone from his face. 'What's your name,' I say.

'Bruno.' His face no longer looks scared, no more tears, no more crying. He gets up and walks off towards the other boys. Within ten minutes, he climbs into a vehicle, all ready to get packed off to training camp. His wife and child look. He doesn't look back at them.

We hang the battered body of Revo on a lamp post, by his scrawny neck. Let everyone see what happens if you cross the Zetas. Later that day Z30 arrives, the fat fuck almost falls out of his SUV. Drunk on wine, high on coke, he congratulates me on a job well done. Tells me that the barrio is mine. Clear the way for shipments to be stored here. Make sure that the Gulf cartel don't come back. I pass him the information Revo gave us. The routes of Gulf shipments, the names and hiding spots where the main-men stay. Another pat on the back.

He takes out his cell phone, he dials, I can hear him talking, Z30 calling the person on the other end "Capo". It must be Z40. The big boss, the head of the Zetas. I hear that fat fuck taking the credit for the information. Information I got for him. My hard work, my plan, the fat fuck — riding high.

***

Toot Tooooooooooot. As much as I can take, get up in there, fucking powder everywhere. We cut and mix our own. Our stash, for our use. Eyes red, nose puffed and swollen. Every day — fucked beyond belief. King of the castle — no one mess with me. I own this motherfucker; the barrio is mine. Bitches every day, sometimes three or four a day. I don't give a shit how old; I don't care where they come from. I see one — I have her. Somebodies wife or daughter, I don't care. They get delivered to me.

Everyone talking about me, I hear: 'Gael, Gael,' called out, I look about no one there. Five maybe six days, powder up the nose, Meth from the pipe. Keep upping my intake, trying to drown out the voices in my head: 'Kill, Kill, Kill.' Keep bringing me bitches to fuck, I like it when they cry and beg me to stop. More crank, more coke. I can take it, keep it coming, got to drown out the voices. I hear: 'Gael, Gael,' called out, I look into the street, it's deserted. Some old guy clearing a front yard. Maybe it's him, maybe he saying this shit. Don't sound like a male voice. I fucking blow him away. Bang, bang, bang. I still hear 'Gael, Gael.' I fire my pistol off in all directions. I run through the barrio, I see people. Gun out — bang, bang, Bang. They run, they hide. I hit some other guy as he walks out of a store. 'Gael, Gael.' Into the store, store keeper, his wife, some other fucker in there — bang, bang, bang. Dead people, still hear the voices: 'Gael, Gael,' followed by 'Kill, Kill, Kill.'

Crank, coke, nose bleeding. Heart pounding, head hurts. Everyone talking about me, everyone saying shit about me. I sit in my room — in someone else's house. It's my house now. I play with the toys in the house, kids won't be needing them anymore, they won't get any older than what they are now. They won't ever get any older. Won't get to talk shit about me. If the parents die at my hand, then kids die also. Don't need them growing old and coming after me. I am Rojo, fucking king of the castle.

Fucked up for days, Christmas time coming up, my favourite time of the year. Like Jesus, the people of this barrio can bring me gifts. They pay me, I let them live. If I take their house, they still pay me, no one leaves. They go off to work somewhere else, their families remain, insurance.

I round up some boys, it's time for school. Through the gates, up the steps and into the halls. Need new recruits, but most of all going to strike those Gulf cartel bastards where it hurts. Take their children.

Toot, toot — fucked up before we go. Seven of us, guns on show. No one stops us. Fucking principle, he tried to talk shit once, he got smoked. Through the halls, Christmas decorations, pictures and artwork by kids. Classroom to classroom — Kids scared — teachers scared. No one says shit. Looking for new boys, new talent. Looking for Narco kids. Rich, spoiled Narco kids. Gulf Narcos still send their kids here, we know the names, and we know the faces. Z30 gives us the mission. Round them up, take them as hostages. Gulf cartel pays the Zetas to get their kids back. One by one we round them up, teachers try and stop us. Teachers get bullets. Such a brave teacher, the papers will read. They tried so hard, but died trying to protect their students. Bang, bang, bang.

Loading kids into our vehicles, ship them out. One girl in the canteen looks familiar, she looks scared, she shakes and trembles, looking at me, looking at the tatts. Can't quite place the face, she is pretty, she is around fourteen, has a sort of oriental look about her, but definitely Spanish. Next to her is another boy, he is tall, skinny, good looking boy. He looks scared, he looks away from me. He is younger than her. Their clothes look ragged; they are poor. Not Narco kids, not looking that way. The boy would be good for my outfit. He would fit in, I think. The girl could be mine, although she looks scared, I can't take my eyes off her, beautiful. Maybe a Queen to my King. Can't quite think where I know her from, maybe in my dreams. I walk towards them, the boy shakes her sleeve, breaks her out of her trance. I want her, I want her now. The boy can come as well; I like the idea of him being on the team.

Sirens in the background, someone called the cops. Raffi takes my arm, breaks me out of my trance.

'Rojo, cops are on their way, let's get the fuck outta here.'

We run out of the hall and get into our vehicles. We captured the armoured carrier off the CDG, it's ours now. Crying and screaming Narco-kid hostages in the back.

As we drive away I say to the boys, 'who was that girl in the canteen? I want to know who she is? where's she from, and the boy, I can see potential with him, who is he.'

'I don't know the girl,' says a voice from the back of the vehicle. 'But the boy is called Tomas; he lives in the east side barrio with his Papa and retard brother. The girl came to stay a few months back.'

I turn around and face the voice. 'How do you know all this?'

'I used to know him.' Says the voice, quiet voice — face looks pale, very young looking, eyes wide, definitely wired on crank and coke, black head band on, all in black. Child soldier: boy Zeta. Can't remember seeing much of this kid, I have so many now, that it's hard to keep up with them all. Faintly remember him.

'What's your name boy?' those big ark eyes look at me, he looks so small, sat in the back of the truck, with his AR15 slung across his chest, the yes look up and that quiet sullen voice comes out.

'My name is Luis.'

Chapter19

Matamoros General Hospital and San Fernando, Tamaulipas, Mexico

December 2010

For weeks, I have been sat in this hospital, reflecting on how I am the antithesis of Laena. My youngest son fighting for his life, because of my own stupidity, my own ignorance. My other son, back at home with Alejandro and Febe. All of them scared and hopeless against the new terror that currently exist within our hometown. I have been brought up to speed with the recent events, I can't leave Joaquin here alone, I shouldn't leave Tomas and Febe. Another of life's difficult and unyielding quandaries I find myself in.

I had to yet again call Antonio and inform him that another of his family has fallen foul of our difficult times. He is concerned, he is agitated, he doesn't judge, he wants to help. I find it difficult to admit that I am failing in everything that I do. I persuade him not to come down here. The roads are blocked; routes in and out are restricted, military and police cordons and blockades, cartel hit squads everywhere — often dressed as police. I am sure that he would come down here as a one-man army and start blasting people. I don't need any more on my conscience.

I have taken one step forward and three back with Tomas. It's only really Febe that is holding him together now. He is too frightened to go out, soccer is over, playing in the fields is over. The barrio is literally under occupation, Alejandro has been a good friend to me, but upon every visit, the news gets worse. Tomas and Febe, no longer go to school. School has shut down; the Zetas have closed it down themselves and the cops are helpless to do anything about it. Teachers have fled, the CDG are locked in a battle with the Zetas over abducted children. Executions and abductions are taking place all over the region. San Fernando is under marshal rule, the CDG are out, and the Zetas are in. Cops running scared, townsfolk clearing out all the time. The massacre was just the beginning, an insight of what is about to come. The barrio is held, no one runs, no one can hide. If we play by their rules, we live. It's an occupation — democracy is dead.

All of this going on and I am stuck here, Matamoros is also like a melting pot. This hospital resembles a field hospital in wartime. It's always the children and the helpless that are the casualties. The ones that never bear arms are the ones that end up being brought in on stretchers and gurneys. Doctors and Nurses struggling to save the lives of the innocent. When they try, fucking cartel scum come in and threaten to kill them if they don't stop what they are doing, and treat some of their Narco associates who have come in with a splinter in their thumb.

My poor boy doesn't even realise the evil that surrounds us. Maybe it's for the best. Despite all his struggles in life, he just wants to build, to be creative, to build his sky scraper, so we can all live in the clouds and be safe.

Joaquin's hospital bed and treatment has been paid for, a mystery someone. Someone who feels guilt, someone who feels sorrow. It doesn't take a genius to work out it was Benito. Despite what I said to him in our last conversation, he tried to help; he was just one honest man amongst many that didn't follow suit. The papers read that he was found face down on a dirt road, shot to death; his body was then tied to a car and dragged for a mile. An entire mile long blood trail along an old dirt road. He couldn't even have an open casket at his funeral. His entire family were wiped out while in their beds. I can't even imagine what he must felt in those dying moments; I say a prayer for him hoping that he wasn't aware they got to his family first. First Suarez and now Benito.

Joaquin's injuries are healing; the bullet struck his shoulder, no permanent damage but massive blood loss and lots of physiotherapy. When we are released from hospital, we must get a bus back to San Fernando. My truck and tools are gone, shot to pieces. My livelihood is now gone. The money that I saved is still hidden away at our home. By the time Christmas comes and goes, there won't be much left. Not enough to get us to El Paso, our visas and permits all up in smoke. Our plans on hold again; what a fuck up I am. To add insult to injury, no sign of Bertrand Le Vell, he didn't even live at that apartment block in the first place. I was used and spat out and now I am on the verge of losing everything else.

It's been over six weeks since we travelled along Highway 101; the horrors seem more evident than before. It's a sullen and quiet journey, Joaquin falls asleep on me. He snores gently, his shoulder and arm in pain; he wakes infrequently to cry in pain. The pain he suffered — saving my life. The boy is a hero; it should be me who is the hero. The one who saves his life, the one that my children look up to, not the parent who almost gets them killed.

As we arrive back at home, Tomas and Febe are elated to see Joaquin, they hug him and kiss him and shower him with attention and affection. The happiness in our home seems strained. Alejandro has forged a relationship with Febe and Tomas, but no sooner has he filled me in on recent developments, he leaves, to go back to his life, his empty house, that once belonged to his parents and where he hoped Maria would one day come to live. He still occupies the house in the hope that one day she may return. I know exactly what that feeling is like.

Febe insists on taking Joaquin to what is now essentially her room. Febe is very astute, she acknowledges that Tomas and I need to talk. She knows that conversation between Tomas and I had to reconvene. We sit together in the dining area of our small shanty house, wondering how this house was once a place of happiness and joy has now become something so very different.

'I need to explain something Tomas,' I say, 'I have made mistakes; more than just a few, I am in no doubt that you probably hate me right now. What happened to your brother is my fault, what happened to your Mama is my fault? I can't change what has happened, but I will change what happens from now on. I will get you across that border and with your grandparents. Once I have, I won't trouble you anymore. It's probably better that I clear out and leave you live with them.'

I don't say this out of pity; I have had my time to reflect, to look at where I have gone wrong.

'Papa, you are a fucking selfish asshole. When things get tough, you clear out!,' he shouts, 'You just feel sorry for yourself, that's all. You just want me to say that it's alright and that it's not your fault. You just want me to tell you that mistakes happen and forget about it. You can't do this all the time, go around sulking and moping and pissing and moaning!' Now he is unleashing it to me.

'Believe it or not, I need you, Joaquin needs you, Febe needs you — we all do. But you just expect your fuck-ups to go unnoticed, you can't stand that your decisions have had consequences, can you? You should have told us what all this was about. You were played for a fool and you didn't even know it. You think you're so clever; with your college degree and your fancy talk. That's not who you are now. You're our Papa; you're supposed to take care of us. You mope around here for months, doing nothing to find Mama, and then suddenly you do this — too much, too late. You should have tried all of this back when she first vanished".

'Don't you think I know that already, don't you think that I have learned my lesson.'

I am agitated, not at Tomas, but at the realisation that it's as clear as the nose on my face, how stupid I have been.

'I am fucking this up, I miss your Mama, every day I miss her more and more. Every day I live with this, it chokes me, it kills me. I want her back; I can't do this without her. I can't raise you both the way that she could. I am scared that I won't ever find her. All I ever wanted to do was make you proud; I just wanted to find the man, who may have the answers.'

Eyes filled with tears, I stop talking.

'What good would that do, if you're dead? What good would it have done if Joaquin would have been killed? She's not coming back; Mama is not coming home. She wouldn't leave us for any other reason other than the worst reason. You keep coming up with some other reason that may explain where she is. She is not coming home.'

He doesn't cry as he says it, Tomas is mature as any man I know. He has grown up so fast, more advanced than a boy of his age should be. This place can age a person. I reach over to him, to hug him, to hold him close to me, I don't want to lose him, I don't want to lose any more of my family.

'The day after Christmas day, we run, all of us together.' I say.

'Yes, we can't leave this any longer,' Tomas sounding more like the person who takes charge.

I go into town with the remainder of the money I have. I buy presents for the boys and Febe. Joaquin's building blocks and some new tools. A new hammer, punch, screw driver set. I can't wait for the look on his face on Christmas morning. For Febe, I buy lots of girlie shit that I think she might like. Music, make-up, books and clothes. Any daughter of mine is not going to walk around dressed in hand-me-downs. For Tomas, I buy the most up to date soccer kit I can get, the tracksuit, the national team shirt, the sneakers. I am going to make this the best Christmas I possibly can. I buy the Turkey and the trimmings, the cake and sweets. We are going to eat until we are can't eat anymore. Decorate the house, just like Laena would have. I am excited, I am never normally this excited about Christmas, but no way am I going to let these kids go without.

The streets of San Fernando are crawling with Narcos, Zetas occupying the roads, SUVs everywhere, they pack guns and like to let us know it as well. Law and order seems a thing of the past here. The cops wander around, never challenging them.

I get on the bus and take up two seats with my goods. The bus stops on the outskirts of town before we get near to the barrio, Zetas get on. They see me; they see my shopping bags with tinsel leaking over the side.

'Hey fat boy,' says one of the group, I look at him, but avoid staring into those wild, wide eyes — pupils like pinholes, 'hey Santa Clause, what you got me for Christmas ese.' I hate rhetorical questions, especially when any answer could get me killed.

'Just some things for my boys.' Polite, avoid anything confrontational.

One of them reaches into my bag, breaks off some bread and stuffs it into his mouth, chews like a dog.

'Hey mano, we didn't ask what you got for your boys, we asked what you got for us.'

Oh fuck, here it comes, but then comes my reprieve.

'Hey Chica,' one of them says, looking at the back of the bus, 'hey baby, almost didn't see you there while we were talkin' to this fat fool.'

The bread eater stares at me, he looks toward the back of the bus. I don't turn around; I can hear them antagonising what sounds like a young girl. I can hear her plead with them. I can hear her beg them to leave her alone, I can hear them making remarks about her, telling her they are going to fuck her, that she is going to enjoy it, sounds of her being pushed down on the seat. The bread eater looking right at me, a gun tucked in his pants. The girl starts to scream. I look ahead, my eyes fill with tears. I do nothing, I don't move, I don't turn around. I let this happen. The driver lets this happen, what are they going to do with her? The bread eater walks to the back of the bus, my heart pounding, sweat coming from my forehead. What about the children? what about *your* children? what would they do if they knew you did nothing? Evil prevails when good men do nothing. I do nothing, I am too scared. I don't want to die, who would take care of the children. I keep telling myself this to excuse myself from the guilt of cowardice.

Suddenly the girl runs to the front of the bus and demands the driver stop, he slams on the brakes and the girl looks back at them. They sit at the back, laughing like a pack of wild hyenas. They taunted her, they wanted her to think that they could just take her whenever they wanted, that's how they operate. Complete compliance and control. A bus full of people, they do what they want and everyone else, including and exclusively me, sits and stares ahead, pretending that it's not happening. Weak, weak, weak.

I decide to get off with the girl, she runs along the deserted street. I am too ashamed to even try and approach her. The bus leaves, from the back window, I see them looking out — fucking vultures, preying on those who are already dead, dead like me. I walk the rest of the way. Through the barrio, the barrio I grew up in, the barrio I don't recognise anymore. Before, the Zetas used to just fight here, now they occupy this place. Of old; Narcos lived outside of the city limits, now they have moved in.

The night before Christmas, the children are in bed. I prepare the food, I wrap the presents, I leave the evidence that Santa came during the night. The glass of milk and the food for his reindeer, just as Laena used to. I lay on the sofa, my thoughts juxtaposed between excitement of having a family Christmas and my shame over my cowardice.

***

The children wake at damn nearest dawn they possibly can. They wake me in the process. Joaquin jumps up and down on the sofa, which is now and has been my bed sine Febe arrived. They are so excited, so much so, they couldn't sit still. I tortured the children, by declaring that tradition said they had to eat breakfast before we opened any presents. They literally flew to the table, where I cooked up Huevos rancheros. They couldn't help enough. Anyone with children, especially those either in their teenage years or nearing them don't generally volunteer for such mundane tasks, but today, I couldn't beat them away from the stove.

After breakfast, they opened their presents, with no haste whatsoever. Permanent smiles on their faces, excitement and joy etched over their facial expressions. I felt myself overcome with happiness and with great sadness. Thinking of Laena at this time of year. I wish she were here now. So much has happened recently that the great anguish that looms throughout our life has been somewhat diluted, diluted for a day, today is going to be special. As I sit and watch them, I think back to all our previous Christmases. There is no point in moping about, yearning for what once was. They show one another their gifts, they are happy, I am happy. I don't want this moment to end.

Throughout the day, they play together, each showing off their presents and playing around the house and the yard. Joaquin studying his building blocks and new tool set, inventively studying them, in his mind carefully piecing what he wants to build and how he will do it. He studies and paints the picture in his head and works at it from there. He has the aptitude one day to make a great architect, and Tomas is so bright that he can do anything he sets his mind to.

We play games throughout the day; we kick the soccer ball around in the yard. It's much cooler this time of year so we wrap up warm. I wish we had snow, it doesn't snow in El Paso either, but one day, my plan is to go to the north, to take the children to New York or Chicago and savour those cold, crisp winters. To play in the snow, to feel what I always wanted to feel at Christmas, just like in the books and magazines I had read about Christmas time. I wanted to have photos taken, just like the ones I browsed through, to see the children playing and laughing, just like in the books and magazines. We will get out of here, we truly will. I don't yet know how, plans have gone awry and money is scarce, but we will.

I serve the Turkey later in the day, helpings of Ensalada de Noche Buena which is a salad of lettuce and nuts and beets. Tamales lay out on the table with Rosca de Reyes traditional sweet bread. Vegetables and potatoes, we drink fruit punch and a solitary cerveza for me. We cannot fit the food onto our plates; we fill our faces with the food after a prayer. I lead the prayer, thanking Jesus for the food on our tables and wishing that we could all be together at Christmas time, wishing that those loved ones, who could not be here at Christmas time were safe with him in heaven. Christmas time is not a time for cynicism or uncertainty in religion. It's for the children, I keep telling myself this — it's for the children. Joaquin's arm and shoulder continue to cause him issues, since the bullet smashed through most of the bone in that area, so I have to cut his food into pieces for him.

The fun and laughter doesn't stop during meal time. Febe and Tomas laugh about the amount food that Joaquin has over his face, he eats with great vigour and has demonstrated that his appetite has returned. His face is a picture of happiness, despite the food around his face, he laughs along with Febe and Tomas. I wait in anticipation that he will suddenly speak again. They are having fun and enjoying the first Christmas since their mother disappeared, and for Febe since losing her father. Despite the no gifts at the table rule, Joaquin has his tools tucked into every pocket his pants can possibly hold. I don't trouble him with such rules at this point. He is eating and being merry, just like a child should be at this time of year. I don't want this day to end.

The day comes to an abrupt halt, when the front door of our house comes crashing through. Four Zetas pour into our dining area, they are drunk, they are high. They wear Santa Claus hats, they shout, 'Ho, ho, ho, Merry Christmas mother fuckers.'

I leap out of my chair, Febe and Tomas freeze, Joaquin jumps up and yelps in shock at these godless heathens storming through our house. He begins to cry; I run to him and take him in my arms. His mouth still full of food. He stops chewing, Febe and Tomas with the very same cowed expression.

'What do you want?' I say.

'Hey, it's Christmas, a time for giving ese, a time for us to receive. I notice you laid on dinner, well, where is our invite. That's not very neighbourly like, is it?'

I can't stand this bullshit passive-aggressive threatening tenue that these scumbags display toward us. I want to shout and scream and fucking romp and stomp on the heads of these bastards. I want to kill them. Not at Christmas time, not on our day, our one day of the year that we hold sacred and so special.

'What is it you want?'

One of them comes toward me, pistol in his hand, now tucked under my chin, Tomas screams: 'Leave him alone, get out.'

'No Tomas — don't say another word, just stay there.'

I am careful around my tone; I don't want to aggravate them anymore than I have to. The children are inconsolable.

One of the little fuckers is shorter than me, in his late teens, spots on his fucking ugly reptile like face. Tattoos around his neck, breath stinking of whiskey.

'You don't want to refuse us, my man. You see we ain't asking, we tellin'.'

The syntax of these fucking parasites annoys me, their gutter talk.

'I don't exactly know what it is you want; you have not said. You just storm in here, terrify the children and make comments such as these. It's Christmas, my children have lost their mother, this is their first without her, can't you just show some compassion, couldn't you have just left it to another time!'

My teeth are gritted; I can feel them grinding away at one another. I am desperately trying not to cry, but I already feel the wave come over me. Our meal, our Christmas day destroyed. As if we haven't suffered enough.

'I will fucking kill your bastard kids, motherfucker,' he shouts in my face. He turns and looks at them, then back towards me, 'but it's Christmas, I am giving something back to you.'

'I don't understand what you are saying,' I say to him.

'We need your house; we are moving you on motherfucker. You want to die being a hero? or give it up now — tonight. It don't matter a shit to us, we kill you and take it anyway. Maybe fuck your kids and kill them afterwards, or you get the fuck out of here!' The others laugh at this puke's comments. 'As its Christmas, we will let you take your clothes; you got ten minutes to pack.'

I am shoved towards the centre of the dining room. The pistol trained over the children. Joaquin screaming and trying to run towards me. One of the Zetas grabs him. Holds him around his neck. Oh fuck, when he is cornered like that, he will lash out.

'Please senor,' I plead with the Zeta, 'don't do that, he doesn't understand. Let him come to me, I can calm him and reassure him, he doesn't understand.'

Sure enough Joaquin kicks at the Zetas leg; so much so, he drops him to his knees. Joaquin runs to me and throws himself into my arms.

'That little shit,' the Zeta holds the gun up towards us, he stumbles, fucking drunk as a monkey, 'He's fucking dead — that little shit.'

I take him in my arms and huddle down, protect him with all the life I have in me. Tomas and Febe jump up, try to grab at the Zeta holding the gun. The others rush in, Tomas and Febe struck with backhands, they fall to the ground. The Zeta who does all the talking steps in.

'What's his fucking problem?'

'He doesn't understand, he has been through a lot, he doesn't speak, please senor,' I am begging him now, on my knees, begging with everything I have. 'Please, we will go, we will leave, we will go right now.'

'Is your kid a fucking retard?' the Zeta says.

'No,' I reply, 'he has been through a lot, his is traumatised, please, he doesn't understand.'

I am doing Joaquin an injustice now. He is fifty times the person you could ever be, I just want to try and stop this madness the best I can.

'That means he is a fucking retard.' The Zeta then laughs, they all laugh. They start doing impressions of what they think someone with learning difficulties talks like. These animals are the fucking retards, not Joaquin. They laugh and point the pistol at me once again.

'Say it fat man, say it — Go on, say it! My son is a fucking retard, say it.' I look at Febe and Tomas on the floor, sat in beaten dismay at their situation, tears streaming down their faces. Not knowing what their fate hold now. Guns pointed at my face.

'Go on, say it, or are you a retard too. Say it; tell me your son is a fucking retard.'

I hang my head, maybe we won't die tonight, resistance is futile. 'My son…is a retard.'

This brings about great laughter from the gang. I am in stunned disbelief that they find this funny. This is their entertainment. This is their idea of enjoyment.

'Get the fuck outta here.'

When I stand up, I see that one of them has found the money — the last of the money I had saved, minus the Christmas presents. He stuffs it in his pants. They throw clothes at us and a suitcase. I stuff the clothing into the bags. They are sticking their fingers into the food. They tear strips off the turkey we were eating. They take my children's Christmas presents. Joaquin's building blocks are thrown about the room. One comes back with a wrapped box from Tomas and Joaquin's room. He pulls the wrapping off and opens the box. He pulls out a watch, silver watch. I had never seen it before. Tomas looks at the watch, he looks at me.

'That was for you Papa; we saved up and bought it for you.' His voice hollow, his eyes dart towards the bastards that occupy our house.His comments are met with laughter from these bastards, who mock him and call him names. We get up and walk out of the front door. Our family home, the home we shared memories is now reduced to a Zeta stash house. I manage to stuff a photo of us all as a family into the bag, our possessions prized into one bag as we are sent out into the cold night air. No place to call home. What is a man, who can't protect his home?

I walk through the yard, defeated. The children in tears, no money to escape, no house to live. I look about the street I once lived, I can't focus on anything. My mind in limbo, which way to go? where to go? what do we do now? It's gone — all gone.
Silent night, holy night.

Chapter20

Tamaulipas, Mexico

September - December 2010

'Please, please, tell my Mama I am a good son; don't let her know I died like this.'

Javier is on his knees, blood splattered, his words come out with almost no emotion at all. The top of his head is split wide open from the bat I laid down upon him. But it wasn't the bat that killed him — it was me. He is as still as a statue; looking directly ahead, his eyes don't blink or move around, he has stopped screaming now, the pain that has been inflicted to his body is probably wearing off. He won't feel pain anymore, time to go to sleep — tell the angels in heaven that you don't feel pain anymore. He slumps forward, straight onto his face, blood gurgling out of his nose and mouth.

I lay the bat on the ground. Javier is face down in the dirt, blood pours from his head. The crowd of young Zetas cheer, Rojo walks over to me, I can see the white powder around his nose, those eyes surrounded by tear drop tattoos, piercing through me, that wide grin and pointed nose, he looks evil, he looks like the devil himself.

'You're in, little man, get your shit together, you're off to training camp,' says Rojo.

He walks away from me, he sounds annoyed, like he was expecting this great battle. Javier was weak, he was injured, he was bleeding, he could barely make his way to his bat before I picked up mine. The sound of the nails on the bat tearing away at his flesh — that look on his already bloody face when I hit him repeatedly, will stay with me forever. As the crowd moves away from the gladiator arena, I walk over to Javier's lifeless body, the pool of blood he lies in, the insects scurrying on the ground, drowning in the pool of his blood. He was just a boy himself, older than me, but he will never be any older than that, because of me, I never killed anyone before, it doesn't feel *like* I thought it would. The stories I was told by the boys in the barrio always sounded heroic, sounded exciting. I never thought I would kill someone I knew. I knew he had a family, I knew he lived somewhere, someone's little boy once. He probably sat in bed with his Papa or his Mama and read stories together, shared dreams of being an astronaut, or a fireman. Sat on his Papa's knee and sang nursery rhymes together, kissed his folk's goodnight, while they tucked him into his bed, in his pyjamas, kissed his head, told him everything would be OK, they were always there for him and told him how much they loved him.

I went down on one knee, he couldn't be alive, he just couldn't. Although I am much smaller, weaker and younger than him, he didn't stand a chance. I don't want any of his family to think he died this way. I feel terrible. For so long I always wanted to be a gangster, a Sicario, a Narco. I always thought I had it in me, but deep down I don't. I killed a boy because I was too afraid to say no, to run or to let myself die in his place. I wish it were me who died; it feels like a piece of me is dying right now.

The Zetas boys are calling over to me, beckoning me to come with them.

'What about him?' I shout over to the boys.

'Don't worry about him,' shouts one of the Zeta boys in return, 'he'll be worm food later; leave him out for the coyotes to eat.'

He laughs after saying it. I can't take it, what if he has a family, if it were my Mama, she would be frantic, she couldn't take it if she thought that were me —dead and left alone out here. I start to search his pockets; I find his cell phone. It's old and very basic. I find a number for his mother and father. I think of an old woman sat at home wondering where her boy is. The last thing she would think is that he is dead in some desert outside of Nuevo Laredo or wherever the hell I am at this point in time. I can't call her; I type a text message as quick as I can:

"Mama I am safe and well and don't worry about me. I am live and well and will speak to you when I can.
Lots of love Javier."

I smash the phone to pieces, I stamp on it and break it up, tears coming out of my eyes, I must stop crying, if they see this, I am dead.

'What the fuck you doin' ese, you fuckin' stupid, we could have sold that phone,' says the same Zeta boy.

'Cops can track phones remember, I smashed it up in case they did some of that fancy shit, like you see in the movies.' I wipe my eyes away, trying to make out I am wiping the blood away from my face, a little kid trying to act tough. I always wanted to be a gangster, now I know what it's like.

We were taken to a kind of army style camp out in the middle of nowhere, other boys who were initiated that night, all quiet, all scared, all realising that being a Zeta is not what we expected. All of us probably thinking the same thing. There is no way out now, we can't go back. Even if we were allowed back to our families, would our families want us? I think of my Mama, how sad she will be, will I ever see her again, all I want right now is my Mama, to touch her, for her to hug me and kiss the top of my head, like she used to. I regret not telling her I loved her enough, I wish I said it to her every day, please Mama, don't cry, I am OK.

After the several hours of driving, we are pulled out of the truck, we are taken to bunk houses, full of older Zetas, these boys have already gone through their training. Lots of mean eyes and nasty stares await us as we get to the bunk house. Rows and rows of bunk beds. Lots of teenagers wanting to kill, excited about being a Zeta, all of them carrying knives and hand guns at their sides, machine guns, AR15's slung over their chests. Young kids playing tough.

Our clothes are taken from us and we are given black combat pants and shirts. Of our group, there are twelve of us. I am so tired; I could sleep for days. No sooner have we got our uniform, we are taken for a run. All the grown men are instructors; all well-built, scars, tattoos, they look hard, and they look mean. All of them were soldiers once, now they fight for Z40, the new leader of the Zetas. The run is exhausting, we run for five miles at a fast speed. My legs are only short, I can't keep up, I fall behind, the instructors shout and holler at me, call me names, hit me with a cane when I tell them I can't go on. All the boys suffer the same as me.

Straight after the run, we eat basic rice and beans and then out again for more physical training: push ups, sit ups, pull ups, log runs, assault courses. After the first day I hit my bunk and fall into a deep sleep. No sooner had my eyes closed; we were back up again, running assault courses throughout the night, eventually falling back into our beds.

Up at five am, do it all over again. Weeks and weeks of this, so tired, don't know what time of day it is, constant shouts of abuse, the older Zetas calling us names, hollering abuse as we undergo the same things that they had to. I wake one day with a fever, I can barely move, I puke over the floor — I can't do this. I am pulled out of bed, fatigues on and made to do it all over again.

Can't think straight, I don't know the names of the other boys, they don't know my name, we just go at it, weeks on end, day and night, night and day. My body become used to the runs, to the pain of not being able to stop and rest, the burning heat of this place, body becoming stronger, forgetting about home, can't even remember where I lived, not heard my name in so long, I must remind myself. I am Luis, I am Luis, I am Luis.

Taken to special rooms by the instructors, told that we must withstand torture, the Zetas kill traitors; no one ever discloses the whereabouts of Zeta camps or places where the Zetas hide out. It's one of the golden rules. To earn your medallion and your badge, you must prove yourself at the camp, prepare to kill and be killed in the name of Los Zetas. We are placed on beds; held down, towels placed over our faces, water poured over us, can't breathe, the towel soaked in water, try to get air into my lungs, sucking in towel, suffocating, I think I am going to die. The towel is pulled away; I am asked questions.

'Who are you?'

'Where are you from?'

'Tell me your name?'

'Tell me the name of your commander?'

I want to give them the answers, just so I fail, and maybe they will take me away and shoot me in the back of the head somewhere. They don't; fucking towel goes back on, more water, can't breathe, I am going to die. Seems like hours, seems like days. Dragged out to rooms and beaten by young, newly trained Zetas, they enjoy it, they kick me, they punch me, they piss on me while I am on the ground.

'I want my Mama.' I cry out, I don't care anymore, I don't try and play tough, I don't care what they think of me, I just want to get away. They laugh and beat me more, same questions:

'Who are you?'

'Where are you from?'

'Tell me your name?"

'Tell me the name of your commander?'

Night into day, day into night, it doesn't stop, weak, hungry and tired. Every time I fall to sleep, I am awoken with army boots kicking me while I lay on the cold wet, hard ground. Night into day, day into night. I don't know the answers to the questions I am being asked, if I did, I would give them — just to get out of here. When the exercise ends, we are told that this is what the Federal policia will do if we are captured. If we give them the information, then the Zetas would find us and kill us and our families.

Our class graduates, I am not sure what I have learned. We move to weapon handling: shooting ranges, pistols, machine guns, shooting houses, target after target, trained how to kill quietly and swiftly with a knife, how to behead an enemy of the Zetas with machetes and swords. Explosives, sniper rifles, surveillance, counter-surveillance, hand to hand combat. All our instructors are either Mexican or Guatemalan Special Forces.

No matter what, we had to kill, our training only taught us one thing, kill anyone who stands in our way.

The barrio where I once lived seems like a distant memory, my Mama, Tomas, school, all of it buried deep inside my head. My mind full of horrible thoughts. I have forgotten the pain I once felt for killing Javier, it's long gone. Now I only know one thing, which is to kill. We are told:

'You fight for Z40, he is our leader, you kill for Z40, he is your leader. You obey every order, do you understand.'

'Yes sir.'

The answer, loud and all at the same time, It's said with meaning. We don't have our own minds anymore; we follow every instruction to the letter. We don't talk back; we only speak when spoken to. We haven't earned the right to open our mouths.

We hear stories of boys who tried to escape and what happened to them when they were caught. They were placed in large drums of acid, where they melted in front of your very eyes. They say the screams woke up the entire camp.

The camp is one mile square. No one tries to run away, the longer the training goes, the more I realise, this is what I am, a Zeta, born to kill, born to die for them. My mind has gone; no more soccer with my friends, no more school, no more Mama or the barrio or Javier and his Mama, I don't care anymore, it's all gone, all blocked out. Like a robot now, I live now, just to take orders, just to kill.

The training ends and we are told that we can celebrate, we are given yerba and tequila and rum. We are told we are men now, not boys. We drink, we smoke, no laughter or frivolity, we only live to serve our leaders. The older Zetas are waiting for their next mission, they are undisciplined, they have forgotten the code, they don't deserve the medallion or the badge, they sit around drinking and smoking yerba. We go to the hut with them. We are given our medallions and badges by the camp commander, we call him sir. The older boys are drunk, they make fun of us, they tease us, they challenge us to drinking games. Feeling woozy, feeling high, feel like I am slipping away, I fall down, they pick me back up.

I wake up in my bed, I feel someone get into my bed, stinks of booze, older than me. It's one of the camp instructors, he is drunk, he kisses the back of my neck.

'Shhh, just stay right where you are, don't say a fucking thing and you will be fine.'

I lay on my side, perfectly still, I don't move, I feel his hands all over me, I feel nothing inside, I am dead inside. We live only now, to serve our leaders.

Town after town, city after city. Matamoros, Ciudad Victoria, Nuevo Laredo, day after day, night after night. Missions they call them. Take out the enemy, take out the Gulf cartel. Our leaders are given the names of those that need to be taken out, the youngest are sent in first, we usually make the most noise —we are the decoys. Time after time, we kill. Kill with guns, kill with bombs, kill with knives. It doesn't matter who gets caught up in it. We are told where to shoot, we do it. If innocent men, women and children are in the way, fuck it, they die.

Empty inside, I don't know how many missions I have been on now, I don't know how many have died. The screams all blend into one; the screams of rival Narcos being chopped up, or cops, reporters, politicians, school teachers, immigrants all howl through my head day and night, night and day. I drink to block it out, it doesn't work, I take cocaine, more and more cocaine. Our commanders hand it to us, like candy. It keeps us tight, it keeps us awake, it keeps us wired, we fight better, we kill better, we don't sleep, we don't eat, we snort and we kill. On and on and on and on and on and on.

I don't remember each day as they pass. I don't know what day of the week it is, I only know what the next mission is. Every time our numbers get smaller, we get more young Zetas delivered. I don't know their names; I don't want to know their names. We hunt in pack. The young Zetas always go in first.

We shoot it out with soldiers and cops, I see children nearby, I shoot over their heads, some of the group shoot the kids, small kids, literally just able to walk, they laugh about it afterwards. I am not the same boy I once was, but I still have some conscience. The pain and the killing get too much. I ask my commander for something else, something to help me. He takes out some brown, he puts it on a spoon, he cooks it up to liquid, syringes it up into the needle, takes my arm, in goes the needle, down goes the plunger.

'This should help you on your way.'

Mellow — feeling easy, slightly drowsy, but it's like flying, memories fade, the bad stuff leaves my head, the sound of the screams get quieter. Fuuuuuck. I want more, I need more, I ask for more, I take more. Snorting to the needle, needle then snorting. Snort to fight — needle to forget. The faces of the dead haunt my sleep, faces of men and women and children always there. Use more; remember more, use a bit more, forget a little more. Day after day, night after night. It seems like years since I joined them. This evil brotherhood of mine. I am woken one day by the commander, he presents me with a silver forty-five calibre pistol, nickel plated, its big and heavy.

'Thank you sir,' I say, 'what have I done to deserve such a fine gift?' always be polite, always be courteous to your superiors.

He laughs and laughs and can't stop laughing. 'Don't you know, it's your birthday today?'

I am thirteen-years-old.

I am assigned to go to my old place of birth, where I used to live, the place that I left a million years ago, San Fernando. I am assigned to go work for Rojo, he has a special mission to complete. I do as I am told as do the other boys. We spend the day killing CDG members, we set fire to them, we burn them, we shoot them dead. We capture one of them. He looks familiar; his name is Revo I think. Made to fight against another man. Revo is killed, the man joins us. It all comes flooding back to me now, I see the look on his face when he is loaded onto the truck and I remember that feeling — the feeling of having to kill someone in cold blood and then join those who made you do it in the first place. That was a million years ago. I hear him say his name. 'Bruno.'

Day after day, night after night, needle — snort — snort — needle again. Empty houses, anyone who gets in the way, kill them. Store the shipments, guard the shipments. Kill anyone suspected of being collaborators with the CDG. Houses used to stash shipments; the barrio I once lived a million years ago is now Zeta territory. I always knew I would come home.

Rojo is getting worse, he cuts off heads and puts them on posts, he wants the Black Widow, he wants her bad. She humiliated him; no one speaks of his humiliation. If they do, they die. I see him playing with childrens toys, when he thinks no one is watching. He talks to himself all the time; he sings to himself, he talks to himself about killing Z30 for taking credit for clearing out the barrio.

The Zetas offer five million pesos for the head of the Black Widow they put up posters of her. It comes back to me; I remember that face, from a million years ago. That was my mother once upon a time ago. I don't have a mother anymore. Rojo shit in his pants when she went after him. I dare not say anything about ever knowing her; they would kill me or use me as ransom for her. If it comes to it, she dies, by my hand or another. I knew that woman a million years ago. She is already dead to me now; I only have the Los Zetas, and the killing, and the snorting, and the needle. I do as I am told; I follow every order no matter how ridiculous. I say nothing; I keep quiet at all times. You never know who is listening. Rojo will kill you if you speak about his leadership. We all know he is crazy, we all know that he is out of control. He isn't a warrior, he is a coward, we know it, he knows it. But we follow orders.

We fight CDG in the town of San Fernando, we take territory piece by piece, slowly but surely, we kick them out. The last of them in this region are still around, they have greater numbers than we do. Rojo wants to strike back.

'Let's take the kids, let's go into that piece of shit school and take those spoilt rich kids, the bastard off-spring of those cunt Gulf cartel honchos.'

His wide grin and yellow teeth on full show, the meth hasn't been kind to him of late, more coke and meth than anyone could take. He wants to take them, to kidnap them and hold them for ransom. His plan is to hand the kids over for the Narcos.

We hit the school, we strike hard. Anyone gets in our way, bang, bang. The dining hall, grabbing Narco kids from their lunch tables. I know the place, Rojo knows the place. He knows which kids to grab. Same kids who called him Gael and beat the shit out of him; when he was just a sissy altar boy, before he killed his parents, before the tattoos on his face, before he was a Zeta.

We move through the dining hall; we grab the kids. Typical Rojo he sees something, someone. He stops and stared, he looks at a boy and girl at the table, both sat together. I look at his face; he has this stupid look on his face, like the fucking pussy has just fallen in love. He is looking at the girl; he can't take his eyes of her. He looks over at the boy, I look at the boy. The boy doesn't look anywhere but at Rojo, he looks scared, that face, that face, that face. The boy, I know the boy. From a million years, ago, I know the boy. I remember that scared face, I seen it a hundred times before. I know him, do I care for him, was he someone who I loved or someone I was friends with. *That fucking face.*

We move out of the dining hall at speed, sirens coming, don't need a shootout with cops right now. We all killed our fair share, but not today, not now. The Narco kids are crying and begging and screaming, Rojo gets annoyed and starts to threaten them. We load them into the SUVs and get the hell out of there. I am not thinking straight; I just think of that face. It's flooding back, I start to remember, through all the screams and the death and the pain — it starts to come back to me. A traitor? someone who should have been my friend? someone who should have had my back? A million years ago, in this shitty little town, he dropped me for a girl, I went to Nuevo Laredo, carrying a bomb, more screams and more death. A boy was beaten and shot to death, we drove to the camp, we met Rojo, I killed Javier. More screams, more pain and more death, all flooding through my head, racing through me like lightning. I remember, he should have come with me, he should have stopped me, it's his fault, he was my friend, I remember the teacher, dead in the parking lot. I remember the boy, cursing me, accusing me, blaming me. I remember the screams from the teacher's wife and son. I add those screams to the many I have, all screaming at once.

Rojo asking about the girl, I hear him talking about the boy, how he wanted the boy, for the boy to join the Zetas, how he looked strong and fit and how beautiful the girl looked. I open my mouth, when he is asking about them. I never address or speak to Rojo normally.

'I don't know the girl,' I say, 'but the boy is called Tomas, he lives in the east side barrio with his Papa and retard brother. The girl came to stay a few months back.'

Rojo says, 'how do you know all this?'

'I used to know him.'

'What's your name boy,' says Rojo, that lousy mother fucker, no good leader, so wrapped up in his little world, he don't even know who I am.

'It's Luis.'

Chapter21

San Fernando, Tamaulipas, Mexico

December 2010 – March 2011

We walk out of our house, carrying our bags of clothes. Papa doesn't speak, Joaquin still crying and Febe just says nothing. She has that look again, like when we first met her, like she is far, far away. It's Christmas night, its colder than usual, we walk aimlessly around the barrio, looking for shelter. Papa doesn't look well, try and speak to him.

'Papa, Papa, please say something, what are we going to do, where are we going to go.'

He doesn't respond, he just walks along deserted streets and then back along the very same path he took. We follow him, Joaquin keeps jumping up, hoping Papa will take him in his arms and cuddle him. Papa doesn't, he just walks and walks.

'Why don't we go to Alejandro's house,' I say. 'Papa, let's go to Alejandro's, come on talk to me,' I shout at him, but he doesn't answer.

He has finally given up. As we walk, I see a shack, just a deserted shack, which was probably some kind of bus stop in the past. I can't get anything out of Papa, I tell everyone to sit in there. I stand in front of Papa; he can't look at me. I put my arms out to stop him from walking. I sit him down in the corner and take out a coat from the bag and place it over him for warmth. In the other corner, I sit down with Febe and Joaquin. I take out coats for all of us and use them as blankets; we sit and huddle in together. Papa just stares ahead, he says nothing, his eyes — he looks hollow, nothing behind the eyes. I put my arms around Febe and Joaquin and we try to huddle against each other for warmth, try to sleep, try to forget. We have nothing, absolutely nothing left now.

Throughout the night, we hear the sounds of drunken Zetas pouring into the streets, sounds of them shooting their guns of in celebration, shouts and screams from people like us, all of them being removed from their homes as the Zetas take over their properties, steal their gifts and money, rob them of the one day of happiness they thought they might get this year. Christmas was so good until then, it was like the old days again, like Mama used to host at our house, before she vanished, before the Zetas took over, before the killings. I kiss both Febe and Joaquin on the top of their heads as they rest against me.

We wake the next day, Papa is still sat staring, he looks as though he hasn't slept all night. I get up and lay Joaquin and Febe against one another; they shuffle, but don't fully wake. I sit next to him and huddle in under his coat.

'It's going to be OK Papa, just think of the ranch, just think of Papa Antonio's ranch next Christmas, just think about the horses and cattle. I can't wait to see you in a cowboy hat, riding a horse around.'

I laugh as I say it, trying to invoke some humour, buts it's lost on him. I just don't want Papa to blame himself anymore; I just want some reaction from him. I try and pull him back, to laugh at himself and the ridiculous thought of him riding any horse. He can barely ride a bicycle.

'Come on Papa, snap out of this,' I plead, 'It's not your fault; there was nothing you could have done. I love you Papa; we all love you. It was the best Christmas since Mama left, until those bastards ruined it. I know how much effort you put in and that's what counts. Please Papa, snap out of it.'

I cuddle into him, wrapping my arm inside of his and pulling myself tight against him. He doesn't move, his face doesn't change. He is lost.

When we eventually all come around, we get Papa off the ground and walk, eventually finding Alejandro's old house, it was a house that his mother and father built, they died some years back, so he lives alone. Now Maria has gone; he spends all his time alone. He answers the door, half asleep. His face is one of surprise as he sees us all standing there, bags in hand, literally leading Papa by the hand. He tries to talk with Papa, but it's no good, no response.

His house is small and littered with empty cerveza bottles, one small bed in the middle of the room, the bathroom has no door, the kitchen looking like it needs a good clean, all the plaster on the walls are coming away, leaving the stone exposed. Clothes and his bus drivers uniform, placed on a chair, creased and wrinkled. I sit down and tell him what happened, tell him everything, about where we slept. He puts an arm around me and then says it's OK, we can stay here as long as we like. He makes breakfast for us, Papa doesn't get up off the chair, he doesn't move, looking dead ahead, staring into space.

Days pass by and a new year comes around. No celebrations, this year is likely to be worse than last. We spend all our time cooped up in Alejandro's house. Too frightened to go outside, always peering out of windows when we see the headlights of the SUVs pass by, Zetas hanging out of the windows, guns poking out, just waiting for an enemy to be walking by. But there are no enemies anymore. It's just us, the ones that were left behind.

The stories get around that the children who were taken from our school that day have been released in exchange for the Gulf cartel members, Parents trading places with the kids. The Zetas shooting the Narcos as soon as they possibly could. The kids have now fled San Fernando, probably to the United States. School is now closed, no school for any of us now. At least that was a distraction for us, at least by going to school; we would learn new things and be told of a world outside of this place. The barrios and the town are deserted at night, the number of Zetas in the town are much larger than before, they are on every street, in every bar and now taking the houses. It's only a matter of time until they take Alejandro's house.

Papa is losing weight, he looks gaunt, he takes on water by the sip and eats very little. He looks terrible, he looks broken, he sleeps all day and paces around at night. The house is too small to do this, but he keeps doing it. He has now started to respond to us, his eyes have black bags underneath, he looks ten years older, he only answers questions, his answers are rambling and sometimes he doesn't make any sense at all. We have been prisoners in Alejandro's house now for several weeks. Alejandro goes to work and we often go with him. Febe and I take turns in looking after Papa at the house. We only go out with Alejandro when he takes journeys, that don't involve going on highway 101, the highway of death. It's too dangerous now to travel on. We hear stories from the other driver's that are friends with Alejandro. They tell stories of Zetas attacking Americans who come down here on vacation, people being robbed and murdered on the highways, road blocks made of Zetas. The local cops too afraid to take them on, *or* even the unbelievable? That the cops work with the Zetas now.

The inevitable happens, the Zetas take Alejandro's house and we are all kicked out into the street. We don't protest, the night they come. We know what they want, we know the drill. Pack up and leave. Again, we walk; bags in hand and sleep out under the stars. Alejandro says we can sleep in his bus, back at the station; we do this for a few nights and move on again. We use as many shelters, old deserted cow sheds, doorways as we can. The people that are still left in and around the barrio give us food and water. They know what we have gone through, they know the pain, they wait for their turn. Several homeless families have built make-shift-camps out on the highway. We often visit and stay, we are given soup and bread and water. Day after day, we wander, not talking to each other, lost souls in our own town. Zetas see us and call us names, call us peasants and bums, comment that we 'Smell like shit.' We wash ourselves and our clothes in the river; we sleep in ditches and in the green area by the river.

We walk through the town like ghosts — amongst the Narcos and the everyday people who are still holding on to some hope. We don't have any means of getting hold of Papa Antonio and telling him to come get us. No army or marines in sight, the cops all stood around, laughing and talking with Zetas. They don't even pretend anymore.

Joaquin hasn't had any medication for his inured arm in weeks, he starts to get sick, we don't have money for treatment. I try and take him to the doctor, Papa doesn't even realise anymore. He is long gone, still in a world of his own. The doctor says that Joaquin has an infection, his arm and shoulder should still have treatment. I tell him I don't have any money; I tell him what happened to us. The doctor gives us medication and pain killers for nothing, he wishes me the best.

We spend some nights asleep in the cathedral, God watches over us while we sleep. Papa kneels at the altar, I hear him praying, telling God that if he had any compassion, that he would rescue his children from this place. Papa rambles, he is getting thinner and thinner. His clothes now hanging off him. We are hungry, some days we don't eat. Papa goes to the bakery and waits for the baker to get rid of his stale bread, Papa brings us the bread, he breaks it up and gives it to us. It doesn't stop the hunger. The local priest finds us asleep in his church, he takes us to his living quarters and gives us hot soup and allows us to sleep in his church.

'Wake up kids, wake up.' Papa on his feet, eyes wide, looking excitable, strange to see him this way. Its morning and the sun shone through the church windows onto the empty church. 'Come on, we can sleep anytime, lest go, let's get out of here, come on, let's go on an adventure.'

He is jumping about, eyes like stalks, his face now covered in a grey and black beard, his untidy thin hair, now a shock of grey. I don't recognise him anymore.

'Papa, what are you talking about?' I say.

'Flip, its early, where do you want to go?' says Febe, still sleepy and most definitely confused at the way Papa is acting.

'Come on, let's go, wake your brother, let's go.'

We leave the church, Papa is buzzing, almost running. He goes into a store and comes running out with food and a large bottle of water. I can't believe what I am seeing. Papa always said thieves were the worst. We all run as the old man tries to chase us.

Luckily, it's a store that we have never gone into before. We walk for hours, eating the food that Papa stole: bread, chocolate, some apples and bananas.

'Papa,' I say 'why did you do that? that man is just trying to earn a living, you always taught us that we shouldn't steal. You always told us it was wrong.'

He turns around and grabs my arm, he has never grabbed me in his life, his grip hurts my arm. 'Stop complaining! stop your whining and complaining all the time I am sick of it I tell you!' We all freeze, he has lost his mind, we have never seen him like this before. 'What would you have me do? What, you expect me buy food? With what? Well come on mister fucking know-it-all?' His eyes pierce through me, I am scared. I feel myself wanting to cry.

'Don't you dare,' he says 'you know, my father had a cure for kids who cry, but I bet you wouldn't want that, would you. If you can think of a better idea, then go ahead, I am all fucking ears. You talk about that fucking ranch and how successful Antonio is, how much money he has, how hard he works. None of you ever said that about me. Not you, not you mother. You're all ashamed of me, because I come from here, because I am a fucking peasant, like my father before me. A no-good drunk, who has no money, no prospects, no ambition.'

Papa is shaking, his face looks frantic, he is not well. I am in shock; I have never heard him talk this way before, about Mama or Papa Antonio or us.

'I didn't mean anything by it Papa.' I say, I don't mouth off to him, I can tell that he is not himself.

'Let's go, let's just enjoy the day, I don't want to fight, let's get out of here.' His whole tone of voice has changed; he returns to being excitable and almost childlike.

We go down by the river, the same river we used to go with Mama, the river where he first met her. We skim stones, Papa being playful with us all; almost trying to overplay his behaviour, over friendly but it scares me. He tells us stories of the First World War, how soldiers would be sent over the top of the trenches into no man's land, where they would charge into certain death, some would be shot down, some would make it to the German trenches and defeat them. He made it sound like a big adventure. He stands up and has us all line up at one end of an open field near the river; he tells us how he used to play this as a boy, with his friends.

'Chaaaaarge,' he shouts.

We all run, pretending we are holding guns, running and zig zagging around, avoiding the pretend enemy fire. Each of us knows what it is like to face gunfire, as we did it for real in Matamoros. We keep it up, Papa seems happy and is laughing and playing out his old boyhood memories, his eyes wild, his thinning hair all over the place, we join in charging across the field, even Joaquin who doesn't normally play like this, does the same, making the sounds of enemy machine gun fire. For once in a long time, I am having fun, I forget about the way Papa spoke earlier that day. He is not himself, he is not well. We run and charge and fall to the ground, pretending we are the last stand against the evil empire that awaits us in the enemy trenches. We do this over and over; Papa truly never getting bored of it, we all join in and play. It feels good, we forget we are hungry, we forget that we have no home or even any way of breaking out of here. It feels like Papa is trying to get out his frustrations that he has, his wishes to be a brave soldier, fighting against evil, maybe even wishing he were fighting the cartels? mowing them down with machine guns and freeing the good people of Mexico.

We sit down on the grass near to the river. We eat the rest of the bread and fruit and some more chocolate.

Febe looks over to Papa. 'Tell us about this place when you were a boy Flip, it wasn't always like this.'

'No Febe, this was a place of farmers and workers, people worked hard, paid their way, no robberies or murders or any of these cartel people roaming around, it was a different place back then.'

'I bet you were happy as a child?' Febe says, looking at him, while he stared at the river, never looking back at us. 'You never speak of your mother and father, where are they now?' Febe follows up. He never spoke of them and I always wondered why.

'My father,' he says, he lets out a snigger: 'What can I say about him. Well what can't I say about him? He was born near to here, when he was young; he moved to Texas with his mother and father and became a citizen. He joined the Marines and fought over in Vietnam, he fought during the Tet offensive, which was a large offensive by the North Vietnamese. My father went all the way through that. When he came back to America, he renounced his citizenship and came back here, he met my mother and they had me. They married almost straight away. The problem was, you see he only came back here, so he didn't get shipped back to Vietnam again. Any poor Mexicans or Latinos with citizenship were sent over there, because they were poor, because they had to prove themselves. He did two tours over there, it changed him, it made him hard, it made him nasty. After a while, he always said that he would go back to the US and take us with him. He was going to state that he served the US oversees and this would place him at the front of any queue.

But he never went back; he said that he couldn't because of us, because of me and my mother. He said that we held him back, that it was our fault.'

Papa pauses for a moment, I see a hand come up and wipe his eye. 'He tried to teach me to be like him, he was a fighter, a boxer and not a bad one either. I was a writer, someone who liked books and education. I liked school and was mediocre at sports. I was sensitive and gentle; he was hard-nosed and unrelenting. He had mood swings and would often get angry, he made me fight him in this ring he built in the yard, he wanted to teach me how to fight. Teach me to be a man, to be a Hernandez. I was scared of him, I hated him and he hated me. My mother was sacred of him and just let it carry on. He never told me he loved me, he never showed me that he loved me. I was just there, this kid who held him back his whole life. You see he needed to blame someone, for not making it, for not being the successful person he always dreamed of. He always went on about America, about being an American citizen, how he spread his wings and went there as a young man and always cursed the day he came back here. The problem wasn't coming back here; the problem was he came back with all his dreams shattered. He thought that fortune grew on trees over there, when in fact he was just another border jumper, another fucking beaner who didn't mean shit — who everyone hated. He thought the military would make him proud, make him a more worthwhile citizen, a respected person. Instead it made him hard and bitter. He couldn't sleep no longer than three hours without waking up screaming in the night. I had a brother, Juan. He was younger than me; he was the apple of my father's eye. He didn't get treated the way I did. When I left to go to college, my father cursed the day. He repaired roofs and did manual work; no son of his was going to be that way. When I went to college in the capital, he died. We never got to speak again. My mother died three months after him. My brother sold their little house and drank himself stupid and moved out of the city. I don't know where he is.'

I struggled to take it all in. I never knew a house without love, it was hard to understand. Febe walked over to him and sat by his side, she looked at him as he stared out at the river.

'You're a great father and now you're my father too.'

We spent the night at the river and slept under the stars. Papa slept like a log that night, Joaquin huddled into him under Papa's long coat. It got quite cold at night, but we were getting used to it by now. I sat down by the river with Febe, it was the first night in a long time that we weren't playing the roles of mother and father to Joaquin and Papa.

'Had Papa ever told you that story before?' said Febe intrigued, but also sounding quite sad.

'No, never. I don't even think he ever told Mama before. I am worried about him; I have never seen him this way before, up and down all the time.'

'He has been through a lot, especially since I came along, I sometimes think that it's me, that I am a curse on this family,' she didn't sound like she was teasing, like she would often do.

'That's ridiculous, he loves you. Before you came along, we never spoke to each other. I blamed him day after day, always thought that it was his fault Mama disappeared. But now I have learned that if he ever had the slightest thought that was ever going to happen, he would have left. He has lost all his pride and everything he ever worked hard for. The last straw would be his family. We have to be strong for each other.'

I put an arm over her; she puts her head on my shoulder. That feeling comes back again. For months now, life has been hard; I had to put those feelings on hold.

'Thank you,' says Febe. 'Does that mean that we are brother and sister now.'

She sounds jovial again. I want to tell her, but I don't know how, tell her how much she means to me, that ever since the first moment I laid eyes on her, that I loved her. I have gone beyond hiding my feeling anymore. I realise that life is too short, after everything we have been through.

'No, I don't want you as my sister;' I say 'I don't think of you that way, I think of you in a different way.'

Febe lifts her head from mine and looks at me. 'What do you mean?'

I can tell now my awkwardness coming through. My heart races and my cheeks blush. I never know when Febe is teasing me. I must tell her, it's now or never

'I love you,' I say. It's done now; I have done it, no turning back. I look at Febe, her face looking as lovely as it has ever been; she is listening to what I am saying. 'I love you, I have ever since you first came to us.' I think of what Papa told me, all those months ago, if he hadn't asked Mama, then he would have regretted it is whole life. 'I wanted to tell you all along, I can't stop thinking about you, I want to be with you all of the time, I thought I was too young to feel like this, but I do. I could never find the courage to tell you, but I couldn't go through life not ever telling you how I feel. If you don't feel the same I would understand, I am just a kid after all, but I don't think anyone would love you like I do.'

She looks stunned; she turns away from me, for what is only a matter of seconds, feels like a life time. My heart pounds and my stomach feels like I am on a rollercoaster, just waiting for her to respond. She looks back at me; she leans forward and kisses me, on the mouth. I respond to the kiss, heart pounding like a drum. I have never kissed a girl before and at this moment; I don't ever want to kiss any other girl than Febe.

She leans back and looks at me, 'I love you too Tomas, I never thought you were ever going to say it. I feel the very same, I am just old fashioned; I want the boy to say it.'

She smiles and I am hooked, forever. We join the others and sleep under our jackets, I lay next to her, I feel her hand slip into mine. Despite all the pain and suffering, I now feel happiness that I have not felt before. I can't ever let her go; I will never let her go.

***

It's now March and spring is coming. In Mexico, it's just hot all year around and we spend our time hiding out from the Zetas at night, sleeping wherever we can, taking food from wherever we can, sometimes people give us food, sometimes we work for food. My father loans himself out, helping people around the town, doing chores and we are paid with food and water. We help too. As a family, we are like something out of Oliver Twist; poor, no home, just working wherever we can. At night, we creep around the town; Papa says that in desperate times, we must resort to whatever to survive. We can't get out of town; the place is patrolled by Zetas. They have set up road blocks all along the main roads out of here; we hear stories of people disappearing, no one knowing where they have gone. People have been caught trying to escape from the town and when they are caught, they are never seen again. Lots of stories, lots of rumours. We have taken to breaking into stores at night and scavenging for any supplies we can get our hands on. It's quite exciting. Joaquin uses his tools to break locks, Febe is usually the lookout, while we rummage through some of the deserted stores in town, we find canned goods or anything that might be of value. During the day, we sell anything of value to people around the barrio.

Febe and I often look at each other and smile; we have not told Papa how we feel about each other, now is not the time. We sometimes share the odd kiss, when no one is looking. It feels exciting; the life we lead now is like something from one of those old stories about Robin Hood. Papa says that Mama would kill him if she knew, so we were never to tell anyone, not even Papa Antonio, when we get to El Paso. The danger of how we live add interest and make the whole thing seem like one big game. San Fernando is a dangerous place; we must keep out of sight.

We see Alejandro doing the rounds; he stops his bus and lets us on.

'Thank Christ,' he says to Papa. 'You seem a lot better, than when I last saw you?' he says.

'Yes, just a blip,' he replies.

'I been looking everywhere for you, I got this.'

Alejandro hands Papa a letter, Papa opens it. I see him studying the letter, his face is one of deep concentration, but his eyes begin to squint, he studies the letter, mouthing the words to himself.

'What is it? who is it from?' I say.

'It's from Bertrand — Bertrand Le Vell, that fucker says he heard I was looking for him, he is at the Almovador hotel.'

Oh god, oh Jesus, this is the man Papa has been looking for, the one who Papa believes has done something to Mama.

'Drive us to the Almovodor.' says Papa, his voice coming out through gritted teeth, he looks crazy.

'But —' replies Alejandro, also as shocked as I am.

'*NOW*, goddamit!'

***

Papa tucks a knife into his waist band and climbs the stairs to the room that the manager gave us. The hotel is old, used by people passing through, although these days not many pass through anymore. The stair case is old wooden and creeks as we climb up. We go to the room that the manager said he was staying. No knock at the door, Papa opens the door, the knife in his hand. I want to stop him, but at the same time I think what if he is the man who hurt Mama, or killed her or is he holding her somewhere. Febe and Joaquin just follow. We are all into the room as soon as Papa opened it.

Sat on the bed, is the man Papa has been looking for. But not the man I expected and neither did Papa as he stops, his angry face changing to a shocked one. Sat on the bed is a tall black man, thin, almost starved thin, his arms thinner than mine. His face is lined with wrinkles, his hair only existing on the sides, bald on top. Grey curls and a grey moustache. He looks like someone's grandfather, rather than a murderer. His left arm crooked, the hand bent in a downward position, almost like a hook. He looks tired, he looks old. He has on old dirt covered pants and a white vest, covered in dust and dirt.

'You must be Felipe,' he says 'and you must be Tomas and Joaquin, your Mama told me all about you.' He looks directly at me and says, 'you look just like her, it's like looking right back at her.' The voice soft and friendly, like you would expect of an older man, he looks like he is pleased to see us.

Papa stands there, with his mouth open, he looks about the room, the bag in the corner, the work clothes; Papa looks as shocked as I did.

'You Bertrand?' Papa says, he seems to have calmed down.

'Yes I am, I understand you have wanted to speak with me. I found a letter at a bar, addressed to me, it was in the name of someone called Benito, I don't know any Benito, but he asked that I contact him. I tried over and over again, so when I got the money, I came back here. This is about Laena, isn't it?'

'Of course, what the hell did you think it was going to be about!'

'Maybe we should excuse the children, before we talk.' His voice sounding concerned.

'No, they can hear this as well, it's their mother, they can hear you out, what have you done with her, you bastard.' Papa almost growls as the words come out.

Bertrand peers down at the ground, his voice sounding lower than before, like he is ashamed of something. 'I didn't do anything to Laena, but I am responsible.'

Papa grabs the old man off the bed; he curls with fright and howls.

'What you say — you old crippled bastard, WHAT HAVE YOU DONE?'

Papa throws him onto the bed, he looks up at Papa, he looks terrified, he doesn't seem like the man that Papa had always believed. Papa holds the knife again in his hand, Bertrand curls and begins to cry, I stand in front of him.

'No Papa, please, you're not a bad man, let him talk.'

Bertrand stops crying after a few minutes and sits back up again and he starts.

'Laena and I worked in the fields at the old ranch out near the highway. We were friends, she would often help me because I struggled with some of the work, but I needed to work, I needed to eat and I drink a lot.' He lifts his crooked arm as a way of explanation. 'She spoke of you all very highly; she loved you all very much. I liked to hear her speak of you. It reminded me of my family back home, I miss them so much. We were friends; she was also someone who looked out for everyone who worked in those fields. One day a local gang arrived at the fields, they were young, they came from the barrio — where

Laena lived. They walked into the fields and began to hassle the men. Laena wanted to confront them; I told her not to, that they would leave in a minute. But they didn't, they kept on and on until eventually they started beating up some of the elderly men. There were small children there also, children of some of the women who worked with us. They pulled out guns and one of them shot an old woman who was shouting at them for hitting people. She stood up and raced towards them. They pointed a gun at her and threatened to shoot her. She told them to leave, that they could take what they want, but just leave. They rounded us all up. I stood next to her and told her to think of her own family.'

Bertrand had to pause, I could see Papa's eyes welling up, his mouth began to quiver.

'Then they started to grab the children and the women, they shot another woman and one of them took a child, just a small child, younger than your boy over there,' pointing at Joaquin. 'They had him by his ankles and swung him like a doll and tried to smash his head into the rocks. They had all the women and children lined up, they had guns pointed at them, they started shooting the men, at least ten of them were shot — there and then. They were about to kill the women and children. Laena stormed up to the man and struck him over the head with a spade. She told them to leave, she cursed them and spat at them and called them cowards and cursed them to hell and back, she went for them, she must have hit at least three or four of them, she was like a banshee — not scared in the slightest, she saved the lives of those children, they all managed to get away, even the small one who they were swinging around. The women too.'

He stopped, he was clearly upset, he was trying to avoid telling us the rest.

'What about Laena? what about my wife?' Papa now in tears, unable to control his emotions.

Bertrand looks up, eyes full of tears. 'They shot her — she was hit several times, she fell to the ground and we all ran away, down to the road, we never looked back. If it wasn't for her, we would all have been killed, the children as well. She was a brave woman, a hero and no one even knows about her. Every day I feel shame, for being a stupid old drunk cripple who ran away, I lived and have nothing, she died and she had everything.'

'That's not true,' says Papa; he has managed to gain control of himself. 'You couldn't have done anything, it's not your fault, it's those bastards, these bastard Narcos. They're everywhere and they kill everything beautiful in the world; it's not your fault.'

'The old farm is deserted; the gang took over the farm and killed whoever was left. They buried the bodies somewhere out on the highway. All the people who worked there fled the region, but the word got out. I called the cops to inform them of what happened, spoke to some cop, he told me to get the hell out of here and if I ever breathe a word of this, then I would be buried as well.'

'What will you do now? where are you going?' asks Papa.

'Back home, back to Belize, I have seen enough here to make me think, it was a bad idea coming here. The people of Mexico are some of the best and some of the worst the world has to offer.'

He looks at Joaquin and I, His story was what I always knew deep down inside, I always knew that she was never coming home. 'Let me tell you something boys, she was very, very proud of you both and loved you dearly. Your Mama was the bravest person I ever met and the best friend I ever had. You should be proud.' He looks at Papa, 'You were her one and only love, she told me this, she said that she would follow you to the ends of the earth, whatever that means — where will you go now.'

'Away from here — far away from here.'

Chapter22

San Fernando, Tamaulipas, Mexico

January – March 2011

'We can't get in there, not a chance, not against that many of them — Maria you've lost your fucking mind?' I am beginning to tire of his supposed pragmatic stance on everything.

'You heard what the fuck is going on down there, you heard about them taking over the town, we are supposed to defend the people, our people, remember.'

I can see him looking at me, like I have lost my mind; I will back this up with an insult.

'Oh, yes I forgot, you're an American at heart of course. These aren't your people, are they! they are mine, and theirs,' as I point to the rest of our group. 'Where are the Americans anyway, the fucking DEA cleared out of here months back, probably sat in Acapulco or Mexico City, sipping cappuccinos and wondering where it all went wrong. You fucking Yankees are something. Maybe, if the cartel members changed their names to Mohammed and prayed to Allah, then you could bet your ass, they would hit this region in droves, by sundown every one of them would be in Guantanamo with car batteries attached to their nuts.'

'You doubt *me* and everything that *I* have done for this cause!' he follows up: 'Its certain death, no glory, no medals, just a one-way ticket to a dirt nap in some shit ass part of the desert. The plan was: expose the fucking cops, expose the local politicians and those who benefit from this. You remember our pact? covert action, more than one way to skin a cat.'

'Manny, I am tired of just sitting back and watching this happen — they killed my boy, they killed innocent people and will keep on doing this, unless we take the fight to them. I want little cocksucker Rojo, I want his fucking head on a stick, then I am going to do the same to Z30.'

After hours of deliberation and putting things in place and planning, and further planning, and more fucking deliberation, we come to a compromise. We take out Z30, weaken the structure, we know his movements; we know how he likes to flaunt himself. We remove his fat ass and they replace him with someone crazier, that's the way it goes.

It's all set; we look to take him out in his own yard, right outside San Fernando. We can't get in close; we don't get to gut him like a fucking pig, as I want to. Kill him from afar; I want to take the shot. I am a quick learner, I can handle a rifle at long distance, Manny showed me, Manny taught me, Manny trained me. Night-time is the best, take him out when he's drunk, when he's stoned, when he least expects it. We know they have a camp outside of the town, just off the highway, the highway of death. Road blocks set up by Zetas, stopping everyone coming in and out, some get in, some get out.

Hours of surveillance at night time across the desert, using night time binoculars, following members back to their hideout — no sign of Z30, where is that fat fuck? We watch the camp from far away, we see the weapon dumps, the SUVs, we see cop cars coming into the camp, we see girls being brought there, girls who don't want to go, screaming and crying and pleading. I can see boys, just young kids, wearing the black combat uniform of the Zetas; they look more like Nazis than anything. Black headbands on, marching around, doing as they are told. It's like something out of a nightmare, like the apocalypse has finally arrived.

After a week of continual observations on this stronghold, Z30 arrives; he takes his time getting out of the SUV. He strolls around the place like some dictator, I can see him slapping the younger boys, I see him shouting and hollering at the older ones, drinking, taking coke, fucking, living life like Caligula.

We watch him at the camp for a further day, study his movements, and see if there is anything he likes to do. Like clockwork — bingo, he likes a cigar at night, around eleven pm, outside his tent, taking in the dry desert air, while he puffs on a Cuban. We can smell it from back here, half a mile away up into the hills, watching intently, studying. As well as watching him, we watch the camp; there must be at least a hundred of them at any one time. No shipments come through here, just Zetas, lots of them, all ready to immobilise at any time. When they're not on duty, they get fucked up on booze and drugs. We plan to put this back on the Gulf cartel, have them take the hit on this, let them kill each other, Z30 is a fucking nobody in the rank structure, the army and federal police don't even have him on their Zeta family tree. We know better, we know he is the king shit down here at the moment, we have the best intelligence, we don't pay for it, we see it with our own eyes.

The day of the hit, I take the first watch, I must accustom myself with the lay-out again, see who is around, how many, wind distance and direction. From this distance, I must be sure I take the shot, it's a tricky one. Even Manny is doubtful of it. I keep my eyes in the night time binoculars, watching each of the Zetas either patrolling or going from one place to another. I watch a line of young Zetas head out and take up positions, like some Latin version of the Hitler youth all marching in time. I look at the size of them, some probably not even in their teenage years yet, no sign of that punk Rojo. Probably crying and whining somewhere or hurting helpless animals for fun. Something keeps drawing my attention to the group of younger ones, one of them near the front of the marching line, those little legs, walking like a rooster, reminds of… Yes — just like his little swagger, he was born with a leg slightly longer than the other, had to wear a hip cast when he was a baby — got to keep my eyes open, can't get distracted. I move the binoculars to watch over the sectors of the camp, but still bring the binoculars back to where the young one is now positioned, can't see him fully yet. It's a morbid fascination of how he reminds me, must be losing my mind, no need to torture yourself, you stupid deranged bitch, must be losing it.

Another scan and I move back to the young Zeta, he is looking in another direction, away from my line of sight. He is positioned looking out of a fence, into the desert. There are watch towers and makes shift huts, trucks and vehicles, over crowded, not quite the military establishment it wants to present itself. Back and forth, back and forth, I scope the place and back to that kid, definitely losing it, I don't know why I am doing it to myself. Back and forth, back and forth. I then see another sentry walk up to his position, he is being relieved. Now he will turn — now he will look this way and now you can satisfy that curiosity. I watch as they talk, the boy still looking in the direction he was supposed to, like a good little soldier. Come on; turn around, let's have a look, just to make sure, it wouldn't be— Wait, he is turning, right around now, looking down at his weapon — looks up —

'Luis,' I say aloud, 'Its Luis, he's down *there*.'

Manny grabs me: 'What the fuck — you're going to get us all killed, what the hell are you doing, you want them to hear us!'

'No, no you don't understand.' Frantic now, shaking uncontrollably, I am sure, it's him, it's him. I grab the Binoculars, the boy is facing the other direction, but after seeing the face and that unmistakable walk of his — its him, its him.

'I have got to get in there; I have got to get in there.' My voice getting louder, Manny slaps my face, pulls me in close.

'No, it wasn't him, it wasn't him. You know that other boy sent the message; you know he lived, and in order to have lived, Luis must have died. We have seen these initiations all over the state, with our own eyes and we all know how they end up. How could a twelve-year-old boy fend off a boy much older? Pull yourself together or I pull the plug on this.'

Luis is thirteen now — would have been thirteen.

I look around at the group; they all look at me, like I have lost my mind, they look dazed by my actions, but I know what I saw. I don't know how to explain them or how this is even possible, I don't try and justify it to them, they would lose confidence if I carried this on, but I can't leave it. Initiate the action, get out of here and then rationalise it later.

I swap the binoculars for the rifle, high velocity, used by Navy Seals and Marines alike. Manny's weapon of choice, try and compose myself, I know what I saw, I know what I saw. More than ever now, I want to kill this bastard. I control my breathing, get it back down, heart rate still up though, control my breathing, let the rifle rise and fall with every breath I take.

I watch the tent he usually stands outside of, all alone, just his thoughts to keep him company. A light wind blowing over the desert, the green vision of the scope — I can see everything. I don't remove my eye from the scope; get the eyes accustomed and ready. Here he comes, but I am still thinking of Luis. The urge to whip the scope about the base, to look is burning — just a quick one. We know he stands out there for eleven minutes, give or take a few seconds, it wouldn't hurt, but Manny would see it, the others would see it.

I studying his movements, I have watched him over several days now, he stands up and generally looks out into the desert, no one disturbs him. I regulate my breathing to shallow, so I don't over compensate. I don't hold my breath because a lack of oxygen can make the body spasm, one move to the left or right, means a shot going at least thirty metres wide either side. Finger against the trigger — take in the slack of the trigger — there he is — I aim for the chest area, with the wind the way it is and the distance, I am more likely to cause a fatal shot by aiming in this region. I fire — I keep my eye in the scope, I realise very quickly at the point of taking the shot, that someone came out to him, this never happened before. Still looking through the scope. Pink mist flies up, he goes down, he his clutching his chest, near to the collar bone, non-fatal shot. I try for another. Zetas running down towards the gate, shots being fired off in all directions.

Rojo — fucking Rojo is crouched down by Z30; he has something in his hand — a pistol. Zetas running everywhere, but Rojo is calm, walking up to Z30, while he lays on the ground, trying to get himself up, howling in pain, I have seen this before from that little shit, he is going to finish the job off for me. All of this in seconds, I see the flash of the pistol — Z30's forehead explodes — he tumbles backwards. Rojo shouting that the shots are coming from the left side, his hand points in a different direction to where we lay in hiding. Behind the rocks, up into the hills. Rojo the manipulator, Rojo the devious one, calculating, cowardly. Definitely a dangerous one. I don't take the shot, if I did, it would be fatal for us, our position now blown. I gather up the round and we clear out, quickly, silently, like all Black Widows.

We move out of the region for a while, let the dust settle as it were, we head up north and hide out, let's see what this brings. Sure enough, the Gulf cartel are blamed, the streets of Reynosa and Nuevo Laredo bathe in blood. Gun battles in the streets; car bomb attacks, kidnappings, beheadings, banners lay out with the Zetas trademark threats to all their enemies, headless corpses handing from bridges and lamp posts. Cops and soldiers intervene, three sided shootouts, the cities awash in violence and blood. Innocent people killed, images of bleeding children being carried by screaming parents stay with me, mothers crying in the streets standing over the bodies of their children and husbands. Banners placed on streets; made by parents begging for any information about their missing sons or daughter, husbands and wives, missing their loved ones, nowhere to be found, the big black hole of Mexico swallows more and more with each passing day.

Z30 is replaced — long live the king. Martín Omar Estrada Luna otherwise known as 'El Kilo' takes his place. One monster for another. The word gets out that he is now the leader, he is brutal, he is calculating, he is crazy, he is a devout Zeta. Tall, large powerful build, close cropped hair with goatee, scars over his face, like Frankenstein's monster. A US born Mexican and one of the men who was involved in last August's killings of busloads of immigrants. The Zetas needed to kick up someone who was ruthless and hungry and willing to do almost anything and everything to keep their control. If he is Frankenstein's monster, then by proxy, I could be his creator, I removed the head of the snake, but it appears that the tail is where the venom lies. With El Kilo and Rojo operating, San Fernando is going to explode.

I lay out my plan to Manny, that I must go back there, I have an itch I can't scratch, I know what I saw and I know who I saw. A mother doesn't forget her child.

'Your boy, he is gone. Even if that was him, and let's just say it is, he is lost, he won't be the same boy you remember. If you even tried and were successful to get to him, what do you think he would do? He is a Zeta now and you're his sworn enemy.' Manny's direct approach, contemplated, but ignored.

'I have been thinking about this one for some time now, I remember the message that Javier's mother showed me that day, I won't ever forget it.'

'Mama I am safe and well and don't worry about me. I am live and well and will speak to you when I can.
Lots of love Javier'.

'Where the message reads "live and well" that is the bit that boggled me, but I never had time to process it. Luis could never get his context right in grammar, he never wrote past and present tense correctly. "Live" should have read "alive." Now unless, both Javier and Luis had the same grammar teacher, who was a complete and utter fucking retard, then I am sure I am on to something here. I know what I saw, the height, the walk, the face. A mother cannot be mistaken about these things.'

'We can't go through with you on this; your leadership is questionable if you are just going to drop everything for something such as this.'

'You fucking asshole — just remember why I started this group, *the Autodefensas* — it was revenge, revenge on those who I thought killed my boy, that was the catalyst, that was why I rose up to fight them, the rest came afterwards. You dare question my leadership, you pompous prick! After everything I have been through, after everything I have done, I was the only one who stood up to them, everyone else followed me. It only takes one to rise and that was me. I have killed for this movement, I have bled for this movement, I never gave an order that I wasn't prepared to do or hadn't done before.'

I can see Manny back away, like anyone, he can say the wrong thing and he knows that's exactly what he did at that point.

'That was wrong of me to say that, and I am sorry, but the fact remains, he could, at any time of come found you, he could have gotten away and got word to you that he was OK, that he was alive. Instead he chose to send some fake message to someone else and carry on regardless. He is a Zeta now if you go into the Vipers nest hoping to lure him out, then you're a bigger fool than I ever thought you were.'

'Don't you see,' I say, still not giving up. 'That's my point, he sent a message to that boy's mother, he didn't want her to think that her son was dead, doesn't that show you, that he isn't lost, that the same boy I raised — all on my own, still has good in him, that he is not passed over the brink.'

'No it doesn't explain anything, not to me. Your blindsided and I understand that and why that may happen, but just think to yourself, he may have done that for the reason you just gave, but why didn't he ever get word to you, tell me why you think that is?'

'Because I am the Black Widow.'

'Exactly my point and what I said back then, when you told me he was out there, in that camp. You're his enemy now.'

'I am going, you and Fidel can run the group and I will meet up with you another time,' I say. Manny's words make sense, he is right, I am blindsided, but that's a mother's love.

'No, Fidel is good enough to lead them, or Sofia, or both. I am coming with you; I will save you.'

'I don't need saving.'

'Yes you do — from yourself.'

***

A ghost town, my old barrio has been cleared of all the good that once lived there. Only the scum live here now. The streets a constant wash of garbage, literal and metaphoric. Narcos and Sicarios. Blank and lifeless faces observe the occupation of their neighbourhood. Generations of honest hardworking people, cast out of their homes; exiled by the occupying cartels. I visit the make-shift camp outside of the barrio. Disguised in a wig and glasses, I dress like I am ten years older than I actually am. Manny does the same. His name is as well-known as mine; Narcos fear him, they know his sort, they know how he operates and they fear him. I speak to no one, I know the faces of the people I walk amongst; I have been to church with them, celebrated with them, talked with them. They look lifeless, they look like ghosts. We sleep there, we stay there, mingle in amongst the many, we go into town, we don't attract attention, we blend in.

I see Alejandro driving his bus, I see him sleep in one of the tents in the camp. I want to approach him, to tell him I am sorry for the way it all turned out; with us, with everything. He was hurt when I told him I didn't want him anymore; he looks like one of the ghosts that haunt this town.

We check out the alleyways and the escape routes should we hit any difficulties. I check out the empty stores, all possible hiding places and observation points. Everything I do now is with military precision. Always searching for a vantage point, always an offensive or defensive tactic. We see a man stood at the rear of one of the stores. He is prizing a lock, a child with him carrying tools in his tiny hands, picking the lock. Manny and I take cover and peer from a distance. Once the lock is picked, the man turns in my direction. Flip, my god its Flip and Joaquin. I suddenly notice Febe and Tomas; they go into the store, followed by Joaquin and Flip, Febe keeping an eye on the door and the alley. She knows what she is doing; she looks like a consummate professional. Someone who has lost so much: a true fighter.

I am overcome with sadness at seeing the family I cared for, for so long, I missed them — I loved them. Good people, having to do bad things to survive, they had lost so much, yet they were still a unit. For survival, they had reached the furthest depths that they could possibly go. I know Flip; a proud man, reduced to stealing and using his children to help, all in the name of survival. I wanted to go to them, to speak with them, but I can't, not now. I watch them scurry away, like feral animals; it breaks my heart to see what this has done to so many good people, to my friends, to my family. Salvation: that is what I search for, and Luis is the only way for me to get my old self back. I am not a killer; that's not me, that's just what I have become, what fate has lead me to. A cruel twist of fate leads me down this path; now I have a redemptive path to take, save my boy, save my Luis.

The Zetas rotate in and out of the city, out of the barrio. I watch and study the patterns, the younger ones stay in the barrio, the sicarios, the older Zetas, generally take the city.

For weeks, we stay in the barrio; searching for Luis, where is he? when is he likely to turn up? We see Rojo; instrumental in all of this, I see. He is the leader of the younger ones. El Kilo, visits often. Two high value targets that we just can't risk taking out or being seen by. Every time I see either one of them, the rage in me fills, I just want to walk over and plunge my knife into their pitch-black hearts.

Eventually the time comes that I have been waiting for, after two months since I first laid eyes on him, watching that camp, I see him. Up close, he looks dreadful, his skin pale, sallow and jaundiced. The shaking hands and jittery tics of a junkie, his eyes are hollow, nothing there anymore. He is my boy in body only. My heart dies again, I relieve the day, when I was told that he was dead; over and over. I think about what he has done, what has he witnessed; what have they made him do? I know about the training camps, the cruelty, the abuse, the elders forcing themselves onto young boys, the suicide missions — everything. All learned along the way. Deep down, a part of me wishes that he had died, maybe then he wouldn't have had to go through all the things he has. How do you bring someone back from that? He is thirteen now, yet he still looks much younger: carrying a weapon, dressed in black; but still my Luis, I won't leave without him, I can't leave without him. We creep behind him, Manny swift and silent; his training has equipped him with the ability to take out any foe.

I stand back; Luis turns and looks directly at me, Manny manoeuvres in the turn — so to stay behind him, Luis doesn't even see it coming. He raises his weapon, Manny comes from behind, a hand across his mouth, arm twisted — weapon relieved. Luis is lifted from the ground, the hand stopping him scream, eventually used to stifle the air out of him, his legs kick frantically, they slow and come to a stop. He is unconscious, he drifts off. Manny carries him to a field adjacent to the east side of the barrio, we lay him down. He sleeps, he still looks my boy — my Luis. That same look he had, when I would come into his room at night and kissed him on his head while he slept.

***

'Luis, Luis, wake up, its Mama.'

I stroke his face, his eyes open, his face looking back at me. No smile, no recognition. I see the track marks on his arms, my heart breaks again. He says nothing, there is nothing behind the eyes, without warning he spits directly in my face.

'You slut, you whore, you fucking no good whore.' I can't believe the words, it's not him, he's possessed, it's not my boy. 'You fucking Black Widow slut-whore. You're dead — you know who I am, who my friends are, wait until I tell them you're here, they gonna rape you and cut you into a thousand pieces, they gonna pour acid into your eyes and your face, you and your whole crew, you bitch whore slut.'

He spits again, he opens his mouth to shout, Manny grabs his mouth and pins him down to the ground again, knife out this time, holds it against his throat.

'You say another word you little shit and it's you who gets cut up.' Manny looks up at me, he nods when Luis can't see, lets me know, it's just words. Manny removes his hand from Luis' mouth.

Luis looks at me again, 'What's this, another man again. You fucking this one now, you make me sick, you're a killer, just like this asshole — we know about you man, and we know all about her, you're dead, it's only a matter of time.'

I slap his face, I shouldn't have, I know I shouldn't have, it's not him, it's not Luis down there, it's another boy, a monster. Deep down inside, my boy is still there. He starts to cry; I reach over to him.

'Don't touch me, don't touch me.'

I lean into him, Manny holding his arm. 'It's OK, It's OK, we won't hurt you, I'm sorry I hit you.'

'You will be, you fucking bitch, you left me, this is your fault.' He sobs, he won't look in my direction, he sits on the ground, staring at the floor. Manny let go of his arm. He doesn't try and run, he doesn't fight or do anything, he just sobs.

'Come with me Luis, this isn't you, you're not one of them, I know you, you're a loving boy, someone who would do anything for anybody. I can get you out of here tonight, out of this city, far away from all of this.'

He doesn't move, he turns to see my face, the venom gone out of his face, the hatred he showed me has faded, he looks at me, I know he knows who I am, I know he is listening, please just say you will.

'I can't.' He replies to me; I know I can persuade him.

'What do you mean, of course you can,' I say, my heart sinks, trying to shift gear from killer to mother again, it's been so long, trying to get back to my old motherly ways, 'Luis, I love you and I know you love me, I am so, so sorry, but you have to know, I searched high and low for you, I went out of my mind, thinking you were dead, I tried everything to find you, you are my life, without you, this is what I become. I need you Luis, let's go, let's get out of her, you and me.'

I am desperate now, without a moment's thought, I sing to him, a song that I used to sing to him when he was small, to get him to sleep. An old song that my mother sang to me. My eyes fill with tears, for the first time in I can't remember, I am crying, my heart had turned to stone, believing that Luis was dead, I try everything I can. Luis is looking at me, his eyes also filled with tears, he smiles. Then he sings it back at me, just like that. From memory, he still remembers it. I hear him singing and it's like it should be, a childlike voice, that hard look on his face melts away, he looks like my boy again, his eyes warmer.

'No!' shouts Manny.

Without a breaking his stride, Luis has raised a pistol, Manny does, what Manny always does. The best he can, he knows that my world would end if Luis was hurt, he doesn't grab his arm, he isn't close enough, he stands in front of the pistol, all in a split second.

Bang, Bang.

Manny drops to his knees, then forward onto his face. My fault, Manny was right all along, as always. Pistol pointed at me now; Luis has stopped singing, face hard, eyes soft, still filling with water. I am dead, rather me than him. I turn around, Luis behind me now. I walk slowly.

'Don't take another step, I will kill you.'

'Then kill me, you were about to anyway, now you have time to think about it. Shoot your Mama in the back, kill me. I would rather be dead anyway.'

I keep walking, five yards, six yards. 'Stop, I said don't fucking move again, I swear it, don't fucking move.'

Seven yards, eight yards, nine yards.

'Mama!'

Bang, bang, bang.

Chapter23

San Fernando, Tamaulipas, Mexico

March 2011

Being back in my home-town feels strange, been away far too long. To that hell pit, far away from here. Little do they know; I am no Zeta. Fuck the Los Zetas, I fucking spit on you bastards. I curse them in my thoughts, in my sleep. Taken away from my wife, my beautiful wife and child. One day my sweet, I will find you again. I went away once before, I tell no one. I was once a Soldier, a real Soldier as well. I think back to the stories in school, the story of Troy and the Trojan horse — well that's what I am. The first chance I get, that evil little bastard with the tear drop tattoos dies. But not by my hand. I was there when Z30 was killed and I see him on the ground, shot, but still alive. I saw that evil little bastard pull his piece and take his head off, right at close range, a smile on his face as he did it. While the others were running around in the name of the Zetas, trying to protect their leader; I was stood by, watching, glad to see our leader on the ground in agonising pain. Anyone shoots him is a friend in my book. I see Rojo, he doesn't see me. I take out my cell phone and turn the camera on, I watched him pussy out before, I wanted everyone to see it for themselves. They think I am just some big, dumb lunk; all brawn and no brains, some peasant, who was good for dying for the Zetas. I intended to show that video of that little pussy and have him kicked out or killed or both, but I managed to catch a bigger fish, him executing his own leader. I got it, you bastard and when the time comes, everyone will know.

I aced the training camp; they suspected I may have been a soldier once.

'What's your name boy.' Said one of the instructors, as loud as he could into my face.

'Bruno Villalobos,' I replied.

'Where you from Bruno Villalobos.'

'From San Fernando, senor.'

'Do you want to Kill Gulf cartel.'

'More than anything in the world.'

'Outstanding, Villalobos, outstanding.'

And so, it went on — for weeks and weeks. While the others flagged, I got on with it, when they wanted to quit, I kept going, when the instructors pushed us to our limits, I pushed back. Not because being a Zeta is what I want, but because I must get back to my wife and child. All cell phones were taken from us when we arrived. We were stripped and checked for anything that we might bring back. I didn't know where the camp was, but on the journey, back to Tamaulipas, I noted the journey, my cell phone has all that information. I knew how to hide a cell phone, lodged perfectly in my ass: go hunting around up there motherfuckers. The strip search at the camp was just a basic pat down. Just need to find the right person to pass it onto. The Trojan horse, the one person who could bring these bastards down, but first, play it cool, play it steady. Get your wife and child to safety, make sure they are safe.

Before I got back here, I was sent to Nuevo Laredo. Missions to carry out, Gulf cartel to kill. I killed and killed and killed for them. Any of my so called fellow soldiers died by the side of me; I left the bastards; let them die, fuck them. Within weeks I was the number one shooter; my commander praised me and got word back to Z40 that they had found a true soldier, like the old breed. I was taken to Z40, where he praised my efforts and rewarded me with money. I didn't want money, so I secured safe passage for my wife, child and mother out of the state, get them over the border, into the US. That is the only gift I wish for, I am yours now, I will fight for you, I will die for you. I just want my family out of the way. Z40 was honoured over my loyalty and my wishes became reality. Within three days in February, they were over in Brownsville, safe and well and Z40's hideout was safely secured into my cell phone. Ready for another time.

Our new leader, El Kilo is a pure savage, mad and bad. He possesses a kind of madness that wouldn't be out of place within the Old Testament, he had a vision, one that he wanted to fulfil. All he wanted was to punish these people, exterminate the people of this town, he would froth at the mouth, when spitting this out in one of his drunken and cocaine induced eulogies. Like a preacher of hate, he would spit this out to his followers. His main disciple was Rojo. Rojo had finally found a kindred spirit.

He knew that the town was his; he had cops in his pocket, the town mayor marked for death. The thousands that had already fled this town after the massacre would not happen again. El Kilo was the one who orchestrated those murders, out of paranoia, out of belief that immigrants travelling to the US were in fact on their way to work for the Gulf cartel, all those people wanted was to cross over.

They sang songs about him. Z30 couldn't control him and sat back, while people like Rojo and El Kilo played out their desires, they wanted the power, they weren't interested in the money, they wanted to play god to the poor and forgotten. The same people who would reap the fury and madness. El kilo was not the only one; there were men above him as equally aggressive and as crazy. The head of the region is known only as El Wache, both El Wache and El Kilo were as mad as one another; both set up and executed the massacre in August.
As the month of March went on, plans were afoot, Plans made of mad men. Listening in on the conversations, it was how I imagined the Nazis sat down and planned their "Final Solution." The reasons were never explained, it didn't make any sense, but sure enough they were planning murder, on a mass scale. The details were incomprehensible, I could only pick up minor detail, but I certainly heard what I heard. How the targets were going to be selected was anyone's guess, Rojo was at the meetings, with El Wache and El Kilo, giggling like a fool, grinning like a deranged madman. They talked about it in tents, only higher ranking Zetas allowed, Rojo present because he led the boys. Maybe it was all talk, the ramblings of absurd deranged lunatics, who smoked too much crank and crack. Even though that was what I thought, it still played on my mind. I couldn't be part of that. I could serve my masters by killing equally deranged Sicarios who fought for the CDG — but not townsfolk, not the people I was raised with. Maybe this Trojan horse needed to get a little closer?

Patrolling the town; ashamed of my uniform, ashamed that I have become one of the aggressors, one of the occupiers. Knowing nods coming from stinking filthy pig cops, who I often saw at our camp, taking money, drinking and even sitting in on the "final solution" as I aptly named it. I had no one to share it with, everyone I associated with now, were either brain dead or just plain dead. All of them wrapped up in the ideology.

I see a man and his children scurrying through the streets, running from a store, carrying groceries, the children with armfuls of food in their arms. Some fat store attendant running out after them. 'That's the fifth time this week, you little runts, you filthy tramps, you come back again and I will tell the Zetas.' I walk over to him.

'What's up?'

'These filthy barrio peasants, fucking stealing from my store, I work for El Kilo now; aren't you supposed to do something in return.'

'I will tell you what I will do,' I say, 'I might open up your fat fucking mouth and put a grenade in it. I remember you, I know you. You were always a turncoat snide son of a bitch, who used to supply the CDG, when they were around. Maybe I tell El Kilo about that. Now you fuck-off back to your store and forget about it, or I pistol fuck your ass in the town square.' He swallows, he shits his pants, off he fucks, as ordered back to his store.

I go to the alley-way, where I see the man and his children scurry. They see me and get up, walk off slowly, trying not to attract my attention, they look back, they look scared. The man looks around, big beard, greying, hair longer than it should be, all over the place and thinning all over, I recognise that face, but it looks older now.

'Hey! hey you: stop,' I call out. They stand still and look at me, all of them look shell shocked, like they are about to be killed or something. I often forget what I represent now, I don't realise. 'It's Flip, isn't it? Flip Hernandez from the east side barrio?'

'Yes Senor,' he says, not recognising me, he looks thinner than I ever remembered; older, long coat on, eyes looking vacant, like he isn't quite fully there at the moment.

'It's me, Its Bruno, Bruno Villalobos, my father used to work with you, back at the local paper, many, many years ago, you remember.'

He looks at my uniform, although he doesn't say it, his expression and lack of eye contact says it all. Traitor to your people.

'Yes, yes I do.' The words, slow and nonchalant. He is afraid, afraid to speak to me, its people like him, like me who suffer. But these bastards found a place for me.

'Please sit down with me. I mean you no harm, I honestly don't. Look that trouble with the store keeper; I straightened it out for you. You can go into that store, take a shit on his nice polished floor, fuck his wife and then steal what you want; he still won't bother you again.'

I realise that my rather vile speech was conducted in front of children, I am not used to this, to being amongst family and friends, just other foul mouthed thugs all the time.

I sit down with him and tell him my story, how this came to be, how I came to be one of them. I even tell him of my plans; which is a dangerous move because that information is invaluable to the Zetas and by the look of him; money is something that he could do with. He starts to warm to me again and tells me of his time working with my father and the regretful incident where he was shot through the head in his office by a Sicario.

I miss my father so much, I was only a boy at the time, but I remember the funeral, people from all over the state came. I remember Flip being there, I remember seeing him mourn my father's death. After that we moved to the barrio, we didn't have the money any more to live in the more salubrious area of the city. I kept up my father's love for writing, I wrote for the school paper, but couldn't make it to college. I made it to the army instead.

Flip told me of what had happened to him, of what he had been up to since that day. How his wife had been murdered, he told me in intricate detail what had been going on in his life, and since I shared my secret with him, he shared his with me. The young girl and who she was, where she came from, what she had witnessed and what happened. We swore a pact, together at that moment, in that dirty alleyway, that we would not speak of each other's secret.

'You have to go Flip, get far away from here and you have to go soon.'

'Easier said than done, I am afraid, unless you have a spare car going for free, then I would take you up on that.'

'I will get you the money; meet me here in a week's time. I will get you enough money to get you all out, I swear.'

'I don't know Bruno; I am not one for charity you know.'

'Don't think of it as charity, think of it as a gift, something that I want to do, for you. You have had some tough breaks, had they not have happened, then you would have been out of here months ago. Promise me, one week from tomorrow.'

He nods at me.

I stay in the alley and then go wandering, not patrolling, but wandering through the city and then get a ride out to the barrio. I don't know anyone any more, they have all gone, all the houses belong to the Zetas now, all stash houses, shipments from floor to ceiling, protected by a team of Zetas all day, every day. All ready to ship to the US. I wander out to some of the deserted fields, fields I played in as a boy, when we moved here from the suburbs, I loved it; as kids we ran through these fields, they neighboured the houses and we would cut through gardens, being chased by the elderly men, who liked nothing more than complain about kids running riot. Better times, innocent time.

Bang, bang.

I see the bright flashes illuminate the vacant, I creep — moving slowly, maybe the shots were fired at me? Definitely gun fire. I move through the line of trees, heading toward the direction of the muzzle flashes. Oh fuck, oh shit, from the tree line, a Zeta kid, pistol raised a man face down in the dirt. A woman with her back to him, she slowly walks away, the boy telling her to stop.

The boy is still pointing the pistol at the woman; she is ignoring him; long hair, wearing oversized glasses; definitely not a Narco; maybe something else.

'Mama,' he shouts; she keeps walking. I run, I was always a fast runner, he is so fixated on her, he doesn't notice me coming, I have my gun trained on him, but the word 'Mama' sticks in my head.

Bang, bang.

I fire two rounds over his head. He falls backwards, and knocks his head on the ground. The woman runs back toward him. My pistol raised, she turns in my direction: 'Who the fuck are you!'

As I see her, I swallow my words, I know exactly who she is, she is screaming, shouting. 'You motherfucker, you killed him, you killed him, you killed my boy.'

I punch out; hit her straight between the eyes, the oversized glasses smashed, the wig falls off as she falls into the dirt. Her nose pours with blood, slows her momentum down, I strike her again, out cold. I tend to the boy; he is OK, but needs attention. As I tend to him, I process what the hell has just gone on, I know what I heard. I manage to calm him down. Better tie the crazy bitch up, I know her, by reputation and by name: Black Widow.

Luis, as I come to know him, is in shock, cold and still. I keep him still, she wakes up. She sees me holding him. 'He is going to be fine, but he is injured and I have to get him out of here, but not before you tell me what the hell is going on.'

'Fuck you, you cocksucker.' What a charmer, I think, I had heard that about her.

Again, twice in one day I have to tell her the whole story, but I don't think that I have endeared myself to her, this may take time, but I tell her everything and how; like the boy, I didn't have a choice, my family and the whole thing. Potentially dangerous when I let on to my enemy, exactly what my true intentions are. I tell her about my cell phone and what it has on it, what information I hold and if I were ever to find someone trustworthy, then I would hand it over to them. I tell her where I lived and about my father. She looks up at me, face looking less like she wants to kill me, but still with certain mistrust.

'So how did you end up in this predicament, tell me about the kid?'

'My son, he is my son.' She weeps.

'You got to get out of here, get far away from here. These boys are damaged goods now. There is no getting through to them. If you stay, he will surely tell them that you came. If they find out he's your son, then he dies as well.'

'I am not leaving without him, you don't know what I have been through, I am not leaving him here.'

'That's your call, but I got to get him out of here like right now, you want to storm the wire and kill everyone, do it another time, hopefully when I'm not there. I will square this away, leave it with me.'

She gets up, staring down at the boy, she leans over and kisses his cheek, he shudders, he is getting cold. She looks over at the lifeless body of the man lying face down in the dirt pile. I know him by reputation as well: The Jackal.

***

I get back to the camp and tell El Kilo and Rojo, what had happened. I tell them that the boy spotted some activity in the field and realised that one of the men was an Autodefensa, he was the Jackal.

'The kids a fucking hero,' shouts El Kilo. 'Get him some medical attention, right now, go get that body back, I want to see for myself.'

The minions run off and a few hours later come back, the Jackal on a stretcher. Photos taken, videos taken; a souvenir, his left ear cut off, El Kilo places it in his top pocket of his plaid shirt.

'That's why you can't trust these locals, they need to learn that there is only one king around here,' El Kilo grinning ear to ear as he studied his prize. Rojo comes into the hut, taking credit for training the boy.

'Yes, Luis is one of my finest, this just confirms what you already said, we need to hit back and hard.' Cryptic comments from two psychos.

For the next few days they tuck themselves away in meeting rooms, charts and maps out on tables. Commanders and team leaders present. No foot soldiers allowed. Within days, Rojo and El Kilo as well as a volume of Zetas leave the camp, word and rumour going about, something about some hi-jacking or some ambush; rumour and conjecture.

A week has passed and I find Flip and the children in the alley, as planned. They have food in their hands, this time no cursing or fat fucks chasing them. Being a Zeta has some merit I suppose? I stuff the wad of filthy drug money into Flip's hand. Blood money for killing Narco scum, a present from Narco scum.

'Look, the buses leave every day, heading north, along highway 101, night buses. Jump on one and get out of here, if you get stopped by Zetas, don't state that you're from here. There is enough spare money for them to take from you, they shouldn't bother you after that.'

Flip stares into his hand, stuffed with cash, flanked by his children, dressed in rags, looking tired and hungry.

'Thank you,' says Flip, looking down into his hands, he looks frail, he looks like he has seen the worst the world has to offer and then some. He scuttles off, children in tow. I wish them all the luck and say a prayer for them.

When I get back to camp, I check in on the boy, Luis as I now know him. He lies there, motionless, I see the track marks on his arms; lying there, looking back at me, bags under his eyes, eyes like something from an old china doll, like they have no life in them at all. I check no one is around.

'Kid, I didn't say anything, not a word, OK. The same goes for you. If they find out about you, you're dead, you hear me, nod if you understand.' He nods back at me.

'We got to get out of here as well, you and I don't belong here, we ain't like them. Tomorrow, we skip out of here, I can use one of the vehicles, move north, get to Laredo or somewhere like that, aim to get over the border, get word to your Mama — come on kid, answer me.'

He doesn't say a word; he just stares at the ceiling. Even if he wanted to run, he doesn't know how to anymore.

The next day I pull patrols around town and get back in the evening. I keep looking at my watch, eight thirty and Flip is out of here, good on him. There has been activity around the camp, but no sign of Rojo or El Kilo. For days now, they have been back and forth with squads of Zetas, all night every night, doing god knows what. Probably a good time to bounce. I go to the boy's tent — he's gone.

'Hey,' I shout to some numb-nuts who is about fifteen and trying to grow some rat hair on his chin around his acne, 'where's the kid?' my heart racing now, hoping he hasn't blabbed.

'Man, he is out on the highway, some other camp we got running out there, crazy shit goin' on over there.'

'What the fuck are you talking about? what the hell is going on?'

'El Kilo — he lost his shit, big time, wants to fucking punish putos who are disloyal, he been roundin' up motherfuckers, taking them out to the desert, straight off the highway, real old school shit.'

'What people? who are they?'

'Motherfuckers from the city, the barrios, people off the buses, he swears they the ones trying to overthrow us, believing that they enemies of ours, working for the Gulf carter, roundin' them up — man it's nothing like you ever seen before.'

I think of Flip, his family and my people, the people of this town, my old friends, people I worked with. Fuck, oh fuck, Flip is heading straight for it.

'What things, what are they doing to people.'

'Been doing it for days now, pulling buses and dragging them off, man sometimes dozens at a time, must be over eighty people now.'

The kid is buzzing with excitement, I want to strangle him, but I need him, he can tell me everything along the way. This sounds bad, those snippets of information I have picked up on, were in fact a plan, put in place by madmen.

'Take me there, NOW!'

Chapter24

San Fernando, Tamaulipas, Mexico

28th – 29th March 2011

The sun sets as we send the last of our balloons. My message is very simple and for once heartfelt, 'Deliver us from evil.' Tomas and Joaquin don't send it to their mother, they no longer live in the hope that she will return to them, they know she died protecting others, protecting children. She lived and eventually died for children. They write messages for Papa Antonio, of their excitement, to be finally leaving San Fernando, travelling to the border and crossing, somehow crossing to be with him, to be with the family they have left. They write to tell him of their Mama's brave deeds. Febe sends one as well, she doesn't tell us what she wishes for, she never does.

We board the bus, heading for Reynosa, Alejandro drives our bus, we chose his bus, I wanted to say goodbye to my oldest and best friend. But first we have to make our way along highway 101, the highway of death. No sooner do we board the bus and sit down, I notice Febe take Tomas's hand in hers. They sit together; she places her head on his shoulder. So, he finally told her of his feelings, my boy is growing up; he has found his first love. I feel a sense of happiness for him, but also that feeling of melancholy, selfishly because of my own personal loss. I know I will never find love like I had for Laena. I just want to remember her the way I do. I can't replace it or substitute it and I wouldn't even try. My family are what's important now. We have made it; we are finally leaving this place. As the bus pulls away from the station, I lean back in my seat, Joaquin places his head against me. We are tired, from fatigue, from the death and destruction that currently exist in this place. The good people are fleeing, the bad are taking over. I drift off into sleep, the rumbling vibration of the bus act as a soothing medium.

I am once again with Laena, Tomas and Joaquin are playing with her, as she gathers them up in her arms and twirls them around. My cognitive senses come into play, I can feel the warm summer breeze, hear birds chirping, the smell of freshly cut grass and taste her lips when I kiss her. Just like I always remembered. In dreams I find my own private island; a place where I am happy and content. No matter where we flee, no matter where we land there will always be a piece of me that is empty. For a long time now, I have lived in the belief that one day Laena may come back to me, that perhaps she was alive and maybe just lost. I want to keep the dream alive, I never want it to end, I am with Laena, I am with the boys, we are happy again, we don't feel pain, we have not suffered. Febe has now become part of the dream, she is with Laena and the boys, playing and laughing. For many months now, my dreams have evaded me; my thoughts have been irrational and displaced. As I watch her, I wonder if she held me responsible, although I am dreaming, I subconsciously think that Laena must blame me. I blame myself day in and day out. She looks at me tells me that everything will be OK. In dreams a man can find redemption, can find peace and amity.

In my dreams, we are young again and the rest of the world is otherwise forgotten. There is no pain or fear or violence. Happiness is unilateral, nothing can penetrate this feeling, no outside influence can disturb us. It's just us. We occupy a world where there are no Narcos, no gangs, and no killings. It's like living in a Mexico that we once knew and loved. We play and dance and the children look so happy, this moment is without replication. My private Island.

I dream of when I When I first saw Laena. I knew she was a step above the rest of the girls. Her father Antonio had a reputation for hard work and high standards and morals. Laena was cut from the same cloth. She was a rancher's daughter, unafraid to get her hands dirty and work hard. She didn't conform to the usual stereotype held for women of such beauty. I knew this, so in no way was I going to bullshit her with fancy talk and caddish one liners. Be myself, but not be too much like myself. This woman was regal; from my point of view and I had to talk to her because it was one of those moments in time, if I didn't speak to her, then I would regret it for a lifetime.

I fell in love for the very first time that night. I stayed in love with Laena from that night onwards. That first night I didn't want it to end. We talked all night, about where we grew up, where we went to school, plans for the future, family and upbringing, which I skirted over somewhat. When Laena asked me to join her at a table for a drink, my heart skipped. She looked radiant; I can still picture that long black dress with her hair worn down, like it was yesterday. We talked for hours, and when the crowds of people got up to dance, Laena asked if I would join her. We danced and laughed, namely because of my lack of coordination and the fact that short stumpy boys from the Eastern barrios of San Fernando move with the grace of a Sherman tank.

At the end of the evening when I asked if I could see her again, she paused. I hung at her word thinking at any moment that I had misjudged the situation and that she wasn't interested in me at all; perhaps she pitied me or wanted to make some of the other boys at the dance jealous. When Laena said 'I would like that very much,' I knew that she was the one, and I swore from that moment on I would take care of her and love her forever.

The brakes of the bus squeak, the bus jolts forward, the momentum causes me to wake up in a state of panic. I recognise, even without opening my eyes that the bus has stopped suddenly and the only reason can be something has caused it to stop. With animal instinct I sense danger; I come too and look down the aisle, toward the large windshield and beyond. We are on the highway, highway 101. I can see headlights, across the road, a road block. Hopefully federal police, probably state or municipal, checking ID's and taking money off people travelling, maybe even Zetas looking to rob passengers. Don't panic, don't panic, don't panic. Get some money from the bag; place the rest where you can safely hide it without being rumbled. Hand it over without protest, after the Zetas have robbed us all, we can travel again, maybe we get robbed again along this road, but soon, we will leave this highway, get on the road for Reynosa. Pay the coyote to get us across the border, get to Antonio's ranch, and live happy long lives.

'Shit,' I hear Alejandro say, 'stay calm everyone, everything will be fine, just do as they ask and no one will be hurt, they probably just want our valuables, please don't do anything to anger them, just do as they ask.'

'They?' I call down to Alejandro, 'who are they?' I touch Joaquin, who grumbles and pushes my hand away.

'Los Zetas, about a half dozen, they have blocked the road, they are probably just after money.' Cool, calm and conservative, Alejandro, always the consummate professional, 'Please, everyone just listen. No heroes, just do as they say.'

Voices start to grumble and I hear panic overcome the passengers. The sounds of people pulling items from their bags and pockets. I reach forward and stir Tomas and Febe, they wake and look about the bus; they too can sense panic, sense danger. They have lived life as feral children for months now, their senses finely tuned.

Alejandro sits and watches the side opening door of the bus; only he can really make out what is going on. I stay seated; Febe and Tomas look back at me. Both have that look on their faces, they are terrified, they know that there is no escape from this bus, we are trapped.

'Papa,' says Tomas, his voice breaking and panic stricken.

'Don't worry, stay calm and stay still, it's OK my son, nothing is going to happen, they are probably after money, I have some for them, we will get to Reynosa in no time and then into Texas, please don't worry, it will be OK.'

I touch both on the head and then look down at Joaquin; he seems oblivious to it all. I feel omniscient in the knowledge that our situation has just become that much worse; the passengers cannot surely know how in danger we truly are. My heart pounds, I look about the bus and the faces of everyone now tell me that they have read the situation to be a dire one. Child passengers cower into the laps and arms of their parents, parents looking visibly panicked. I look to my left side and notice a small girl, she looks at me, I give her a smile, one that I hope tells her everything will be OK. I try the same with Febe and Tomas, but they are wily enough to know that we are in grave danger. Maybe it's just a robbery, but the Zetas have more money and power than I can fathom, maybe that's the question that niggles me and everyone else on the bus. Why us, why people like us. We are not part of your war; we are merely the casualties of it.

I see Alejandro looking toward the closed door of the bus, he switches the engine off. From outside I hear: 'Open the door asshole, move it you son of a bitch, unless you want me to shoot you.'

I see Alejandro's shaking hand raise and pull the lever to the door, it opens. A black clad Zeta boards the bus, machine gun pointed at Alejandro; he points it down the aisle, machine gun trained upon us. He looks wired, crazy eyes, a wry grin. Behind him, more gunmen embark, forcing the first Zeta closer towards us.

'You are all fucked,' he yells. The silence is now broken and the crying and panic that was once contained, has now overcome the passengers. The sounds of pleading and begging, prayers to god that will remain unanswered, echo throughout the bus. Children screaming and clinging to parents. Familiar sounds; sounds that the Hernandez family know all too well. Passengers offering money and jewellery, begging comments shot down with the comment of, 'we will take your shit anyway.'

Febe and Tomas, jump over their seats and sit with Joaquin and I. All of them huddled down, arms wrapped tight around each other, the sobbing played down, so not to attract too much attention, but the fear is uncontainable in them. I sit in resolute acceptance, my mind counting to ten, calm myself and think of a way to get out of this. What are my options? How can I save the children? What are they likely to do to us? While it seems obvious, I remain as calm as my subconscious will allow, study the Zetas on-board this bus, who looks like they could be corruptible or maybe so smashed that I could try and overpower one and mow the rest down with his machine gun? how many passengers would be killed? Would I inadvertently get my own children killed? My options seem limited and above all, I am a coward, someone who will no doubt quake and just accept my fate as it now stands.

'Drive the bus where we tell you and only where we tell you,' says the first Zeta, he looks and sounds like he is in charge. Alejandro starts the engine and pulls away. The vehicles in the road pull away, to allow the bus to pass, from the rear window; I see their headlights on the black highway night sky follow us.

'Turn down there,' shouts the lead Zeta, Alejandro pulls the bus onto a dirt road, a bumpy old deserted road, the Zetas keep a watchful eye on us, paying no attention to anyone but ensuring its cargo gets to the right place. The dim lights of the bus go out. My eyes become accustomed to the night.

The children squeeze tighter to me, as I look around, the road shows no sign of life, no one around to alert the police or the army or anyone. I then realise what I am thinking, there is no one to save us, the police are as much a part of this as the Zetas. The army don't come out here anymore; we are at the mercy of our enemy. Through the darkness, the sobs and crying can be heard, the softly spoken prayers for salvation heard in tandem. I can't help, but think that we are doomed to never leave this road alive.

Joaquin huddles into me, he hates the noise, he senses that there is danger, I see his little hand pushing his screwdriver and hammer into his cargo pants. All I can think of is how his mind must be working. Joaquin rationalises his situation, that they are likely to steal his beloved tools. I don't answer him; I squeeze him tighter to me. I feel my eyes well-up, my mouth starts to quiver, the highway is disappearing from the horizon, the depths of hell wait for no man.

***

The bus drives for what feels like an eternity, the road becoming more and more uneven, giving the impression of desolation, no one would even care to come down here, what reason would anyone ever take this road. I look out of the window, the desert landscape shrouded in darkness, if they were going to kill us outright, then why go this far, why continue down this road?

The Zetas say nothing, they don't laugh or joke with each other, they don't even move from their positions within the aisle of the bus. The only sound comes from the engine of the bus, delivering us to our fate. The chassis of the bus rattling and shaking as the shock absorbers fail to prevent the bus jumping about and throwing the startled and scared passenger around in their seats. No one dare speak or address the Zetas. Maybe it is a robbery and they just want to take us off the road? maybe they just want the bus itself? dump us off, take our belongings and leave us to the mercy of the treacherous highway. It has happened this way before, I remember Alejandro telling me about it. We are not immigrants, not like those passengers in August of last year, we are Mexicans, I keep telling myself, trying to rationalise the situation, filling my head with answers to my own questions.

The bus descends into a dip in the road and struggles to make its way up the incline, I estimate we have driven for around thirty minutes along this road, we are now reaching some form of higher ground. I look toward the front of the bus; I see lights again. Not street lamps or the headlights of oncoming traffic, but fire, what looks like burning oil drums, off into the distance? The bus drives towards its conclusion, this is the place, time to focus, observe the surroundings, where are we? Is there any way of escape? Why are we taken here?

As the bus comes to a halt, Alejandro is removed from his seat and the door is opened, being near the rear of the bus, I still can't make out what is waiting for us here. From the front, passengers are pulled out of their seats and out of the bus.

'Move it, get the fuck up,' Zetas pulling passengers out of their seats. My children cling tighter to me, I can't let go of them, I won't let go of them. What in god's name is this place?

From the open door, I can hear voices and laughter and Narco music blaring out. As the passengers are unloaded I can hear commands coming from the people waiting outside. Eventually it's our turn to get up.

'Get up, get out of your fucking seats, move it puto.'

A hand grabs Tomas and pulls him up, he is crying and holding on. I can't stand up, with the weight of Febe and Joaquin, still clinging onto me, at the same time, passengers to my sides are struggling also. Febe takes Tomas's hand and I stand, tightly gripping Joaquin's small and trembling hand.

We shuffle to the front of the bus. 'Do as they say children,' I say aloud, voice remaining calm and controlled, don't panic, don't try and sound panicked, just try and keep the children calm, keep them safe. As we stumble from the bus, there are Zetas everywhere, dozens of them, drinking cervezas from bottles and tins, women embraced in the arms of their heroes, laughing and pointing at us. Stumbling around and drunk, shouting obscenities; passengers lined up ready to view their entertainment.

I can see four other buses, just like the one we have been taken from. One of them is riddled with bullet holes, windows blown out, congealed blood poured from the foot step of the passenger door onto the dust covered ground. From complete darkness, now into unbearable light of the burning oil drums, my eyes are strained. I hold onto the children as we are pushed to line up, next to our buses. I see a barn of some kind, music blaring out of it, Zetas pouring in and out of it. It's a fucking party; the bastards have taken us so they can entertain themselves.

The line of passengers cry and beg for their lives, the child who was seated next to us, clings to her mother's dress, her dark hair across her tear-covered face. I look down at my own children, Joaquin stands with his hands over his ears, trying to block out the noise that startles him, scares him, and confuses him.

Tomas and Febe stand together, Febe's hand grips his, I see Tomas look at her, 'It will be OK, please don't be scared.' The same words that I would use — even when it's hopeless, he tries to comfort her.

I see Febe turn and face her aggressors, once again, she is in the belly of the beast, this poor girl has endured so much and by some cruel twist of fate has ended up back in the hands of the Zetas. She wipes her eyes and turns toward Tomas and I. She gives a faint smile, in acceptance that she will face whatever is likely to come.

Away from the barn, is a smaller animal shed, the door is open; it's a walk of about twenty metres, from the doorway of the main barn, I see a familiar face, teardrop tattoos pouring from each eye, three rows, down to his neck, hands and arm covered in blue and black ink. That pointed thin nose, that wide grin. He walks towards us, he stands next to the adult Zetas who took us from the highway, further down the line another adult Zeta arrives. Rojo, the Zetas junk-yard dog. He is jumpy, an eerie sense of excitement in his demeanour. It can mean only one thing?

'Commander Forty,' shouts one of the Zetas, 'how do you like these miserable motherfuckers.'

He walks up and down the line, observing each of us, looking us over. He was pure military style, dressed in black military regalia of the Zetas. The younger Zetas appeared to be in awe of him, especially Rojo He paces up and down the line of terrified passengers. 'Let's see assholes. Who wants to live?'

No one of us answer him, he approaches a young boy at the far end of the line and looks down toward the front of his pants, oh Jesus, the poor boy has wet himself, he is shaking and crying. Commander Forty, pulls out a pistol and shoots him in the forehead. Tomas and Febe begin to tremble.

I look down at them and whisper, 'not now, hold it in please.'

I can feel the tears stream down my face as my voice breaks. Oh no, not my boy, please not my boy. Tomas props himself up again and wipes his eyes. He looks straight ahead. Zetas are being directed to separate us, I hear the words I have been expecting and dreading all along.

'Take the women and the children away, just leave the boys and the men.'

The Zetas, in numbers begin to pull the women away from the line. They are pushed into a huddle and face the men. Men cry out for their wives and girlfriends, the children cry out for their mothers. Febe is taken out of the line and pushed toward the group, Tomas squeezes her hand and she looks at him. No tears, no crying, she looks in acceptance of her fate — whatever that may be?

'No please, she is not a woman, she is too young,' says Tomas, the Zeta back hands him across the mouth.

My fists clench in anger, I look at Febe, she looks back at me and I see her mouth the words, 'Don't worry about me.' She smiles at me and is thrown amongst the huddle of crying and hysterical women.

'No Tomas, don't do or say anything, she is OK.' I knew that wouldn't be the case, these fucking animals would violate them all.

The children are next, pulled out of the line into a group, Joaquin is grabbed from me. 'No, no wait, let him go — you motherfucker! no, not my boy, no you lousy fucking pig!'

I grab the shoulder of the Zeta and swing him around to face me, two others stand in front of me, guns pointed at my head, Joaquin is taken and led towards a group of crying children, all hysterical, all crying out for their Mama's and Papa's.

I am held against the side of the bus by my sentries, I take a blow to the stomach and lurch forward, I end up face down on the ground, boots on my hands, one boot-sole pushing my face into the dust, Tomas shouting for Joaquin; cries coming from Febe. We are all separated. Within myself I find a strength that I never knew I had, the strength that comes when you have nothing to lose, when the survival of your entire family depends on it, I pull my hands out from the boots that pin me down, skin pulled from the knuckles, I push my hands into the dust-laden ground and push myself up. Zetas falling away from me — super human strength I never knew I possessed. I get myself into a standing position in order to charge, I don't care what's there: machine guns, knives, pistols — I will not let you take my boy, he is scared, he is young — not my little boy. I feel my voice turn into a roar rather than any scream, I am up — a rifle butt strikes me in my back and my legs. I feel hands grab my collar and I am again back against the bus. I look in the direction of where the children were lined up; they are being led away, toward the small shed. The children are crying and looking towards their parents, not knowing what will happen to them, not knowing what they are likely to endure themselves. I see Joaquin at the back of the line, he takes the hand of the girl who clung to her mother's dress, the little girl is crying; Joaquin's face expressionless, he holds her hand and walks with her — off to their fate, even in his last moments, he tries to comfort a scared child. Selfless as always, my boy.

I try and break free, I am crying, in the knowledge that this is the last time I will see him alive again. Joaquin walks off, not knowing and having no comprehension at all of what is about to become of him, I am glad of that, I would hate to think of him being alone and scared. I pray to god, that it's quick, that he doesn't see it coming, sleep tight my little boy.

'You bastards, you murdering fucking puke, you fucking murdering godless motherfuckers.' I shout, not caring anymore, not scared, wanting to rip the throat out of the nearest Zeta I lay my hands on.

Commander forty stands in front of me, Rojo by his side.

'How very exciting,' he spits. Rojo lifts a rifle and smashes me to the temple. Light headed, falling, deep darkness where I don't dream of Laena and the family that once was.

***

Papa's head reels back against the bus, blood coming from the side of his head, he falls forward, his body rigid, he hits the ground like a boxer hitting the canvas. He doesn't move, Rojo stands there laughing, the gun is pointed at me, I look over to the huddle of women, who are holding one another now, an hour ago, they never knew each other, never even spoken to one another, but now they held each other for fear of what was going to happen next.

I look at Febe, she stands there looking back at me, it's a look that tells me that I wouldn't see her again, she doesn't cry, she doesn't even look afraid anymore. The women cry out for their children who are walking in a line, they too are crying in return for their parents. Except for Joaquin, he is holding the little girls hand; it looks strange to see these crying faces and one that is totally without any emotion. Maybe he doesn't understand? maybe he does? If I know Joaquin and his temper, when they try and get him to do something he doesn't want to, he will give them hell. Short and barrel like, he is strong and can be very difficult to handle. He carries on walking, focused on holding the girls hand while they are led into the small barn.

As the gun points at me, I am in a state of helplessness, I don't know what to do, who do I help? Papa lies on the ground, I don't know if he is dead or unconscious? Febe is about to be killed or raped or god knows what? and Joaquin, maybe he will suffer a similar fate? Febe looks at me, her eyes are a calming influence, it's almost like she knows me too well, she knows I am scared and her look tells me that it will be OK, to remain calm, despite my entire world has hit rock bottom. My family is being torn apart in front of my very eyes.

My heart is pounding, I can feel the rush inside, wanting to fight my way out, rescue Joaquin, rescue Febe, save Papa. Seconds feel like hours, Rojo is staring right at me, his eyes begin to squint, I can tell that he recognises me, maybe from the barrio, maybe from when he came to school that time and kidnapped those kids; but why would he care anyway, we are just people to murder for his entertainment. I wipe my eyes, I look straight at him — fuck him, fuck the little runt bastard. What have I got to lose now, maybe I should just call him Gael, right in his face, spit in his eye and have it done with.

'I know you,' says Rojo, 'you're the boy from the canteen, the one who looked at me.' I don't know why he would remember me. 'I have an opening for you, I knew from the first moment I saw you, that you would make a fine addition to my crew, bet you want to kill me right now puto, especially after I hit your old man down there.' He kicks Papa in the side, a murmur, a sound comes from Papa, he is alive, just done in.

'Why me,' I say, too scared to tell him to fuck off.

'Do you see what we are doing here, little man. This is a recruiting station, it's like the fucking army, they conscript people, so do we. You go with the men, you're tall, you're young, you could beat any of these pussy old motherfuckers and join us.'

I don't understand what this crazy bastard is talking about, probably talking crazy as usual.

'I heard you're a bright boy, very smart, going to be big when you get older, you're going to be an asset. Don't you fucking dare pussy out or say no, you see what Commander Forty did, just because that kid pissed his pants.'

It hits me as I see the line of men being told to make their way onto the large barn, where the Zetas seem to be hanging out. The women are also led in through the same way.

'I saw a girl with you, that day in the canteen, she was sat with you, where is she now.' I remain silent.

'I don't know, what girl?'

No sooner had I said it, quick as a flash a knife is pressed at my throat.

'Don't ever fucking lie to me — not ever. You're fucked my man, you have the choice, talk or die right now. I will gut you like the peasant fool you are".

'Over here,' shouts Febe. She must have overheard him; I don't know how through the sounds of the screaming and crying and that fucking Narco music?

The two lines of men and women are led into the barn separately, Rojo signals to the young Zetas to leave us here. He puts us next to each other, trains the rifle on us both. One young Zeta stays with Rojo to keep watch over Febe and me. The line reluctantly moves away, the passengers terrified of what will happen in that barn. Rojo stares at Febe, he steps closer to her, his face in hers. That grin of his disappears, his eyes begin to soften, he gives her an awkward smile. Febe turns her head, so she doesn't face him. He takes grabs her with one hand around the jaw and pulls her face within an inch of his.

'Don't fucking sass me, you know who I am? Bitches don't ever turn away from me, when I am talking,' he hisses at her as he says it, spitting over her face, with every word that comes from his mouth. 'You don't have choices anymore; we have taken them away from you. You're either mine, or you're fucking dead, but not before the boys run a train through you, you hear that OK?'

Febe nods, it's the only way to survive at the moment, extend our chances of survival at every cost.

'What about my brother?' I say, 'We will do anything you ask, but what about him? Please, please bring him to us.'

Rojo turns and hits me in the stomach, I crouch, the wind taken out of me, I struggle to breath, the pain shoots through to my back, I can hear laughter from the boys who have now joined him.

'Don't think I don't know what you're up to, little puto, don't think I don't know you or your family. I grew up in the same barrio as you, that fucking dead beat on the ground is Flip Hernandez, your bitch whore Mama bailed out on you, because you're all worthless fucking dead beats, stupid kids and a fucking pussy for an old man, no wonder she got the fuck out when she did.'

I can feel myself well-up, but this time with anger as well, the pain keeps me on my knees, 'you don't have choices, or are you fucking deaf, you both come with us and join us, the bitch as my "whenever fuck", whenever I want to fuck you, you drop them panties and I get to fuck you and you. You little shit — you get to clean my boots, clean my weapons, feed my dogs, wipe my ass. Now GET THE FUCK UP!'

I stand, holding my belly. The boys kick Papa, who grumbles and eventually lifts his head, blood down his face, temple to his jawline, matted in his hair and around his left ear.

'My boy, where's my boy?' Papa says, he stands and stumbles.

'Save it old man, save it for the tournament.'

Papa looks at me and Febe 'Where is Joaquin? what's going on? Are you hurt? What is going on? Where's Mama? What the hell…'

His face looks confused, he turns and faces the Zetas, he looks at them, like it's the first time he ever saw one before, he stumbles and jolts around, his eyes are wild, he can't get the words out, he stops in his sentence and has seemed to forgotten what he was talking about and what had happened before he was hit in the head. Why the hell would he mention Mama?

'Move it!' shouts one of the young Zetas and hits Papa in the back, Papa turns and faces him, that look of surprise and confusion, his eyes beady and squinting, like he doesn't know what is going on. He probably has concussion; he makes snorting sounds, like a pig and turns away from the Zeta. What the hell is he playing at? he then starts jumping up and down, lightly on the spot, moving his arms and legs, like an athlete preparing for a sprint, he starts gurning and twisting his face, then stops and stands still and moves with us, almost like he has come to his senses.

'Come on move it!' Shouts one of the boys, Rojo holds onto Febe's arm and leads her towards the entrance of the barn, I can see her trying to move wide, keeping herself away from Rojo's body, it's obvious that he repulses her.

'Move it, move it,' Papa repeats and giggles like a child, then suddenly stops and I notice his eye starts to twitch, my god I hope that he gets to his senses quicker than this. As we move closer to the doorway, my stomach starts to turn, I taste bile in my mouth, I want to puke. As we enter the main barn, it's full of Zetas, one big guy in the middle, closely shaved head, goatee, scars on his face. Everyone hanging around him, he waves over at Rojo and Rojo pokes his tongue out and looks at Febe, he makes obscene gestures with his tongue at her, making sure this guy sees it. The guy doesn't, he turns away to speak with the man I now know as Commander Forty. Cops are stood around, mixing it up with these bastards, fucking state police, still in uniforms, the one with the mirrored sunglasses watches as we are led in, like stray cattle for slaughtering. He looks, but doesn't laugh, or smile or do anything. He turns away and talks to another cop, like we are not even there.

It's hotter than hell in here, towards the far end of barn there is a separate room, like a cattle hold. The women from the bus are now being pulled inside, they scream, Zetas pulling them in, slapping and punching them. The women are holding onto whatever they can, so not to get pulled in. I look away; I can't look any longer, only evil things happen here. The men are on their knees, looking on as their wives and daughters and siblings are being taken off to be playthings for these evil bastards.

I am placed with the men, Rojo stands with Febe, tightly holding onto her arm, every now and then looking at her, looking at her in a way I don't like one bit. I can tell, he wants her, but not in a tender way, like I want her. The Zetas come forward and gather around the men, Commander Forty calls for quiet, everyone listens in, the only sounds are those coming from that room at the back of the barn, awful cries for help and mercy, sounds of voices begging for them to stop. Words I know I will never forget, no matter how long I live.

'I will ask you all one more time, who the fuck wants to live.' Commander Forty shouts at the line of men, I notice some other men behind us, they look haggard, they were not on our bus, they must have been earlier passengers. Dried blood and pieces of flesh still on the ground, an awful smell, coming from a circle that has been drawn on the ground in white chalk, most of the chalk is blood stained. A Zeta enters the circle and empties a bag of hammers, baseball bats, knives, swords and iron bars; each weapon has blood on them. Every man raises his hand; everyone wants to live.

'Good,' says Forty, 'we will test your abilities to see how capable you are. If you make it, you'll survive; if you do not, you're fucked.'

I already knew what was coming next, I had heard the stories, heard Maria tell us about Luis, what had happened to him. I looked on the ground at the blood covered weapons; I puked on the ground, to a roar of laughter from the Zetas.

'Look, each of you will get into pairs and beat the shit out of each other. Those who survive will work for Los Zetas, those who don't, well they're fucked.'

A man from the bus leaves the line and drops to his feet, he is elderly, he begs Forty not to have to do this, he offers money and his watch, anything to get away.

'Go then, you asshole, leave,' says Forty.

I know what's coming, the man turns quickly heading for the door, Forty picks up a club, from the pile of weapons and takes a full swing, placing the club in the centre of the back of the man's head, he goes down, Forty raises the club above his head and brings it down again and again and again. Blood takes flight as the man's skull cracks wide open, we all look away; Forty drives the bat into the wide-open skull ensuring that the brain is totally crushed. He then strikes over and over and over. When the beating stopped, I looked back and saw that the elderly man's head was now just a mush of skull, brain and blood — nothing left. Forty was completely coated; his face now bore the colour of El Diablo.

The message was clear, Zetas began pulling some of the much older men out of the two lines and took them to another part of the barn and made them form another line, guns were raised, the men each raised their hands in prayer, to beg for their lives, sound of the gunfire rang through the barn and through my ears — bodies fell. The Zetas reloaded and fired some more. No one would ever get out of that one.

We were given five minutes to select our partner, in order to fight. I could see men heading towards me. They would pick me, because I am young and weaker than them, they stood a chance. One man approaches me and declares he wants to challenge me. Papa took hold of me and pulled me against his chest.

'Fuck off, this is my boy, you don't get to kill my boy, go find yourself some other child to butcher, you fucking coward.'

The man promptly left, Papa had a look on his face that no one would mistake as being anything but serious about his threat. Even in times of shear desperation such as this, the man would rather take his chances, than be killed outright by Papa; he looks insane, with the blood over his face, his overgrown grey and black beard and wild twitching eye.

A man comes over to Papa and me. He looks older than Papa, a shock of grey hair and beard, tears in his eyes, his face looking as though he had seen all the horror that the world had to offer. He leans in close to us.

'Senor,' he addresses Papa, who literally snarls at the old man, 'put me up against your son, I — '

Papa takes the old man by the collar: 'I will fucking kill you, you come anywhere near my boy, you fuck, I swear to — '

'You don't understand, 'says the old man, tears in his eyes, that same broken look on his face that every innocent man in this place possesses, 'I don't want to hurt your boy, far from it. I am Raul, my wife and daughter were taken away from me a few days ago, to the same place the women from your bus were taken. I haven't seen them since.' It was hard to hear him over the roar of the Zetas in the barn, they were pushing people to pair up to fight, money being laid out on the ground, betting taking place, they were gambling over our lives. 'They took my grandson — took him to that shed, the one outside.' The man breaks down; Papa takes a hold of him again, and tries to shake him back to telling his story.

Papa leans in closer again. 'What is in that place, where they took your grandson".

Raul breaks down; the Zetas are looking at their watches, counting down the five minutes. 'I heard these bastards — laughing and joking about what they did to the children, from the bus.'

'Come on, please just tell us, we don't have time, my boy is in there.' Papa is flexing the fingers of his right hand as he does this, like he has cramp or something.

'They were locked in cages, while the Zetas poured acid into large oil drums, they then threw the children in one by one, they made the children watch, you could hear the screams from in here, oh god, oh Jesus, I just want it to be over.' He grabs a hold of me and looks into my eyes, I can't control myself now, I am so scared — not Joaquin, not that way, not like this, not in this evil place. Raul looks back at Papa and says, 'Senor, I will pair off with the boy, I swear to the almighty, that he will get out of here, I wouldn't hurt a fly — especially a boy, just get out of here, do what you have to do.'

Papa looks at me, 'don't be scared Tomas, we have to do this, I will be watching you.' Papa turns towards Raul, 'you harm my boy in any way, I am taking you out.'

Papa's eye twitches again, the right side of his face drooping, maybe the shock of everything recently has just taken its toll again, maybe he is going mad. I have never heard him threaten anyone like this before, even with Bertrand, I felt as though it was idle threats, but now he looks ready to kill.

'I promise you senor, nothing will happen to your boy. Godspeed to you Tomas.'

I look about the barn; the pairs are slowly getting together. Each picking up a weapon. Raul picks up a knife for each of us. He smiles again and then signs the crucifix across his chest. He looks up toward the roof, looking for god. God Is not here. Everyone looks ready to fight or as ready as anyone could possibly be. My hands are shaking, although I know that Raul has promised that he wouldn't fight back, I am frightened of killing him — I don't want to kill anyone, I am twelve years old, I am a boy, a child. Children shouldn't have to do this.

Papa moves away and looks for a partner. Stood behind him is Alejandro. Alejandro smiles at Papa. 'Looks like you and me old buddy.'

'Looks like you and me old buddy,' Alejandro looks at me with a wry smile. He looks hazy, my eyesight is blurred, head all fucked up, noises from this unholy gathering pierce through my brain. Woozy — dizzy — hyped up. Not feeling right, that knock on the head had best sort itself soonest. I rock on my feet, balance all over the place. Feeling like I want to crack some fucking heads! Not like me at all, what the fuck is going on with me? Alejandro passes me a bat, I reach for it, but it's all fucked up, I am seeing two bats, I reach for the imaginary one. Come on, come on, get yourself together. Oh no Joaquin, my boy, where the hell is he? I can't see any further than about twenty feet. Can't make out the girl, what's her name again? You dumb stupid fuck, its Febe, its Febe, what's going on with you. Snap out of it.

I look around for that fuck, who approached Tomas, wanted to take on my boy did you, you fuck — I will crack you wide open, Peasant motherfucker, yeah come on, come get some, come get … Alejandro looking at me, concentrate on his face, what's he saying? Tears in his eyes, holding the bat by his side. I think I have to fight him, not sure what the guy said, I see my old man, my father stood in the crowd, can't see shit all else, but I see him.

'Come on Flip, you little fat waste of fucking oxygen, what you gonna do, your worthless, you ain't shit.'

I look away from him — Laena stands in the crowd, watching, I knew she would come back to me. 'The boys,' she says, 'don't lose the boys.'

Fuck it, fuck it all. 'Fuck it all.' I shout it out, why did I say it? I am losing it, got to focus — I get up close to Alejandro, can't make out what he is saying, the noise is piercing through my ear drums, head feels like someone is sticking something sharp right through it. I seem my Father and Laena, stood in the crowd, watching over me, I close my eyes — try and shake it away.

'You and Tomas, together, you get to that Zeta camp, that's your only chance to get away.' Alejandro says to me, struggling to hear him over the noise coming from this place.

'We can all go together; all get the hell out.' I say.

'No,' says Alejandro, the look on his face says it all, I may be fucked up, but the message is clear. 'Only room for you two on that bus ride out of here, I think I made my last one tonight. I can't deal with this anymore, I seen what they are capable of.'

What the hell is he saying, he is talking shit again, when the hell has he seen anything.

'You're talking shit again, what the hell have you seen. It's me who is all over the place, yet you're the one talking like some kind of Quaker after his first whiskey chaser,' even now, I can't help injecting some humour. I don't feel scared anymore, I feel hyped up, like I could take on the world.

'When they capped those Guats and Salvadorians last year, I was there, I was one of the drivers, they pulled them from my bus. I let it happen, I didn't say shit, they told me I would be dead if I ever told anyone, the same bus that Febe was dragged from. They let me go, they let me live.'

I look at him, I study him, the best I can at the moment. He is crying, tears now streaming down his face.

'I done the worst thing imaginable — I said nothing. I told no one, you're the first person I ever told. Maria would be so ashamed of me, I am nothing but a gutless coward, I live with this day after day. The only thing I am worth now is to give you both a fighting chance, get your boy out of here alive.'

'I am not going kill you Alejandro.'

'If you don't, then we both fucking die, that's the only way.'

He lifts the bat, Zetas all around us, 'what the fuck are you pussies doing, get to fucking work, five minutes are up.'

The end of Alejandro's bat pokes me in the chest, and again, and again. 'Come on motherfucker, what are you waiting for.' He is shouting at me, taunting me to fight, trying to hurry me along. Laena watches from the side-lines. She says nothing, but her words are with me.

'Don't lose the boys.'

A Zeta pushes Alejandro toward me, he hits the shinbone of my leg, I feel the impact — no pain. I am expecting that sudden sharp sensation, but nothing. He has a look of fury on his face, the noise is deafening now, I can't see Tomas, too busy trying to focus and blank out dead people, Alejandro lifts the bat above his head, as if to strike me down, like a gladiator would, I can't do it, I can't kill another person, I am not cut out for this, I am better than this.

'Don't lose the boys.' Again and again and again.

I step to the side and strike Alejandro, to the left side of his hip. The bat was lifted over his head; he drops it and it falls behind him. Zetas cheering, rage burning through me.

'Don't lose the boys,' echoing through my head, Laenas face, solemn and stoic as she watches on, the dead watching me, judging me.

'Come on Flip, you fucking faggot, no good pussy bitch.' My father chanting from the background, rage burns even greater, I must fight, I must get my boy.

Swing! Crack! — Alejandro takes one to the side of the head, he falls, blood pours from his hairline, he is screaming — blood from his nose, he looks up at me like a wounded animal, he looks at me as if to beg for his life, he looks and sounds as if he regrets his promise — couldn't bear the sound of my best friends cries for mercy of begging for his life.

'Flip, wait, Flip no.' Alejandro's cries out, my heart sinks, forevermore I will never forget those cries, he didn't want to die.

'Don't lose the boys,' again and again and again.

I silence the cries of mercy, like some form of Neanderthal I bring the bat down upon my best friend, over and over and over. The cries of pain and fear stop. The cheers of bastards become louder. My arm is grabbed and held aloft, 'Winner' is called by the Zeta bastards who watch over the monstrous battles to the death with frenzied excitement, their blood lust satisfied; for now.

My vision is coming back, a haze still apparent, but I can see further now than before. I can see Tomas; he is stood to the side of the old man. A knife protrudes out of the old man's neck from an upward angle. He kept his word, someone else who couldn't take the burden of having to pay witness to such evils. As I look around the macabre scene of murder and mayhem, like bearing witness to the fate of Sodom and Gomorrah; judged because of their sins; cities destroyed by the hand of god.

The bleeding battered bodies are loaded onto trucks by the winners; we are informed of our impending transit to a training camp. Rojo comes over to us; the underling must supervise the removal of the bodies. Pools of blood, throughout the barn, drunken Zetas slipping in the blood of innocents, as they stumble drunkenly to fraternise with each other, to revel in the excitement of the gladiatorial entertainment they had just witnessed. The smell of booze and blood hits me, my senses feel heightened. The winners are rounded up again, lifting the bodies and given shovels.

'Your first duty as fully fledged members of Los Zetas is to bury these assholes out back,' says one of the Zetas; Commander Forty and El Kilo watch over us, the survivors tired, blood stained and helpless. I wobble on my feet again; I trip and go down on one knee. Tomas helps me back up, I look at him, the poor child has endured more than anyone can. I kiss him on the top of his head, as we are led away by Rojo, the attack dog of this inhuman scum. Febe is by his side, she looks over at us as we leave the barn. In the background, I can hear gunfire again. The female passengers have served their purpose, now they can rest in peace.

I look towards the smaller barn where Joaquin was taken. Guns are trained upon us as we carry the bodies outside; we lay them down and are ordered to dig. We pile the bodies, one on top of the other and all of us dig together, while the debauched party continues inside of the barn, the sounds of laughter and music can be heard from inside.

Tomas stands close to me as we dug our hole. 'I didn't kill that old man Papa, I swear, he did it to himself,' as if I needed reassurance that my son was still pure of heart.

'You don't have to justify yourself to me my boy. Even if that were not the case, we must do everything to survive. We are going to be separated soon, all of us. We can't go to Reynosa, Zetas are everywhere. Get to Juarez, we don't have time to talk now, they are listening, so we must be quick. Get to Juarez and cross the border — call Papa Antonio when you get there.'

'But Papa, it's just as bad over there and we don't know anyone.'

'Zetas don't go there, believe it or not, it's probably the safest place to get to at this moment in time.'

'What about Joaquin? What about Febe? We can't leave them like this.'

'Joaquin is — ' I couldn't bring myself to say it, after what Raul told us, I just knew that he would be gone by now. The barn where he was led, was silent, all the little children silent now — all gone to heaven.

'Don't say that Papa, you can't give up on him, we don't know that yet!'

'I am sorry, but we do know.' I start to cry, my head spins, I feel like I am falling again, sounds piercing through my head.

'No Papa, stop this, now. We got this far, we can't just give up now, you're clever and will think of a way, I know you will, please we can't leave him here, we have to find out, we have to get him out of there.'

He is right, time to think, think of a way — head all fucked up, feeling dizzy, the fingers on my right hand are stiff, flex the muscles, get the circulation going again. He is right, we have to try, we all have to get out of here — somehow.

I look over at the small barn — think goddamn it, think. I keep shovelling; I hear a voice in the background obeying orders, but it sounds familiar, Tomas recognises it too. We both turn around. Holy Mary mother of god, it Luis.

I blink — I must be completely fucked up, my head is spinning. We both look over, so it can't be my imagination, it is, it's him. Pale, wide unblinking eyes, looks completely out of it, looks shell shocked.

'Papa, did you see that? It's him, its Luis.'

'I saw him, but look at him, he isn't the same kid as before, we can't trust him — don't even try.'

While I try and look away, Tomas stands tall, trying to get his attention. I look on; Luis looks in the direction of Tomas. Luis stares, he looks like a zombie, emotionless, no act of recognition, no sign of friendship. Rojo stands in the distance with Febe, the bastard hasn't let her out of his sight. He starts to make his way over, holding Febe by the arm, she looks better than I thought, she looks like she is prepared for anything.

'Tomas, don't look at him, I told you before, look away.'

It's then Luis face seems to break from the far out look, his eyes soften, his mouth curls slightly, but the attempts at emotion disappears as soon as Rojo arrives. He walks straight up to Tomas and slaps him across the face, red marks left behind.

'So, you and this bitch are in love? Is that so motherfucker!' He squeals his words out, his voice sounding like he is disappointed — as if a girl like Febe would ever consider this little shit over my son. 'Answer me — what you deaf, you retarded like that fucking brother of yours.' Everyone carries on digging, no one dare look up, my eye glances Luis, he stands there, obedient as a guard dog.

'Yes, yes we are.' Febe answers for Tomas.

'Quiet whore, you fucking slut, I was going to have you as my girl, but not now, not now I know you prefer little peasant boys like him.'

He sounds broken, like a lovesick puppy. I see it now, he *is* insane, from just one look at her, he has fallen in love, I know that love sick look anywhere, but he is trying to play it cool, play it like a tough guy. You can't hide that emotion; his voice is broken as the venomous words are spat at Tomas.

'Don't you get it,' says Febe, 'no matter what you do to me; you can force yourself on me, you can hurt me, but you can never stop me from loving him. He is a million times the person you will ever be. I could never be with you, you make my skin crawl, I hate you, more than I could ever hate anyone. You're just too stupid to see it, get it over and done with and kill me, I can't even pretend to want to be with you, you're evil, just an evil little hateful boy, a spoiled little brat who couldn't get enough of his Mama's attention.'

The look on his face — he is furious, puffing and panting, his eyes filled with tears, Febe's words spat out with the same level of venom, she doesn't pause, she then turns to condescension.

'Oh what's the matter — little Rojo going to piss his pants is he. You're not a man, you're just a lap dog, someone who they have around to use and abuse, you're a joke, do you honestly think that they desperately want some spoiled little Mama's boy around? You look like some fucking clown with your stupid tattoos, strutting around like some big shot. Go on, fucking do it, FUCKING KILL ME!'

Rojo finally snaps — he hits Tomas again, Tomas hits the floor, Luis steps forward to back him up. Tomas goes to the ground, Luis trains his rifle at Febe, I step out of the hole I am stood so fucking helplessly in. Rojo kicks Tomas in the face, he rolls over, blood from his nose, he is crying, Rojo fucking laughs and kicks him again and again and again about the body, Tomas in agony, fury rushes through my veins.

No one sees me coming — raging now, head fucked, dizzy. Before I know it, I have my hands around Rojo's neck, I lift him from the ground. I feel the strikes of rifle butts to my back, over and over. I swing around and Luis is hitting me with his rifle, Febe charges him and hits him to the ground, she sits on him. Rojo's feet are lifted from the ground; I slam him against the side of the mud pile. I raise my hand and slap, slap, slap. I can't stop slapping him. I clench a fist, smash him in his nose — blood sprays and he is screaming like a baby.

'Fucking pussy bitch, fucking pussy bitch, what's the matter Gael, am I fighting back, you sissy motherfucker, you pussy ass bitch.'

I am out of control; I lay into him, while yelling at him. Rojo screams upon hearing me call him Gael, I keep on slapping him about the face and head with the free hand, I keep one hand around his neck, I slam his back against the mud pile. My head spins out of control, the rage and adrenaline keeps me going, no filter for the rage that is pumping through me.

'So you want to hit my boy, go try that again, you fucking pussy ass motherfucker, come on Gael, come on Gael, Gael, Gael, Gael.'

He tries to overpower me, but he can't, I have him, I am going to kill this little putrid shit. In a flash, I think that killing him would be amoral, but I already killed my best friend tonight, killed him because these animals made me do it. I stop the hitting and pin him to the ground, with feelings of rage that have never surfaced before I raise a rock above my head and look down on him. He is just a boy, a boy not much older than Tomas or Febe. Indeed he is a monster, but he is just a boy. I look over at Tomas, who has lifted himself from the ground now, the rest of the survivors look on in horror, they say nothing, they to, as shell shocked as Luis. As I look up, there are a group of young Zetas stood watching over me, all teenagers, all holding guns at me.

'What are you waiting for, fucking kill him,' says Rojo, spitting his words through loose teeth and a mouthful of blood.

This isn't me, I am not an animal, I loosen my grip on him. I stand up and put my hands in the air.

'Let's do the three of them, right now, right here,' screams Rojo.

'Not now and not here,' says an older boy, he doesn't look or sound scared of Rojo.

'Fuck you Raffi, I am in fucking charge, El Kilo put me in charge, not you. You open your mouth once more; you're a fucking dead man.'

'Like I am scared of you, you took a beating of some puto from the barrio, he whipped your ass, you just don't want the others to know — fucking pussy, what's up Gael, can't take charge of a load of bus passenger, you fucking — '

Bang!

Raffi shot through the back of the head, down to his knees, straight onto his face. Luis stands there, pistol in his hand, smoking barrel.

'Not here Rojo, the others see this, they will know we fucked up, take the three of them to the small barn, put them in the acid barrels. The children are all dead anyway, just add these three, it don't take no more than about ten minutes to boil them up. Me and you, maybe one other, just in case they try any funny shit?'

My boy — Joaquin gone, I drop to my knees and cry, Febe and Tomas come to me. Rojo splits his sides with laughter. I look up from the ground, Rojo stands over me, rifle in hand.

'Got some unfinished business with you, old man.'

He slams the rifle, yet again into my temple, hearing gone in my left ear, can't see through my left eye, not at all. Feels like I am going down, deeper down the rabbit hole.

***

'Mammy, Mammy — let me out of here, I want my Mammy.' The boy keeps shouting this out, I don't like the noise, I try and block it out of my ears by covering them.

It smells bad in this place, locked in a cage with this boy, who keeps crying for his Mammy. There are cages next to us, lots and lots of cages, like the ones dogs are kept in. Some are children I remember seeing on the bus, some were already here, when these bad men with guns and knives took us to this barn, took me away from my Papa, from Tomas and Febe. One girl was very young, I held her hand, she is in a cage next to me, she keeps crying, I don't want her to be sad; I want to stop her being sad. The men have not told us why they are keeping us in the cages; I think they want to hurt us. I don't like being hurt, I don't like these men, they scare me. They have bad eyes; they pushed us into the cages and hit the cage when we cried too much.

A boy came in, a friend of Tomas, Tomas's friend from school, I remember his face, I remember he used to talk to me. Luis is his name; he told some of the men to help him, I heard him say that we wouldn't get out of here and come and help him, heard him say that Rojo needed help. The boys hurry after him, leaving us alone.

I take out the screwdriver from my pants; I also hid the hammer in the side pockets. The teachers at school always took my tools away from me, but they would give them back. These men are bad, they took watches and money from people when we first got here, they would have taken my tools away and they wouldn't have given them back. The lock on the cages is easy; Papa taught me how to take a lock apart — even from the inside. I think the one in this cage will be easy to unlock.

I unscrew the rear plate, it comes off and I can see the mechanism, it's a tubular mortice type lock, I know these locks quite well. I use the screw driver and hammer to try and hammer the catch, so it slips back, so I can then push the catch fully out of its housing, if I hit it too hard, then it will jam and I will never get it open.

'Hey, what are you doing,' whispers one of the boys from one of the cages.

I ignore him, I don't even look at him, no time to be distracted, he tells me to stop what I am doing, he keeps saying that if they find me doing that then we will be in big trouble. It is taking a long time to try and get this right. I use the right amount of pressure, by hitting the catch with the screwdriver and hammer to make the latch pop back, I then twist the screwdriver so the latch doesn't pop back into its housing. I push the door and it opens.

I hear footsteps, so I close the door, not fully, just enough to make it look like its closed. A man walks in, not a boy, but a man, he is in black, he is one of the bad ones. He hits the cages with an iron bar. It makes a terrible sound, I block my ears, I hid my hammer, the children start screaming and crying loud again.

'Let's deal with you little shits,' says the man; he is smiling when he says it. He picks up a toy doll of the floor and throws it into a drum; the drum spits hot water and gives off a horrible smell.

'That's what will happen to you little shits in a second, a nice hot acid bath, to wash away the smell of you fucking barrio kids.'

Papa used to use acid to clean rust from metal fences, he always told me never to touch it, I saw his arm once, when he spilled some, it looked nasty, I don't want to get thrown in there, got to get out of here, that bad man wants to throw us in. He goes to the cage next to us and unlocks it, he takes the little girl out and lifts her up, she kicks and screams, he slams the cage shut as another girl tries to run out. Got to think, got to think fast. I kick the door open of my cage, it flies wide open. I scream and scream and scream, I don't stop, I don't want him to hurt the girl, she is scared, she is only small. I need to draw him over to my cage.

'What the fuck, who didn't close the cage door? fucking assholes not doing what they're supposed to do, fucking shit.' He is very angry; he carries the girl over to my cage. I know what I am going to do. I stop screaming as he stands close to the opening of the cage.

'What the fuck you looking at dummy?' he says to me.

I'm not a dummy, I can build large models with wood and metal, I can fix fences and roofs and walls. I am going to build a sky scraper and live high up in the clouds, so I don't have to be scared anymore. I can break any lock that needs breaking. I hate him, he wants to hurt us, he wants to burn us. I pull out my hammer, the one he didn't know I had, who is the dummy now.

Whack.

I hit him in the face —blood pours out of his nose so I hit him again on the head; he falls to his knees. I hit him again on the head as hard as I can, he doesn't move.

I get to work, I hold the little girls hand, she cries and cries. I smile back at her. Just in case she is afraid. I don't want her to be afraid anymore.

I start using my screwdriver to pick the locks, when I remember the man on the floor has the keys. I go through his pockets and find a key. I open the cages, one after another, after another, after another. Some of the older boys and girls stop the younger ones from running out of the door; the bad men would see us and throw us in the acid. I can see a door at the back of the barn, I lead the children over to the door, we try and push it, but it's stuck, it won't budge, I can't get it to open.

I can hear voices and footsteps coming towards the barn, oh no we are stuck, we must hide.

'Get them in here now, let's show these motherfuckers what we did with that little retard, let's show them the soup we made.' He laughs as he says it, I remember that voice, it's the boy with the ink over his face.

My ribs and stomach hurt as I am pushed towards the barn, Rojo looks frantic, he has blood over his face, pouring out of his nose. Papa humiliated him, right in front of his own people. He is going to hurt us, hurt us in ways that only exist in my nightmares. The boys drag Papa by his arms as the rest of the passenger bury the dead bodies in the holes, dug be the victors of the victors of our initiation; thrown in, one on top of each other, the women were going to be next.

As we are taken to the barn, out of the corner of my eye I can see beyond the farm and notice a vacant lot, rows and rows of buses parked, riddled with bullet-holes. Buses that at one time or another contained people heading for a better place, only to end up like this. I look at Luis as we walk, I can't hold back any longer.

'All your wishes come true, you get to be a Zeta, all you ever wanted to be, now you're going to waste us, the family that treated you like one of our own. I hope you rot for this — hope you rot in hell.'

That fucking Luis even told Rojo to take us somewhere quiet, so he wouldn't get found out. He doesn't look at me, he can't look at me. Febe takes my hand as we make the short walk, to where Joaquin was taken, to where he probably died, calling out for us — the bastards. I look back and Papa is waking, he is moaning and making some very strange sounds, a kind of snorting sound, his eyes rolling around in his head, Rojo walks ahead, he says something to us, something he thinks is funny, something about Joaquin.

As we walk into the smaller barn, the cages are open, the acid drums full of a milky-red substance, the smell awful, ammonia burning through my nostrils. They killed them; they killed my brother and the other children. Some of them just babies. Rojo is looking about, when he suddenly shouts and kicks a man who is led on the ground. The man rolls over, face smashed in and two golf ball size lumps to his forehead. Febe looks at me, suddenly she seems tense, she looks about the barn.

'What the fuck, what the fuck, what the fuck!' shouts Rojo, he is jumping about like a madman, kicking the man on the ground, the man barely able to speak or even get up. 'Who was supposed to be keeping an eye on the kids, oh fuck, oh fuck, I am dead, I am fucking dead. Go find them, GO FIND THOSE FUCKING LITTLE BRATS,' he shouts at the boy Zetas.

He is panicked now, he knows that his failure will cost him — good I am glad, now he is starting to make mistakes, starting to fuck up, his masters will put him down, like all vicious junk yard dogs.

'Hey.' shouts a voice from the doorway. I look behind me, it's Bruno. Suddenly my heart starts to race, while all this has been going on, the fights and the killing, it all starts to look like Joaquin got out and freed the rest of them. Things are starting to look up for our predicament. With Bruno here, we stand a chance, all of us stand a chance. Febe squeezes my hand a little tighter in the knowing that some kind of plan has been underway the whole time, by some shear miracle and the intervention of others that we all had been thinking along the same lines, we each worked out a way to get out of this. Febe caused the distraction, Alejandro and Raul offered themselves up as the sacrificial lambs, Papa managed to get us in here, Joaquin got out — probably using that fucking tool set, he hid in his pants again. This is either a fantastic plan that's gone ahead or just sheer luck or intervention of God, or just that when the chips are down; the good people can fight back, when trapped in a corner.

I start to feel a pang of guilt over those that had already died here and around the area, like this, in these horrible ways, just to entertain these bastards. It's no time to start maudlin over this, it's time we got to it, got creative and got out of here, were not out of the woods yet.

'Don't tell me the kids got out, don't tell me they escaped. Z40 and El Kilo are going to be pissed as hell about this,' said Bruno, he walks over to Rojo. Rojo turns and glares at him.

‘What did you just fucking say to me, what the fuck — who do you think you are, you’re just some fucking lump from the barrio, I saved your ass, you got in with us, because I put you up against some lame ass who couldn’t fight his way out of a kid’s party.’

‘OK tough guy, maybe you want to do the man dance with me then,’ says Bruno, he stands up to Rojo.

At that moment, Luis shouts, ‘There here,’ he is stood behind a row of cattle troughs; he points his rifle at them. I see Joaquin’s head pop up, my heart leaps inside my chest, without thinking I run toward Luis, who is twenty feet from me and jump directly in front of his rifle and stand right up to the barrel.

‘Go on, do it then,’ I say, absolutely petrified of death, but at the same time unable to stand by any more.

‘Tomas — don’t,’ shouts Febe

‘It’s OK,’ I shout back, “Luis won’t hurt the children; I know he won’t, just like he won’t hurt me. I am his friend, his best and only friend.’ I look directly at him, his eyes softening up again.

‘What the fuck are you waiting for, WASTE THEM,’ shouts Rojo, his bloody face, looking more and more like he wants to cry out loud and run off back to his mother, rather than keep up the tough guy image, he so hoped to maintain.

‘Go on Luis, waste them, waste me while you’re at it, then you kill my Papa and go on inside and waste anyone else who may still be alive. You can go on killing women like my Mama, or your own Mother, you can go from town to town killing and destroying everything that used to be good about this place — you’re one of us, not one of them.’

I notice the other boys, who stand with Rojo, they look confused, they have that look of unease on their faces, they know that this falls on them, the mistakes made by Rojo will mean that they get to suffer also, I notice this — Bruno also notices it.

‘You boys better get the hell out of here, when the others find out about this he’s the one who will be fucked. You want to be the ones who die with him. Raffi is lying with a bullet in his head; don’t think he wouldn’t do the same to you. When they ask him why a bunch of farmers and repairmen and kids got out and ran amok, he will put that on you, just so he can worm his way out of here. Who do you think wasted Z30?’

‘You fucking prick,’ shouts Rojo, he pulls his pistol out from his belt and points it at Bruno.

'I got it all on video motherfucker,' Bruno holds a cell phone in his hand, 'all I got to do is push that button and its sent to Z40's cell phone, you think I am fucking around — pull the trigger. When a bullet hits the brain, the muscle reflexes cause a person's grip to tighten, my finger tightens and Z40 gets to watch one of his faithful lieutenants shot to shit, by some jumped up little pussy twerp who just got too big for his boots.'

Rojo looks around, looking at the rest of the boys, looking for some form of solidarity.

'He's bluffing, there is no video, fucking waste the kids, waste these barrio hillbillies and let's get back to it.'

'Your talk is tough, but you still ain't pulled the trigger, you know I ain't bluffing, because you know you done Z30 and you know that I know. You listen in boys, pay attention now because if that video hits Z40, then anyone who stood by Rojo is going to get whacked out as well.'

'Come on Luis,' I say, 'Let's stop this now, I know you can't do it, I remember how bad you felt about Mr Lingala, how bad you felt for Javier's mother, so much so you sent her a message that he was OK.' His eyes move away from mine; he lowers the rifle; he points it at the ground.

'Don't you fucking do it, you son of a bitch, you fucking gutless cowardly little shit, I will fuck you up,' shouts Rojo, watching his whole house come down around him, the loyalty he commanded, now falling apart. Rojo's hands shakes as he holds the pistol, still pointed at Bruno. 'Fuck you puto,' he says to Bruno.

Bang — I close my eyes at the sound.

I hear the bullet strike something metal, high above us in the metal rafters of the roof. I open my eyes, Rojo is squealing and wailing. Papa is up and off the ground; he has him from behind, in a bear hug, like the phoenix from the ashes. He has lifted Rojo off the ground. Bruno steps in and grabs the pistol. Papa lets out, what I can only describe as a roar as he runs, carrying Rojo towards the cages, he throws him inside, Rojo hitting the back of the cage, the loud vibrating sound of him colliding head first into the bards. Papa slams the door and turns around, waiting for his fate, waiting for the Zeta boys to mow him down in a hail of gunfire.

The gunfire doesn't come, the boys stand blank faced, looking at Papa, his mouth lopsided, sweating heavily, and struggling to regain his breath. Bruno holds the pistol, waiting for one of the boys to point their rifles at him. They look at each other, the words of wisdom finally hitting home. They drop their weapons and flee out the front door.

Rojo runs at the cage, screaming and screaming and screaming. Every time he runs into the cage door he hits the floor; he gets up and runs at it again and again and again. Screaming continually, like a trapped wild animal, screams turn to howling, like a coyote. He just gets up again and again and again, howling and running at the cage door. He kicks and head-butts it, smashes it with his hands — but it doesn't move. His eyes wide, like a crazy deranged lunatic, doing all he can, not giving up, desperate to break free, unable to get out, running and hitting the bars, falling and doing the same, over and over and over. Bruno walks towards the entrance to make sure the boys don't go straight in to their masters.

'It's clear,' he says.

Luis stands still, his weapon still in his hand. Bruno approaches the second door and kicks it through. Outside the dark night waits, we slip out through the door. I wait for Papa to get out; he is slower than before; he seems to be limping. Bruno leads us to one of the buses parked in the vacant lot, far away from the barn; far away from the evil laughter, smell of blood, Narco music ringing out along with the sounds of the voices of evil men, plotting evil deeds. I look and see Luis running with us, silent, he doesn't say a word.

We get to a bus, a deserted bus, with shot out windows and blood down the side.

'Get in,' says Bruno, I stand with him, loading the children on-board.

They jump on, rushing to get seated, still upset and tearful, still wanting their Mama's and Papa's. Mama's that are now dead, Papa's who now have to wear the Zeta badge and fight for these monsters, Papa's who are buried dust-laden graves with other Mama's and Papa's. Like my Mama, buried somewhere out in the deserted fields, outside San Fernando.

Papa limps at the very back, he looks pale, his face bloodied, his mouth drooping on the left side, I look at him and he says:

'Let's find paradise.'

His voice sounding like he is drunk — no time to worry about that now. He laughs as he says it, but it sounds more like he is just trying to be optimistic rather than finding something funny. As he gets on board, he flexes his fingers of his left hand again, I can see the frustration in his face, it's a struggle to get the hand working.

Out of nowhere, Maria comes from behind the bus, she jumps on, as she does she leans in and kisses the top of my head.

'I knew you could get him to come, I knew you could get Luis back again.'

Maria goes to see Papa briefly, she hugs him and Febe. She takes Luis in her arms and squeezes him tightly. She looks so different now, her hair short, dressed in Army type clothes, no longer plump. He doesn't lift his arms, he doesn't speak — he shows no emotion at all.

I hear Bruno speak with Maria, while she is still holding onto her son, her boy, the reason why she fought so hard all along. She truly did show the people of Mexico the meaning of fighting for her family.

'Get them out of the area, I can stall them for now, pull the bus out quietly, it's dark enough and noisy enough they won't hear you. Most of them are dusted and drunk, get far away from here, somewhere the Zetas won't go.'

'You were right to come find me,' says Maria, 'I can't believe they went and did this, no one will believe how far they went; we thought it was bad before. I am going to come back here with an army and wipe them out, what about you?'

'Not me Mama, I got a certain tattooed freak to deal with, got myself a video to show the bosses. You go on back to being a mother again. I got a wife and kids of my own to get back to as well. I got some stories of my own to tell the authorities. You get these kids out of here and I will blow the fucking lid on this place, I will do the talking, now get the hell out of here, I got one last duty to fulfil as a Zeta.'

Bruno jumps off the bus and keeps an eye out while Maria starts the engine; she crawls wide around the lot, so not to be seen. Papa sits holding onto Joaquin, almost suffocating him, squeezing him and never wanting to let him go. I sit down with Febe, she kisses me softly on the cheek. I have my family again, or what's left of us. Papa limps down to the front of the bus, to assist Maria, Joaquin stays with me. The bus creeps onto the deserted track, heading back out onto the highway.

'Anywhere in particular,' says Maria.

'Juarez,' says Papa, 'I got a ranch in Texas to get to.'

***

I got to get out, I got to get out, I got to get out, I got to get out, I got to get out.

'Fucking let me out of here.'

No one comes; those gutless fucking turds have left me in this fucking cage. I will kill those bastards, those peasant barrio bastards for this, I will hang their headless bodies from the town cathedral, I will kill anyone who has ever been involved with them, I will hunt them down like fucking dogs, I will slaughter them for this. Those traitors who didn't stand by me, they die next; I know the towns where they came from, their mothers and fathers, brothers and sisters, all of them, dead. That fucking Bruno motherfucker — traitor, fucking cowardly traitor, I made his sorry ass, without me, he would have never got into the Zetas, who the fuck does he think he is, I could take, I will take him. I'm ready now, I wasn't before, he took me by surprise, I didn't pussy out, I just wasn't ready to fight him, but I will fucking whip his fucking faggot ass, right in front of El Kilo and Z40. They will all see what I can do, that I am a good soldier.

I shake the cage, I been in here for ages now, I bet he is showing that video to them. Got to get my story straight, Z30 was a coward, he was planning on taking over and having you all killed — so I killed him, shot him down like the pussy coward he was.

No, wait, maybe I could say that he was planted by the Gulf cartel or Sonora or Juarez — yes, he was planted by them, I heard him talking on his phone telling them all the shipping routes, the transportation so I killed him and I didn't tell you because? Because?

No wait, he was planted by aliens from fucking Mars who wanted to take over the world, by destroying the Columbians and shipping it themselves through Mexico, wiping out the cartels and serving the best shit at Hollywood parties because they want to fuck Lindsay Lohan and meet Johnny Depp and take over Hollywood by supplying the best imaginable shit. Ha ha ha ha ha ha ha ha ha ha.

I am fucked, they are going to seriously take their time in killing me for this, no point in making excuses, I fucked up over the bus, I fucked up by allowing them to escape, I fucked up for killing Z30, I fucked up, I fucked up, I fucked up. I am just a kid, maybe they will go light on me, maybe they will show me mercy. Oh God, all the things I have done, even God wouldn't forgive me for. But fuck him, he don't live down here, he don't live in Tamaulipas, he don't even watch over his flock down here. I did what I thought I had to do, fuck all of them.

El Kilo and Z40 come storming from the bigger barn, a group walking with them. They stand facing me, locked like a pathetic animal at a rescue home, begging to get out. Bruno stood behind them.

'So Mano, what you got to say for yourself,' says El kilo.

'The video; we saw it, saw what you done, so what about it then? Speak motherfucker,' says Z40, he doesn't seem to have the same sympathetic understanding that El Kilo may have.

'I treated you like a little brother,' says El Kilo, 'you betrayed us, the only family you ever wanted, the only family you have.' He looks at the empty cages; he looks at the oil drums full of bubbling acid. That smell is rancid, the smell of burned flesh, the smell of dead children, boiled alive, the screams of pain and horror, I remember laughing as I did it. I was a good soldier, I was their best.

'I bet this is down to you, didn't have the balls to go through with it, or was it something else, maybe those kids fucked you up and ran off, where are your fucking boys, they piss themselves and run off too?'

El Kilo just wants me to answer him, I smile at him, the biggest smile I possibly can. Maybe he would like a little song, one of my favourites, the priest liked this one and it's fitting for the occasion.

'Ave Maria,
gratia plena,
Maria gratia plena,
Maria gratia plena,
Ave ave Dominus
Dominus tecum.

Benedictus tu in mulieribus,
et benedictus
et benedictus fructus ventris
ventris tui, Iesus.
Ave Maria.'

'Stop singing, you little faggot,' shouts El Kilo, now he is pissed, I can feel the tears stream down my face. He pulls out his pistol and shoots the lock off. El Kilo, Z40 and Bruno, all looking at me, looking at me confused, confused why I am not begging for my life. El Kilo pulls me out of the cage, by my neck, Z40 helps him, they shout at me, while I hum the tune, they slap me, trying to get me to stop. They say I am a traitor, some crazy little punk and a coward, not fit to wear the uniform, not fit to be a Zeta, this is all my faulty, they ask how the people fled , which way, how many, how did it happen. I keep on humming the tune. They walk me over to the drums of boiling acid, I keep on humming, I don't respond to them, I hear one of them say it's my last chance, to tell them. I break out into song again. They shout at me continuously.

'Do you know what sort of shit we will be in, if this gets out? Answer me faggot.'

I got an answer for you

'Ave Maria,
Mater Dei,
ora pro nobis peccatoribus,
ora ora pro nobis
ora pro nobis peccatoribus,
nunc, et in hora mortis
in hora mortis nostrae.
in hora mortis mortis nostrae.
in hora mortis nostrae.
Ave Maria'

They just look at me, they realise it's a lost cause, the rest of them lift my feet off the ground and hang me over the oil drum, they shout and curse, but I don't hear them anymore. All I can think of was the girl, the one they called Febe, so beautiful, the most beautiful girl I had ever seen, why didn't she want to be with me? I would have treated her like a princess, why did she have to say those horrible things about me? I loved her, I loved her from the first moment I saw her, way back, last August, I had to remove my mask, I wanted to see her with my own eyes, I wanted her to see me. I never wanted her to die, when I saw her again; sat in that canteen at that school, it was like she was an angel, sent down to earth again, resurrected to walk amongst us. I love you Febe.

The voices are shouting and shouting as I stare into the boiling acid, I can feel the hands slip away from me, let me go, head first to my peril, slipping and slipping, they are trying to get me to talk to them, but all I can think about is that angel, the angel Febe. The voices stop, it's a waste of their time trying, I am lifted high above the drum my arms are released, hanging right above the oil drum, I can feel the heat as they lower me down. Sudden weightlessness and in I fall.

'Ave Maria.'

Chapter25

Monterrey - Torreon - Ciudad Delicias – Ciudad Juarez

29th – 30th March 2011

She smiles at me — Laena smiles at me, she is proud of what I have accomplished. The boys are safe, Febe is safe. She stands by the river bank; she looks young again, the children pulling at her arms, desperately wanting to play. She calls out to me, her hand out for me to take. I want to feel her again, I want to touch her again, I reach out to take her hand.

The bumps in the road stir me, I keep my eyes closed, hoping that I will drift off again, but I don't. Whenever I am woken from my dreams of Laena, I can never return to the point that I left. I sit up, Tomas is sat with Febe, she rests her head on his shoulder and he looks so content, so much in love. Although he is young, he is mature; he is intelligence, his intelligence far surpassing that of any other twelve-year-old boy. Joaquin asleep on separate seat, he looks so peaceful. They have seen more in their short life times than a child should ever see. My hope is that peace will find them, that they can live out their lives never having to endure such horrors as they have in the last year. It has been a year since Laena disappeared; a year without her feels like a lifetime. I try to stand, but my left leg is locked tight, the fingers of my left-hand stiff, I try and flex them, but the hand is drawn into a permanent fist. My vision is hazed and I have a feeling of almost drunkenness. My balance is off, my ears ring and I can feel the left side of my face and mouth numb. I draw my good hand across my mouth, to wipe the excess saliva away that is pouring onto my chin. My head spins and it's hard to trust what I actually see.

The children from the barn all sit in silence. They have lost so much and now face an uncertain future, unanswered questions swimming around in their heads, questions that children so young should not have to confront. There is no conversation or blithe merriment that you would associate with children being together. They have been scarred by the events they have witnessed; their faces tell the whole story. I almost feel a sense of guilt being party to their saviour. Their lives are potentially marred by the fact that they have lost everything and now face uncertainty and danger again on our route to Juarez.

Although this weighs heavy on me, I know that children have a resolute way of overcoming tragedy. I have an obligation to keep them safe, not only to my own children, but now also to them. I have obtained a sense of grandiosity in escaping from a place as I can only describe as Hades in its earthly form. I am starting to believe that my life has purpose and meaning again, but I am also duly aware that my condition in the present time is a grave one. My mind is failing in its functions; my body is also following suite. I feel a level of euphoria, but I also know that brain damage can lead to such beliefs. Medical attention is what is needed, but we must get over the border.

I gaze out of the window, across the deserted highway and surrounding desert, the sun is coming up across the landscape; it's a picture to behold. I always took for granted what a beautiful place my homeland is. The rural farms and houses still occupied by decent hardworking folk. From the bus, I see them continuing with their daily chores. I am proud of my homeland, proud of my people, people like me. People who work hard and endure no matter what is thrown their way. I will miss this place; I will miss my people. When I try to think of America I can't maintain any reasonable thought. I have never left Mexico, despite only living one hundred miles from the border, I have never crossed over. It's not that I never wanted to, but I have always felt a certain reticence to travel to a place of such enormity. I am used to the easy going feel of where I am from, knowing that I can go anywhere and whoever I speak with, they would always reply, never having that feeling of being inadequate or poor. Maybe I will be wrong, maybe I have just misjudged America all this time, but that is always how it has felt to me. The feeling has always been with me; it's how I was raised and what I have come to believe. It's a mind-set that is very difficult to shake.

Maria drives the bus throughout the journey and Luis sits behind her, he has not spoken a single word since we got out of there. It is hard for me to look upon him with sympathy, but I wonder what he has been through, what has he seen, what has he done, how will he ever be cured, he shakes throughout the journey, he pukes in a garbage bag — coming down off smack, he is pale and sweating. Maria talks with him, but there is no reply.

Maria has no option but to go underground, she is a wanted woman, but also a woman of status, a folk hero, a saviour of the people, an insurgent, a killer. One man's freedom fighter is another's terrorist. My heart goes out to her, a victim of circumstance; just like me, just like Tomas, Joaquin and Febe, just like the children we now have in our care.

When we get to Ciudad Delicias, I find a taverna and ask to use their phone, I call Antonio, I tell him that we are headed to Juarez and looking to cross the Bridge of the America, possibly sometime later today. I drool over the receiver of the phone and struggle to remain standing in the booth; he asks me if I am OK, I know that he can tell my voice is wavering. Shooting pains in my head and my neck, the left leg, totally locked up, walking with what looks like an over exaggerated limp. I tell him some of what had happened, that we couldn't cross anywhere else and that we were running for our lives. I tell him how our passage using a coyote is not possible as we have no money. He says that he will meet us on the Juarez side.

I leave the taverna and thank the host, he looks at me, in a concerned like fashion, I catch a glimpse of myself in the mirrored drinks cabinet. I am pale, my brow is sweat covered, yet I shiver with cold, my lopsided grin seems like a permanent fixture. Two blasts to the head with the butt of a rifle was never going to make anyone feel too good. Although I look like shit, I don't feel weak or unable to continue, I am good. No bleeding, no real headache, I can carry on, get to the other side in a few hours, get to a doctor, get some medication inside of me, some rest and some food and I will be right as rain. I fall to the ground as I step out of the tavern — must have been that high step, the host should get a fucking sign, I look back, there is no step. As I stand up I feel giddy.

The children remain on the bus, A man has joined our merry band, he is about my age, he introduces himself as Adan and tells me that he has food for us, but he also needs to get to Juarez, he pays for the fuel for the bus, he tells me that he is on the run from Monterrey, that his family have been killed in the recent violence, he recognises Maria, that she is the Black Widow, that she has inspired people in his region to fight back, that they had heard of her plight and followed suite. I pat his arm and speak with him, but I don't know what I say, my voice sounds far off in the distance, like it's not me talking, like some out of body experience, I wipe my mouth again and drag my left leg, the left hand is totally closed now.

I sit on the bus and we hit the road again, back out onto the highway, heading towards Juarez. Not a city that I would travel to by choice, but one that I need to get to. I feel excited about going over the border, the cars, the food, the cities, the people. The land of the free. I sit back and think about the life ahead for us, for my family. The schools and the opportunities, the life we will lead. The opportunities for Joaquin; a place where his needs could be catered for, where Tomas could continue his learning, where Febe could finally settle.

The journey is long, but Maria has driven the entire way, this man Adan, has now taken over the driving, Maria sits with Luis and puts her arm around her boy, I notice he reciprocates and hugs her back. The other children have started talking, but I am struggling to hear what is said. Feeling tired now, feeling weak, need some rest before Juarez, before I go to sleep I must tell Tomas, Joaquin and Febe that I love them and give them a kiss. It's a ritual taken every night, I don't know why I choose to do it now, but I must. Before bed I kiss them and tell them that I love them and reassure them it's all going to be OK, we are going to America and we talk about our journey. I gather them round and they all sit with me; the other children crowd around also. I say the words to them, but I feel myself going off on a tangent, I am aware that I am forgetting my words, forgetting the simple things. I can see Tomas nod at me, as if to reassure me, I can see that he is upset, I tell him I am OK, just tired.

I continue with my vigil as I do every night. We talk about the journey and how we are now doing it, rather than just talking about it. Joaquin listens when I tell him about the big buildings, the bridges and the shopping malls with glass roofs and how he is going to build one as soon as he gets there. His face alights with joy as I describe the modern architecture. Tomas telling me about how he will have to start playing American football and baseball rather than soccer. I tell them not long now, almost there, just a few more hours. I put my arms around them all, my left hand now merely a useless appendage, starting to forget how I came to be hugging them, what did we talk about, struggling to understand what Febe and Tomas are saying to me, their mouths are moving — can't hear the words, just able to hear the greatest words to ever come from the mouths of children.

'We love you too Papa.'

Those are the only words I need to hear; the rest is inconsequential. Starting to feel like I am locked in now, the body won't do what I tell it to, can't talk anymore, feel too weak, couldn't move my limbs even if I wanted to. Need to rest now, nearly in Juarez, got to get to the bridge, get over to the other side, need to cross over, never crossed over before, need my rest, it's a big task, will cross over soon. I close my eyes.

I walk down to the river bank, Laena stands there, looking as beautiful as I remember, she is young and beautiful, just like the very last time I saw her. She is addressing me, she is paying attention to only me now, and she smiles that beautiful smile and holds out her hand. I take it. It's real, it feels real. I walk hand in hand with her down to the river, we stand looking at it flow, she rests her head on my shoulder. A balloon bounces off the steady flow, a piece of paper attached to the string.

‘It’s one from the children,’ she says.

I look at her and she smiles again. Tomas, Joaquin and Febe stand by our side; they all look so happy, so content. I just want to remember this moment. I want this moment to stay with me forever; I don’t want it to end. If I were to have one thing, just one thing in life, it’s for this to be my forever, I never want to leave this place, to be here and stay like this forever.

This is my forever, my last memory, my last dream.

Chapter26
Ciudad Juarez, Chihuahua, Mexico
30th March 2011

High up into the hills overlooking Juarez, the bus descends the narrow roads, it's dusk and already the sky is lit up with tracer rounds, coming from the machine-guns of rival cartels fighting it out. No sooner had my eyes fixated upon that sight; I could hear the cries coming from the back of the back of the bus. I release Luis from the grip I have had on him since Adan took over the driving from me. I have not been able to let him go, I have him back, by a shear miracle or gods work, I have my son back, however the cries coming from the back of the bus are coming from Joaquin, a boy who cries so infrequent, which can mean only one thing. I stumble down the aisle, where I see the rest of the children, all gathered around the seat, where Flip was spent most of the journey, his head slumped forward, blood coming from his left ear. Tomas continues to call out, 'Papa' and tries to stir him.

'Maria, he is asleep, he is only asleep, please can you wake him up,' he cries out.

Joaquin cries uncontrollably; I have never seen him this way before. I reach forward and place my fingers to the left side of Flip's neck; no pulse. I lift his head back, his eyes closed the slightest of smiles on his face, he didn't suffer, he died outright. He had been in bad shape since he got on the bus; he told me that he took two hits to the head with a rifle butt. That would be enough to finish him off. Poor Flip, he had been slowly dying this last year since Laena disappeared — dying of a broken heart.

'Move away children,' I say and I lay him down on the seat. I feel my own heart break, not just for Flip, but for his own children. I kiss him on the forehead. Goodnight sweet, gentle Flip, a man who never harmed anyone, a man who cared and loved his family so deeply; taken away just moments before he could find happiness again. The world is such a cruel place; this place can be the cruellest place on earth sometimes. I gather Joaquin, Tomas and Febe in my arms and hug them.

'I am so, so sorry.'

It's the only thing I can say; I don't have the words to make all this better. I tell Adan to stop the bus on the outskirts of town, he questions my decision and I show him the colt 45 I have tucked into my waist band — no more questions asked. I get off the bus and speak an old man, who is sat on his porch of his old cottage.

'Good evening senor,' I say.

'What's so good about it senorita,' he responds offering some sarcasm.

'We have a man on-board, he passed during the journey, we need to lay him to rest and we cannot take him on the rest of our journey.'

'I am not an undertaker, why don't you take him to the one in the city; it's not like their novices at burying the dead, three thousand dead in our city last year and already a third of the year gone and we are looking to top that number already. What brings you here anyway? you have come in from the east, why have you come here.'

I feel as though I need to humour this old buzzard, there is no point in bullshitting him, he can see right through it. 'We are trying to get the dead man's children over the border, we need to get them to the bridge, their grandfather is crossing over to collect them.'

'No he ain't, no one is crossing over tonight, or tomorrow night.'

Getting tired of this now: 'And why is that.'

'The Sonorans and the Juarez cartel are having a little street party, can't you hear the firecrackers going off, plus there are demonstrations going on as well, the cops are caught between them and the cartels fighting it out. The demonstrations are over Calderon and his government taking no action over the Femoniciados, you know the number of murdered women and children in the city.'

We don't need a lecture on that now. 'OK old timer, you seem like a man in the know, you give me something and I will give you something. You give me a place where I can get those children safely, but not necessarily legally over the border and I will give you something I got.'

'You're not my type,' says the old buzzard, 'you got a nice set of hooters on you, but I am more into the younger ones with smaller asses, you know like those girls in the MTV videos.' He smiles at me, knowing he is enjoying yanking my chain.

'I'm a virgin anyway, waiting for the right man, I got something that will pay, if you find the right journalist, how would you like to stick it to a load of cops and politicians in Tamaulipas?'

'I hate Tamaulipas, but I hate cops and politicians more. You can cross over in Nogales, it's about a four or five-hour drive from here, ask for a man called Diego Jimenez, you will find him, everyone knows him, you got any money?'

'No, we can't afford a coyote.'

'Diego ain't any coyote I can assure you of that, but I better suggest that it ain't you who does the asking.'

'And why is that old timer?'

'Cus you're the Black Widow, everyone knows your face.'

'And I know you ain't just some old cussing buzzard sat out on your porch either, you a lookout for the Sonorans or Juarez.'

'Whoever on the day pays the most, I see you got a whole load of kids on that bus, I don't know why and I don't want to know why, but I do know you had better get the hell out of here, you know the gangs sell kids off don't you? get shipped off to work in some sweat shop or factory or some perverts from over in the US. Or even worse than that?'

'What could be worse than that?'

'Working in fucking McDonalds.' He lets out a laugh and gets out of his chair, he comes out of the house with a bag of food for us and some water, he tells me of a can of gasoline out back and lets us have that. As I go around back he whispers in my ear.

'That man on-board, the driver?'

'Yes,' I say

'Get shot of him, he doesn't look right.'

'Well he told me his family were killed and needed a lift to Juarez.'

'The only people who come here are crazy,' the old buzzard's eyes look directly at me at this point, 'or they got some other agenda, and he definitely got that look about him, like he got an agenda, he catches on to you and who you are, before you know it, you're behind bars or being skinned alive by the cartels, mark my words, you get shot of him.'

Now is not the time to question it. I get back on the bus and ask Adan to get off. No time for questions or threats, the butt of my colt goes straight over his head — down he goes. Probably not the most thoughtful thing to do, since I have a friend on-board who died subsequently from being hit over the head with a gun, but I am not taking any chances. I leave him in the dust outside of the buzzard's house. I pull off the thick file that I have saved for that rainy day, the months of work, espionage and surveillance against the San Fernando and Tamaulipas officials and cops — my own special little fuck you from the Black Widow, and hand it to the buzzard.

'Take it to the press first, get a copy to go to Mexico City, to the Attorney General, trust me he will thank you for it.' He nods and accepts it

'Don't worry; if it's likely to pay, then it's there already.'

We set off on the road again, another five-hour journey, across to Nogales, lots of tunnels in Nogales, Narcos sending people through carrying bags of powder to their counterparts in Arizona. Not what Flip had in mind for his children, but now the mantle is handed on to me, got to save the kids, he saved my Luis and I will return the favour. Fuck, Laena would kill me if she knew what I was up to.

I call for Tomas to come down to the front, he sits with me.

'I am sorry about your Papa; he truly turned out to be a hero didn't he?' I say.

'Yes, yes he did. He saved my life and he saved those kids back there, well with a little help from Joaquin of course.'

I noticed that although in mourning, he made light of things, the love for his father and the knowing that he was a hero had softened the blow slightly. These kids were tough, they had a strong disposition, they were fighters and no matter what came, they fought back.

'Tomas, we have to get to a place called Nogales to get you across, we can't cross in Juarez and your grandfather can't get over either. It's your only way to cross over.'

'What about you and Luis and the rest of the children,' he says, the look of guilt clearly etched all over his face.

'You cannot worry about the rest of us, it was your Papa's plan to get you over, get you somewhere safe and I am not about to let him down. As for the rest of us, don't worry, you and your family saved them, saved Luis as well. They owe you their lives, you have done your part. My work here isn't finished yet and I am in no position to take a load of children with me, I just can't do it myself either.' As I say this I now feel the burden of guilt replicated overcome me, Febe joins us at the front.

'Maria, we can't leave the rest of them, they are only small children, most of them would die if they are left to fend for themselves,' says Febe.

'Look, you don't understand, I am hunted, anyone found with me will be killed, that includes Luis, but I can't just turn off this thing I have started, even if I wanted to I can't, the Zetas wont rest until I am dead, they know what I know and I am about to make matters worse for them, just to let you in on this, Bruno has offered to turn himself in to the authorities and tell them everything. What happened last year is nothing compared to what they have been doing recently. Bruno told me that he learned they had been doing this continually for days; he says there are hundreds of people buried in and around San Fernando. The bus you were on was just the last of many, and it may not have been the last. Bruno is going to lead the Federales to the burial sites and spill his guts about all the murders and the shipments, he is about to put one hell of a dent in the Zetas, but it won't be one that will see them all go away forever. That's why we must run. Luis and I are hunted and maybe even killed, these kids stay with us, they die, just like us. I promise I wouldn't just drop them off in the desert, I will get them somewhere, maybe to the Nuns or an orphanage or something, but I can't take them, I pose more of a danger to them, than if they lived on the streets.'

Both look back at me, they know the predicament, they know what I am saying makes sense, but in its comprehension, it seems callous, they each in turn look back at the huddle of small children, remembering their own predicaments, Febe seeing her father shot down like a sick animal in some cowshed in San Fernando. Tomas, how his own Mama never came home and now that his Papa had just died. They had become what I hoped they wouldn't, their environment had now made them hard. They lost their father only a matter of hours ago and rather than grieve, they must deal with further problems. Despite this, they still have a heart, it is still their natural instincts to protect the small children, the baton of responsibility has passed from Laena to Flip and now Flip to the two of them.

Far behind us a city destroys itself with mass shootings and violence, we hit the highway cloaked in darkness, only the headlights on the road, we can see nothing around us. Tomas, Joaquin and Febe kiss their father one last time and lay his coat over his head, knowing that he will be buried in some shallow grave in Nogales, not a fitting burial for a man who raised and cared for them. Further and further we travel, not stopping, heading to an uncertain future yet again.

Chapter27

Nogales, Sonora, Mexico

31st March 2011

I look down over Papa as he lies on the seat. I feel guilt; I feel guilt for lying to Papa all this time. There is no ranch, there is no livestock and horse riding. Papa Antonio works as a ranch-hand and lives in a shack near to a ranch, just outside of El Paso. When he went across with Grandma, they hoped we would all come with them. Papa Antonio foresaw the troubles and made his decision to cross over, his business in Mexico suffered because of the rise in violence and anyone with any businesses or money were threatened by the cartels. Men came to extort money from him, so Papa Antonio killed them, shot them down and fled. They were connected to the cartels, so Papa Antonio had to leave. He crossed over and took the first job he could find, working as a ranch hand. He didn't tell anyone about what he did, not even Mama. The only reason I know is that I overheard him telling Mama on our last visit.

Mama and I concocted the lie in order to get Papa to come over with us. We lied to him about Papa Antonio's wealth and the ranch, we did it to try and convince him that we would have a better life in America. Papa Antonio and Grandma are US citizens now, but they crossed illegally. They work for pittance; they were once people of stature and respect, now they are just another Mexican family, who jumped over the border, just refugees who live as second class citizens in America, just so they can stay alive. I feel bad for lying to Papa. I lied to Febe as well, I told her where Papa lived and explained that it was a ranch, just not that he worked on one. He was amongst the other Mexican families, all living in shacks and working for some rich Texan.

He feels cold to the touch now; we have travelled throughout the night with Papa on this bus. Joaquin doesn't understand, he puts a coat over Papa. His face is pale and for a while it looked like he was just asleep, but not now. That once appearance of a wry smile, now looks like a grimace. I lay a coat over his head, I don't want to remember him this way, I just want to remember him as he was when Mama was around. I wanted to remember those drunken conversations on the porch with Alejandro, where they would laugh and curse and Mama would go out and tell them to be quiet, how he would laugh and smile and poke fun at Mama, because she was so organised and he was not. That is how I want to remember him.

Maria drives the bus into Nogales, from the hill tops as we enter the rows and rows of stucco type houses give the appearance the town is wealthy and far more civilised than our town. I can see the Fence that runs through the town, separating Nogales Sonora with Nogales Arizona. The Americans are so desperate to keep us Mexicans out of their beloved country. Mexican border cops patrolling the fence lines in jeeps and on foot, happily helping the good old US. As we drive into town, it is apparent that the town certainly looks cleaner and better kept than where we are from. The main roads having restaurants and fancy bars and tavernas, expensive cars travelling the streets, healthy and happy families walking the streets all smiles and happy faces, looking well fed and probably putting on a show for their American neighbours, who could peer through the fifteen-foot fence to look at what could be.

On the edge of town Maria drives to a small street that runs alongside the border fence. An old beat up truck with men hanging out alongside is parked, they look like traffickers, they have that Narco look about them. Our bullet ridden bus sticking out a mile along these streets, Maria takes us there to find Diego, the man who may or may not get us all across. Maria gets off the bus and goes to speak with the men, as we wait on the bus.

'I think this is risky,' says Febe, 'we don't know these guys at all, I heard stories about these types of people selling kids to people, what if they tell Maria one thing, but do as I just said. Why don't we just climb that fence, we could all get over that, it doesn't look so bad.'

'No!' I say 'there are cops patrolling that fence all the time, we would never get over without being seen, either by the cops on this side or American police, we have to do it this way.'

'There has to be somewhere else to cross, maybe we head further west?' Febe looks jittery, she has a sixth sense for this kind of thing, probably brought on by what she has done through before.

'We can't go further west, that's the Sonoran Desert, we head out into that straight off and we die, we have to stay as close to Nogales as possible.'

'You think a band of kids wandering through Nogales isn't going to arouse suspicion, any tunnel they may have is always going to drop us out into the desert, otherwise they wold be shipping drugs straight into the main street, no Narco would dare do that. We should split — do it another way.'

'That fence runs for miles past this town, either way we got to use the tunnels. Please Febe trust me, we are almost there, we just got to get this bit done and we are out of here.'

She looks at me, her eyes seeing right through me, just like Mama used to. When she looks at me like this, I know she can see through right through to my soul, she instinctively knows what I am feeling and how I am feeling.

'Do you hate it here that much; that you feel you have to get across, even if we get killed doing it?'

'It's not that, I love this place, I don't want to leave, but we don't have any choice, look what happened to Mama and now Papa and all of the many others.' I look over at Luis, sat down the front of the bus, just sat staring into his lap; Febe turns to look in the same direction. 'Just look at him, you didn't know him like I did, a year ago he was just another boy, just like me. Look at him now. All my friends have split from San Fernando and are living in camps or sleeping under bridges or by the side of the highway, I don't have a school, I don't have a family here anymore, I can't go back to Tamaulipas ever again, so what do I do.'

'We cross,' Febe says, 'but what about the children? we can't just dump them when we get to the other side, they can't help what has happened any more than we can, but I can't just leave them like this, they would be thrown back no sooner than landing in the US. What do we do about them?'

I am stumped at this question, I must get across, mainly for Joaquin, I have to get him out of here, but inside I start to feel guilty about what I really think, how I selfishly just wanted to get us all to El Paso and fuck the rest.

'We don't have a choice, we have to get them over, it's the only safe place for them at the moment, they will have to come with us, Papa Antonio will sort the rest once we get there.'

'Your family can't take care of these children, it's not possible, not unless they are huge fans of the "Sound of music" and before you say it, yes they did show that movie in El Salvador.'

I laugh, 'My family will understand, I don't want to leave them anymore than you do, I didn't want to just pick and run from here, neither did Mama or Papa, but it has just gotten worse, look at the shit you been through, we been through, Maria and Luis. How many people have we alone seen killed in the last few months? We have to cross this way, I know we can't trust these guys, but it's our last hope.'

Febe leans in and kisses me on the cheek; I feel my heart flutter, like it does every time she does that. I love her so much; I can't be without her. Maria returns to the bus and climbs aboard. She sits with Febe and me.

'Those guys will take you to Diego, it's tonight or never, so you have to go with them right now,' Maria says, that look of sorrow painted all over her face.

'Who is this Diego?' I say, intrigued and slightly suspicious that some guy would just help us at absolutely no cost at all.

'He works for Sonora, that's all you need to know, he will let you use his tunnel, all of you.'

'Did you pay him?' says Febe.

'No, to get through, you all have to do something in return.' Maria hangs her head.

"Do what exactly? what do we have to do?'

'Carry something; each of you has to carry something with you. Once you get through there are others waiting to collect? Then you're free to go, get to your grandfather's place and don't ever look back.' Maria sounds saddened by the whole turn of events.

'So they want us to carry drugs into the US, that's what they want, isn't it?' says Febe, 'and what if we are caught? how many years in jail is that? or do they just send us back over — to go to jail, so we can be killed by the Zetas in jail!'

'No Febe, you just don't get caught, it's as simple as that, you get across, you do as they want and you get the hell out of there, any cops or feds waiting on the other side, you get the hell out of there.'

Maria grabs a hold of me and pulls me in, she squeezes me tight and then does the same to Febe and then turns to Joaquin and does the same, she starts to cry.

'I will take your Papa with me, I will lay him to rest somewhere peaceful, somewhere he would want to be laid to rest.' Maria looks down upon the covered body of Papa.

'He never crossed over, not once. All he wanted to do was cross over, to go live in the US in the end, that's all he spoke about was getting over and now he will never know,' I say to her.

'No Tomas, he just wanted to get you over there. Not because he hated it here, far from it, he loved this place, like I love this place; he just hated what had become of this place. All he really wanted was to get you all over, so you didn't have to live this way any longer. One day you may all come back, and I hope you do, but for now, get over to your family. Be safe, all of you. You're the adults now, look after the children, and make sure they get there safely. Say goodbye to your father, one last time.'

I lean over and lift the coat that covers his face; I kiss him gently on his forehead.

'Goodnight Papa, sleep well. You are the bravest man I know.'

Febe kisses him next and lastly Joaquin.

Maria leads us to the front of the bus, I look down at Luis, as he sits silently, as he had been all the way along this journey, his eyes dead, his face emotionless, yet a flicker of sorrow seemed to be present as I looked at him for the very last time. I put my arms around him, he was my friend, my best friend and all I wanted was for him to be his own self again.

'I will see you again Luis, I promise,' I say to him, I notice a tear in his eye, but he doesn't speak. I continue to look into his eyes, to see if there is anything more, but it doesn't show. He has seen so much and been to places and has done things that I couldn't even imagine.

We get off the bus and all of us walk in one line toward the old truck waiting at the bottom of the street. Joaquin takes the hand of the small girl with the long hair again and walks with her. He is her protector and has been throughout. I take one last look back and see Maria standing there, next to the bus, looking back at us. I hope that she finds peace; I hope that she lives a long and full life, but I know that the odds are stacked against her, both will be hunted, living their lives looking over their shoulder. We get on the truck and all sit in silence, knowing that once again, we face uncertain danger.

***

The truck rumbles out of town, no one speaks to us, no one tells us anything. The men on the bus sit in silence, they have guns tucked into their waist bands, they never even look at us throughout the journey. We leave Nogales and head out into the desert, the heat beating through the exterior of the truck. The sweat rolls down my face, the road becoming more and more uneven. After several hours, the truck stops and we wait; again no one telling us anything. I watch the sun go down over the desert. Bright red, burning through the sky, the clouds that lay underneath are dark, but the sun looks beautiful as it starts to set over the hills and mountains of Sonora. My last sunset in Mexico, I start to get that feeling of homesickness, like I am beginning to regret even considering leaving the place that I call home; the only place I know as home.

Within an hour, we are in complete darkness, the truck starts up again and heads along the road, we travel again for another hour or so until we eventually come to a stop. The driver of the truck flashes his beams and in the distance a flash comes from the desert and we start up and head towards the flashlight. The light keeps flashing; the truck driver keeps his headlights switched off. Like a ship in days of old, we are led to our destination.

When the truck stops, the back doors are opened and men stand there with flashlights, hurrying us off the truck. Amongst the men a tall dark-skinned Mexican stands, he is dressed in the typical Narco cowboy style — this has to be Diego. He walks over to me, being the tallest and looking like the eldest.

'So you must be the boss man, is that right?' he says, he has an authority about him, like he could be both charming and deadly in equal measure.

'That's right.' I try and stand tough and match him. With everything that has happened in the last few days, nothing could scare me here.

'You ever done this type of thing before,' he says.

'Yes, lots of times,' Febe interrupts, 'your people on the other side ready for us because we don't want to be stood there waiting, we got to shuffle on.' She sounds tough and sassy, maybe a little too much sass.

Diego laughs to himself, 'I like it, lots of tough kids. Just remember you fuck this up, we take you out, kids or no kids. You get pinched on the other side, you don't say shit, you don't mention me or the tunnel, you got that, if you have a problem understanding that, just remember, we got people in jails in America and over here. This operation is small, but it's important. You get across and head for the hills, there will be a truck waiting for you.'

We are led over to a van; the rear doors open and bricks upon bricks of pure white powder. The powder is so white that it even provides light in the darkness. We are each given a backpack and bricks are loaded into the packs. We are led to a trench where we are all told to jump in. We walk along the trench until we get to a dug-out hole, about five feet in height, small enough for a child or a small adult. The hole leads down under-ground — down the rabbit hole again I think to myself.

I am up front, being the leader, I get to go first, I get to play at being the man of the family. The backpack weighs heavy on my back; I look back up to ground level and see Diego stood watching over us. The van is driving away.

'What about the rest of the bricks,' I say to Diego.

'You know what they say about curiosity and the cat don't you?' said Diego.

I lead the way inside, Joaquin walks behind me, still holding the little girls hand, Febe stays at the very back, making sure that we all get through.
I shuffle through as its completely black inside, placing my hands against the walls of the tunnel, trying to keep thoughts out of my head, like 'what if the tunnel collapses' and thoughts about rats, wild animals or ogres and monsters. I keep breathing and making sure that everyone is keeping up.

We shuffle through the tunnel, the smell of damp overwhelming — the heat excruciating, the sweat pouring off me. It's so dark in here and I start to feel claustrophobic. That feeling of what if? constantly on my mind. What if we get so far and the tunnel suddenly stops? if it falls through, do we all die down here — like rats, eating each other, clawing each other to death through fear and madness. My mind plays constant tricks on me, telling me that we are doomed, that we are going to die down here; right about now, the only thing I want is Papa, stood with me, telling me it's going to be OK, like he did back in that barn, how he calmed me down. The further we get through, the more I hear the cries of panic coming from the children. I stop and announce to the children that everything will be fine, that we won't be in here much longer, tell them to be quiet or someone may hear us and we will end up being caught.

As we make our way through the tunnel, it seems to become narrower, the tunnel walls seem to close in, the back pack scuffing against the roof of the tunnel, still no sign of fresh air — I can taste the dirt and dust in my mouth, the pace slowing as the line of children start to slow down again. The sound of screams can be heard from amongst the line. The sounds of clawing and desperation as one of our group screams out, declaring they can't go through, that they want to turn back. I hear Febe trying to calm the child; a boy who I can only guess would be around a similar age to Joaquin, begging her to let him go back, how he can't go through here any longer, sobbing and screaming, causing others to fall against the ground of the tunnel.

The darkness closing in on us; panic overcoming us all. The boy has set off a chain of events that cause us all to start doubting our journey. I can hear Febe pleading with the boy, telling him that he cannot go back, if he does then the men would not take kindly, that they would kill him. This doesn't seem to be working, I hear Febe becoming more and more forceful with the boy, trying as much as she can to keep him moving, her words fall on deaf ears as he screeches like a wild animal, people falling down inside, a pile of children suffocating each other as the line becomes a mass of tangled bodies, claustrophobia now reaching a climax, the cries of the children echoing through the tunnels, I reach to Joaquin, who now sits on the ground, covering his ears and rocking, petrified of the noise. The small girl behind him, clinging to him as she falls. The only voices of reason coming from Febe and I as we try and play responsible adult, to a child who has become so overcome with fear and panic that all reasonable thought has gone.

'He's gone, he's gone, I had to let him go, he's gone back the way we came,' shouts Febe.

'OK,' I say, 'come on let's move again, not far now.' My words sound hollow as I have been saying that for hours now. I lead us along, wondering what will become of that boy, another child off to his death.

We shuffle along — thirsty, tired and week, the air becoming more and more dense, difficult to breathe, we are all becoming weak, the sounds in the tunnel now consist of coughs and heavy breathing. I turn to check on Joaquin, who seems to be struggling to breathe, I can tell that he is struggling, he holds onto his injured shoulder, the shoulder that he suffered a gunshot only a few months ago. It feels hopeless; I have led us from dangerous situation straight to another. Catch 22, I remember Papa using that phrase once as we sat doing homework. This is exactly what catch 22 is, even if we do make it out of here, what awaits.

It amazes me how much the mind plays tricks, even shuffling through this tunnel, I start to analyse what has occurred and start to question the purpose of what we are doing.

Why would Diego send us through this tunnel, carrying what seems to be only a small portion of the bricks of cocaine from that van? Who on earth would take such a risk for such little reward? Where was that van going after we started the journey? Why was Diego so keen on reiterating the point about if we were caught by the police on the other side?

This starts to make sense now, that fucking bastard has set us up. There is a second tunnel near here, one where the large shipment goes through, probably on a pulley system or something, he sends us through as bait, the cops snatch us and they think that was the route and that is the shipment, when all along the Sonorans send through the bigger shipments and the cops get distracted, we are a fucking decoy. Keep it to yourself, don't say anything, we can't go back now, we go through, we still have a chance, we go back and who says that they don't shoot us as we pop out.

Eventually I feel the tunnel start to lead to an incline, a draft of cool air blows down upon me. Fresh air, desert air. The best air I have ever smelled. I turn and whisper back to the group, that we are on the other side. No whoops of excitement or joy, just the sounds of desperation as they each clamber towards fresh air. I stand at the mouth of the tunnel and help each one out, I place Joaquin next to me, while I steer each child to stay down until I go and check out the surrounding area.

Febe clambers out last of all. Her face covered in dirt and sweat, she throws her arm around me and drops to her knees. We each remove the bottle of water that the Sonorans kindly packed in each bag and take large gulps, I regulate the water and make sure no one takes on any more, as we have the desert to take on next. I tell Febe of my suspicions of Diego and us being used as a decoy, she nods in agreement, sensing the same as I.

A small gulley path leads us down a rocky slope; it's the only path that looks like it leads to any destination. Two boys gallop ahead, only young boys; I still don't know any of their names just yet. They are excitable and keen to get out of here. It hits me like a lightning bolt, the obvious path for us, would be an obvious path for someone else. Suddenly one of the boy's trips and lands face down on the slope, a flare shoots up into the sky and lights up the canyon, in full view and for all to see, border agents and uniformed cops rush toward us.

'Quick, everyone, get the hell out of here, get off the path!' I yell.

The agents and cops come running up the pathway, they grab the two boys who rushed and tripped the flare. Not only were we a decoy, but the bastards set us up, they tipped the cops. I climb up onto the rocky hillside, pulling Joaquin and Febe up, next the small girl; the two boys flay their arms and legs about and kick out, but the cops over power them. I slip my back pack off and get the others to do the same; I push the children in the direction of higher ground, heading off towards the east, into the night. Back packs are removed as cops make their way behind us, flashlights dancing around, no place to hide, just keep running.

Exhausted and scared, we run off into the darkness, no idea where we will end up, no idea of our future. As we run we hear one of our group fall, the cries coming from a girl this time, it's not from Febe, it's not from the little girl who Joaquin protects, I hear her cry and call out. Febe stops to go back. I follow her and tell the others to stay put.

We follow the cries, we try and lift her, the girl screams out, obviously in pain, must have hurt during the fall.

'What is it, where does it hurt,' says Febe.

'My leg, my leg, it hurts, oh please, please make it stop, make it stop.'

The girl howls; from the slope of the rock face, the flashlights can be seen, they are following the cries, they know the direction. I look at Febe, the sky is clear and bright and I see every expression on her face. We look at each other and we know the situation we are in, we know it's no use; we have that difficult decision to make and no time for discussion. We lay the girl down, she looks back at us 'Please, don't leave me, don't leave here like this, I beg you, please don't leave me here.'

I look into that scared face, the face of a child, probably around ten years old, I don't even know her name, I don't even know anything about her, I don't remember her at all, not from the escape, not from the bus journey, I never even tried to become acquainted. I know I must make one of the most difficult decisions of my life. I turn my back on her, her cries become louder as she knows what my intentions are. Febe does the same; we turn our back on her and run off, across the rocky slope, heading into the night. Twelve children went into a tunnel in Sonora, only seven remain.

'No please don't go, please don't leave me like this, please, please, please!'

Chapter28

Santa Cruz County, Arizona, USA

1st April 2011

I cuddle in between Tomas and Febe, the other children all try and squeeze in. I am cold and I am hungry, the ground is hard and I can hear rattle-snakes in the bush. Tomas told me that we are in America now, but I don't feel safe, I am still scared. The people here don't seem very friendly. I can't sleep out here in the desert; I keep thinking what happened to the children who didn't get away? What would the policemen with the torches do to them, would they hurt them like they tried to do with us? Would they pass them over to other bad men who would hurt them?

In the pictures of America, I remember seeing big tall buildings — lots of big tall buildings, but there is nothing here, it's a desert, hot and full of dangerous snakes and wolves and coyotes and bad men who grab children and throw them in cages, like the policemen back home. I want Papa, I miss him, I want him here right now. Tomas and Febe told me he was sleeping, so I tried to keep him like that, he felt cold so I covered him up. Then they told me that he had died — so why did they lie to me? Why did they say that he was asleep, when in fact he was dead? I just want him back, I want Mama back as well, I want them to come find us and take us away from here. The little girl doesn't let go of my hand, she even sleeps holding my hand, she is scared. She said her name was Ximena and she also said she is six years old and lived near to Abasolo. She said her Mama was a teacher, but had gone to heaven.

In church the priest always said that when a person dies, that they go to heaven and their spirit comes back to look over you. That's just silly, the priest was stupid because Mama and Papa, well they didn't come back, where are they now, if their spirit returns to watch over us. He lied, the priest lied, it's not true, when you die, you just die and that's it.

***

I wake up at sunrise and watch the sun come up over the craggy and hilly mountain range of the desert. For miles, I can see the cactus, old leafless trees spread out along the range and the hills and paths we would have to walk to get anywhere near to any town. So far, it looks the same, although we were told the tunnel lead to America and the voices of the cops that grabbed the children last night were American, I could still be in Mexico for all we knew, it all looked the same.

As I sit up I look around and take my water bottle out and take a gulp, I look back to the direction of where Mexico lay and I have a funny feeling run through me, I wish I were there right now. When I was over there I wanted to be here, but now I am here I start to feel like it was a bad choice. Everything that we have tried to get us over here has led to bad luck, it was supposed to be a happy occasion, we were supposed to be happy in getting over here, but so far I don't feel that at all.

I look down on the sleeping children; Febe included in that, they look ragged, dirty, exhausted. What we have been through would be unimaginable to any child in America right now. The children on this side of the border are probably waking up to loving parents, who care for them, who take them from their beds and kiss them and hug them and send them off to the rest of their day, knowing that they are likely to get back home after school and they will be together as a family. I look at us and we are counting our lucky stars that we survive the rest of the day. I am sure that not all kids have a bed of roses over here, but at this moment in time, I am blinded by my own selfish thoughts of our predicament.

I wake the group up and tell them that we must head off; each child takes a gulp of water, the younger ones, especially the girl who has seemed to have formed a bond with Joaquin, complains that her stomach hurts, that she is hungry and feels too tired to walk.

'Just walk for a little while longer, I promise you, when we find a town, we will stuff ourselves with hamburgers and fries and apple pie and all that other junk they sell here.'

I tickle her belly and she laughs. We head off east, into the rising sun, hoping to find what we all came here for — hope.

Hours and hours of walking, no idea what time of day it is, the sun is up and we head over the rocky and uneven terrain, away from the border fence, away from patrolling border cops. Every now and then we take cover in the brush, watch the border cops driving around in their trucks, we even see them chase down a group of Mexicans who have gotten across, we watch the guns being pulled, the trucks chase them, shots fired at their feet, men bundled to the ground, handcuffed, placed in a van — adios muchachos.

Keep walking, keep moving, one line of children as the walkways are narrow. We have not eaten anything since yesterday; we don't speak during the journey. I take the front of the line, Joaquin behind me, Ximena as I now know her behind Joaquin, Febe at the back. I don't want to know the other children, one boy and two other girls, just in case, can't get too close, just in case anything happens to them. The girl who fell on the rocks, I heard the voices shout out to her, the flashlights popping around in the night sky, the American voices tell her that they were not going to hurt her, all in the distance as I ran to save my own ass.

It was a four-hour drive from Juarez to Nogales, now we have that journey again on this side of the fence, but on foot, with border agents looking to throw our assess back over to the Mexican side. For most, it would be an inconvenience, but for us it's certain death. No one can know where we are, the Zetas would most certainly come for us. We keep on walking; I remind myself that no hunger or pain of walking is going to stop me from getting to where I need to go. To El Paso, to my people, to be once again loved and cared for.

The ground starts to level out and we walk in small cluster. I walk with Febe and Joaquin. I take her hand in mine, for once it's me who takes the lead, despite everything that has gone on before this moment, I am happy once again. I am with the girl I love; the one I want to be with forever and ever. I can't imagine life without her.

'We made it Febe,' I say, 'You will love El Paso, Papa Antonio and Grandma will make a fuss of us, you see they will. Grandma still has my Mama's old toys and dresses at the house. We can ride horses, help with the cattle, go to the mall in El Paso, I could even hold your hand on the school bus. You're going to love it.'

Part of me feels guilty about exaggerating about my grandparents.

'I can't wait,' she says, the exhaustion sounding in her voice, but smiles none the less, 'are you serious about us being together, forever I mean.'

'Of course I am. I know I am just a kid, but I don't think I could ever imagine being without you. I love you Febe, I loved you from day one.'

I turn to her as I say it, her face gentle and soft; her eyes twinkle as she looks at me.

'I love you too Tomas and I don't want to ever be without you.' My heart hits that beat again, just like when I first saw her, 'we have to make sure nothing happens to the children though, we can't dump them, you know that right.'

‘Of course, we are like adults now, fussing over a bunch of kids.’ I laugh about it, only a few days ago I was the one who needed looking after, now I am some sort of father figure, these kids don’t move a muscle unless I say it’s safe to do so.

We keep walking, satisfied that life is good, despite the current situation, that I have my one true love with me, heading off towards a certain future.

Bang, Craaack.

A familiar sound, the echo thunders through the valley. We hit the ground, face down; even the young children recognise that sound and instinctively go to the ground.

Bang, Craaack.

The ground exploding before our very eyes. A second shot then a third. Then a voice calls out, an American voice. None of us speak English; we don’t know what is said. I peer up towards where I could hear the shots come from, two men in desert camouflage move through the brush, they are dressed like soldiers, American soldiers, but they are too old, one is too fat — they can’t be. They stop in front of us and their guns aimed at us. They have badges on their arms, not the usual military style badges, some form of dagger, underneath the words “Arizona peoples militia.” I read English, just about, but I don’t speak it and looking at the situation now, I probably never will.

‘Stay down, don’t you fucking move an inch.’

I don’t understand what they are saying; it’s just words, words I don’t know the meaning of. I stay down, because I can’t imagine that they want us all up and jumping around.

‘Look here Reggie,’ the fat one says, ‘looks like the fucking dope peddlers got kids to do their work for them.’

‘Oh yes, I bet. I bet these kids are out of Juarez or some shit, well they gonna’ understand some constitutional rights in just a second. Fucking rice and beans all round, I bet these little fuckers will be stitching fucking T shirts in Houston by tomorrow, if they had their way?’

We don’t understand what they are saying; we don’t know who they are or what they are. I hear cries coming from the children, they, like me probably believe that these men are cops or border agents or something.

‘Anyone of you speaks fucking English, habla Inglés.’

‘No señor,’ I say

‘Well look here, we got the fucking boss man.’

'Yes a smart Mexican, hey you a smart one, you the one runs these kids through here, bringing your fucking filth across into our country, to poison our kids, that you boy.'

I still don't know what they are saying, I can't address them, and so I stay quiet.

'This is the United States boy, this is Arizona boy, we don't take kindly to your kind coming over here, with your cocaine and your bloodthirsty ways, border-jumping from Nogales or Juarez or somewhere. We defend the constitutional rights; we bear arms against foreign invaders motherfucker, and we certainly going to straighten you right out now.'

They pull me off the ground, I am on my feet, I look over at Febe and Joaquin. Here it is, go through all this, to get killed in America. I don't know what they are saying to us, but I know they aren't cops or agents or anything like that, these men want to spill blood and they are going to do it right now.

'You,' the fat one shouts, 'we gonna hand you over, the fucking patriot act says that if under threat then by foreign invaders, then you little fucks are off to New Mexico, got a nice little camp there.' He laughs.

The skinny one says, 'but not this one, not the boss man, because we throw him back over and he comes back.' The skinny one pushes me, I shunt forward. He kicks me in the backside: 'Vamanos, muchaos, move it motherfucker, go on, make a run.'

I know what's going on, I don't have to speak the language, they want me to run, so they can cut me down. I turn and face them, I smile.

'You pissing me off now boy.' the fat fuck shouts at me. He raises his gun and points it at me.

'Fuck you, you fat pig!' I shout at him, he doesn't flinch, he doesn't speak enough Spanish.

'Tomas, what are you doing,' shouts Febe.

'They think I fear them, after all we been through, they think I am scared of them. We have been through hell and back and some hillbillies dressed as fake soldiers and get their rocks off by shooting kids are not going to scare me.'

'What the hell you saying boy,' the skinny one shouts.

'You fucking cowards, go on, make yourselves feel like men, shoot me, shoot me you fucking cowards, you're just like them, just like the fucking men we ran from.'

'What's he saying Reggie?'

'How the hell do I know, maybe he's signalling for the others, maybe it's a trap, fucking do him and round these little bastards up, hand them over to the Nogales PD.'

‘We can’t do him and hand witnesses over Reggie, you dumb fuck, we can’t drill them all, we will never explain that away.’

‘What the fuck are you waiting for?’ I scream, I can feel the tears roll down my cheeks, ‘fucking kill me then!’

‘Tomas shut up! don’t do anything stupid.’

‘Now the bitch is gabbing on,’ says the fat one, ‘What we gonna do now?’

‘Febe,’ I call over to her, ‘when I tell you to go — run, back down the pass and around, head east. Take the kids with you, all of them.’

I move to the side, I can see their gun hands shaking, these assholes are going to shoot us all, even if they don’t want to, they are spending too much time thinking about it, got to get the kids away.

‘He’s making his move, the boss man here, let’s plug the little shit.’

‘I don’t know what you’re saying, but you’re going to rot in hell for this, you fucking gutless pieces of shit,’ I say as I stand in front of the children; I lean back to look at Febe from over my shoulder.

Joaquin stands up and runs to me; the fat one swings his gun at us. Joaquin stands in front of me, oh shit, oh Jesus; I thought he was going to shoot him then. They really are planning to do us.

‘What the fuck is this little one doing; almost took him out Reggie, almost, fuck me, they got a gun on them, I can tell, they playin’ us, so one of these little bastards pulls a piece and we all get done in, fuck this, do the boss man and search them all.’

‘Febe,’ I say again, ‘the ranch is just outside of El Paso, take the kids, down the pass, run as fast as you can, get there, get to the ranch, I will meet you there, I promise — Joaquin and I will make our dash up to the high ground. Febe you listening to me?’

She looks at me, her eyes filled with tears, she smiles at me, but somehow it looks different than before, I just can’t tell myself why, but it seemed different this time. I move closer to the trembling gun hand of the fat one, he is sweating, he looks nervous; I stand so my belly is right up to the barrel, Joaquin by my side. The skinny one walks forward and joins his friend.

Like a flash, I hear the scrambling sounds behind me, Febe and the children are scrambling off the floor, my distraction worked, they shove me aside and go to the edge of the ravine, to look at where they fled. I run at the fat one as he points his gun towards them. With all my might, I shove him over the side, he drops fifteen feet onto the hard-rocky ground, the skinny one comes at me, grabs me and pulls me toward him. He bear-hugs me, he slips his arm around my neck and chokes me, his skinny arms around my throat, I feel week, I can't breathe, feel myself falling away, drifting off.

I am on the floor, Joaquin stands over me, the skinny one led on top of me, Joaquin has his hammer in his hand, the skinny one out for the count. I push him off me and look out towards the flat ground, I see the children, and I see Febe, far off into the distance, running, not looking back, heading off into the horizon. Below us, I hear scrambling, the fat one coming around, the fall not far enough to kill him, but we got lucky that time, we must flee.

'You and your hammer.' I say to Joaquin as I run my hand across the top of his scruffy mop of hair.

We run over the high ground heading east, looking back to see if the men come after us, got to get to the ranch, Febe will be there soon, Febe and the children, our ever-increasing family.

***

As the sun sets and we have used up all our water we reach a highway, we hitch a lift with a kindly old man, who happens to come from our side of the border, we tell him where we are heading and he drives us into Nogales. It's amazing, only a few days ago, we were in Nogales, but this time we peer through a fence at the side we came from. The old man takes us to the bus stop and slips us American dollars and shows us the bus to El Paso.

We travel through the night on the overnight bus; Joaquin soon falls asleep and rests his head on my shoulder. No one on the bus pays us any attention, people don't even look at us, we are hungry and thirsty, but the three-hundred-and-fifty-mile journey travels straight to the City. From there we can call Papa Antonio. An old Mexican man stops for us and even gives us the money to get on the bus, no questions, just gives it. I look around the bus and I fail to see any friendly faces, we drink from the sink in the toilet that is at the back of the bus.

Not long now and we will have made it, months and months of planning, many months and months of pure hell on earth and we will have made it. I have this constant feeling of dread throughout the journey. Something bothers me about the look Febe gave me before we were separated, almost a look of finality. I am being stupid, Febe knows the way, she knows how to get there, we can be together again, together for all time. Just like Mama and Papa were destined to be, they can rest easy now, knowing their boys will be safe. I am buzzing with excitement, the thought of America and all it has to offer for us. Febe will love it here, Joaquin will love it also. It's just going to be us from now on, living a good life, a life where we don't have to be scared anymore, don't have to run from gunfire or worry about our houses being taken over by Narcos. All I think about is seeing Febe again, and my grandparents, my aunt and uncle and my cousin. I just hope that Febe made it onto the highway, like we did.

She is a clever girl, not one to be taken for a fool, in some ways she is one of the most intelligent and strong willed people I know. I love her for it and I can't wait to tell her that I love her again.

The sun is starting to rise when we arrive in El Paso, the sun shines down on the city on the desert, the high-rise building, the city streets quiet, all but for some early morning traffic and a few people out jogging, I look along the streets and see the chains of stores and restaurants and bars, its unlike anything we ever had across the border. The funniest thing is happening to me, I start to feel bad about crossing, I am starting to miss my people already, I miss the place where I once lived. Despite everything that has happened I feel regret for fleeing, I start to feel like maybe Febe was right all along, maybe we should have stayed, why should we be pushed out of the place we were born, pushed around by thugs and gunmen.

I start to think of all the good people that suffered, Mama and Papa, Alejandro, Maria and Luis, I even think of Bertrand Le Vell, the man who came to Mexico looking for a better life, I think of Mr Lingala and his family, I think of Bruno and hope he is safe. I think of the children that made it, the children that got away and are with Febe right now, of Ximena and how she wanted Joaquin as her protector and I think of the children who didn't get away. The children that were caught, they tasted American air for just a few seconds and now probably on their way back to Mexico, homeless and without parents, like lambs to the slaughter. I think of the old man, who sacrificed himself so I could live. All the faces; some I don't even know their names, all going around in my head, the lost people, the good people of my homeland.

We reach the bus station, American faces looking down on us, not speaking, no one asking if we are OK, or did we need help, just looking at us, no smiles, no friendly gestures, just cold, hard stares. In the station, there are local cops, so we decide not to hang around, it's obvious what we are and where we just came from, we have some money and find a taxi, one with a Spanish driver and ask for him to take us to the ranch.

The taxi pulls onto the long driveway, Joaquin looks out of the window and is excited to see the horses and the cattle, the ranch hands leading the cattle out to graze, we pull up to the small shack where Papa Antonio comes out with grandma, they run to us and gather us out of the taxi, Papa Antonio picks us both up, still very strong for being a man in his sixties, he wraps his arms around us and grandma stoops down to do the same; both crying, both saying that they thought we were gone forever, saying sorry that they couldn't get to us.

'Where is Febe,' says grandma, 'I thought she was coming over as well, where is she Tomas?'

'She will be here, trust me on that,' I say.

***

We run and we run and we run, can't slow down, running like animals, hunted by everybody. I have found purpose in my life, I must care for the children, I was lucky to have been found in my hour of need, by a great and wonderful man and his family. I met the most wonderful, gentle and caring person I could ever hope for, a person who I love with all my heart. They took me into their family when they had nothing of their own, they treated me like one of their own, they never let me down, they didn't throw me to fend for myself, they cared for me and treated me like I was theirs. I will always love them for that and I will always love Tomas for that, a sweet and loving boy, who wanted only to care for me and love me forever. One day I hope to make my way to him again, to be with him forever, my little Tomas, my knight in shining armour my soulmate, the one and only true love I have ever known. One day I will fulfil my dreams and be with him, but now I can't. Without me these children will never survive, without me, who would care for them. without Flip I would have surely died in a foreign land, without me these children would perish the same way. I must protect them, it's my role now I would never let any harm come to them. Poor sweet Tomas will be heartbroken but he will understand, he has nothing but goodness in his heart, his offer of taking them to the ranch was kind — it couldn't and wouldn't work. I love you Tomas, but these children need me, my job here is done. If in anyway took away some of the pain that you have suffered, then my job

is done, if I gave you any happiness in your life, then I am happy also.
You saved us, you saved me, forever I am in your debt, you will be happy now
no need to be scared anymore, you can live without fear. I owe everything to Flip
the only favour I can offer in return is the safe passage of your sons. One day
Tomas I hope to see you again, always my heart belongs to you. We keep running
Deep into the night, hopping trains and trucks, on deep dark highways that
don't seem to end, got to keep moving, keep running, got to save the
Children.

***

Every night I sit outside of the small wooden shack where we all live, looking out across the plain, waiting for her, just waiting for Febe to arrive, I can't wait to see her face again, to hold her hand, to have that feeling again, that feeling in my heart when she is near me, not long now, she will be here soon. I sit on the porch looking out, Joaquin sits with Papa Antonio. He seems happy again, he likes it here. I am happy also; soon Febe will be here to share it with me.

Chapter29

El Paso, Texas, USA

August 29th 2016

'Built that wall! build that wall! build that wall! build that wall!'

The rhetoric blares out the television set over various parts of the country; at conventions, rallies, repeated over and over along the campaign trail. As the months went on the crescendo had taken full momentum, it rang through my ears and attacked my sense of belonging. I am an alien, a refugee, six years on and the place I call home feels like a hostile land. The hostility more nuanced than blatant. The sideways glances, the sly comments, disapproving looks from a minority of people who resent my being here.

It's been five years, five long and very difficult years. I am soon to be eighteen years of age, Joaquin and I are now US citizens, Papa Antonio and grandma are our legal guardians and that was our only saving grace. I am soon to leave Texas to head off to college, an education that I have worked hard for, that my grand-parents worked hard to support me. No hand-outs, no pleas to the US government for assistance, we did it all and we did it alone. The Mexican fighting spirit fully ingrained in me, the virtues and values that my Mama and Papa taught me. In a bizarre and ironic way, I miss home, I miss the people — despite everything that happened, despite the loss of everything I held dear to me, I can't turn it off.

Even now my sleep is restless one; I wake and look around the room I share with Joaquin. I look for him; sometimes I even get out of bed and check that he is there. Despite the passing of time, I still look upon him as that six-year-old boy, being led away from us, believing we would never see him again.

Soon after our escape, Bruno went to the Attorney General's office and handed himself over, giving them the accounts of what happened between 24th and 29th March 2011. No sooner had he handed himself over the authorities as the star witness, the package that Maria gave that old man in Juarez landed on his desk. The Attorney General's office had no choice, but to send investigators into the region. Bruno led them the burial sites, he gave testimony of how Los Zeta commanders and hierarchy gave the order to capture buses and use the passengers for their own entertainment. To indoctrinate them into the Zetas by making them fight, by raping and murdering female passengers, by throwing the children into oil drums full of acid and then burying the dead nearby. The Federal Police recovered one hundred and ninety-three bodies alonc, all from those fateful days back in March 2011.

The testimony of Bruno led to the arrests of El Kilo and a number of other Zetas. The Federal police and the government linked their investigation back to the massacre in August 2010 of the seventy-two immigrants. Bruno now lives somewhere in the US, but under federal protection.

The Army took position in San Fernando in an attempt to restore order. The army stepped in and took over law and order in the city, many officers were arrested and indicted, I keep the newspaper cutting of the Tamaulipas state captain who wore the mirrored sunglasses, a photo of him being taken to prison in shackles, lifting his glasses to dry his eyes.

As for Rojo, he was never seen again after the night we escaped. He is the quintessential bogey man, an urban myth — haunting the towns and barrios of Northern Mexico. Children who misbehave are told of him as a means of scaring them into being good. Children are told, if they hear singing from their bedroom window, the Rojo has come for them, to steal from them from their beds.

Maria remains on the run, I last heard that after she left us, she travelled to Sonora, where she spread the word of the Autodefensas, she actively encouraged those who were tired of living under cartel rule, to rise up and fight. Until this very day, the name Black Widow can still be heard within the barrios and shanty towns of Juarez, Nogales, Nuevo Laredo and Matamoros. She is seen less and less these days; her legend will live on.

As for Luis, he was never the same again. The last I heard and this was from Old Man Chavez, who writes now and again, was that Luis was committed into an Asylum somewhere in Monterrey, but had to be continually moved around because the Zetas were looking to take his head. Another young life ruined by the violence.

The name of Felipe and Laena Hernandez remain something of a little known and mythical folklore in San Ferndando. They are known as salvador de los niños — Saviour of the Children. There are no plaques or shrines for them, just the stories around campfires of their exploits, testament of the courage of the people of Tamaulipas.

Joaquin is twelve now, a boy older than his years, a product of the environment in which he was raised. Joaquin built his own wall around himself, he has regained the will to speak again and does so, but he speaks infrequently, he remains guarded. Joaquin is often prone to melancholy and often reflects upon the last year of living in San Fernando; how Mama and Papa came to their demise, of the escape from that compound, if the Zetas still hunt for us now? He often ponders on what became of Febe and Ximena; how he hoped they made it somewhere safe. Joaquin's hope indicative of my own, our bond of brotherhood in an unbreakable one. In many ways we have both built a wall, we both have friends, but they are always observed with suspicion, trust is a valuable commodity, if they aren't family, then always keep them at an arm's length.

It's time for us to leave El Paso now, Papa Antonio and Grandma have to move out of the house, they are too old to work this ranch any longer, the below minimum wage pittance they have supported us on doesn't allow for us to live in Texas any longer. I have obtained a scholarship in Journalism at a college in Los Angeles and we have found a Mexican family in South Central who fled San Fernando at the same time as us, and are willing to provide us with lodgings. Papa Antonio and Grandma will search for jobs once we arrive.

We have to keep moving, get away from here, a new threat dawns now.

'Build that wall! build that wall! build that wall.'

Our documents are false, obtained from some back-alley shark who charged the earth. We live and work here, but we are refugees from our homeland. A homeland that we wish we could return to. A homeland that remains unstable, if we return, an uncertain future waits. Our safe-haven was short lived; the change in America is evident, the recent political agenda and shift in ideology is a sign of things to come. The beginning of the end for us, yet again we have to flee from here, we are too obvious. The ranch owner has attracted the attention of the Immigration and Customs Enforcement agency; they have applied untold pressures on the ranch owner. It's only a matter of time.

We pack up our meagre belongings and load them into Papa Antonio's car. I don't want to leave this place, in Los Angeles we will be just another poor Mexican family, hiding out in South Central, living at the bottom of society; every knock at the door spent wondering if we will be deported, living amongst the huge urban sprawl, the pull and attraction of gang life waiting for Joaquin and I, drugs and guns on every street corner. We take our seats in the car and pull away from the house that we have called home for the last six-years.

I look out toward the plains; even now, still wondering if she will ever return to me. I have never forgotten her; I can't forget her. As the years have passed, I still remember her, just like it was yesterday. I wonder what she is doing now? what she looks like? has she found a new love? is she even alive? In my heart, I know that I will never see her again, I know that she had other plans, she felt responsible for the children, I hope that they have found a beach somewhere or a remote place, where the evils of the world will never find them.

As the car pulls away I look out of the window one last time, hoping that Febe has found her way back to me once more. I look toward the plain one last time, with every prayer left in me, I want to see her run towards the house, to come back to me, to tell me that she will never leave me again and that we will be together for all time — but she doesn't come. We move along the long and winding road onto the highway, just another highway on a journey into the unknown once more.

The End.

36612047R00174

Printed in Poland
by Amazon Fulfillment
Poland Sp. z o.o., Wrocław